Get **more** out of libraries

Please return or renew this item by the last date shown.
You can renew online at www.hants.gov.uk/library
Or by phoning 0845 603 5631

Hampshire
County Council

MURDER AT
MANSFIELD PARK

LYNN SHEPHERD

THORNDIKE
WINDSOR
PARAGON

LIBRARY OF CONGRESS CATALOGING-IN-PUBLICATION DATA

Shepherd, Lynn, 1964–
    Murder at Mansfield Park / by Lynn Shepherd.
        p. cm. — (Thorndike Press large print historical fiction)
    ISBN-13: 978-1-4104-3258-2
    ISBN-10: 1-4104-3258-0
    1. Austen, Jane, 1775–1817—Characters—Fiction. 2. Young women—Crimes against—Fiction. 3. Murder—Investigation—Fiction. 4. Country homes—England—Fiction. 5. England—Social life and customs—Fiction. 6. Large type books. I. Austen, Jane, 1775–1817. Mansfield Park. II. Title.
PR6119.H465M87 2010b
823'.92—dc22   2010036720

BRITISH LIBRARY CATALOGUING-IN-PUBLICATION DATA AVAILABLE

Published in 2010 in the U.S. by arrangement with St. Martin's Press, LLC.
Published in 2011 in the U.K. by arrangement with Beautiful Books Ltd.

U.K. Hardcover: 978 1 445 85469 4 (Windsor Large Print)
U.K. Softcover: 978 1 445 85470 0 (Paragon Large Print)

Printed and bound in Great Britain by the MPG Books Group
1 2 3 4 5 6 7 14 13 12 11 10

For S & S
who were there at the start.

NAMES OF THE PRINCIPAL PERSONS

AT MANSFIELD PARK

The family:
Sir Thomas Bertram, Baronet
Lady Bertram, his wife
Thomas Bertram, his eldest son
Miss Maria Bertram, his eldest daughter
William Bertram, his second son, away at
   sea
Miss Julia Bertram, his second daughter
Miss Fanny Price, niece to Sir Thomas;
   daughter to Mr Price of Lessingby Hall,
   Cumberland, and his wife Frances, sister
   to Lady Bertram

The household:
Baddeley, the butler
Mrs Baddeley, the housekeeper
Mr McGregor, the steward
Mr Fletcher, the bailiff
Mrs Chapman, attending Lady Bertram

Mme Dacier }
Hannah O'Hara } attending Miss Price
Kitty Jeffries, attending Miss Bertram
Polly Evans, attending Miss Julia Bertram

AT THE WHITE HOUSE

Mrs Norris, sister to Lady Bertram
Edmund Norris, her stepson

AT THE PARSONAGE

The Reverend Dr Grant
Mrs Grant
Henry Crawford, half brother to Mrs
Grant
Miss Mary Crawford, his sister

AT SOTHERTON

James Rushworth, son to Sir Richard
Rushworth
The Honourable John Yates

FROM LONDON

Charles Maddox, a thief-taker
George Fraser }
Abel Stornaway } his assistants

CHAPTER I

About thirty years ago Miss Maria Ward, of Huntingdon, with only seven thousand pounds, had the good luck to captivate Sir Thomas Bertram, of Mansfield Park, in the county of Northampton, and to be thereby raised to the rank of a baronet's lady, with all the comforts and consequences of an handsome house and large income. All Huntingdon exclaimed on the greatness of the match, and her uncle, the lawyer, himself, allowed her to be at least three thousand pounds short of any equitable claim to it. She had two sisters to be benefited by her elevation, and her father hoped that the eldest daughter's match would set matters in a fair train for the younger. But, though she possessed no less a fortune, Miss Julia's features were rather plain than handsome, and in consequence the neighbourhood was united in its conviction that there would not be such another great match to distinguish the Ward family.

Unhappily for the neighbourhood, Miss Julia was fated to confound their dearest expectations, and to emulate her sister's good luck, by captivating a gentleman of both wealth and consequence, albeit a widower. Within a twelvemonth after Miss Ward's nuptials her younger sister began upon a career of conjugal felicity with a Mr Norris, his considerable fortune, and young son, in the village immediately neighbouring Mansfield Park. Miss Frances fared yet better. A chance encounter at a Northampton ball threw her in the path of a Mr Price, the only son of a great Cumberland family, with a large estate at Lessingby Hall. Miss Frances was lively and beautiful, and the young man being both romantic and imprudent, a marriage took place to the infinite mortification of his father and mother, who possessed a sense of their family's pride and consequence, which equalled, if not exceeded, even their prodigious fortune. It was as unsuitable a connection as such hasty marriages usually are, and did not produce much happiness. Having married beneath him, Mr Price felt justly entitled to excessive gratitude and unequalled devotion in his wife, but he soon discovered that the young woman he had loved for her spirit, as

10

much as her beauty, had neither the gentle temper nor submissive disposition he and his family considered his due.

Older sages might easily have foreseen the natural sequel of such an inauspicious beginning, and despite the fine house, jewels and carriages that her husband's position afforded, it was not long before Miss Frances, for her part, perceived that the Prices could not but hold her cheap, on account of her lowly birth. The consequence of this, upon a mind so young and inexperienced, was but too inevitable. Her spirits were depressed, and though her family were not consumptive, her health was delicate, and the rigours of the Cumberland climate, severely aggravated by a difficult lying-in, left young Mr Price a widower within a year of his marriage. He had not been happy with his wife, but that did not prevent him being quite overcome with misery and regret when she was with him no more, and the late vexations of their life together were softened by her suffering and death. His little daughter could not console him; she was a pretty child, with her mother's light hair and blue eyes, but the resemblance served only to heighten his sense of anguish and remorse. It was a wretched time, but even as they consoled their son in his affliction, Mr and Mrs Price could only congratulate themselves privately that a marriage contracted under such unfortunate circumstances had not resulted in a more enduring unhappiness. Having consulted a number of eminent physicians, the anxious parents soon determined that the young man would be materially better for a change of air and situation, and the family having an extensive property at the West Indies, it was soon decided between them that his wounded heart might best find consolation in the novelty, exertion, and excitement of a sea voyage. Some heart-ache the widower-father may be supposed to have felt on leaving his daughter, but he took comfort in the fact that his little Fanny would have every comfort and attention in his father's house. He left England with the probability of being at least a twelvemonth absent.

And what of Mansfield at this time? Lady Bertram had delighted her husband with an heir, soon after Miss Frances' marriage, and this joyful event was duly followed by the birth of a daughter, some few months younger than her little cousin in Cumberland. One might have imagined Mrs Price to have enjoyed a regular and intimate intercourse with her sisters at Mansfield during this interesting period, but her husband's family had done all in their power to discourage any thing more than common civility, and despite Mrs Norris's sanguine expectations of being 'every year at Lessingby', and being introduced to a host of great personages, no such invitation was ever forthcoming. Mrs Price's sudden death led to an even greater distance between the families, and when news finally reached Mansfield that young Mr Price had fallen victim to a nervous seizure on his journey back to England — intelligence his parents had not seen fit to impart themselves — Mrs Norris could not be satisfied without writing to the Prices, and giving vent to all the anger and resentment that she had pent up in her own mind since her sister's marriage. Had Sir Thomas known of her intentions, an absolute rupture might have been prevented, but as it was the Prices felt fully justified in putting an end to all communication between the families for a considerable interval.

One can only imagine the mortifying sensations that Sir Thomas must have endured at such a time, but all private feelings were soon swallowed up by a more public grief. Mr Norris, long troubled by an indifferent state of health, brought on apoplexy and death by drinking a whole bottle of claret in the course of a single evening. There were some who said that a long-standing habit of self-indulgence had lately grown much worse from his having to endure daily harangues from his wife at her ill-treatment by the Prices, but whatever the truth of this, it is certain that no such rumour ever came to Mrs Norris's ear. She, for her part, was left only with a large income and a spacious house, and consoled herself for the loss of her husband by considering that she could do very well without him, and for the loss of an invalid to nurse by the acquisition of a son to bring up.

At Mansfield Park a son and a daughter successively entered the world, and as the years passed, Sir Thomas contrived to maintain a regular if unfrequent correspondence with his brother-in-law, Mr Price, in which he learned of little Fanny's progress with much complacency. But when the girl was a few months short of her twelfth birthday, Sir Thomas, in place of his usual communication from Cumberland, received instead a letter in a lawyer's hand, conveying the sorrowful information that Mr and Mrs Price had both succumbed to a putrid fever, and in the next sentence, beseeching Sir Thomas, as the child's uncle, and only relation, to take the whole charge of her. Sir Thomas was a man of honour and principle, and not insensible to the claims of duty and the ties of blood, but such an undertaking was not to be lightly engaged in; not, at least, without consulting his wife. Lady Bertram was a woman of very tranquil feelings, guided in every thing important by Sir Thomas, and in smaller day-to-day concerns by her sister. Knowing as he did Mrs Norris's generous concern for the wants of others, Sir Thomas elected to bring the subject forward as they were sitting together at the tea-table, where Mrs Norris was presiding. He gave the ladies the particulars of the letter in his usual measured and dignified manner, concluding with the observation that 'after due consideration, and examining this distressing circumstance in all its particulars, I firmly believe that I have no other alternative but to accede to this lawyer's request and bring Fanny to live with us here, at Mansfield Park. I hope, my dear, that you will also see it in the same judicious light.'

Lady Bertram agreed with him instantly. 'I think we cannot do better,' said she. 'Let us send for her at once. Is she not my niece, and poor Frances' orphan child?'

As for Mrs Norris, she had not a word to

say. She saw decision in Sir Thomas's looks, and her surprise and vexation required some moments' silence to be settled into composure. Instead of seeing her first, and beseeching her to try what her influence might do, Sir Thomas had shewn a very reasonable dependence on the nerves of his wife, and introduced the subject with no more ceremony than he might have announced such common and indifferent news as their country neighbourhood usually furnished. Mrs Norris felt herself defrauded of an office, but there was comfort, however, soon at hand. A second and most interesting reflection suddenly occurring to her, she resumed the conversation with renewed animation as soon as the tea-things had been removed.

'My dear Sir Thomas,' she began, with a voice as well regulated as she could manage, 'considering what excellent prospects the young lady has, and supposing her to possess even one hundredth part of the sweet temper of your own dear girls, would it not be a fine thing for us all if she were to develop a fondness for my Edmund? After all, he will in time inherit poor Mr Norris's property, and she will have her grandfather's estate, an estate which can only improve further under your prudent management. It is the very thing of all others to be wished.'

'There is some truth in what you say,' replied Sir Thomas, after some deliberation, 'and should such a situation arise, no-one, I am sure, would be more contented than myself. But whatever its merits, I would not wish to impose such a union upon any young person in my care. Every thing shall take its course. All the young people will be much thrown together. There is no saying what it may lead to.'

Mrs Norris was content, and every thing was considered as settled. Sir Thomas made arrangements for Mr Price's lawyer to accompany the girl on the long journey to Northampton-shire, and three weeks later she was delivered safely into her uncle's charge.

Sir Thomas and Lady Bertram received her very kindly, and Mrs Norris was all delight and volubility and made her sit on the sopha with herself. Their visitor took care to shew an appropriate gratitude, as well as an engaging submissiveness and humility. Sir Thomas, believing her quite overcome, decided that she needed encouragement, and tried to be all that was conciliating, little thinking that, in consequence of having been, for some years past, Mrs Price's constant companion and *protégée,* she was too much used to the company and praise of a wide circle of fine ladies and gentlemen to have any thing like a natural shyness. Finding nothing in Fanny's person to counteract her advantages of fortune and connections, Mrs Norris's efforts to become acquainted with her exhibited all the warmth of an interested party. She thought with even greater satisfaction of Sir Thomas's benevolent plan; and pretty soon decided that her niece, so long lost sight of, was blessed with talents and acquirements in no common degree. And Mrs Norris was not the only inmate of Mansfield to partake of this generous opinion. Fanny herself was perfectly conscious of her own pre-eminence, and found her cousins so ignorant of many things with which she had been long familiar, that she thought them prodigiously stupid, and although she was careful to utter nothing but praise before her uncle and aunt Bertram, she always found a most encouraging listener in Mrs Norris.

'My dear Fanny,' her aunt would reply, 'you must not expect every body to be as forward and quick at learning as yourself. You must make allowance for your cousins, and pity their deficiency. Nor is it at all necessary that they should be as accomplished as *you* are; on the contrary, it is much more desirable that there should be a difference. *You,* after all, are an *heiress.* And remember that, if you are ever so forward and clever yourself, you should always be modest. That is by far the most becoming demeanour for a superior young lady.'

As Fanny grew tall and womanly, and Sir Thomas made his yearly visit to Cumberland to receive the accounts, and superintend the management of the estate, Mrs Norris did not forget to think of the match she had projected when her niece's coming to Mansfield was first proposed, and became most zealous in promoting it, by every suggestion and contrivance likely to enhance its desirableness to either party. Once Edmund was of age Mrs Norris saw no necessity to make any other attempt at secrecy, than talking of it every where as a matter not to be talked of at present. If Sir Thomas saw any thing of this, he did nothing to contradict it. Without enquiring into their feelings, the complaisance of the young people seemed to justify Mrs Norris's opinion, and Sir Thomas was satisfied; too glad to be satisfied, perhaps, to urge the matter quite so far as his judgment might have dictated to others. He could only be happy in the prospect of an alliance so unquestionably advantageous, a connection exactly of the right sort, and one which would retain Fanny's fortune within the family, when it might have been bestowed elsewhere. Sir Thomas knew that his own daughters would not have a quarter as much as Fanny, but trusted that the brilliance of countenance that they had inherited from one parent, would more than compensate for any slight deficiency in what they were to receive from the other.

The first event of any importance in the family happened in the year that Miss Price was to come of age. Her elder cousin Maria had just entered her twentieth year, and Julia was some six years younger. Tom Bertram, at twenty-one, was just entering into life, full of spirits, and with all the liberal dispositions of an eldest son, but a material change was to occur at Mansfield, with the departure of his younger brother, William, to take up his duties as a midshipman on board His Majesty's Ship the *Perseverance*. With his open, amiable disposition, and easy, unaffected manners William could not but be missed, and the family was prepared to find a great chasm in their society, and to miss him decidedly. A prospect that had once seemed a long way off was soon upon them, and the last few days were taken up with the necessary preparations for his removal; business followed business, and the days were hardly long enough for all the agitating cares and busy little particulars attending this momentous event.

The last breakfast was soon over; the last kiss was given, and William was gone. After seeing her brother to the final moment, Maria walked back to the breakfast-room with a saddened heart to comfort her mother and Julia, who were sitting crying over William's deserted chair and empty plate. Lady Bertram was feeling as an anxious mother must feel, but Julia was giving herself up to all the excessive affliction of a young and ardent heart that had never yet been acquainted with the grief of parting. Even though some two years older than herself, William had been her constant companion in every childhood pleasure, her friend in every youthful distress. However her sister might reason with her, Julia could not be brought to consider the separation as any thing other than permanent.

'Dear, dear William!' she sobbed. 'Who knows if I will ever behold you again! Those delightful hours we have spent together, opening our hearts to one another and sharing all our hopes and plans! Those sweet summers when every succeeding morrow renewed our delightful converse! How endless they once seemed but how quickly they have passed! And now I fear they will never come again! Even if you do return, it will not be the same — you will have new cares, and new pleasures, and little thought for the sister you left behind!'

Maria hastened to assure her that such precious memories of their earliest attachment would surely never be entirely forgotten, and that William had such a warm heart that time and absence must only increase their mutual affection, but Julia was not to be consoled, and all her sister's soothings proved ineffectual.

'We shall miss William at Mansfield,' was Sir Thomas's observation when he joined them with Mrs Norris in the breakfast-room, but noticing his younger daughter's distress, and knowing that in general her sorrows, like her joys, were as immoderate as they were momentary, decided it was best to say no more and presently turned the subject. 'Where are Tom and Fanny?'

'Fanny is playing the piano-forte, and Tom has just set off for Sotherton to call on Mr Rushworth,' replied Maria.

'He will find our new neighbour a most pleasant, gentleman-like man,' said Sir

Thomas. 'I sat but ten minutes with him in his library, yet he appeared to me to have good sense and a pleasing address. I should certainly have stayed longer but the house is all in an uproar. I have always thought Sotherton a fine old place — but Mr Rushworth says it wants improvement, and in consequence the house is in a cloud of dust, noise, and confusion, without a carpet to the floor, or a sopha to sit on. Rushworth was called out of the room twice while I was there, to satisfy some doubts of the plasterer. And once he has done with the house, he intends to begin upon the grounds. Given my own interest in the subject, we found we had much in common.'

'What can you mean, Sir Thomas?' enquired Lady Bertram, roused from her melancholy reverie. 'I am sure I never heard you mention such a thing before.'

Sir Thomas looked round the table. 'I have been considering the matter for some time, and, if the prospect is not unpleasant to you, madam, I intend to improve Mansfield. I have no eye for such matters, but our woods are very fine, the house is well-placed on rising ground, and there is the stream, which, I dare say, one might make something of. When I last dined at the parsonage, I mentioned my plans to Dr Grant, and he told me that his wife's brother had the laying out of the grounds at Compton. I have since enquired into this Mr Crawford's character and reputation, and my subsequent letter to him received a most prompt and courteous reply. He is to bring his sister with him, and they are to spend three months in Mansfield. Indeed, they arrived last night; and I have invited them and the Grants to drink tea with us this evening.'

The family could not conceal their astonishment, and looked all the amazement which such an unexpected announcement could not fail of exciting. Even Julia checked her tears, and tried to compose herself. Mrs Norris was ready at once with her suggestions, but was vexed to find that Sir Thomas had been amusing himself with shaping a very complete outline of the business. He had, in fact, long been apprehensive of the effect of his son's departure, and the contraction of the Mansfield circle consequent thereon. He had reasoned to himself that if he could find the means of distracting his family's attention, and keeping up their spirits for the first few weeks, he should think the time and money very well spent. Such careful solicitude was quite of a piece with the whole of his careful, upright conduct as a husband and father, and the eager curiosity of his family was just what he wished. Questions and exclamations followed each other rapidly, and he was ready to give such information as he possessed, and answer every query almost before it was put, looking with heartfelt satisfaction on the animated faces around him. One question, however, he could not answer; he had never yet seen Mr Crawford, and could not answer for any thing more than his skill with a pen. Had he known all that was to come of the acquaintance, Sir Thomas would surely have forbad him the house.

The Crawfords were not young people of fortune. The brother had a small property near London, the sister less than two thousand pounds. They were the children of Mrs Grant's mother by a second marriage, and when they were young she had been very fond of them; but, as her own marriage had been soon followed by the death of their common parent, which left them to the care of a brother of their father, a man of whom Mrs Grant knew nothing, she had scarcely seen them since. In their uncle's house near Bedford-square they had found a kind home. He was a single man, and the cheerful company of the brother and sister ensured that his final years had every comfort that he could wish; he doated on the boy, and found both nurse and housekeeper in the girl. Unfortunately, his own property was entailed on a distant relation; and this cousin installing himself in the house within a month of the old gentleman's sudden death, Mr and Miss Crawford were obliged to look for another home without delay, Mr Crawford's own house being too small for their joint comfort, and one to which his sister had taken a fixed dislike, for reasons of her own. Having been forced by want of fortune to go into a profession, Mr Crawford had begun with the law, but soon after had discovered a genius for improvement that gave him the excuse he had been wanting to give up his first choice and enter upon another. For the last three years he had spent nine months in every twelve travelling the country from Devon-shire to Derby-shire, visiting gentlemen's seats, and laying out their grounds, gathering at the same time a list of noble patrons and a competent knowledge of Views, Situations, Prospects and the principles of the Picturesque. What would have been hardship to a more indolent, stay-at-home man was bustle and excitement to him. For Henry Crawford had, luckily, a great dislike to any thing like a permanence of abode, or limitation of society; and he boasted of spending half his life in a post-chaise, and forming more new acquaintances in a fortnight than most men did in a twelvemonth. But, all the same, he was properly aware that it was his duty to provide a comfortable home for Mary, and when the letter from the Park was soon followed by another from the parsonage offering his sister far more suitable accommodations than their present lodgings could afford, he saw it as the happy intervention of a Providence that had ever been his friend.

The measure was quite as welcome on one side as it could be expedient on the other; for Mrs Grant, having by this time run through all the usual resources of ladies residing in a country parsonage without a family of children to superintend, was very much in want of some domestic diversion. The arrival, therefore, of her brother and sister was highly agreeable; and Mrs Grant was delighted to receive a young man and woman of very pleasant appearance. Henry Crawford was decidedly handsome, with a person, height, and air that many a nobleman might have envied, while Mary had an elegant and graceful beauty, and a strength of understanding that might even exceed her brother's. This, however, she had the good sense to conceal, at least when first introduced into polite company. Mrs Grant had not waited her sister's arrival to look out for a desirable match for her, and she had fixed, for want of much variety of suitable young men in the immediate vicinity, on Tom Bertram. He was, she was constrained to admit, but twenty-one, and perhaps an eldest son would *in general* be thought too good for a girl of less than two thousand pounds, but stranger things have happened, especially where the young woman in question had all the accomplishments which Mrs Grant saw in her sister. Did not Lady Bertram herself have little more than that sum when she captivated Sir Thomas? Mary had not been three hours in the house before Mrs Grant told her what she had planned, concluding with, 'And as we are invited to the Park this evening, you will see him for yourself.'

'And what of your poor brother?' asked Henry with a smile. 'Are there no Miss Bertrams to whom I can make myself agreeable? No rich ward of Sir Thomas's I can entertain? I ask only that they have at least twenty thousand pounds. I cannot exert myself for any thing less.'

'If that is your standard,' replied Mrs Grant, 'then Mansfield has only one young woman worthy of the name. Fanny Price is

Sir Thomas's niece, and has at least twice that sum, and will inherit her grandfather's Cumberland property, and some vast estates in the West Indies, I believe. And she is generally thought to be by far the handsomest of the young ladies — quite the belle of the neighbourhood. But I am sorry for your sake, my dear brother, that she is already engaged. Or at least, so I believe, for no announcement has actually been made, but Mrs Norris told me in confidence, that Fanny is to marry her son Edmund. He has a very large property from his father, though you would scarcely believe it from the way his mother carries on. Such assiduous economy and frugality I have never known, and certainly not from a person so admirably provided for as Mrs Norris must be. I believe she must positively enjoy all her ingenious contrivances, and take pleasure in saving half a crown here and there, since there cannot possibly be any other explanation.'

Mary heaved a small sigh at this, and thought of the considerable retrenchment she had been forced to make in her own expenditure of late. Mrs Grant, meanwhile, had returned to the young ladies of the Park.

'You will be obliged to content yourself with Miss Bertram, Henry. She is a pretty young lady, if not so handsome as Miss Price, and has a nice height and size, and sweet dark eyes. But I warn you that you may encounter some competition in that quarter. A Mr Rushworth has but lately arrived in the neighbourhood, and I believe we may even see him at the Park this evening. He is the younger son of a baronet, with an estate of four or five thousand a year, they say, and very likely more.'

Henry could not help half a smile, but he said nothing.

The dinner hour approaching, the ladies separated for their toilette. Although Mary had laughed heartily at her sister's picture of herself as the future mistress of Mansfield Park, she found herself meditating upon it in the calmness of her own room, and she dressed with more than usual care. The loss of her home, with all its attendant indignity, had been a painful proof that matrimony was the only honourable provision for a well-educated young woman of such little fortune as hers. Marriage, therefore, must be her object, and she must resign herself to marrying as well as she could, even if that meant submitting to an alliance with a man of talents far inferior to her own.

As the weather was fine and the paths dry, they elected to walk to their engagement across the park. If she could not share her brother's professional interest in the disposition of the grounds, Mary yet saw much to be pleased with: lawns and plantations of the freshest green, and nearer the house, trees and shrubberies, and a long lime walk. From the entrance hall, they were shewn into the drawing-room, where everyone was assembled. They soon discovered, however, that the family had been frustrated in their hopes of Mr Rushworth; he had sent Sir Thomas a very proper letter of excuse, but regretted that he was required directly in town. The immediate disappointment of the party was rendered even more acute by the fair reports Mr Bertram brought with him from Sotherton. In the course of the afternoon Mr Bertram had perfected his acquaintance with their new neighbour, and was returned with his head full of his recently acquired friend. The topic had evidently been already handled in the dining-parlour; it was revived in the drawing-room, and as coffee was being poured Mary was standing near enough to Mr Bertram for her to overhear a discussion with her brother on the same engrossing subject.

'I tell you, Crawford, you never saw so complete a man! He has taste, spirit, genius, every thing. He intends to re-establish Sotherton as one of the foremost houses in Northampton-shire. It has lain empty for so long, and the house itself is sadly neglected, but Rushworth has great hopes for it. I will take the first opportunity to introduce you — he has above seven hundred acres, and all of it needing as much attention as the house.'

Mr Crawford bowed his thanks. 'I am always happy to make the acquaintance of gentlemen of extensive and unimproved property,' he said with a smile.

The card tables were soon placed, and Sir Thomas and his lady, and Dr and Mrs Grant sat down to Casino. Mrs Norris called for music, and Mary was prevailed upon by Mr Bertram to sit down at the piano-forte. After listening for a few minutes, Mrs Norris said loudly, 'If Miss Crawford had had the advantage of a proper master she might *almost* have played as well as Fanny, do you not agree, Edmund?'

'You are too kind, ma'am,' said Miss Price, colouring most becomingly. Mr Norris said nothing, and Mary looked up to see how warmly he assented to his lady's praise; but neither at that moment nor at any other time during the evening could she perceive any visible symptom of love; and from the whole of his behaviour to Miss Price she derived only the conviction that he was an arrogant, weak young man, driven by motives of selfishness and worldly ambition into a marriage without affection. Miss Price herself was more of a puzzle. The good-natured Mrs Grant had extolled her beauty so highly, that Mary had the pleasure of being disappointed. But it was not merely Miss Price's looks that attracted Mary's notice. With an uncommon quickness in understanding the tempers of those she had to deal with, and no natural timidity to hinder her, Mary rarely had any great difficulty in making out the characters of the people she encountered, but Miss Price, at first, was in every view unaccountable. That a young woman possessed of so large a fortune should have consented to an engagement without further proof of attachment than Mary was able to discern in Mr Norris, was beyond her comprehension. Mary loved to laugh, and she fancied she might find much in the situation to amuse her in the weeks to come, but to her reason, her judgment, it was inexplicable. Further observation of Miss Price in the evening circle shewed her to be vain, insincere, and possessed of a quite excessive degree of self-consequence, despite her studied appearance of modest self-denial. Mary could only conclude that so far, at least, the foremost position in the family which the supposed engagement afforded her, had been reason enough to assent to it. But despite the long-standing nature of the connection, and the apparently unanimous wishes of the two families, Mary did not give much for Mr Norris's chances if a more prepossessing rival were to step in before the articles were signed.

The other young women of the family were more easily accounted for. Julia Bertram spent the evening with her mother on the sopha, engaged in her needlework, but from one or two remarks Mary heard her make, and from the little shelf of books at her side, she judged the youngest Miss Bertram to have both a tender disposition, and a fondness for reading. Her sister Maria seemed to be a pleasant, accomplished girl, but one whose natural sweetness of temper was not equal to the severe trial of holding but a second place in every thing to Miss Price. Despite her beauty and acquirements, Miss Bertram's fortune was so markedly inferior, and her footing in the family so subordinate, as to have pressed very hard upon the patience of a saint, much less the feelings of a pretty young woman of twenty.

Mary wondered at Sir Thomas, whose conduct seemed in so many other respects to be most just and reasonable. Could he be blind to a state of affairs that was plain to Mary after little more than an evening's acquaintance with the family? Could he not see what the consequences of such a misplaced distinction might prove to be? Could he, in fact, have so little insight into the disposition of his niece — a young woman who had been brought up under his eye since she was twelve years old?

CHAPTER II

After breakfast the following morning Henry proposed that Mary accompany him on a survey of the park. The enthusiasm produced by their walk of the previous evening was excited still more by the loveliness of the day; it was really April; but it was May in its mild air, brisk soft wind, and bright sun, occasionally clouded for a minute. Every thing looked beautiful under the influence of such a sky, even a bowling-green and a formal parterre laid out with too much regularity for his improver's eye.

'Well my dear Mary,' said Henry, drawing her arm within his, as they walked along the sweep, 'how do you like Mansfield?'

'Very well — very much. Our sister is all kindness, and I am sure our three months here will be marked by many such evenings at the Park.'

'And Mr Bertram?' he asked.

Mary shook her head with a smile. 'I fear

our sister will be disappointed if she persists in her expectations of him, even supposing him capable of attaching himself to a woman of no fortune, and no connections. I concede that Mr Bertram has easy manners and excellent spirits, as well as a long list of intimate friends that he seems to add to on the strength of the most meagre acquaintance, but these are not sufficient qualities to attract *me,* notwithstanding the reversion of Mansfield Park, and the baronetcy he will one day assume.'

Henry laughed. 'You are far too old for your twenty years, my dear Mary. I will leave it to you to break the news to our poor sister! And the young ladies?'

Mary decided to keep her more perplexing observations to herself for the present, stating merely that Miss Bertram seemed to be a very pleasing young woman.

'Quite so, but I do not know what to make of Miss Julia. I do not understand her. Why did she draw back and look so grave at me? She hardly said a word.'

Mary laughed. 'Henry! Miss Julia is not *out.* No wonder you could not get her to speak. She should not be noticed for another six months at least — or until Miss Price marries.'

'Oh, Mary, these outs and not outs are

beyond me! But you have now introduced a subject in which I must confess the most profound interest. What think you, my dear Mary, of the said Miss Price? The sweet and amiable and modest Miss Price? Did you not see her last night? Writing that note for Lady Bertram? Attending with such ineffable gentleness and patience, her colour beautifully heightened as she leant over it, her hair arranged neatly, and one little curl falling forward as she wrote —'

'I am sure that Miss Price's ringlets are quite as artfully contrived as her deportment,' interrupted Mary with a laugh. 'I can respect her for doing her hair well, but cannot feel a more tender sentiment. Nor, I am sure, can *you*. I know you are merely teasing.'

'No, no, I am quite determined, Mary. My mind is entirely made up. My plan is to make Fanny Price in love with me.'

Mary shook her head with a smile. 'My dear brother, I will not believe this of you. Even were she as perfectly faultless as she appears — even were she the angel Mrs Norris claims her to be — we are told that Miss Price is engaged. Her choice is made.'

'All I can say to *that* is that if Miss Price has given Mr Norris her heart as well as her hand, then she will be safe from any attack from me. But Mary,' he said, stopping short, and smiling in her face, 'I know what a thinking brain you have, and I know full well that you saw exactly what I saw — you cannot dissemble with me. Miss Price does not care three straws for Mr Norris, nor he for her; *that* is your opinion. And I do not blame her — what woman would care for such an undersized, solemn, gloomy fellow! Did you not hear him discussing his wretched dog last night? I never heard so much fuss made over such a trifle, or so many long words expended over such a small puppy — if it was necessary to say any thing at all on such a desperate dull subject. In his place I would simply have said "I have given the thing a basket in the stables", but clearly such plain and manly dealing is beyond the wit of our Mr Norris. What was it he said? "I at length determined on a method of proceeding which would obviate the risk of unnecessary expense." Honestly, Mary, what is one to do with such an insufferable fellow?'

Mary laughed and replied, 'Perhaps he will improve upon acquaintance?'

'I rather doubt it,' he said, with sarcastic dryness, 'as I am sure his lovely Fanny is only too aware.'

'Oh! Henry, how shall I manage you? But

I know you are not serious.'

'Forty thousand pounds is a serious enough matter, would you not say?'

It was lightly said, and lightly taken, and without attempting any farther remonstrance, Mary left Miss Price to her fate, and they continued their walk. Henry led the way; every vista was pointed out, every prospect noted, until an opening in the trees finally afforded them a view of the house. They stopped some minutes to look and admire, until they noticed Miss Price and Mr Norris on horseback, riding side by side, followed by the Mansfield coachman, making directly towards the spot where they stood. Mary turned to her brother with a smile. 'It seems you will have an early opportunity to begin your wicked project. I shall observe how you succeed, though if I am to judge by her behaviour last evening, I do not think you should expect very much encouragement. If there is not hope in her disdain, there is hope in nothing else.'

'I fear we interrupt you in the exercise of your profession, Crawford,' said Mr Norris, as soon as he was within hearing. 'I suspected we might encounter you on our ride; the weather is exactly suited for your purpose. Well, how do you go on? Have you been able to form an opinion?'

Henry protested that a survey such as he felt necessary to be done was not the work of a moment, but, if he would, Mr Norris could be of inestimable assistance to him in pointing out the various divisions of the park.

Before Mr Norris could answer, Miss Price ventured to say, 'Edmund, I am sure my uncle's steward would be happy to offer his services to Mr Crawford by way of a guide.'

Mr Norris made no reply and continued, 'Is there any thing you particularly wish to see, Crawford?'

'Sir Thomas's letter talked of an avenue. I should like to see that.'

'Of course, you would not have been able to see it last night, for the drawing-room looks across the lawn. Yes, the avenue is exactly behind the house; it begins at a little distance, and descends for half a mile to the extremity of the grounds. You may see some thing of it here — some thing of the more distant trees. It is oak entirely. But have a care, Crawford, you will lose my cousin Julia as a friend if you propose to have it down. She has a young girl's romantic attachment to the avenue; she says it makes her think of Cowper.'

' "Ye fallen avenues, once more I mourn

your fate unmerited,"' said Mary, with a smile. 'The park is certainly beautiful at this time of year. The woods are some of the finest I have ever seen.'

'Indeed,' said Miss Price, looking at her with evident surprise. 'I had not expected someone so used to the bustle and dirt and noise of London to feel the pleasures of spring so keenly. The animation of body and mind that one can derive from the beginnings and progress of vegetation, the increasing beauties of the earliest flowers — when all is freshness, fragrance, and verdure!'

There was a short silence, then Mr Norris returned to Henry. 'It is some distance, I am afraid, from this spot to the avenue, and I fear Miss Crawford may have had walking enough for this morning.'

'I am not tired, I assure you,' said she. 'Nothing ever fatigues me but doing what I do not like, and nothing pleases me more than accompanying Henry on his visits. I rarely have a gratification of the kind.'

Mr Norris nodded gravely, and then continued to address Henry, 'All the same, the park is large — full five miles around — and your survey of the grounds would be better taken on horseback.'

'My dear Edmund,' said Miss Price, 'you

forget that a man such as Mr Crawford can scarcely afford to keep three hunters of his own, as you do. But there must be some horse or other in my uncle's stable that nobody else wants, that Mr Crawford could use while he is here?'

Henry made a low bow. 'Miss Price is all consideration, but I can assure her that her generous concern is quite unnecessary. Dr Grant has offered me the loan of his road-horse, and as for Mary, well, she is no horse-woman, so the question does not arise.'

'Would it interest you to learn to ride, Miss Crawford?' asked Mr Norris, speaking to her for the first time. His addressing her at all was so unexpected that Mary hardly knew what to say, and felt she must look rather foolish, but whatever her confusion, she was still able to observe that, although endeavouring to appear properly demure, Miss Price's disapprobation was only too evident. Mary thought that Mr Norris must perceive it likewise, and presumed that no more would be said on the subject. What, then, was her increase of astonishment on hearing Mr Norris repeat his offer, adding that he had a quiet mare that would be perfectly fitted for a beginner. What, thought Mary, could he mean by it? Surely he could not be unaware of Miss Price's views on the subject? But quickly recovering her spirits, she decided that if he saw fit to ignore Miss Price's feelings, there was no reason for her to respect them, and she accepted the offer with enthusiasm, saying that it would indeed give her great pleasure to learn to ride.

The next morning saw the arrival of Mr Norris at the parsonage, attended by his groom. Henry, who had been waiting with Dr Grant's horse, lingered only to see Mary lifted on hers before mounting his own and departing for a day's ride about the estate.

With an active and fearless character, and no want of strength and courage, Mary seemed formed to be a horsewoman, and made her first essay around Dr Grant's meadow with great credit. When they made their first stop she was rewarded with expressions more nearly approaching warmth than she had so far heard Mr Norris utter, but upon looking up, she became aware that Miss Price had walked down from the Park, and was watching the two of them intently, from her position at the gate. They had neither of them seen her approach, and Mary could not be sure how long she had been there. Mr Norris had just taken Mary's hand in order to direct the management of her bridle, but as soon as he saw Miss Price, he released it, and coloured slightly, recollecting that he had promised to ride with Fanny that morning. He moved away from Mary at once and led her horse towards the gate. 'My dear Fanny,' he said, as she approached, 'I would not have incommoded you for the world, but Miss Crawford has been making such excellent progress, that I did not notice the hour. But,' he added in a conciliatory tone, 'there is more than time enough, and my forgetfulness may even have promoted your comfort by preventing us from setting off half an hour sooner; clouds are now coming up, and I know that you dislike riding on a hot day.'

'My dear Edmund,' said Fanny, with downcast eyes, 'it is true that my delicate complexion will not now suffer from the heat as it would otherwise have done. I *was* wondering that you should forget me, but you have now given exactly the explanation which I ventured to make for you. Miss Crawford,' she said, turning her gaze upon Mary, 'I am sure that you must think me rude and impatient, by walking to meet you in this way?'

But Mary could not be provoked. 'On the contrary,' she said, 'I should rather make my own apologies for keeping you waiting.

But I have nothing in the world to say for myself. Such dreadful selfishness must always be forgiven,' she said with a smile, and an arch look at Miss Price, 'because there is no hope of a cure.'

And so saying, Mary sprang lightly down from the mare and after thanking Mr Norris for his time and attention, she walked hastily away, turning only to watch the two of them slowly ascend the rise, and disappear from her view.

Mary found her spirits unexpectedly unsettled, and carried on walking for some while, hardly knowing where she was heading, and engrossed in her own thoughts, until she suddenly became conscious of a line of ancient oak trees stretching to her right and left. She perceived at once that she must be in that very avenue of which she had heard so much, and was surprised to find that she had walked so far. She was on the point of turning back when her eye was caught by a figure seated under one of the trees, and a moment later she recognised the youngest Miss Bertram, intent on her sketch-book, inks, and pencils.

'Will I disturb Miss Julia if I join her for a few moments?' Mary asked as she approached the bench.

Julia looked up with a sad smile. 'In truth, Miss Crawford, I would welcome the interruption. I have been trying to capture the exact effect of the sunlight on the leaves, but it is, for the moment, eluding me.'

Mary looked over the girl's shoulder at the drawing, and was agreeably surprised at what she saw. There was a peculiar felicity in the mixture of the colours, even if the more disciplined guidance of a proper drawing-master seemed to have been wanting. Mary could not but wonder why Sir Thomas had not provided such tuition for his daughter; the expense would be nothing to a man in his position. But putting the thought aside for the moment, she resolved to speak to Henry when she returned to the parsonage; as far as she was able to judge, Miss Julia had a more than everyday talent, and her brother might perhaps be able to offer some assistance. The two of them sat companionably for some minutes more, looking at the view and talking of poetry. Their taste was strikingly similar — the same books, the same passages were loved by each, and Julia brought all her favourite authors forward, giving Thomson, Cowper, and Scott their due reverence by turns, and finding a rapturous delight in discovering such a coincidence of preference.

'And your sister?' Mary enquired, after a pause. 'Does she share your enjoyment of reading?'

Julia smiled gravely. 'Alas, no. Maria and I used to read together at one time, but her thoughts now are all of balls and gowns and head-dresses, and other such idle vanities. No,' she said, with a faltering voice, and tears in her eyes, 'now that my beloved William is at sea, there is no-one in whom I can confide.'

She sighed, and was silent for a moment, gazing at the vista before them. 'I had hoped to follow the course of his ship on the map in the school-room, but he could not be sure of his exact route. My father has promised that this picture I am drawing will be sent to William in Bahama, if I can perfect it.'

Mary gently touched her arm, and observed, 'I am sure the gift will be all the more precious to him, because it comes from your own hand.'

'This was our favourite place,' Julia continued, with more animation. 'How many times have we sat together under these beloved trees! I always come here when I wish to think of him. We so loved to watch the progress of the seasons, and see the leaves change colour from the freshest green to the autumn glories of gold and red and brown.'

'In that case I am sure you must spend many happy hours with your cousin,' said Mary. 'Only yesterday I heard Miss Price rhapsodising about the beauties of spring.'

In spite of herself, Julia could not help half a smile. 'That does not surprise me — Fanny is much given to "rhapsodising" of late. She believes it shews her to have elegant taste and — what was her phrase? — "sublimity of soul". And such romantic sensibilities are, of course, exceedingly fashionable just at present.'

It was Mary's turn to smile at this, and an unexpected gust of wind then nearly shaking the sketch-book from Julia's hands, the two of them jumped up and began to walk back towards the house. By the time they reached the terrace some thing like friendship had already been established between them, notwithstanding their differences in age and situation. They parted with affectionate words, and Mary returned at last to the parsonage.

Julia said nothing to her family of her encounter in the avenue, and spent so long in adding new touches to her drawing that her mother was already ringing the bell for dinner when she joined the other ladies of the family.

Mrs Norris began scolding at once. 'That is a very foolish trick, Julia, to be idling away all the day in the garden, when there is so much needlework to be done. If you have no work of your own, I can supply you from the poor-basket here. There is all this new calico that your mother bought last week, not touched yet.'

Julia was taking the work very quietly, when her aunt suddenly exclaimed once more. 'Oh! For shame, Julia! How can you shew yourself in the drawing-room in such a disgraceful state! — Look at you, quite *covered* with paint, and to be sure you have ruined this entire roll of cloth with your thoughtlessness. Do you have *no* thought for the waste of money? Be off with you now, and wash yourself, before your father sees you and mistakes you for one of the lesser servants.'

There was indeed a very small speck of ink, quite dry, on Julia's hand, but she knew better than to contradict her aunt, however unjust her accusations, and returned to her room to remedy it, her heart swelling with repressed injury at being so publicly mortified for so little cause. When she reappeared downstairs she was just in time to hear the name of her new friend. Maria had not long returned from her daily ride with the old coachman, and related, with much liveliness, that he had never seen a young lady sit a horse better than Miss Crawford, when first put on.

'I was sure she would ride well,' Maria continued, 'she has the make for it. Her figure is so neat and light.'

'I am sure you are a fair judge, Maria,' said Lady Bertram, 'since you ride so well yourself. I only wish you could persuade Julia to learn. It is such a nice accomplishment for a young lady.'

Mrs Norris, who was still in a decidedly ill temper, seemed to find this inoffensive remark particularly provoking, and after muttering some thing about 'the nonsense and folly of people's stepping out of their rank and trying to appear above themselves', she observed in a louder tone, 'I am sure Miss Crawford's enjoyment of riding has much to do with the fact that she is contriving to learn at *no expense to herself.* Or perhaps it is *Edmund's* attendance and instructions that make her so unwilling to dismount. Indeed, I cannot see why Edmund should always have to prove his good-nature by *everyone,* however insignificant they are. What is Miss Crawford to *us?*'

'I admit,' said Fanny, after a little consideration, 'that *I* am a little surprised that Edmund can spend so many hours with Miss Crawford, and not see more of the sort of fault which I observe every time I am with her. She has such a loud opinion of her own cleverness, and such an ill-bred insistence on commanding everyone's attention, whenever she is in company. And her manners, without being exactly coarse, can hardly be called *refined*. But needless to say I have scrupled to point out my observations to Edmund, lest it should appear like ill-nature.'

'Quite so,' agreed Mrs Norris. 'Miss Crawford lacks delicacy, and has neither refinement nor elegance. Ease, but not elegance. No *elegance* at all. Indeed, she is quite the vainest, most affected, husband-hunting butterfly I have ever had the misfortune to encounter.'

The gentlemen soon joined them, and Mr Norris took a seat by Miss Price, and being unaware of the conversation that had passed, ventured to ask her whether she wished him to ride with her again the next day.

'No, not if you have other plans,' was her sweetly unselfish answer.

'I do not have plans for myself,' said he, 'but I think Miss Crawford would be glad to have the chance to ride for a longer time. I am sure she would enjoy the circuit to Mansfield-common. But I am, of course, unwilling to check a pleasure of yours,' he said quickly, perhaps aware of the dead silence now reigning in the room, and his mother's black looks. 'Indeed,' he said, with sudden inspiration, turning to his cousins, 'why should not more of us go? Why should we not make a little party?'

All the young people were soon wild for the scheme, and even Fanny, once properly pressed and persuaded, eventually assented. Mrs Norris, on the other hand, was still trying to make up her mind as to whether there was any necessity that Miss Crawford should be of the party at all, but all her hints to her son producing nothing, she was forced to content herself with merely recommending that it should be Mr Bertram, rather than Mr Norris, who should walk down to the parsonage in the morning to convey the invitation. Edmund looked his displeasure, but did nothing to oppose her, and, as usual, she carried the point.

The ride to Mansfield-common took place two days later, and was much enjoyed at the time, and doubly enjoyed again in the evening discussion. A successful scheme of this sort generally brings on another; and the having been to Mansfield-common disposed them all for going some where else the day after, and four fine mornings successively were spent in this manner. Every thing answered; it was all gaiety and good-humour, the heat only serving to supply inconvenience enough to be talked of with pleasure, and to make every shady lane the more attractive. On the fifth day their destination was Stoke-hill, one of the beauties of the neighbourhood. Their road was through a pleasant country; and Mary was very happy in observing all that was new, and admiring all that was pretty. When they got to the top of the hill, where the road narrowed and just admitted two, she found herself riding next to Miss Price. The two of them continued silent, till suddenly, stopping a moment to look at the view, and observing that Mr Norris had dismounted to assist an old woman travelling homewards with a heavy basket, Miss Price turned to her with a smile. 'Mr Norris is such a thoughtful and considerate gentleman! Always so concerned to appear civil to those of inferior rank, fortune, and expectations.'

Seeing that her companion was most interested to observe the effect of such a remark, Mary contented herself with a smile. Miss Price, however, seemed determined to continue their conversation, and after making a number of disdainful enquiries as to the cost of Mary's gown, and the make of her shoes, she continued gaily, 'You will think me most impertinent to question you in this way, Miss Crawford, but living in this rustic seclusion, I so rarely have the opportunity of making new acquaintance, especially with young women who are accustomed to the manners and amusements of London — or at least such entertainments as the public assemblies can offer.'

At this she gave Mary a look, which meant, 'A public ball is quite good enough for *you*.' Mary smiled. 'In my experience, private balls are much pleasanter than public ones. Most public balls suffer from two insurmountable disadvantages — a want of chairs, and a scarcity of men, and as often as not, a still greater scarcity of any that are good for much.'

'But that is exactly my own feeling on the subject! The company one meets at private balls is always *so* much more agreeable.'

'As to that,' replied Mary, 'I confess I do not want people to be very agreeable, as it saves me the trouble of liking them a great deal.'

She hazarded a side glance at her companion at this, wondering whether she was as accustomed to being treated with contempt, as she was to dispensing it, but Miss Price seemed serenely unaware that such a remark could possibly refer to her.

'Oh! My dear Miss Crawford,' she said, 'with so much to unite us, would it not be delightful to become better acquainted?'

To be better acquainted, Mary soon found, was to be her lot, whatever her own views on the matter. This was the origin of the second intimacy Mary was to enjoy at Mansfield, one that had little reality in the feelings of either party, and appeared to result principally from Miss Price's desire to communicate her own far superior claims on Edmund, and teach Mary to avoid him.

The weather remained fine, and Mary's rides continued. The season, the scene, the air, were all delightful, and as the days passed Mr Norris began to be agreeable to her. It was without any change in his manner — he remained as quiet and reserved as ever — but she found nonetheless that she liked to have him near her. Had she thought about it more, she might have concluded that the anxiety and confusion she had endured since her uncle's death had made her particularly susceptible to the charms of placidity and steadiness; but for reasons best known to herself, Mary did not think very much about it. She had by no means forgotten Miss Price's insinuations, and could not fail to notice Mrs Norris's rather more pointed remarks; and in the privacy of the parsonage her brother continued to ridicule Edmund as both stuffy and conceited. He began a small collection of his more pompous remarks, which he noted down in the back of his pocket-book, and performed for his sisters with high glee, mimicking his victim's rather prosing manner to absolute perfection. Perhaps Mary should have apprehended some thing of her own feelings from the growing disquiet she felt at this continued raillery, but unwelcome as it was, she chose rather to censure Henry's lack of manners, than her own lack of prudence.

Mary rode every morning, and in the afternoons she sauntered about with Julia Bertram in the Mansfield woods, or — rather more reluctantly — walked with Miss Price in Mrs Grant's garden.

'Every time I come into this shrubbery I am more struck with how much has been made of such unpromising scrubby dirt,' said Miss Price, as they were thus sitting together one day. 'Three years ago, this was nothing but a rough hedgerow along the upper side of the field, never thought of as any thing, or capable of becoming any thing.'

'It may seem partial in *me* to praise,' replied Mary, looking around her, 'but I must admire the taste my sister has shewn in all this. Even Henry approves of it, and his good opinion is not so easily won in matters horticultural.'

'I am so glad to see the evergreens thrive!' answered Miss Price, who did not appear to have heard her. 'The evergreen! How beautiful, how welcome, how wonderful the evergreen!'

But as Miss Price happened to have her eyes fixed at that moment on a particularly fine example of an elm, Mary merely smiled and said nothing.

A few moments later, Miss Price began again in a rather different strain, 'I cannot imagine what it is to pass March and April in London. How different a thing sunshine must be in a town! I imagine that in — Bedford-square was it not, my dear Miss Crawford? — the sun's power is only a glare, serving but to bring forward stains and dirt that might otherwise have slept. And old gentlemen can be *so* particular about such things. I always pity the housekeeper in such circumstances. *You,* of course, know the trials of housekeeping only too well.'

Miss Price having exhausted for the present even her considerable talent for the underhand and the insulting, began to pull at some of the trimming on her dress. 'This cheap fringe will not do at all. I really must ask Lady Bertram to remonstrate with that slovenly dressmaker. I am hardly fit to appear in decent company, but thankfully there is no-one of consequence *here* to see me.'

Mary watched her for a moment, reflecting that she did not have such an ornament on even her finest gown, before commenting thoughtfully, 'I am conscious of being even more attracted to a country residence than I expected.'

'Indeed?' said Miss Price loudly, with a look of meaning. 'What had you in mind? Allow me to guess. An elegant, moderate-sized house in the centre of family connections — continual engagements among them — commanding the first society in the neighbourhood, and turning from the cheerful round of such amusements to nothing worse than a *tête-à-tête* with the person one feels most agreeable in the world? I can see that such a picture would have much in it to attract *you,* Miss Crawford.'

'Perhaps it does.' Mary added to herself, leaving her seat, 'Perhaps I could even envy *you* with such a home as that.'

Miss Price sat silent, once again absorbed in the vexations of her gown, and pulling at it until it was quite spoilt. Mary relapsed into thoughtfulness, till suddenly looking up she saw Edmund walking towards them in the company of Mrs Grant. The very consciousness of having been thinking of him as 'Edmund' — as Miss Price alone was justified in thinking of him — caused her to colour and look away, a movement which was not lost on the sharp eyes of Miss Price.

'Well, Miss Crawford,' she said archly, 'shall I disappoint them of half their lecture upon my sitting down out of doors at this time of year, by being up before they can begin?'

Edmund met them with particular awkwardness. It was the first time of his seeing them together since the beginning of that better acquaintance which he had been hearing deprecated by his mother almost every day. He could hardly understand it; there was such a difference in their tempers, their dispositions, and their tastes, there never were two people more dissimilar. But even if he saw the force of such a contrast, he was not yet equal to discuss it with himself, and seeing them together now, he confined himself to an insipid and commonplace observation about the wisdom of judging the weather by the calendar, which would have merited an entry in Henry's pocket-book, if he had but heard it.

As the four of them returned to the parsonage house, Edmund recollected the purpose of his errand; he had walked down on purpose to convey Sir Thomas's invitation to the Grants and the Crawfords to dine at the Park. It was with strong expressions of regret that Mrs Grant declared herself to be prevented by a prior engagement, and Miss Price turned at once to Mary, saying how much she would have enjoyed the pleasure of her company, 'but without Dr and Mrs Grant, she did not suppose it would be in their power to accept,' all the while looking at Edmund for his support. But Mr Norris assured them that his uncle would be delighted to receive Mr and Miss Crawford, with or without the Grants, and in her brother's absence Mary accepted with the greatest alacrity.

'I am very glad. It will be delightful,' said Miss Price, trying for greater warmth of manner, as they took their leave. Edmund took her arm and they walked home together; and except in the immediate discus-

sion of this engagement, it was a silent walk
— for having finished that subject, Edmund
grew thoughtful and indisposed towards any
other. Miss Price narrowly observed him
throughout, but she said nothing.

CHAPTER III

At ten minutes after four on the appointed day, the coachman drove round and Mary and Henry set off across the park. As it happened, the Mansfield family had received a first letter from Mr William Bertram that very morning, and a whole afternoon had been insufficient to wear out their enthusiasm for accounts of how he had fitted up his berth, or the striking parts of his new uniform, or the kindnesses of his captain. The letter was produced again when the Crawfords arrived, and much made of its frank, unstudied style, and clear, strong handwriting. This specimen, written in haste as it was, had not a fault, and Mrs Norris expressed herself very glad that she had given William what she did at parting, very glad indeed that it had been in her power, without material inconvenience, to give him some thing rather considerable to answer his expenses, as well as a very great deal of invaluable advice about how to get every thing very cheap, by driving a hard bargain, and buying it all at Turner's.

'You are indeed fortunate that Mr William Bertram intends to be such a good correspondent,' said Mary, examining the letter in her turn. 'In my experience, young men are much less diligent creatures!' with a smile at Henry. 'Normally they would not write to their families but upon the most urgent necessity in the world; and when obliged to take up the pen, it is all over and done as quickly as possible. Henry, who is in every other way exactly what a brother should be, has never yet written more than a single page to me; and very often it is nothing more than, "Dear Mary, I am just arrived. The grounds shew great promise, and thankfully there are not too many sheep. Yours &c".'

'My dear Miss Crawford, you make me almost laugh,' said Miss Price, 'but I cannot rate so very highly the love or good-nature of a brother, who will not give himself the trouble of writing any thing worth reading, to his own sister. I am sure my cousins would never use *me* so, under any circumstances.'

'I doubt there is a man in England who could so neglect Miss Price,' said Henry gallantly, but received no other reward for his pains than Miss Price at once drawing back, and giving him a look of scorn.

A table was formed for a round game after tea, and Henry ventured to suggest that Speculation might amuse the ladies. Unwilling to cede the arrangement of the evening to anyone, and certainly not to either of the Crawfords, Mrs Norris protested that she had never played the game, nor seen it played in her life.

'Perhaps Miss Price may teach you, ma'am.'

But here Fanny interposed with anxious protestations of her own equal ignorance, and although this gave Mrs Norris a further opportunity to press very industriously, but very unsuccessfully, for Whist, she quickly encountered the warm objections of the other young people, who assured her that nothing could be so easy, that Speculation was indeed the easiest game on the cards.

Henry once more stepped forward with a most earnest request to be allowed to sit with Mrs Norris and Miss Price, and teach them both, and it was so settled. It was a fine arrangement for Henry, who was close to Fanny, and with two persons' cards to manage as well as his own — for though it was impossible for Mary not to feel herself mistress of the rules of the game in three minutes, Fanny continued to assert that Speculation seemed excessively difficult in *her* eyes, that she had not the least idea what she was about, and required her companion's constant assistance as every deal began, to direct her what she was to do with her cards.

Soon after, taking the opportunity of a little languor in the game, Edmund called upon Mr Crawford to discuss his plans of improvement, it being the first time that the ladies had had the opportunity of questioning him on the subject.

'Mansfield's natural beauties are great, sir,' he replied, 'such a happy fall of ground, and such timber! (Let me see, Miss Price; Mrs Norris bids a dozen for that knave; no, no, a dozen is more than it is worth. Mrs Norris does *not* bid a dozen. She will have nothing to say to it. Go on, go on.) With improvement Mansfield will vie with any place in England.'

'And what in particular will you be suggesting, Mr Crawford?' asked Lady Bertram.

'My survey is not fully complete, ma'am, but I anticipate one or two major works that may put the estate to some expense.'

'Well, the *expense* need not be any

impediment,' cried Mrs Norris. 'If I were Sir Thomas, I should not think of the expense. Such a place as Mansfield Park deserves every thing that taste and money can do. For my own part, I am always planting and improving, for naturally I am *excessively* fond of it. We have done a *vast* deal in that way at the White House; we have made it *quite* a different place from what it was when we first had it, and would have done more, had my poor husband lived. I am sure you would learn a great deal from the White House, Mr Crawford,' finished Mrs Norris carelessly. 'You may come any day; the housekeeper will be pleased to shew you around.'

Henry merely bowed; even had he intended taking Mrs Norris up on her condescending offer, what he had seen of the house from the road, had already confirmed his opinion that its owner was a person of more fortune than taste.

'I hope the Mansfield estate will bear any expense you care to propose, Crawford,' said Sir Thomas solemnly after a few minutes, as another deal proceeded. 'But, unhappily, I have suffered some recent difficulties on a property I own in Yorkshire, and as I explained to my family this afternoon, I fear I will be obliged to go there myself, to prevent any further losses. And as I will be travelling north I will go first to my niece's estate in Cumberland, and conduct my annual review with the steward and the bailiff. It is rather earlier in the year than I usually undertake this journey, but my niece's forthcoming birthday will require certain alterations to the superintendence of the estate, which I must settle on her behalf with the attorney. Nonetheless I am in hopes that the whole business may be concluded within three months, and that I will be able to return to my family well before the winter. In the mean time, Crawford, you have my permission to proceed with the improvements as you see fit; I only stipulate that you keep me informed of your progress by regular correspondence. However,' he continued with a grave smile, 'in the light of what we have already heard of your epistolary style from Miss Crawford, I hope that you can be persuaded to supply rather more detail to *me* than observations about my sheep.'

Henry laughed, then bowed his assent, and wished his patron a pleasant journey. The conversation resumed, and the rest of the company turned their attention once again to the game, but seated as she was near to her brother, Mary soon after found herself overhearing a further brief exchange.

'May I enquire, sir,' said Henry in a low voice, 'whether you would wish me to consult Mr Bertram on any decisions of note that arise in your absence?'

Sir Thomas shook his head. 'Between the management of the estate, and his own shooting parties and horse races, I fear my son will have more than enough to occupy him. Should you need advice, I would recommend your applying to Mr Norris in my stead. He is careful and methodical, and his judgment can be relied upon. Indeed,' he continued, lowering his voice still further, 'I had hoped to have the benefit of his company in Cumberland, especially as I will have to instruct the attorney to prepare the settlements, but Mrs Norris has persuaded me that he should remain here, not only to assist my son, but also for his own happiness, at this particular time.'

Mary struggled to contain her agitation, but the case admitted of no equivocation. All doubt was at an end. There was no other way of accounting for Sir Thomas's words than by supposing that preparations were now in hand for the marriage of Miss Price and Mr Norris.

She made a hasty finish of her dealings with Maria, and exclaimed, 'There! I have finally learned to harden my heart, and sharpen my self-command. I play for victory like a woman of spirit, but I will only pay for it what it is worth.'

You may imagine her surprise when she found that the game was hers after all, and returned her far more than she had expected, from what she had given to secure it.

It was a silent walk back across the park by moonlight for the parsonage party, with each absorbed in their own private thoughts. Mary had never believed Henry's attachment to Miss Price to be serious, and how he might be affected by the news of her impending marriage, she could not say; she was too vexed at her own weakness and susceptibility to have much time to consider his feelings. What had she been thinking? To allow herself to become attached to a man destined for another! She could not even claim ignorance as an excuse — the whole county had known of the planned union, and she herself had been informed of it on the very day she arrived in Mansfield. She had been thoughtless and vain, allowing herself to fall, almost unconsciously, into an attachment that could only injure her peace.

The following morning she awoke to the

same thoughts and meditations which had at length closed her eyes. It was impossible to think of any thing else, and she was quite amazed at her own discomposure. Edmund was no longer the same Mr Norris to whom she had taken such an early dislike, taking for coldness and pride what was in reality only shyness and diffidence. True, his manners required intimacy to make them pleasing, but they had enjoyed some thing nearly approaching intimacy every morning for almost a month, and now that his natural shyness was overcome, his behaviour to her gave every indication of an open, affectionate heart. And now the advancement of his marriage, which should have confirmed him as the husband of another woman, had on the contrary, only served to make her understand her own heart; and never had she thought she might have loved him, as she did now, when all love must be in vain.

Remembering that they had agreed to ride again that morning, and feeling herself quite unequal to it, she sent word to the Park that she would not go out that day, and attempted to persuade Henry to walk with her, and conduct that morning's observations on foot.

'I wish I could oblige you, my dear Mary,' he replied, 'but I am currently sketching plans for a Grecian temple on the hill behind the house. It is full two miles from the parsonage, and I should not have time to complete what I have set myself to do today if I were to walk there and back. But,' he said, smiling, 'I would be delighted to have your company to the stables. I hear we are to meet the celebrated Mr Rushworth tomorrow, and I am most eager to know what kind of a man to expect. I am sure the young ladies of the Park have made it their business to discover all there is to know on such a promising subject. You must enlighten me, so I may be fully prepared.'

Henry meant only to divert her, and at any other time he would have succeeded; she would have entered into his lively speculations as to the cut of Mr Rushworth's frock-coat and his preferred blend of snuff with genuine enthusiasm, for she usually took a great delight in any thing ridiculous, and in self-conceit most of all. But she had never been more at a loss to make her feelings appear what they were not. It was necessary to smile, and smile she did, but the effort required was so far beyond her, that it was a welcome relief to watch him ride away.

After wandering in the park alone for two hours, a recollection of her long absence made her decide at length to return home. She was on the point of turning back when she was surprised by the sight of Mr Norris approaching her, and at no great distance. Composing herself and forcing a smile, she began, as they met, to comment upon the beauty of the day.

'I did not know before that you ever walked this way, Mr Norris,' she continued, but then, recollecting that this might suggest she had sought the place purposely to avoid seeing him, her colour changed, and she said no more.

'I have been making a tour of the park,' he replied, looking in her face, 'as I generally do on days when I do not ride. Are you going much farther?'

'No, I should have turned back in a few moments.'

Mary was surprised to find that he intended to accompany her, and accordingly they both turned, and walked together. She was afraid of talking of any thing that might lead them to Miss Price, or his engagement; and, having nothing else to say, was determined to leave the trouble of finding a subject to him. It was some minutes before he did so, but at last, and as if it were an effort, he said, 'Are you enjoying your stay in Mansfield? Your sister must be glad of your company.'

'I think she is, yes. But I suspect that as far as Dr Grant is concerned, my brother is an even more welcome guest, since he provides a perfect excuse for drinking claret every day.'

Mr Norris smiled. 'I should also take this opportunity to thank you, Miss Crawford.'

'Thank me, Mr Norris?' she said, in a voice of forced calmness. 'What occasion could you have to thank me?'

'For your kindness to my cousin,' he said, with a serious look. 'I have been observing your new intimacy with the greatest pleasure. Julia is a dear child, but she has, perhaps, rather too much feeling for her own tranquillity. The companionship of a rational, unaffected woman like yourself can only be of the utmost advantage to her.'

It was not the prettiest compliment she had ever been paid, but now that she knew Mr Norris better, Mary was sensible of his sincerity, and valued his words all the more.

'The rest of us have so many cares and preoccupations of our own,' he continued, 'that we may not have understood how lonely she has become since William's departure. And even in a large and happy family the position of a youngest offspring can be a solitary one.'

There might, perhaps, have been the suspicion of a sigh at this, and Mary wondered, for the first time, about his own childhood, and what it might have been to have had such a stepmother as Mrs Norris.

For a moment she thought he was about to say more, but he seemed to think better of it, and another long silence succeeded. But when he spoke again he surprised her exceedingly by asking whether she would be staying on in Northampton-shire when the work on the park was completed. She did not know what to make of it. What was it to him, after all, whether she went or staid?

'I hardly know,' she stammered, blushing in spite of herself. 'We — that is, my sister — has not yet invited me. But Henry will certainly be off,' she continued, recovering her spirits. 'Surry or Shrop-shire, I forget which, but in any case some where beginning with an S.' She smiled. 'But then Henry loves to be continually travelling. Even now, when he may pick and choose his engagements, I have known him to accept commissions simply for the pleasure of being on the road.'

'I can see that such a man as Mr Crawford would like to have his own way,' replied Mr Norris in a serious tone. 'But we cannot all have his same luxury of choice. I envy him that. Most of his fellow men are condemned to self-denial, and an enforced submission to the will of others.'

Mary laughed. 'I doubt that the nephew of Sir Thomas Bertram can know very much of self-denial. Now, seriously, Mr Norris, what have you ever known of hardship? When have you been prevented from going wherever you chose, whenever the fancy took you? When have you been forced to rely on the kindness of others to supply the necessities of board and lodging?'

She stopped, knowing she had said a great deal too much, and averting her eyes, was unable to see the look on his face as he replied, 'Miss Crawford is pleased to remind me of the differences in our situations. But,' he said, in a softer accent, 'in some matters of great weight, I too have suffered from the want of independence.'

'Is this,' thought Mary, 'meant to refer to Miss Price?' Her embarrassment appeared in an agitated look, his in a rush of colour; and for a few minutes they were both silent; till the distant apparition of Henry promised to save them both from further discomfiture. He met them with great affability, saying that he had returned to the parsonage, and finding Mary still absent, had walked out to meet her. Mr Norris took the first opportunity of consigning Mary to her brother's care, and when Henry then turned to her and asked what the two of them had been talking of so earnestly, she hardly knew how to answer.

CHAPTER IV

As she dressed for dinner the following day, Mary struggled to achieve at least the appearance of composure; her brother might make such public shew of his own attachment as he chose, and not care for the consequences; Mary must be more guarded and more circumspect. And now that she was fully apprised of her own feelings, she was apprehensive lest Henry's discernment or her sister's shrewd eye might discover the truth; she did not know, in reality, whether it was her brother's raillery she feared more, or the sisterly concern of Mrs Grant's warm and affectionate heart.

For the time being, however, Mrs Grant seemed more concerned with the small cares and anxieties of her toilette. 'What dreadful hot weather this is!' she said, working away her fan as if for life, as the carriage made its way across the park. 'It keeps one in a continual state of inelegance.'

'We shall, at least, find the company somewhat enlivened this evening by the presence of another guest,' remarked her husband, rather sourly. 'A larger group is always preferable — tiny parties force one into constant exertion.'

As they approached the Park, they passed close by the stable-yard and coach-house.

'Ha!' cried Henry in delight. 'The much-anticipated Rushworth must be here already! You were right, Mary, 'tis a barouche. And a very fine one, at that! Quite as gaudy and ostentatious as I expected. This is much better than I had dared to hope; I anticipate an evening of the keenest enjoyment.'

As it was, the parsonage party heard Mr Rushworth before they saw him, for the sound of his voice reached them even as the servant led them across the hall.

'My dear Lady Bertram,' he was saying loudly, 'the insufferable dilatoriness one endures at their hands! The thousand disappointments and delays to which one is exposed! The trouble that is made over the slightest request, the tricks and stratagems that are employed to avoid the simplest tasks, make one quite despair. Only this morning I decided that blue was *quite* the wrong colour for the drawing-room and directed the painter that the entire room should be done again in pea-green. One would have thought that I had asked him to undertake one of the labours of Hercules.' "For Heaven's sake, man," said I, " 'tis nothing more than a little distemper — no more than half an hour's work for a great lubberly fellow like you. Go to it, man! You will have it done before dinner-time!" But needless to say, when I left Sotherton two hours ago he was still there, on his hands and knees with a sponge and a pail of water. They have no capacity for diligence, Mrs Norris, no enthusiasm for honest toil!'

'Oh! I can only agree with you, Mr Rushworth,' simpered Mrs Norris, 'and if he were here, my dear husband would concur *most* heartily. When we had the dining-parlour at the White House improved, we had to insist that the work was done over three times. I told Mr Norris not to pay them a shilling until we were *completely* satisfied with the results.'

Mr Rushworth was just beginning to commend Mrs Norris's good management when the Grants and Crawfords made their entrance. When Mary was introduced he addressed her with affected civility, and gave a haughty bow and wave of the hand, which assured Henry, as plainly as words could have done, that he was exactly the coxcomb he had been hoping for. However, the smiles and pleased looks of those standing round him by the fire shewed that many of the family had already formed a completely contrary opinion. Mary soon observed that Miss Bertram looked particularly happy; her countenance had an unusual animation, which was heightened still farther when they went in to dinner and she was seated opposite to their principal guest.

Henry took a place near to Miss Price, but she very pointedly gave her whole attention to Mr Rushworth, who was sitting beside her. With both Miss Bertram and Miss Price claiming a share in his civilities, Mr Rushworth had much to do to satisfy the vanity of both young ladies, but it soon became obvious to Mary, that despite paying the most flattering courtesies on either side, their visitor's eye was far more often drawn to Maria than to her cousin. Miss Price saw it too; of that there could be no doubt. Her face crimsoned over and she was evidently struggling for composure. Mary saw that she was piqued, and found herself divided between a hope that Miss Price might derive some benefit from such a lesson in humility, and a degree of sympathy she would not have anticipated, had she pondered the question with cool consideration. Accustomed as the young lady was to constant deference and an easy pre-eminence, no-one seemed to have thought it useful to teach her how to govern her temper, or sustain a second place with patience and fortitude.

Of the tumult of Miss Price's feelings, however, her family seemed perfectly un-aware. Mary thought, however, that she observed a look and a smile of conscious-ness from Miss Bertram, which shewed that *she* could not but be pleased, *she* could not but triumph, meeting with such a delightful and unwonted event. Mary wondered what such an unexpected development might lead to, but even her foresight was not equal to imagining what was eventually to ensue.

When the dessert and the wine were ar-ranged, the subject of improving grounds was brought forward again, and Mr Rush-worth turned to Henry with all the careless insolence of imaginary superiority. 'Know-ing some thing of your reputation, nothing could be so gratifying to me as to hear your opinion of my plans for Sotherton. After all, it is so useful to have one's genius confirmed by a *professional* man.'

Henry coloured, and said nothing, but Mr Rushworth's eyes were fixed on the young ladies. 'In my opinion it is infinitely better to rely on one's own genius,' he continued, 'or, at *most,* to consult with friends and disinterested advisers, rather than throw the business into the hands of an improver. I *had* considered engaging Repton. His terms are five guineas a day, you know, which is of course a mere nothing, but in the end I could not see what such a man could possibly devise that I could not do fifty times better myself. How could it be otherwise? I own that he *may* be blessed with natural taste, but he has no education, none of the instruction that improves the mind and informs the understanding.'

Henry's mortification was apparent, at least to some, and Mr Norris hastened to ask him about his proposals for Mansfield.

'We have all, at one time or another in the last few weeks, attempted to divine your intentions, Crawford, but so far you have always stood firm. But we will not be denied tonight — come, you must let us into the secret. Mrs Grant, Miss Crawford, you must join me in persuading your brother.'

Henry laughed, but protested that it would be impossible to do justice to the imagination and invention of his proposals (this with a look of meaning in the direction of Mr Rushworth) without his sketches and drawings shewing the park as it now was, and as it would be after his improvements.

'But surely you can give us some idea?' cried Tom Bertram. 'A general picture of what you propose?'

'With Sir Thomas's permission, I will be happy to do so.' Sir Thomas bowing his consent, Henry began his narration; and Mary smiled to see him now the centre of attention, with even Miss Price gazing intently upon him.

'I will begin with the river, or perhaps rivulet is a more apt term; a place such as Mansfield should not be dishonoured by such a thin brook that floods with every shower. No, Mansfield deserves the splendid prospect of an abundant river, majestically flowing. But,' he said, turning to his neighbour, 'I see a question in Miss Price's eyes. She is wondering how this is to be done. And the answer is that I propose to build a new weir, a weir that will augment the flow of the river, and create a cascade within view of the house.'

There was the greatest amazement at this, and expressions of astonishment and admiration on all sides.

'And yet,' he said, smiling, 'I have barely begun, and my next scheme is even more ambitious than the first. I will open the prospect at the rear of the house and create a vista that will be the envy of the whole country!'

' 'Open the prospect?' said Julia, speaking for the first time, the colour rushing from her cheeks. 'But you could not do that — that would not be possible unless — unless — you felled the avenue. Surely you do not — you *cannot* — intend to do that?'

'My sincerest apologies to Miss Julia Bertram,' said Henry in a gentler tone, 'but I do not see how else it is to be done.'

Seeing her distress, her father took her hand, and pressed it kindly. 'My dear,' said Sir Thomas, 'I know your attachment to the avenue, but we have brought Mr Crawford here to give us his advice. There can be no use in that if we do not take it when it is given.'

'Did not I hear that you did some thing similar at Compton, Crawford?' asked Mr Rushworth in a complacent accent. 'Cut down some twisted old trees near the house? I am often asked for my opinion on such matters, and on this occasion, I was forced to acknowledge (though rather against the bias of my inclination, I confess) that it appeared to have been some thing of a success. That horrid dark house at Compton has become *almost* liveable.'

Miss Price turned at once to her uncle. 'I

hope you will consider Mr Rushworth's proposition, sir,' she said. 'Those gloomy old trees quite overwhelm the view from my room. Julia's silly girlish attachment to them cannot be allowed to compromise the comfort of everyone else in the house.'

She spoke in a cross tone quite unlike her usual simper, which Mary took as proof that discontent and jealousy had made her briefly forgetful of the appearance of demure and tender sensibility she normally studied to affect. The effect of her words on Julia was equally apparent; it pained Mary to see that the girl had turned of a death-like paleness, and was too intent on suppressing her agitation to eat or speak any thing more.

'I quite agree with you, Fanny,' said Mrs Norris quickly. 'Indeed, I was saying much the same to Lady Bertram only this evening. At fourteen Julia is in far too many respects exactly as she was at ten. Running about wild in the woods, tearing her clothes, and indulging in all manner of juvenile whims. If you had seen her in the drawing-room the other day, Sir Thomas — *quite* ragged and covered with paint from head to toe! I am sure you would have agreed with me — it is time she was taken in hand. I am at your service, sir, whenever you command me.'

As a general reflection on Julia, Sir Thomas thought nothing could be more unjust, and seeing that his daughter's tears were about to shew themselves, he tried to turn the conversation, tried repeatedly before he could succeed, but the volubility of his principal guest came at last to his aid. Mr Rushworth was a great deal too full of his own cares to think of any thing else, or notice what had passed, and he resumed the subject of improvements in general, and Sotherton in particular, with unimpaired enthusiasm. After a lengthy description of the work he was intending to undertake — which was all to be done in the *very* best taste and without a *thought* for the expense — he returned once more to Compton, which he now appeared to consider owed all its picturesque new beauty to his having once had a brief conversation on the subject with its owner, more than a twelvemonth before. Mary hardly dared look at her brother, but when she did have the courage to glance across at him, she found to her surprise that he was deep in conversation with Miss Price. Judging by that young lady's expression, Henry was doubtless supplying all the compliments Mr Rushworth had neglected to provide, but Mary wondered at the wisdom of such a proceeding for either party. Miss Price might make use of her brother's flattery to console a wounded vanity, and he might profit from such a capital opportunity to advance his own suit, but in neither case could Mary see much good resulting from it, and a glance at Mr Norris shewed that he was not entirely free from similar apprehensions. Mary could not but agree, though to think of Edmund as agitated by *jealousy,* was a bitter blow indeed.

Mr Rushworth concluded his discourse with a second and even more lengthy expatiation on the new prospects that had been opened up by the felling of the avenue, and turned in conclusion to Julia, seemingly unaware that he was only adding to her distress. 'But if the youngest Miss Bertram is still unpersuaded, and would prefer some blasted tree-trunks to the openness of a fine view, perhaps a visit to Compton might convince her?'

'It is a capital idea, Rushworth,' said Tom quickly, 'but unhappily Mr Smith is not among our acquaintance, though perhaps Mr Crawford might be able —'

'Oh! If that is all the difficulty, then you need say no more,' replied Mr Rushworth in a grand way. 'Smith is an intimate friend of mine, and that alone will suffice to gain admittance. It is, what? Ten or twelve miles from Mansfield? Just the distance for a day's excursion. We may take a cold collation *à la rustique,* and wander about the grounds, and altogether enjoy a complete party of pleasure.'

Miss Bertram clapped her hands together, her eyes sparkling with anticipated enjoyment; even Miss Price smiled her acquiescence, and Sir Thomas was pleased to give his approbation; but the person for whose benefit the visit had been proposed, remained wholly unmoved. Julia looked first at Henry and then at her father, and then, rising from her chair, she ran out of the room, dashing her plate to the floor. There was an awkward pause before Lady Bertram rose, and suggested to the ladies that this would be an appropriate time for them to withdraw. Mary wondered if she might contrive to see Julia, and console her, but not knowing where she might find the girl's room, she was obliged to hope a member of the family would shew a similar solicitude; though as far as she could ascertain, no-one slipped away upstairs, either then, or at any other time that evening.

When the ladies attained the drawing-room the subject turned immediately to their visitor. Mr Rushworth was not handsome; no, was Miss Price's judgment, he was absolutely plain — small, black, and plain. Further impartial consideration by Miss Bertram proved him not so very plain; he had so much countenance, and his nose was so good, and he was so well made, that one soon forgot he was plain; and after a quarter of an hour, she no longer allowed him to be called so by any body, whatever Miss Price's views were on the matter. Mr Rushworth was, in fact, the most agreeable young man Miss Bertram had ever met; Miss Price's engagement made him in equity the property of her cousin, of which she was fully aware, even without the nods and winks of Mrs Norris, and by the time the gentlemen appeared, she was already wrapt in her own private and delicious meditations on the relative merits of white satin and lace veils.

When the gentlemen joined them a few minutes later, it became apparent that they had been talking of a ball; and no ordinary ball, but a private ball in all the shining new splendour of Sotherton, with its solid mahogany, rich damask, and bright new gilding. How it came that such a capital piece of news should have fallen to the share of the gentlemen and the port, the ladies could not at first comprehend, but the fact of the ball was soon fixed to the last point of certainty, to the great delight of the whole party. In spite of being somewhat out of spirits, the prospect of a ball was indeed delightful to Mary, and she was able to listen to Mr Rushworth's interminable descriptions of supper-rooms, card-tables, and musicians, with due complacency. Miss Bertram had never looked so beautiful, and Mary was almost sure that in the general bustle and joy that succeeded Mr Rushworth's announcement, he had taken the opportunity to speak to her privately, and secure her for the two first dances. As for Miss Price, there could be no doubt whom *she* would open the ball with, but when Mary looked around for her, she found that she was, once again, engaged in an animated conversation with Henry, while Edmund was standing alone by the fire, lost in thought.

The following morning Mary called early at the Park, only to find that Julia Bertram was indisposed and in bed. Having sent her best compliments to the invalid, she was on the point of departure when she found herself being ushered with some ceremony into the morning-room, where the other ladies of the house were assembled. After paying her respects to Lady Bertram, who was sitting on the sopha on the other side of the room, absorbed in her needlework, she saw Miss Price gesturing to her, and as soon as Mary drew near she said in a low voice, 'May I speak to you for a few minutes? I wish to ask your advice.'

The look of surprise on Mary's face shewed how far she was from expecting such an opening, but Miss Price rose immediately and led the way upstairs to her own room. As soon as the door closed behind them, Miss Price began to explain the nature of her request.

'It is the ball at Sotherton that I seek your advice upon, Miss Crawford. I am quite unable to satisfy myself as to what I ought to wear, and so I have determined to seek the counsel of the more enlightened, and apply to *you*.'

Miss Price then proceeded to lay before her such a number of elegant gowns, anyone of which might bear comparison with the latest London fashions, as left Mary in no doubt that Miss Price had no real value for her opinion, and wanted only to display her own superior wardrobe. For the next two hours Mary was obliged to listen to a minute enumeration of the price of every head-dress, and the pattern of every gown.

Her own dress being finally settled in all its principal parts, Miss Price turned her attention to Mary.

'And what will *you* wear, Miss Crawford? The gown you wore at dinner last night? Or do you have another? And what about ornaments? Do you possess any thing that would be considered rich enough for company such as we shall have at Sotherton?'

'I have attended assemblies in London many times,' said Mary firmly, 'and I have always worn a very pretty topaz cross that Henry bought for me some years ago.'

'I recollect the very one!' cried Miss Price, 'but do you really have only that meagre bit of ribbon to fasten it to? Surely Mr Crawford might be prevailed upon to buy you a gold chain as well?'

'Henry had wanted to buy me a gold chain,' said Mary, concealing her anger, 'but the purchase was beyond his means at the time.'

'But surely, *not* to wear the cross to Mr Rushworth's ball might be mortifying him?'

'My dear Miss Price, such a trifle is not worth half as many words. Henry will be delighted to see me wearing the cross, even on a piece of *meagre* ribbon, and I do not care for anyone else's opinion, whatever it may be.'

'Not care how you appear in front of so many elegant young women! *I* would be ashamed to stand up so. My dear Miss Crawford, pray let me be of assistance.'

Turning to her table, she immediately presented Mary with a small trinket-box, and requested her to choose from among several gold chains and necklaces.

'You see what a collection I have,' said she grandly, 'more by half than I ever use, or even think of. My family is always giving me some thing or other. I do not offer them as new, I offer nothing but an old necklace. You must forgive the liberty and oblige me.'

Mary resisted for as long as she could without being thought ungrateful, wondering all the time what Miss Price's real motive might be in such a shew of generosity; but when her companion urged her once again, Mary found herself obliged to yield, and proceeded to make the selection. She was determined in her choice at last, by fancying there was one necklace more frequently placed before her eyes than the rest, and she hoped, in fixing on this, to be choosing what Miss Price least wished to keep. She would rather perhaps have been obliged to some other person, but there was nothing to be done now, but to submit with a good grace and hope for the best.

CHAPTER V

The weather remaining resolutely unsettled, the proposed excursion to Compton was postponed. Luckily the young people of Mansfield had another prospect of pleasure, and one that promised yet keener delights. Invitations to the Sotherton ball were sent with dispatch, and Mr Rushworth calculated to collect young people enough to form twelve or fourteen couple. He had fixed on the 22nd as the most eligible day; Sir Thomas was required to depart for Cumberland on the 24th and was to be accompanied on the first stage of the journey by Mr Norris. The preparations duly began, and Mr Rushworth continued to ride and shoot without any inconvenience from them. He had some extra visits from his housekeeper, his painters were rather hurried in finishing the wainscot in the ballroom, and all the while Mrs Norris ran about, enquiring whether she or *her* housekeeper might be of any assistance, but all this gave *him* no trouble, and he confidently declared that, 'there was in fact no trouble in the business'.

As for Mary, she had too many agitations to have half the enjoyment in anticipation which she ought to have had, but when the day came she awoke in a glow of genuine high spirits. Such an evening of enjoyment before her! She began to dress for it with much of the happy flutter which belongs to a ball. All went well — she had chosen her finest gown, and left her room at last, comfortably satisfied with herself and all about her.

Henry was impatient to see Sotherton, a place of which he had heard so much, and which held out the strongest hope of further profitable employment, and as they drove through the park he let down the side-glass to have a better view.

'Rising ground,' he commented, 'fine woods, if a little thinly spread, and the pleasure-grounds are tolerably extensive. All in all, very promising. I must make more of an effort to be civil to our Mr Rushworth in future. After all, if he can employ Bonomi for the house, he can certainly afford Crawford for the park.'

In the drawing-room they were introduced

to one of Mr Rushworth's intimate friends, the Honourable John Yates, who had arrived from Bath expressly for the ball. The Mansfield party was also present, and had all been walking about together, inspecting the house and exclaiming over its fine proportions and splendid furniture. All the young ladies were most elegantly dressed, and Miss Price's *ensemble* of satin and embroidered gauze was much admired. This did not surprise Mary; she had never seen such a gown before outside a fashion-plate. When the guests began to arrive, Mary was soon solicited by Mr Bertram for the first two dances, and when the company were moving into the ballroom she found herself for the first time near Miss Price. Mary saw her eye glancing for a moment at her necklace with a smile — she thought there was a smile — which gave her a feeling of unease that she could not get the better of for some minutes.

'My dear Miss Crawford,' she cried, 'Mr Rushworth has been shewing us the house, and by that I mean the *whole* house from attic to cellar: drawing-rooms, summer breakfast-parlours, winter breakfast-parlours, dining-rooms, bedrooms, picture galleries, and even a private theatre!'

Seeing Mary's astonishment, she continued, 'I assure you, I do not jest; Mr Rushworth has built an entire theatre, completely fitted up with pit, curtain, stage, and gallery. He and Mr Yates are wild to be doing some thing, and in consequence, everyone else has caught the itch for acting. All they need do now is decide upon a play that will suit every body. As we came down, Tom was saying that he would prefer a comedy, while Maria and Mr Rushworth incline towards tragedy, but I doubt not that, with perseverance, they will find a piece which will please them all.'

'And you, Miss Price? Have you a preference?'

'Oh! As to acting myself,' said Miss Price, '*that* is out of the question; unless, of course, I am particularly wanted.'

Mr Bertram now appeared at her elbow, and Mary was led to the top of the room where the set was forming, couple by couple. Mr Norris and Miss Price soon joined the rest of the dancers, and finally Mr Rushworth conducted Miss Bertram to the head of the set. The ball began, and Mary was more than satisfied with her partner. Tom Bertram was just the sort of young man to appear to great advantage in a ball-room, for he had easy manners, excellent spirits, and a great deal to say, and the two of them went down their two dances with sufficient gaiety to provoke the curiosity of many lookers-on. Miss Crawford was known only by name to half the people invited, but she was pretty, she was lively, and she was soon said to be admired by Mr Bertram. It was enough to excite a general interest, and an unusual degree of attentiveness on the part of the chaperons sitting by the fire, each of whom had fully intended that Mr Bertram should marry one or other of their daughters. Of this Mary herself was perfectly unaware, and when the first two dances were over she returned to her brother, only to find herself straightaway addressed by Mr Norris, who took her very much by surprise in gravely applying for her hand. Having secured her for the two next, he walked away again immediately, and rejoined Miss Price by the fire. Mrs Norris, who happened at that moment to be standing just behind Mary, saw it all, and immediately began to address her companions in a voice loud enough to be heard by half the room.

'Well, my dear Mrs Sneyd, however much you admire Fanny's dancing, I am afraid that there will be little satisfaction in looking on *now*. I think it is rather a pity she and Edmund should be obliged to part.

Young folks in their situation should be excused complying with the common forms.'

'Quite so, Mrs Norris,' replied the other in an obsequious tone, 'I wonder your son did not propose it.'

'Oh! I dare say he did. Edmund is *never* remiss. But dear Fanny has such a strict sense of propriety, so much of that *true* delicacy which one seldom meets with now-a-days, Mrs Sneyd. Only look at her face at this moment, as they are standing side by side.'

Miss Price did indeed look happy; her cheeks were glowing with delight, and she was speaking with unusual vivacity. Mr Rushworth and Maria had just joined the group by the fire, and it was evident that he had requested the honour of the two next.

Mrs Norris was still chattering in the same complacent tones. 'And what say you, Mrs Smart, to the chance of *another* match? Such things are very catching.'

'I take it you mean Miss Bertram and Mr Rushworth? Yes, indeed, they would be a very pretty couple. Lady Orr was saying much the same thing to me only a few moments ago. What is his property?'

'Oh, some four or five thousand a year, I believe. Nothing to my dear Edmund's, *of course,* but those who have not more, must be satisfied with what they have, and make the best of it. But, to be sure, ma'am,' she continued, more confidentially, 'to be sure it is not quite settled, *yet.* We only speak of it among friends. But I have very little doubt it *will be.* He is growing exceedingly attentive, is he not?'

'Oh yes, indeed.'

The music soon recommenced, and when Mr Norris approached to claim her hand, Mary saw that the expression of his face was grave and contemplative. They stood for some time without speaking a word, till suddenly fancying that it would be the greater vexation to Mrs Norris to be seen to be in conversation, Mary made some slight observation on the ball-room.

Mr Norris looked her in the face for the first time, seemed about to speak, but then stopped, his eyes fixed intently on her.

'Good heavens,' he exclaimed. 'What is this? What can be meant by it?'

To Mary's astonishment, his complexion became pale, and the disturbance of his mind was visible in every feature. Nothing could explain such a complete change of humour and countenance; he had always been polite, even if rather quiet and reserved, but now he made every effort to avoid her eye, and every subject of conversation she attempted was firmly and resolutely repulsed, with the result that they concluded their two dances in a most unpleasant and uncomfortable silence.

As soon as the set was ended Mr Norris made the briefest of bows and walked quickly away towards Rushworth and Miss Price, leaving Mary quite at a loss as to how to proceed. She made her way slowly back to where her brother was standing on the other side of the room, watching the group by the fire in a fit of jealous agitation. Miss Price had refused to dance with him, despite the conspicuous encouragement he believed he had received when they last met at the Park.

'It appears I was a useful distraction for an hour or two,' he said, with evident irritation, 'but now she has once again succeeded in attracting the attention of that chattering coxcomb Rushworth, I am no more use to her.' Mary had feared it would be so, and was about to express her sympathy when they were accosted by Mrs Norris.

'Well, miss,' she said loudly, 'it has been quite clear to *me*, from the very day you arrived in the neighbourhood, that you Crawfords are just the sort of people to get all you can, at other people's expense — but I had not thought even *you* capable of stooping quite so low.'

'I — I —' stammered Mary, her face like scarlet.

'Mrs Norris,' said Henry coldly, 'I beg leave to interject on my sister's behalf. To what do you allude, ma'am?'

'That necklace,' she replied, 'belongs to Miss Price. I am therefore at a loss to imagine how *your sister* can have come by it.'

'I can assure you, ma'am,' said Mary, recovering herself, 'that the necklace was a kind gift, most freely given.'

'I beg your pardon,' replied Mrs Norris, 'but I cannot quite believe you. Fanny would never have presented *you* with any item of the slightest value. The cost alone makes such a thing unthinkable. I know for a fact its price was *at least* eighteen shillings.'

Henry was too angry to speak; but Mary stood her ground, and quietly explained the circumstances of the gift. Mrs Norris was, at length, satisfied, if being forced to concede an ill-founded accusation, formed on mistaken premises, may be termed satisfaction, and without making any apology for her error, hastened away. Mary immediately expressed a wish for the relative seclusion of the supper-room, and she was soon after joined by Henry, who, sitting down next to her with a look of consciousness, said, 'My own cares are vexing enough, but I am very sorry if any thing has occurred to distress *you.* This ought to have been a day of happiness.'

'Oh! It shall be. It *is,*' said Mary, making an effort for her brother's sake. 'Let us say no more about it, I entreat you. I shall have forgotten the whole affair by morning.'

'I fear it may prove more enduring than that,' he replied in a low voice. 'Just now, when I was with them, I heard Norris asking Miss Price about the necklace.'

'Mr Norris?' asked Mary, the colour rushing to her face.

'The very same. That necklace you are wearing was evidently *his* gift.'

The truth rushed on Mary in an instant; all of Mr Norris's unaccountable conduct in the ball-room was now explained; his surprise, his seemingly unintelligible words, and the way he had looked at her, *that* was fully accounted for by the extraordinary spectacle of a gift he had presented to one woman being conspicuously displayed around the throat of another.

'I must find an opportunity to explain,' she said, in distracted tones, rising from her chair. 'I must speak to him instantly, I cannot let him think that I —'

'My dear Mary,' replied Henry, detaining her, 'you have not heard the end of my story. When Miss Price gave no immediate answer to his question, *Mrs* Norris hastened to explain to him that your necklace is, in fact, an entirely different ornament, of a similar pattern to the one he gave Fanny, but — and here I had difficulty in holding my peace — of *inferior workmanship.*'

'But why?' stammered Mary. 'What can be the justification for such an unnecessary deception?'

'Perhaps because Mrs Norris's beady little eyes have detected some part of the truth? That Miss Price no longer cares for her son — that is, if she ever did — and her making his gift over to you is proof of that. But, one thing you may be sure of — one thing we may *both* be sure of,' this with a look of meaning, 'is that old Mother Norris will not let it go as easily as that. That marriage is the favourite project of her heart, and she will do any thing necessary to secure it — even if it means practising deceit on her own son.'

'But why should *Fanny* do such a thing?' said Mary. 'She must have known the effect it would produce on Edmund — Mr Norris. I can quite believe that she would connive most happily at any thing that caused *me* embarrassment, but what can she hope to gain by behaving so discourteously to Mr Norris? What can be her motive?'

'I do not pretend to understand Miss Price,' said Henry grimly, 'but could it be that she wishes to put his affection to the test? Or to ascertain if he has feelings for another?'

He stopped. By this time Mary's cheeks were in such a glow, that curious as he was, he would not press the article farther.

'I do not like deceiving Mr Norris,' said Mary after a few moments, oppressed by an anguish of heart.

Henry sighed, and took her hand. 'But unless you propose to *un*deceive him, and therefore to contradict Mrs Norris (which would cause no end of vexation, and not least to you, my dear Mary), then I do not see how it is to be avoided.'

In such spirits as Mary now found herself, the rest of the evening brought her little amusement. She danced every dance, though without any expectation of pleasure, seeing it only as the surest means of avoiding Edmund. She told herself that he would soon be gone, and hoped that, by the time of his return, many days hence, she would have succeeded in reasoning herself into a stronger frame of mind. For, although she could see that, contrary to his earlier reserve, he now very much wished to speak to her, she could not yet bear the prospect of listening politely to apologies that had been extorted from him by falsehood.

CHAPTER VI

The house was very soon afterwards deprived of its master, and the day of Sir Thomas's departure followed quickly upon the night of the ball. Only the necessity of the measure in a pecuniary light had resigned Sir Thomas to the painful effort of quitting his family, but the young ladies, at least, were somewhat reconciled to the prospect of his absence by the arrival of Mr Rushworth, who, riding over to Mansfield on the day of Sir Thomas's leave-taking to pay his respects, renewed his proposal for private theatricals. However, contrary to Miss Price's more sanguine expectations, the business of finding a play that would suit every body proved to be no trifle. All the best plays were run over in vain, and *Othello, Macbeth, The Rivals, The School for Scandal,* and a long etcetera, were successively dismissed.

'This will never do,' said Tom Bertram at

last. 'At this rate, my father will be returned before we have even begun. From this moment I make no difficulties. I will take any part you choose to give me.'

At that moment, Mr Yates took up one of the many volumes of plays that lay on the table, and suddenly exclaimed, '*Lovers' Vows!* Why not *Lovers' Vows*?'

'My dear Yates,' cried Tom, 'it strikes me as if it would do exactly! Frederick and the Baron are capital parts for Rushworth and Yates, and here is the rhyming Butler for me — if nobody else wants it. And as for the rest, it is only Count Cassel and Anhalt. Even Edmund may attempt one of *them* without disgracing himself, when he returns.'

The suggestion was highly acceptable to all; to storm through Baron Wildenhaim was the height of Mr Yates's theatrical ambition, and he immediately offered his services for the part, allowing Mr Rushworth to claim that of Frederick with almost equal satisfaction. Three of the characters were now cast, and Maria began to be concerned to know her own fate. 'But surely there are not women enough,' said she. 'Only Agatha and Amelia. Here is nothing for Miss Crawford.'

But this was immediately opposed by Tom Bertram, who asserted the part of Amelia to be in every respect the property of Miss Crawford, if she would accept it. A short silence followed. Fanny and Maria each felt the best claim to Agatha, and was hoping to have it pressed on her by the rest. But Mr Rushworth, who with seeming carelessness was turning over the first act, soon settled the business. 'I must entreat Miss *Bertram,*' said he, 'not to contemplate any character but that of Amelia. That, in my opinion, is by far *the* most difficult character in the whole piece. The last time I saw *Lovers' Vows* the actress in the part gave quite the most deplorable performance (and in my opinion, the whole play was sadly wanting — if they had accepted my advice, they might have brought the thing round in a trice, but though I offered my services to the manager, the scoundrel had the insolence to turn me down). But as I was saying, a proper representation of Amelia demands considerable delicacy — the sort of delicacy we may confidently expect from Maria Bertram.'

For a moment Miss Bertram wavered: his words were of a piece with his previous compliments; but that was before the ball, when he had danced with her only once, and with Fanny three times. Since then he had hardly spoken to her. Was he now seeking only to induce her to overlook these previous affronts? She distrusted him; he was, she now suspected, at treacherous play with her, but as she hesitated, her brother interposed once again with Miss Crawford's better claim.

'No, no, no, Maria must not be Amelia,' said Tom. 'The part is fit for Miss Crawford, and Miss Crawford only. She looks the part, and sounds the part, and I am persuaded will do it admirably.'

Maria looked narrowly at Fanny; the smile of triumph which she was trying to suppress afforded a yet stronger suspicion of there now being some thing of a private understanding between her and Rushworth, the man Maria had been thinking of as her own avowed admirer only a few days before. Maria knew her cousin, and knew that opposition would only expose her to public shame and humiliation. She had had enough.

'Oh! Do not be afraid of *my* wanting to act,' she cried; 'I am not to be Agatha, and as to Amelia — such a pert, upstart girl. Most suitable for someone such as —'

She stopped and reddened, and then walked hastily out of the room, leaving awkward feelings for more than one.

The concerns of the theatre were suspended during dinner, but the spirits of evening giving fresh courage, Tom, Mr Rushworth, and Mr Yates seated themselves once again in committee, when an interruption was given by the entrance of the Grants and the Crawfords, who had come, late as it was, to drink tea with them. Mr Rushworth stepped forward with great alacrity to tell them the agreeable news.

'We have got a play,' said he.

'I must congratulate you, sir,' said Dr Grant. 'And what have you decided upon?'

'It is to be *Lovers' Vows.*'

'Indeed,' said Dr Grant, who had once attended a performance in London. 'That is not the play I would have chosen for a private theatre.'

'Now, Dr Grant, do not be disagreeable,' said his wife. 'Nobody loves a play better than you do. And are you to act, Miss Price?' she continued, taking a seat next to her by the fire.

'I am to play Agatha,' replied Miss Price with happy complacency.

'And *I* take Frederick,' said Mr Rushworth carelessly. 'I was equally willing to have the Baron, but the others pressed me so hard, insisting that the whole play would be indescribably the weaker unless I should undertake it, that at the last I agreed to take it on, merely to be obliging.'

'I see,' replied Dr Grant, in a heavy tone. 'In that case, I must tell you, sir, that I think it exceedingly improper, in the circumstances, for you to act with Miss Price.'

'You must excuse me, sir, but I cannot agree,' said Mr Rushworth peremptorily. 'We shall, of course, shorten some of the speeches, and so forth, but otherwise I can see no objection on the grounds of propriety. The play has been staged in many respectable private theatres — indeed, I saw it put on at Pemberley only last year, though *their* cast was infinitely inferior to our own, even if I do say so myself.'

'That may be,' said Dr Grant heavily, 'but my opinion remains the same. I think certain scenes in this play wholly unfit for private representation.'

'Do not act any thing improper, Fanny,' said Lady Bertram, who had heard some part of their conversation from her position on the sopha. 'Sir Thomas would not like it.'

'I hope you will never have cause to reprove my conduct, Lady Bertram,' said Fanny, modestly. 'I am sure you never have before.'

'Well, *I* have no such fears, sir, and no scruples worth the name,' said Mr Rushworth, severely displeased with the clergyman's interference. 'If we are so very nice, we shall never act any thing, and I could not wish for a finer *début* for my little theatre at Sotherton.'

'I was just about to say the very same thing,' said Mrs Norris, looking angrily at Dr Grant. 'I do not know this particular play myself, but as Edmund is to act too, there can be no harm. I *think* I may answer for my own son, and I will venture to do the same for Sir Thomas. I only wish Mr Rushworth had known his own mind when the scene painter began, for there was the loss of half a day's work on trees and clouds, when what we want now is cottages and alehouses.'

'Pray excuse me, madam, but in this matter it is *Miss Price* who is to lead,' replied Dr Grant, turning to Fanny. 'You might simply say that, on examining the part of Agatha, you feel yourself unequal to it. That will be quite enough. The part will be made over to Miss Bertram or to Mary, and your delicacy honoured as it ought.'

This picture of her own consequence had some effect, and for a moment Miss Price hesitated; but it was only for a moment. 'Why, Dr Grant, that cannot be,' she replied sweetly, with a glance across at Mary, 'for Miss Crawford already has a part of her own. She is to be Amelia. Do you know the play, Miss Crawford?' she continued, rising and approaching Mary's chair. 'I would be very happy to lend you my copy. I am sure you will find it instructive; especially the third act, where you will find a scene which will interest you most particularly.'

Mary had never seen *Lovers' Vows,* but she knew enough of Miss Price to know that whatever her meaning, there could be no kindness intended to *her* in the remark. But Mr Rushworth having need, at that moment, of Miss Price's advice on the subject of his dress, Mary was able to take up the book and retire to a seat next to Henry, who had likewise been perusing the play with no little curiosity.

'I am to be Count Cassel, I find,' he said gloomily. 'And, as such, to play the part of your suitor, my dear Mary. Knowing that we are to act together is the only piece of enjoyment I foresee in the entire business. This Count is a complete buffoon — nothing but empty-headed foolishness from beginning to end. Upon my word,' he continued in an undertone, 'we have made a pretty blunder in our casting of this confounded play! Here am I playing Count Cassel, a man who is *"rich, and of great consequence"*, two qualities to which I cannot, alas, lay any claim, whereas the whole part might have been written for Rushworth! This line here — *"my elegant gun is inlaid with mother-of-pearl. You cannot find better work, or better taste"* — and here — *"The whole castle smells of his perfumery"*. It is the man entire!'

Mary could not help laughing, and he continued, 'My only remaining hope is that Count Cassel may succeed where Henry Crawford has failed.'

'How so?'

'Why, by reclaiming the attention of Miss Price, who clearly admires the Count Cassels of the world more than the Henry Crawfords. But that being so,' he said in a more serious tone, looking over towards the fireplace, 'I fear for my fair disdain, for I suspect that Mr Rushworth resembles Count Cassel in more ways than one. Where is that speech in Act IV? Ah, here it is — *"for a frivolous coxcomb, such as myself, to keep my word to a woman, would be deceit: 'tis not expected of me."* '

Mary did not know how to contradict him, and the two sat for some time in a thoughtful silence. It was some minutes more before Mary turned finally to the scene Miss Price had mentioned, and as she read it the colour flooded into her cheeks.

She knew they had cast Edmund as Anhalt, but had known nothing of the part itself beyond the fact that the young man was a clergyman. That had seemed to promise few terrors, but she now comprehended that she would be required to act a scene with him in which the whole subject was love — a marriage of love was to be described by the gentleman, and very little short of a declaration of love to be made by the lady. She read, and read the scene again with many painful, many wondering emotions, and was thankful that Miss Price's attention was still engrossed in the various refinements of Mr Rushworth's attire. She could not yet face Fanny's knowing looks, much less contemplate saying such words to Mr Norris before the rest of the company.

Every thing was quickly in a regular train; theatre, actors, actresses, and dresses, were all getting forward, and the scene painter being still at work at Sotherton, a temporary theatre was quickly fitted out in the billiard-room at Mansfield. As the days passed Mary reasoned herself into a greater degree of composure, and could even derive some amusement from the actions of the others, both on and off the stage. Henry had proved to be considerably the best actor of them all, despite the trifling nature of his part, and his consequent frustration was severely aggravated by being constrained to witness the repeated, and soon unnecessary, rehearsals of the opening scene between Mr Rushworth and Miss Price. Everyone else had their own little cares, their own little anxieties — there was so much employment, solicitude, and bustle that the unhappiness of the one member of the party who did *not* act was soon overlooked. Maria had loved Mr Rushworth — or thought she had — and now endured all the suffering of such a public disappointment, made worse by a strong sense of ill-usage. Her heart was sore, and she was not above hoping for some scandalous end to the affair, some punishment to Fanny for conduct so disgraceful towards herself, as well as towards Edmund. Such bitter feelings might have escaped the notice of the rest of the family, but Mary saw them, though the few attempts she made to shew her kindness or sympathy were repulsed as liberties. Nonetheless Mary could not see her sitting by disregarded with her mother and Julia, or walking alone in the garden, without feeling great pity.

A day was soon set for the first regular rehearsal of as much of the play as could be managed without Edmund. The actors were in the theatre at an early hour; Julia, though still delicate after her recent indisposition, was invested with the office of prompter, and the first scene began. Rushworth made his entrance, and Frederick encountered his mother with much amazement.

'*For God's sake, what is this!*' cried Mr Rushworth, beholding Miss Price kneeling in an attitude of elegant despair. '*Why do I find my mother thus? Speak!*'

'*My dear Frederick!*' she said, embracing him with ardour. '*The joy is too great — I was not prepared —*'

'*Dear Mother, compose yourself. How she trembles! She is fainting,*' he cried, as Miss Price leant gracefully against him, observing the directions with the most scrupulous exactness. The pause that then followed was so prolonged that Julia felt it necessary to prompt Miss Price with her next speech. Casting a look of some irritation in her cousin's direction, Miss Price continued. '*He talked of love, and promised me marriage,*' she said, in tones of becoming modesty. '*He was the first man who had ever spoken to me on such a subject — don't look at me, dear Frederick! I can say no more,*' and indeed she did not, though there was a certain half-glance at Mr Rushworth that seemed designed to convey a private meaning.

Mr Rushworth composed himself into yet another attitude of manly vigour, and pressed his companion's hand next to his heart.

'Oh! My son!' she sighed. '*I was intoxicated by the fervent caresses of —*'

'You must excuse me, Fanny,' said Julia, rising from her seat, 'but this passage has been omitted.'

'Yes, yes,' said Miss Price quickly, returning to her own voice, 'I recall. Mr Rushworth, we now move on to the next page. You begin again with *"Proceed, proceed".*'

Lady Bertram and her sister happened to choose this moment to join the small audience, and therefore witnessed only the closing moments of the scene. Mrs Norris was loud in her disappointment at missing Fanny's triumph, but eventually accepted her assurance that there were several more scenes of equal potential, and took her seat.

The next scene brought Mr Yates to the stage for the first time. He had been severely displeased to find that his blue cloak was still unfinished, a failure he did not scruple to attribute to Mrs Norris's insistence on completing it without sending out for another roll of satin. It took some moments for him to rant himself back into a good humour, but by the point of Mary's entrance he was in full voice.

'The name of Wildenhaim will die with me!' he stormed. *'Oh! Why was not my Amelia a boy?'*

Mr Yates's voice was so thunderous, his manner so ridiculous, that it was as much as Mary could do to avoid laughing aloud. In consequence, she did the comedy of the scene some credit, and they proceeded with great *éclat,* especially after the entrance of Henry, whose appearance in a cocked hat he had discovered in the Mansfield schoolroom was such a piece of true comic acting as Mary would not have lost upon any account.

They were obliged to stop half way through the act, where Mr Norris's character would have entered, and Mary returned to her seat to watch Rushworth and Yates roar through the next scene. Frederick drew his sword upon his unknown father, and the Baron imprisoned his unknown son, both hallooing at one another from a distance of less than a yard. The act closed with the solemn pronouncement from Mr Yates that *'Vice is never half so dangerous, as when it assumes the garb of morality',* and the fervent applause of the spectators. Both audience and actors then repaired to the dining-parlour, where a collation had been prepared, and the company began upon the cold meat and cake with equal enthusiasm.

Everyone was too much engaged in compliment and criticism to be struck by an unusual noise in the other part of the house, until the door of the room was thrown open, and Maria appearing at it, with a look of meaning at her cousin and Mr Rushworth, announced in trembling tones, 'Edmund has come! He is in the hall at this moment!'

Not a word was spoken for half a minute, but there was no time for further consternation, for Edmund was following his cousin almost instantaneously into the dining-room, intent on losing no time in giving them a full report of his uncle's health, and the particulars of their journey.

'And what of you all?' he asked at the end of it. 'How does the play go on?'

'We have chosen *Lovers' Vows*,' replied Mr Yates, his voice still rather hoarse from his exertions. 'And I take Baron Wildenhaim.'

'I see,' said Edmund, then, 'I am afraid I do not know the play,' unaware of the relief this declaration afforded to at least one person present.

'You are to be Anhalt, Edmund,' said Tom quickly. 'We have cast all the other men.

Indeed, we were in the midst of a rehearsal when you arrived.'

'Pray do not leave off on my account, Tom,' said Edmund with a smile. 'I will join the audience and spur you on.'

'Would it not be better,' began Miss Price, with a look at Mr Rushworth, 'if Anhalt were to read through his scene with Amelia here, in the dining-parlour? The rest might then take the opportunity to have another rehearsal of the first act.'

No-one making any objection, and some amongst them being anxious to be gone, the greater part of the party returned to the theatre. Mr Norris was evidently surprised to see that Miss Price made one of them, while Mary made no movement to leave the room.

'He must have thought they were to act together,' thought Mary with a sigh, as she rose and called Julia back again. 'Miss Julia! Forgive me, but I am sure Mr Norris would welcome your assistance as prompter. As, indeed, would I.'

Edmund took up a copy of the play, and directed by Julia, found the scene in question.

'I am at your service,' he said, looking from one to the other, 'but clearly I will only be able to *read* the part.'

They began, and Mary had never felt her opening lines so apt as she did now: *'I feel very low-spirited — some thing must be the matter.'*

Mr Norris stumbled over his first speeches, but it was soon apparent that he had the happiest knack of adapting his posture and voice to whatever was to be expressed, and whether it were dignity or tenderness, he could do it with equal beauty. It was truly dramatic, and caught between their theatrical and their real parts, between their present embarrassment and their past misunderstanding, they both gave such nature and feeling to the parts they were playing that Julia could not always pay attention to the book. In some confusion Mary watched as Edmund finally began upon the long-dreaded words, *'When two sympathetic hearts meet in the marriage state, matrimony may be called a happy life.'* He was in the middle of the speech before he suspected its purport, and his reading gradually slackened, until at last, the eyes which had been fixed so studiously on the book were raised towards Mary. Their eyes instantly met, and the cheeks of each were overspread with the deepest blush.

'This picture is pleasing,' continued Edmund, rising from his chair, *'but I must beg*

you not to forget that there is another on the same subject. When convenience, and fair appearance, joined to folly and ill-humour, forge the fetters of matrimony —'

He turned away to recover himself, and when he spoke again, though his voice still faltered, his manner shewed the wish of self-command.

'I must apologise,' he said after a pause, turning back to the young ladies, both of whom had risen from their seats in surprise and concern. 'The fatigue of so long a journey is proving to be no trifling evil. I beg your indulgence and your pity. I deserve the latter, at least,' he said, his voice sinking a little, 'more than you can ever surmise.'

He was gone as he spoke, and Mary followed him almost as quickly, very much afraid lest he should choose this moment to look in upon the rehearsals taking place in the billiard-room. She proved, however, to be too late. As she reached the theatre she found Edmund at the door, his hand still on the lock, his eyes fixed on the performers before him. Mr Rushworth's indefatigable Frederick was supporting Agatha in his arms, as she fainted most charmingly against his breast.

'I will, now, never leave you more,' he stormed. *'Look how tall and strong I am*

grown. These arms can now afford you support. They can, and shall, procure you subsistence.'

Rushworth was so totally unconscious of any thing beyond the stage that he did not notice the uneasy movements of many of the audience, and it was not until Tom gave a decided and uneasy 'hem' that he was at all aware of Edmund's presence, at which he immediately gave perhaps the very best start he had ever given in the whole course of his rehearsals.

'Ah — Norris! — my dear Norris! —' he cried, 'you find us at a most interesting moment! Miss Price's character has just been recounting her sad tale to her son. It was most affecting; we are fortunate indeed to have such an excellent Agatha, there is some thing so *maternal* in her manner, so completely *maternal* in her voice and countenance.'

Mr Rushworth continued in the same eager tone, unmindful of Mr Norris's expression as he turned to look at Miss Price. She, however, returned his gaze with a bold eye; even now, Mr Rushworth retained her hand, and the very circumstance which had occasioned their present embarrassment, was to her the sweetest support. Ever since the ball her manner to Edmund had been careless and cold, and she wanted only the certainty of a more eligible offer to break off an engagement that had now become a source of regret and disappointment, however public the rupture must prove to be.

The eyes of everyone present were still fixed on Miss Price, and only Mary was so placed as to see the expression of shock and alarm on Mrs Norris's face. It was apparent at once that she was under the influence of a tumult of new and very unwelcome ideas. She looked almost aghast, but it was not the arrival of her son that was the cause of it; for many weeks now she had considered Mary to be the principal threat to a union that she had looked forward to for so long, and which was even now on the point of accomplishment. But in devoting so much energy to hindering Mary, and disparaging her, she had entirely overlooked another, and far more insidious development. There was now no room for error. The conviction that had rushed over her mind, and driven the colour from her cheeks, could no longer be denied: the true daemon of the piece was not the upstart, under-bred Mary, but the smooth and plausible Mr Rushworth, a man she had been flattering and encouraging all the while, thinking him to be the admirer of Maria, and a good enough match for her and her seven thousand pounds. But now Mrs Norris's eyes were opened, and her fury and indignation were only too evident.

'If I must say what *I* think,' she said, in a cold, determined manner, 'it is very disagreeable to be always rehearsing. I think we are a great deal better employed, sitting comfortably here among ourselves, and doing nothing.'

Edmund replied with an increase of gravity which was not lost on anyone present, 'I am happy to find our sentiments on this subject so much the same, madam. There will be no more rehearsals.'

There was indeed no question of resuming. Mr Rushworth clearly considered it as only a temporary interruption, a disaster for the day, and even suggested the possibility of the rehearsal being renewed after tea. But to Mary, the conclusion of the play was a certainty; the total cessation of the scheme was inevitably at hand, and the tender scene between herself and Mr Norris would go no further forward.

CHAPTER VII

The price to be paid for the doubtful pleasure of private theatricals was in Mary's thoughts the whole of the following day, and an evening of backgammon with Dr Grant was felicity to it. It was the first day for many, many days, in which the households had been wholly divided. Four-and-twenty hours had never passed before, since April began, without bringing them all together in some way or other. At the Park the evening passed with external serenity, though almost every mind was ruffled, and the music which Lady Bertram called for from Julia helped to conceal the want of real harmony. Maria kept to her room, complaining of a cold, while Fanny sat quietly with her needle, a smile of secret delight now and again playing about her lips. In the more retired seclusion of the White House, Mrs Norris gave way to a bitter invective against Rushworth, inciting her son to exert himself, it being within his power to remedy all these evils, if he would but act like a man, with fortitude and resolution. Edmund's private feelings in the face of such a tirade may only be guessed at.

'I was sorry to hear that the play is done with,' said Mrs Grant, when Henry and Mary joined her and Dr Grant in the breakfast-room the next morning. 'The other young people must be very much disappointed.'

'I fancy Yates is the most afflicted,' said Henry with a smile. 'He is gone back to Bath, but, he said, if there was any prospect of a renewal of *Lovers' Vows,* he should break through every other claim. "From Bath, London, York, Heath Row — wherever I may be," he announced, "I will attend you from any place in England, at an hour's notice." ' 'I confess I did wonder at the Heath Row,' he continued, helping himself to more chocolate. 'Indeed I was not even sure at the time where he meant. It appears it is a small village some where to the west of London. Yates is thinking of buying a place there, but by all accounts the area is damp, low-lying and disposed to fog, and I therefore gave it as my opinion that it was unlikely much would ever be made of it.'

'Still,' said Mrs Grant, returning to the subject of the lost theatricals, 'there will be little rubs and disappointments every where, but then, if one plan of happiness fails, human nature turns to another; if the first calculation is wrong, we make a second better; we find comfort some where.'

Mrs Grant's confidence proved to be well founded, for the weather clearing, the excursion to Compton was reinstated, and the next time they all met together at the Park an early day was named, and agreed to. Lady Bertram having a slight cold, she was persuaded to stay at home by her sister. At any other time Mrs Norris would have very thoroughly relished the means this afforded her of directing the arrangement of the whole scheme; now, all her considerable efforts would be needed to keep Mr Rushworth away from Fanny, while throwing him, if she could, in the way of Maria.

'You must excuse Lady Bertram on this occasion, Mr Rushworth,' she said coolly, 'and accept of the girls and myself without her.'

Julia began to protest, saying she had just as rather not go at all, but her aunt at once addressed her in a whisper both angry and audible: 'What a piece of work here is about nothing — I am quite ashamed of you, Julia, to make such a difficulty when the whole party has been arranged for *your* pleasure and convenience — accept the invitation with a good grace, and let us hear no more of the matter.'

'Pray do not urge her, madam,' said Edmund. 'I am sure my cousin will find herself quite equal to the visit, when the day comes.'

Mrs Norris said no more, contenting herself with an angry look before turning to the subject of transport. 'Your barouche will hold four perfectly well, Mr Rushworth, independent of the box, on which one might go with you. And as for the young gentlemen, why, they can go on horseback.'

'But why is it necessary,' said Edmund, 'that Rushworth's carriage, or his *only* should be employed?'

'What!' cried Maria quickly. 'Go box'd up five in a postchaise in this weather, when we may have seats in a barouche! No, my dear cousin, that will not quite do.' After the ruin of *Lovers' Vows,* and the wreck of her own hopes of Rushworth, Maria had confined herself to the house, seeing nobody, but for some days past she had begun to affect a brittle and reckless gaiety that seemed precisely calculated to convey an indiffer-

132

ence Mary could not believe she really felt. She appeared to have decided that even if the loss of James Rushworth had destroyed her happiness, neither he nor her cousin should know that they had done it. She would not allow them to think of her as pining in a self-imposed solitude for *them.*

'There is no hardship, I suppose,' continued Edmund, 'in going on the barouche box?'

'Hardship!' replied Maria; 'Oh! I believe it would be generally thought the favourite seat. There can be no comparison as to one's view of the country from the barouche box.'

'Quite so,' said Fanny, with a look at Edmund. 'I have no doubt that *Miss Crawford* will choose that seat. She has a great desire to see Compton.'

'Miss Crawford has not often an opportunity to see her brother's work,' was Edmund's only reply, and the subject was dropped.

Friday was fine, and soon after breakfast Mr Rushworth arrived, driving the barouche. Miss Price was clearly meditating how best, and with the most appearance of obliging the others, to secure the barouche box, while Miss Bertram was equally clearly intent on thwarting her, an aim in which she was warmly seconded by her aunt. 'You were saying lately, Maria,' Mrs Norris said quickly, 'that you wished you could drive; I think this will be a good opportunity for you to take a lesson.'

Happy Maria! Unhappy Fanny! The latter took her seat within, in gloom and mortification; the former was assisted in ascending the box by Edmund, who saw it all, but said nothing.

When they approached Compton, Mr Rushworth appropriated the role of guide, and regaled them with a succession of observations on the property on each side of the road.

'Now we shall have no more rough road, Miss Bertram, our difficulties are over. Mr Smith had it made when he first purchased the estate. His original intention was to keep the old road as it was, since it passed by some very pretty cottages — delightfully picturesque objects, all ruined and over-grown with ivy — but the wretched tenants made so many difficulties about living in them that he was forced to undertake renovations, with the result that the houses now look quite ordinary and dull. Happily he lighted on the idea of moving the road entirely, so one is no longer troubled by the sight of villagers as one approaches the house. Miss Bertram will be able to see the church tower now, through the trees. Some reckon it tolerably handsome, but Smith tells me the annoyance of the bells is terrible, and I myself can testify to the clergyman's wife being a remarkably ill-looking woman. Ah,' he said as the barouche rounded a bend, 'we are about to gain our first sight of the house. Here lies the prospect, Miss Julia,' he said, turning back to her where she sat silent and pale at the back of the barouche, 'and I am sure you will agree that the approach *now,* is one of the finest things you ever saw: you will see the rear facade in the most surprising manner. People tell me it is the admiration of all the country, but I assure you it was a mere nothing before — well — before your brother took it in hand, Miss Crawford,' he concluded, with a momentary embarrassment, recollecting that the architect of this marvellously improved prospect was not, after all, his friend Mr Smith, but the man riding silently alongside him. Henry proved, moreover, to be close at his elbow at that moment, making so instantaneous a change of expression and tone necessary, as Mary, in spite of every thing, could hardly help laughing at.

'Capital, my dear Crawford! I was just saying to the ladies, you have out-Repton'd Repton! We are all anticipating the view of the house with the keenest enthusiasm.'

They turned in at the lodge and found themselves at the bottom of a low eminence overspread with trees. A little way farther the wood suddenly ceased, and the eye was instantly caught by the house. It was a handsome brick building, backed by gently rising hills, and in front, a stream of some natural importance had been swelled into a series of small lakes, by Henry's skill and ingenuity. The barouche was stopped for a few minutes, and the three gentlemen rode up to join them. Mary's heart swelled with pride and pleasure, to see her brother's genius and taste realised in the beauties of a landscape such as this. Even Mrs Norris was forced into admiration, though evidently against her will. 'I wish my dear husband could have seen this,' said she. 'It is quite like some thing we had planned at the White House.'

Henry was excessively pleased. If Mrs Norris could feel as much as this, the inference of what the young ladies must feel was indeed gratifying. He glanced at Miss Price, to see if a word of accordant praise could be extorted from her, but although she remained resolutely silent, his spirits were in as happy a state as professional pride could furnish when they drove up the last stretch of road to the spacious stone steps before the principal entrance.

The housekeeper met them at the door, and the particular object of the day was then considered. How would the ladies like — in what manner would they choose — to take a survey of the grounds?

'I wonder,' said Mr Crawford, looking round him, 'whether the party would be interested in an account of the improvements so far? Seeing the park as it is now, it is difficult to imagine it as it was. Shall we summon a council on the lawn? And what does Miss Julia say?' he continued more gently, turning to where she stood at the edge of the party. 'How should you like to proceed?'

Julia did not at first appear to have heard, but when Mary touched her gently on the arm she roused herself, and acknowledged in a sad voice, 'I suppose I am here to be persuaded, and I cannot give my approbation without knowing how it has been altered.'

'Very well,' began Henry. 'Since I came to Compton we have turned the whole house to front the south-west instead of the north

— the entrance and principal rooms, are now on that side, where the view, as you saw, is very fine. The approach was moved, as Mr Rushworth described, and this new garden made at what is now the back of the house, which gives it the best aspect in the world.'

'You speak of turning the house with as much ease as I might turn my horse!' cried Tom. 'Crawford, is there no limit to your exertions in pursuit of your object?'

'Indeed not,' replied Henry, with a look at Miss Price, who affected not to notice. 'My role is to improve upon nature, to supply her deficiencies, and create the perfect prospect that *should have been* from the imperfect one that is.'

'A trifling ambition, upon my word!' rejoined Tom. 'I will remember to call upon your services when I want a river diverted, a hill removed, or a valley levelled.'

'All feats which I have indeed performed!' laughed Henry. 'But, to conclude my narration, the meadows you can just see beyond the wilderness have all been laid together in the last year. The wilderness on the right hand was already here when I came — it had been planted up some years before. As such it is further advanced than much of the planting in the new garden, and I commend it to you as not only a pretty walk, but the one affording the best shade on a hot day.'

No objection was made, but for some time there seemed no inclination to move in any direction, or to any distance. All dispersed about in happy spontaneous groups, though there was, perhaps, a degree of premeditation in Mrs Norris's determination to accompany Mr Rushworth and Fanny. For her part, Mary made sure to keep close to Julia, who had relapsed once again into silence and sadness. A moment later she found, to her surprise, that Mr Norris intended to join them, and the three began with a turn on the lawn. A second circuit led them naturally to the door which Henry had told them opened to the wilderness; from there a considerable flight of steps landed them in darkness and shade and natural beauty, compared with the heat and full sunshine of the terrace. For some time they could only walk and admire, and Mary saw at once that the felling of the trees in the park had indeed opened the prospect in a most beautiful manner, even if she forbore from voicing this opinion aloud. At length, after a short pause, Julia turned to Mary and said, 'I suppose it must be my late illness that makes me so tired, but the next time we come to a seat, I should be glad to sit down for a little while.'

'My dear Julia,' cried Edmund, immediately drawing her arm within his, 'how thoughtless I have been! I hope you are not very fatigued. Perhaps,' turning to Miss Crawford, 'my other companion may also do me the honour of taking an arm.'

'Thank you, but I am not at all tired.' She took it, however, as she spoke, and the gratification of doing so, of feeling such a connection for the first time, assailed her with satisfactions very sweet, if not very sound. A few steps farther brought them out at the bottom of the walk and a comfortable-sized bench, a few yards from an iron gate leading into the park, on which Julia sat down.

'Why would you not speak sooner, Julia?' said Edmund, observing her.

'I shall soon be rested,' said Julia quickly. 'Pray, do not interrupt your walk. I will be quite comfortable here.'

It was with reluctance that Edmund suffered her to remain alone, but Julia eventually prevailed, and watched them till they had turned the corner, and all sound of them had ceased.

A quarter of an hour passed away, and then Miss Bertram unexpectedly appeared on another path, some distance away. She was walking quickly, and with some purpose, and did not seem to notice her sister, or have the slightest notion that any other person was nearby. Julia was about to rise and greet her, when she saw with some surprise that Maria was intent on concealing herself behind a large shrub on one side of the path, to the very great danger of her new muslin gown. The reason for this unaccountable behaviour was soon revealed. Julia heard voices and feet approaching and a few moments later Mr Rushworth and Miss Price issued from the same path, and came to a stop before the iron gate. They had clearly been engaged in a most earnest conversation; Miss Price looked all flutter and happiness, and the faces of both were very close together. Neither was sensible of Miss Bertram's being there, nor of Julia sitting motionless on the bench only a short distance away. It struck the latter all of a sudden as being more like a play than any thing she had seen in the theatre at Mansfield Park, and though she knew she ought to draw their attention to her presence, some thing constrained her, and she remained fixed in her seat. The first words she heard were from her cousin, and were to this effect.

'My dear Mr Rushworth, I have not the *slightest* interest in attempting to find Mr Norris. Why, we have but this moment escaped from his horrible mother. No — I have had *quite* enough of that family for one morning. After all, what is Mr Norris to *me* that I should get myself hot and out of breath chasing about the garden looking for him?'

'Your words interest me inexpressibly, Miss Price,' said Mr Rushworth, with some earnestness. 'I had no idea, when I first came into the area, but that you were the intended, indeed the engaged, bride of that very same Mr Norris. A steady respectable sort of fellow, no doubt, but no match for a woman of character and brilliance such as yourself.'

'Mr Tiresome Norris bores me more than I can say,' said Miss Price with feeling. 'So dull, so wretchedly *dull!* He pays no compliments, he has no wit, and if that were not bad enough, his taste in dress is deplorable, and he has no refined conversation; all he wants to do indoors is talk about books, and all he ever does outside is ride. A deadly tedious life mine would be with the oh-so-estimable Mr Norris.'

Mr Rushworth laughed knowingly. 'Perhaps Mr Norris has recently found someone who might share these dreary interests of his?'

Miss Price gave him a look which marked her contempt. 'She is welcome to him. A woman who has the audacity to attach herself to a man already promised to another, as *she* has done, will surely have no scruple in taking up that other's cast-offs.'

'And you, my dear — my *very* dear Miss Price,' said he, leaning still closer, 'what will *you* now do? There must surely be countless suitors contending for the honour of your hand.'

Miss Price drew away slightly, and began to circle the small glade before the gate. 'Not so many as you might imagine, sir. But I have no doubt of acquiring them, once it becomes known that the engagement with Mr Norris is broken off.'

'So if there happened to be another gentleman who professed the most sincere attachment to Miss Price — nay, not merely an attachment but the most ardent, disinterested love — it might be as well for that gentleman to declare himself without delay?'

Miss Price looked at him haughtily. 'It might be as well for that gentleman to begin by demonstrating, beyond question, that all those ardent feelings are for Miss *Price,* and not for Miss *Bertram.*'

'My dear Miss Price,' he cried, making towards her, 'how could you even imagine — you are so *infinitely* her superior. In beauty, in spirit, in —'

'In *fortune,* sir?'

He stopped, and looked for a moment exceedingly foolish, but Miss Price turned away, smiling privately to herself, content, for the moment, with so complete a conquest, and not above a wish to sport with her new-declared lover a little, by way of punishment for his recent neglect.

'What is that knoll, I wonder?' she said, looking through the gate. 'Might we not obtain a more comprehensive view of the park from there? Such a survey being, after all, the principal reason for our visit?'

'Indeed — I am sure,' said Mr Rushworth, in evident embarrassment. 'That is, I imagine —'

'Oh, but of course, the gate is locked,' she said, a moment later, in a tone of some vexation. 'Why is it that it is only ever the *gardeners* who can go where they like in places like this?'

'I did wonder whether I should bring the key,' he stammered. 'Indeed, I was on the point of asking the housekeeper whether I might have the key —'

'That may very well be so,' she said archly,

144

'but it does not advance us very far. We cannot get through without it.'

Mr Rushworth bowed. 'I will remedy my mistake at once,' said he in a tone of decision. 'If Miss Price would do me the infinite honour of awaiting me here, I will return without delay.'

Miss Price bowed her complaisance, and Mr Rushworth set off at some speed towards the house.

Miss Price was on the point of resuming her circuit of the glade, and to judge of her expression, with no very unpleasant sensations, but no sooner was Mr Rushworth out of sight when Miss Bertram emerged from her hiding place to confront her startled and affrighted cousin.

'So this is your plan, is it?' said Maria in an angry tone. 'You mean to discard our gentle, upright, honest cousin for such a — a — *fop* as Rushworth?'

'As to *that,*' said Miss Price, reddening with astonishment and disdain, 'even were he the most infamous fop in England, I do not think *you* would have refused him, had he made you an offer. But he did *not* make you an offer, did he?'

'No,' said Maria bitterly, seizing her cousin by the wrist, 'because *you* saw to it that he did not. Can you never allow me anyone or any thing of my own, but you have to seize it from me? He admired me, I know he did, and it wanted only a little encouragement to turn that admiration into a decided attachment. A very little encouragement, and a very reasonable forbearance on your part. But no — even *that,* you could not permit me. Even though you were already pledged to another man — and honourably, publicly pledged at that.'

'Do not delude yourself,' said Fanny angrily, snatching her hand from Maria's grasp. 'You may have seen admiration; *I* saw only an idle flirtation — a passing and frivolous gallantry. Whatever you may have hoped, you and your pitiable portion would never have been sufficient to attach a man like Mr Rushworth. You may take *my* word for that.'

These words drew a gasp and a cry of anguish from Maria. 'I wish you had *never* come to Mansfield,' she sobbed: 'We were all of us perfectly happy before *you* came — I wish I had never seen you — I wish — I wish you were *dead.*'

For a single dreadful moment Julia thought her sister was about to strike her cousin; but the next thing she knew, Maria had turned away without another word, and was making her way, not very steadily,

146

towards the house. When she reached the steps Julia saw her stumble blindly, and put her hand out to break her fall. Fanny, for her part, stood motionless for some minutes, leaning against the gate for support, her face and lips quite white.

Julia was thrown into a state of dreadful indecision, uncertain whether to remain where she was, or go to offer her sister some assistance, and thereby reveal what she had overheard; but she was soon relieved of the necessity of action by the appearance of Henry Crawford, who had been wandering about the grounds for some time, in search of Miss Price. He had seen her with Rushworth half an hour before, but had been detained at the critical moment by the housekeeper. Having but this minute extricated himself, he was now in the happy but unexpected situation of being face to face with the real object of his attentions. More gratifying still, the young lady was alone, and — to his eye — very much in need of all the relief and support he was only too willing to proffer. She was trembling, and at first she could only cling to his arm, as he helped her to a small rustic seat some yards farther on. The first fit soon passed, however, and in another moment she was able to recollect herself, and make a strong effort for composure, while still refusing in the most strenuous terms to disclose the cause of her distress. Mr Crawford elected not to press her on the subject, while indulging in the private hope that the whole blame of it might be laid to his rival's account.

'I believe I saw Rushworth on my way here,' he said, curious to see her reaction. 'He was posting away as if upon life and death.'

Miss Price smiled, roused from her indisposition by such pleasing evidence of her power. 'He is gone to fetch the key to the gate,' she said. 'I wanted to see the view from the knoll.'

'Then I am delighted to be in a position to assist you,' said Henry, taking the key from his pocket, while carefully omitting to mention that it was this very key that Mr Rushworth was at that moment in quest of.

Miss Price rose from her seat, and took Mr Crawford's arm. 'So much you have done here, Mr Crawford!' she said, with forced gaiety. 'And to think that Mansfield may look like this in another summer! I confess I long for such freedom and openness as you have created here. Mansfield seems to me more and more like a prison — a dismal old prison. "I cannot get out", as the starling said.'

'To tell you the truth,' replied Henry, speaking rather lower, 'I do not think that *I* shall ever see Mansfield again with so much pleasure as I do now. Even my own plans will hardly improve it in *some* ways.'

He moved closer to her as he spoke, and they were too far away for Julia to discern what happened next, but when she saw her cousin's face again her colour was heightened, and she was breathing rather faster than usual.

'You are too much a man of the world not to see with the eyes of the world,' Miss Price continued, somewhat abstractedly. 'If other people think Mansfield improved, I have no doubt that you will.'

Henry smiled, and took her arm with more confidence and cheerfulness than he had thought possible even an hour before. 'I am afraid that there is little prospect of that. *Your* prospects, however, are too fair to justify want of spirits.'

'Do you mean literally or figuratively? Literally I conclude. Yes, certainly, the sun shines and the park looks very cheerful. And I am absolutely at liberty to command my *own* path.'

'I am very glad to hear it,' said Henry, with a serious look, as he unlocked the gate and the two of them disappeared from view.

Julia was again left to her uneasy solitude. She began to be surprised at being left so long, and to listen with a very anxious desire of seeing her companions again. But soon the voice of Miss Crawford once more caught her ear. They were just returned into the wilderness from the park, to which a side gate, not fastened, had tempted them very soon after their leaving her.

'We have been admiring the view,' said Mary, though in truth, they had passed a greater part of the time in silence. As soon as they were alone, Mr Norris's politeness and cordiality had vanished, and he had become silent and thoughtful. Mary had been at a loss to think of a subject that they might attempt with impunity; every thing brought back some painful recollection — the play, the ball, the ride to Compton, all were equally impossible, and she had at length given up the endeavour.

Julia rose at once from the bench at their approach, and drew Mary to one side. 'I must speak with you,' she said, in the utmost perturbation.

'Certainly,' said Mary, looking at her with some concern. 'I hope nothing has occurred to distress you. Do you wish me to find a place where we may be more private?'

'No,' said Julia with uncharacteristic firmness, glancing across at Edmund. 'I cannot discuss this here. Could you come to the Park tomorrow?'

'Of course. I shall call as early as politeness permits.'

'Thank you, thank you!' said Julia, the colour rushing to her face. 'My dear Miss Crawford, I shall have no peace until I can confide in you!'

They returned to the house together, where they found Tom Bertram, who had for some time been lounging on the sopha reading reviews, awaiting the arrival of tea.

'There you are at last!' he cried as the three of them came in. 'I have had quite enough of improvements for one day, I can tell you. What with wildernesses and terraces and pleasure-grounds, I managed to get myself thoroughly lost. Quite where the rest of you were I cannot tell, but thankfully I came unexpectedly upon the gamekeeper, and spent a capital half hour discussing snipe and pheasant. The covies here are some of the best in the country.'

It was late before the other young ladies and gentlemen came in; Miss Price and Henry Crawford arrived first, followed by Miss Bertram, and finally Mr Rushworth in the company of Mrs Norris. By their own accounts they had been all walking about after each other in the heat, and none but Henry appeared to be entirely happy with the day's events. *He* certainly looked contented — triumphant even — while Miss Price was more withdrawn and thoughtful, and there was a slight disorder to her dress that could not be entirely explained, even by the rigours of a walk to the knoll. Mr Rushworth, by contrast, was positively ill-tempered, and looked all the more so when he found Miss Price in the company of Henry Crawford, but received no apology for her earlier disappearance. Maria, meanwhile, looked pale and troubled in mind, and was holding her shawl wrapped close around her shoulders; nor could all Mrs Norris's attempts to put her in the way of Mr Rushworth, and procure her the seat on the barouche box, suffice to restore her to the state of artificial high spirits with which she had begun the day.

The last arrival was soon followed by tea, a ten miles' drive home allowing no waste of hours, and from the time of their sitting down, it was a quick succession of busy nothings till the carriage came to the door. It was a beautiful evening, mild and still, and the drive was outwardly as pleasant as the serenity of nature could make it; but it was altogether a different matter to the ladies within. Their spirits were in general exhausted — all were absorbed in their own thoughts, and Fanny and Maria in particular, seemed intent on avoiding one another's eye. The party stopped at the parsonage to take leave of the Crawfords, and then continued on to the Park, where Mr Rushworth was invited to come in and take a glass of wine, before resuming the journey to Sotherton. But the company had scarcely entered the drawing-room when Lady Bertram rose from the sopha to meet them, came forward with no indolent step, and falling on her son's neck, cried, 'Oh, Tom, Tom! What are we to do?'

Chapter VIII

Nothing can convey the alarm and distress of the party. Sir Thomas was dead! All felt the instantaneous conviction. Not a hope of imposition or mistake was harboured any where. Lady Bertram's looks were an evidence of the fact that made it indisputable. It was a terrible pause; every heart was suggesting, 'What will become of us? What is to be done now?'

Edmund was the first to move and speak again. 'My dear madam, what has happened?' he asked, helping his aunt to a chair, but Lady Bertram could only hold out the letter she had been clutching, and exclaim in the anguish of her heart, 'Oh, Edmund, if I had known, I would never have allowed him to go!'

Entrusting Lady Bertram to her daughters' care, Edmund turned quickly to the letter.

'He is *not* dead!' he cried a moment later,

anxious to give what immediate comfort was within his power. Julia sat down in the nearest chair, unable to support herself, and Tom started forward, saying, 'Then what is the matter? For God's sake, Edmund, tell us what has happened!'

'He is not dead, but he *is* very ill. The letter is from a Mr Croxford, a physician in Keswick. It appears my uncle elected to undertake an inspection of the property on horseback, and suffered a dreadful fall, and a serious contusion to his head. It was some hours before he was missed, and several more before he was discovered, by which time he was unconscious, and very cold, and had bled a good deal. This Mr Croxford was sent for at once, and initial progress was good. That afternoon he opened his eyes —'

'So he is better — he is recovered!' cried Julia in all the agony of renewed hope.

'— but soon closed them again, without apparent consciousness, and by the evening he was alternating between fits of dangerous delirium in which he scarce knew his own name, and moments of lucidity, when he seemed almost himself. At the time of writing, Mr Croxford admits that the signs are still alarming, but he talks with hope of the improvement which a fresh mode of treatment might procure. *"Before he sank into his present wildness,"'* Edmund continued, his voice sinking, ' *"Sir Thomas begged me to ensure that this letter should go to Mansfield at once, and by private messenger. Knowing himself to be in danger, and fearing that he may never see his beloved family again, he demanded a promise from me, with all the strength and urgency which illness could command, that I would communicate to you his wish, perhaps his dying wish —"'*

Edmund stopped a moment, then added, in a voice which seemed to distrust itself, 'I think, perhaps, that it would be better if we deferred the discussion of such a subject until tomorrow — it is a matter of some delicacy.'

Mr Rushworth offered at once to withdraw, but Miss Bertram stopped him, saying, 'What is it, Edmund? What are my father's wishes?'

'Very well,' said Edmund, with resignation. 'Mr Croxford writes as follows: *"Sir Thomas directs that there should no longer be any delay in the celebration of the marriage between his niece and Mr Norris. If he should be doomed never to return, it would give him the last, best comfort to know that he had ensured the happiness of two young people so very dear to him. He only wishes that he could be sure that his own children were as nobly and as eligibly settled."* '

Every eye turned upon Miss Price, who, conscious of their scrutiny, rose to her feet and said in an unsteady voice, 'You must excuse me, indeed you must excuse me,' before running out of the room.

Mrs Norris made to follow her, unable to suppress a look of triumph and exultation at such an unlooked-for resolution to all her difficulties, but Edmund firmly prevented her. 'She is distressed, madam. It will all be better left until tomorrow, when we will have had the advantage of sleep. In the mean time, Mr Rushworth, I would be most grateful if you would assist us in keeping the whole affair from public knowledge for the time being, until we receive further news.'

Mr Rushworth readily assured them of his secrecy, expressed his sorrow for their suffering, and requested their permission to call the following morning, before taking his leave.

The evening passed without a pause of misery, the night was totally sleepless, and the following morning brought no relief. Those of the family who appeared for breakfast were quiet and dejected; Tom was the only one among them who seemed disposed for speech, wondering aloud how he would ever be able to assume all his father's responsibilities.

'Someone must speak to the steward, and then there is the bailiff,' he said, half to himself, 'and of course there are the improvements. I will walk down to the parsonage this morning and see Crawford myself. He should know immediately. I think we may safely confide in the Crawfords. Knowing my father, as they do, they will be genuinely distressed at this dreadful news.'

The Grants were not at home, but the Crawfords received the news with all the sympathy and concern required by such painful tidings; Mary had barely comprehended the consequences of his disclosure, and Henry was still expressing their wishes for a happier conclusion to his father's illness than there was at present reason to hope, when Mr Bertram threw them into even greater amazement.

'I am grateful for your kind condolences, which I will convey to my mother and sisters,' he said, 'and if Miss Crawford were to favour them with her company at the Park tomorrow, I am sure they would be thankful for any assistance she might be able to offer with the preparations. Though needless to say, we intend to keep matters within a much smaller circle than was originally intended.'

He stopped, seeing their looks of incomprehension. 'Forgive me, my thoughts are somewhat distracted. But every thing considered, I see no reason why you should not know. Sir Thomas has expressed his wish that the marriage between Edmund and Fanny might take place at once. Indeed I was hoping to see Dr Grant, that I might consult him about the service.'

'I see,' said Mary, rising from her chair and going over to her work-table to hide her perturbation.

'So Miss Price and Mr Norris are to marry at last,' said Henry, with studied indifference. 'And when, precisely, are we to wish them joy?'

'As soon as Edmund returns. He left this morning for Cumberland. In the mean time, we await further news,' he concluded, in a more serious tone, 'but I fear that the next letter may simply confer an even greater obligation upon us to hasten the accomplishment of my father's wishes.'

Mr Bertram departed soon after, and Henry following him out, Mary was left alone. Her mind was in the utmost confusion and dismay. It was exactly as she had expected, and yet it was beyond belief!

'Oh, Edmund!' she said to herself. 'How can you be so blind! Will *nothing* open your eyes? Surely Sir Thomas would not insist on this wedding if he knew your true feelings! Or those of his niece! Oh! If I could believe Miss Price to deserve you, it would be — how different would it be! But it is all too late. You will marry, and you will be miserable, and there is nothing anyone else can do to prevent it.'

The agitation and tears which the subject occasioned brought on a head-ache. Her usual practice under such circumstances would be to go out for an hour's exercise, but she dreaded meeting anyone from the Park, and took refuge instead in her room. In consequence, her head-ache grew so much worse towards the evening that she refused all dinner, and went to bed with her heart as full as on the first evening of her arrival at Mansfield.

The next morning brought no further news, and her head-ache easing, Mary prepared herself to fulfil her promise, and pay a visit to the ladies of the Park. It was a miserable little party. Lady Bertram was a wretched, stupefied creature, and Julia was scarcely less an object of pity, her eyes red, and the stains of tears covering her cheeks. Maria Bertram was by far the most animated of the three, but hers was the animation of an agitated and anxious mind. Fear and expectation seemed to oppress her in equal degrees, and she was unable to keep her seat, picking up first one book and then another, before abandoning both to pace impatiently up and down the room. There was no sign of Fanny, and when Mary made a brief enquiry she was told merely that Miss Price was indisposed, and Mrs Norris was attending to her.

Mary sat for some minutes more in silence, impatient to be gone, but constrained by the forms of general civility, until the appearance of Baddeley with a tray of chocolate, which, by rousing Lady Bertram to the necessity of presiding, gave her the opportunity to speak privately to Julia.

'I hope you will soon receive more encouraging news from Cumberland,' she said, regretting she could think of nothing more to the purpose, but relieved to see the girl's face lighten for a moment at her words.

'It is very good of you to come. I have some satisfaction in knowing that Edmund will soon be at my father's side — it will be such a relief to us all! As it is, we do not seem to know what to do with ourselves.

My aunt has been scolding me all morning about the needlework for Fanny's wedding, but I can hardly see to sew.'

At this, her eyes filled with tears once more, and she turned her face away and began to weep silently. Mary took her hand in her own, and offered her assistance, but it was not without a wondering reflection that she might find herself helping to adorn wedding-clothes for the very woman who was to marry the man she herself loved.

They drank their chocolate in heavy silence, until the stillness of the room was suddenly broken by the sound of violent screams from another part of the house. In a residence of such elegance, tranquillity, and propriety, such a disturbance would have been unusual at any time, but doubly shocking in a house silenced by sorrow. Mary was on her feet in an instant, and going quickly to the door she flung it open, and went to the foot of the staircase. There was no mistake; the noise was issuing from one of the rooms above, and the briefest of glances at the footmen was enough to confirm that this was not the first burst of feeling from that quarter they had witnessed that day. Miss Price was giving vent to tumults of passionate hysterics, and although Mary could not distinguish the words, it was clear that Mrs Norris was doing her utmost to comfort and quiet her. Mary was surprised, and not a little ashamed, wondering for a moment whether she had misjudged Fanny, and formed an unjust estimate of her fondness for her uncle. She felt the indelicacy of listening unseen to such a private grief, and turned back towards the drawing-room, where Maria was standing at the open door. Mary felt her face glow, as if she had been caught in the act of spying, but when she saw the expression of the young woman's face she quickly forgot her own embarrassment. She doubted if Maria was even aware of her presence; she was wrapped in her own meditations, her cheeks were flushed, and her eyes unnaturally bright.

'Are you quite well, Miss Bertram?' Mary asked gently.

Maria roused herself with some difficulty from her reverie. 'Perfectly well, thank you, Miss Crawford,' she said coolly. 'As far as one can be, in such a situation.'

Mary returned to the drawing-room to take her leave of the other ladies, and she was half way across the park before recollecting that she had not asked Julia what she had wished to discuss with her at Compton: every other consideration had been swept away by the news from Cumberland. There was nothing to be done now but to return to the parsonage, and endeavour to find an opportunity to speak to Julia the following day. The rain began to fall once more, and she quickened her pace, noticing, however, that there seemed to be a group of workmen with mattocks gathered around a man on horseback, some distance away. The light was uncertain, but she thought she could discern the figure of her brother, and as she was drying herself in the vestibule, he came in behind her, dripping with wet.

'I have just been giving the men instructions to commence the felling of the avenue, and the digging of the channel for the new cascade,' he said, as he shook out his coat. 'How do they go on at the Park?'

Mary sighed, and related the events of the afternoon, too preoccupied, perhaps, with her wet shoes to notice the look in his eye as she described what she had heard on the stairs. 'I had not expected her to be so affected,' she concluded.

'I suppose it rather depends what exactly she is affected *by*,' observed Henry, deep in his own thoughts.

At that moment Mrs Grant appeared, armed with dry clothes, and the promise of hot tea and a good fire.

'I hear there is still no news of Sir Thomas,' she said. 'Poor man! To be cut off at his time of life, when Lady Bertram depends on him so completely! But then again, I have no doubt Mrs Norris will be more than ready to step forward, and supply his place. She never misses an opportunity to interfere, even where she is not wanted. Did you see her at the ball? Taking it on herself to make up the card-tables, as if *she* were the hostess, and plaguing the life out of the chaperons because she wanted them moved to another part of the room. But at least we will not have to endure all *that* again in a hurry. There will be no more balls at Sotherton for the present.'

Henry looked up from where he was sitting removing his boots. 'What is this? No more balls at Sotherton? Do not ask me to believe that Mr Rushworth has all of a sudden lost his taste for gaudy display, or acquired a preference for the modest and discreet.'

'No, indeed, Henry,' said Mrs Grant, with a look that was only half reproving. 'But I heard this morning that he has left the neighbourhood. I am told that when he returned to Sotherton last night, there was a letter awaiting him from his father requesting his presence in Bath, and his father's requests are not, apparently, of the kind to be trifled with. They say he will not be back before the winter. Did you not hear about it at the Park, Mary? Mr Rushworth called there this morning, on his way to the turnpike road — or so Mrs Baddeley told me. The ladies must have heard the news by now.'

'I am certain they have,' thought Mary, 'and I do not doubt that it was *this* news, unexpected and unwelcome as it must have been, that was the real cause of Miss Price's hysteria, rather than any excessive solicitude for her uncle's health.' A glance at her brother proved that he was of much the same mind, but Henry refused to meet her gaze, and a moment later he was on his feet, and hurrying away to dress for dinner.

CHAPTER IX

The weather worsening the next day, Mary was forced to give up all notion of a walk to the Park, and resigned herself to the probability of twenty-four hours within doors, with only her brother and the Grants for company. In the latter, however, she was mistaken. They were just beginning breakfast when a letter arrived for Henry; a letter of the most pressing business, as they soon discovered.

'It is from Sir Robert Ferrars,' he said, as he turned the pages. 'You remember, Mary? I had the laying out of his pleasure-grounds at Netherfield last year, after he acquired the estate from Charles Bingley. A small job, hardly worth the trouble, but one that obtained for me some invaluable new connections. Indeed, I still have hopes of a commission at Bingley's new property on the strength of his recommendation. However,' he continued, his brow contracting, 'it seems that an officious gardener has been interfering with the drains, with the result that most of the gravel walks are now under half a foot of water. Ferrars is reluctant to entrust the repair work to anyone but me — as well he should be, in the circumstances.' He folded the letter and put it carefully in his pocket-book. 'He writes to request my presence without delay. I will pen a note to Bertram to inform him, if you would be so good as to send one of the men to the Park? The affair requires my immediate departure, and if the weather is at all the same in Hertford-shire as it is here, I dare not imagine the dirt and disorder I will find on my arrival. It will be a miracle if my magnificent statues are not up to their knees in mud.'

The rest of the morning was devoted to packing Henry's trunk, and preparing for his journey. When the whirl of departure was over, and they had watched him disappear into the mist and gloom of the afternoon, Mary returned to the parlour to warm herself by the fire, and reflect on the slow monotony of a wet day in the country, with nothing but the prospect of cribbage with her brother-in-law to enliven it. The only slight communication from the Park was a short note from Tom Bertram by way of reply to Henry, but it contained no further tidings from Cumberland, and consideration for the footman standing shivering in the dark at the outer door prevented Mary from sending any word to Julia. She would have to wait for better weather, and as she was used to walking, and had no fear of either path or puddles, she was confident that she, at least, would not be too long confined to the house.

However, in this, she was to be disappointed. It was a further four days before even Mary could venture outdoors, four days that brought no further news, either from the Park, or from Henry, though in truth she had not expected a letter from her brother so soon. The next day was Sunday, and a brief cessation in the rain making it possible to attend church in the morning, Mary was in eager expectation of the Bertram carriage at the sweep-gate. She had no great hope of Lady Bertram, but the sight even of Mrs Norris would be a relief after so many days without seeing another human creature besides themselves; and while Mary's sympathy was for Sir Thomas's wife and children, she could not but acknowledge that his sister-in-law might prove a more useful and communicative source of intelligence.

The church was crowded — especially so, given the unfavourable weather — and it soon became apparent that all the lookers-on of the neighbourhood had heard of Sir Thomas's misfortune, and hoped, like Mary, to gain some further news as to his condition. Mary felt ashamed to be part of such a general and importunate inquisitiveness, and all the more so, when she saw Julia Bertram being hurried to the family pew by her aunt, to the audible whisperings of the rest of the congregation. A brief exchange of civilities was all that was possible before the service, and Mary was relieved to find that Dr Grant made no reference to the events at the Park in his sermon, and the text for that Sunday was mercifully insipid; in Mary's experience, Holy Writ had an unpleasant habit of being only too horribly appropriate.

When the service was over, the congregation hurried out into the church-yard, where the clouds had dispersed across the sky, and the sun had appeared for the first time in days. Mary shrank from the throng surrounding Mrs Norris, especially when it became evident that she was more intent on receiving congratulations on her son's forthcoming wedding, than commiserations for the family's sufferings. 'If poor Sir Thomas were fated never to return,' she was saying gaily, 'it would be peculiarly consoling to see Edmund and our dear Fanny married. And then, of course, I will be taking up residence with them at Lessingby Hall, which is unquestionably one of the *finest* houses in the country. The interiors alone cost the late Mr Price over eight thousand pounds.'

Mary took Julia's arm, and led her gently to one side. She judged it best not to press her on the subject of her own health, and confined herself to asking after her mother and sister.

Julia shook her head sadly. 'There is no change. My mother has been reduced to a pitiably low and trembling condition, starting at every knock at the door, impatient for every new message, and then distraught when it comes, and brings no relief.'

'And your sister?'

'My dear Miss Crawford, I cannot tell you. She is one moment overwhelmed with grief, the next unaccountably light of heart, as if some intolerable weight had been lifted from her. And as for Fanny, she keeps mostly to her room. Her maid tells me she has taken to walking in the garden in the early morning, before anyone else has risen, but the rest of the day she hides herself away, and will see no-one.'

Julia would have said more, but they were interrupted at that moment by Mrs Norris, who began to scold her niece for dawdling, when there was so much employment awaiting them at the Park.

'Really, Julia, this is hardly the time for idle tittle-tattle. You know as well as I do that we still have the bridesmaids' gowns to finish this afternoon. And after I have been slaving myself half the night to contrive yours from what remains of that blue satin, you can at the very least give me your help in putting it together. There are but the seams, you know; you may do them in a minute. I should think *my*self very lucky to have nothing but such a simple task to do, but I will have to give all my attention to the filigree for dear Fanny's veil — *that* will not stitch itself, I can tell you. And we have *still* not received those shoe-roses from Northampton, despite all the haberdasher's assurances, and no doubt the task will fall to me to resolve, as usual, and meanwhile here *you* are wasting your time gossiping.'

Seeing tears in Julia's eyes, Mary hastened to renew her offer of assistance. Mrs Norris was evidently surprised, and looked her up and down for a moment before replying, 'Well, I suppose you *might* be of some use for the hems. Any thing that does not shew, and requires little refinement, may *perhaps* be entrusted to you. If you care to come to the Park in the morning, the housekeeper will direct you as to what you should do.'

She then gave a stiff bow, and led her niece away to their carriage before Mary was able to reply.

Mary rose early the following morning, and left for the Park as soon as she had break-fasted. After so many days of rain, it was a bright, clear morning, and as Mary made her way towards the house she thought of the task that awaited her, and could not suppress a smile. If Mrs Norris had only known, she would not think of wasting her talents on the tedious drudgery of hems. Mary had been taught fine needlework when still a young girl, and shewed a rare aptitude for the most intricate and delicate lacework. Indeed, after their uncle died there was a time — a very short time — when she had been obliged to support herself by placing her skills at the disposal of the fashionable ladies of Hanover-square and Berkeley-street. Her work was highly prized, and much sought after, especially for wedding gowns, but Mary took no pleasure in it, and nothing but the direst necessity would induce her to adopt such an expedient again. It was long indeed, before she could take up her needle for any thing but the most common-place work, but it still gave her pleasure to devise beautiful things for those she loved, and she had smiled to herself more than once when a shawl she had embroidered for Mrs Grant was admired in the Mansfield Park drawing-room.

Sir Thomas's graceful, elegant house looked particularly beautiful in the bright sun, and the walk from the parsonage shewed it to best advantage, the lawns dotted over with timber, and the handsome, stone house standing well on rising ground. There was mist in the hollows, and in the curve of the valley, the workmen were beginning their labour on the channel for the new cascade; the sound of their voices carried across to Mary on the mild morning air. It was a charming view, of a sort to ease the mind, and lift the spirits, and Mary entered the house with a lighter heart than she had known for some days past.

But what was peace and harmony outside, was uproar and disorder inside. Servants were running hither and thither, doors were banging, and the house was all noise and confusion. Mary stood in the entrance, as motionless as she was speechless, scarcely knowing what to think or do, when the door to the drawing-room flung open, and Julia came rushing towards her, threw herself into her arms, and cried, 'Oh Mary, Mary, thank God that you are here!'

For some minutes the girl could say no more, and Mary held her gently, allowing her sobs to subside, fearing that she knew only too well the cause of her distress.

'Is it your father?' she said at length. 'Has there been news from Cumberland?'

Julia raised a face that was as white as death, and wiped her eyes. 'No,' she said softly, shaking her head, 'it is not my father I weep for. It is Fanny.'

'*Fanny?*' repeated Mary, in amazement. 'I fear I do not understand you. Am I to understand that some thing has happened to Miss Price?'

'She is gone,' gasped Julia, her handkerchief to her mouth. 'When her maid went to wake her this morning, she was not there.'

'Not *there?*'

Julia shook her head. 'She has fled from the house, with nothing but the gown she had on, and we have no idea where she can be — or,' she continued, her voice dropping to a whisper, and her face crimsoning over, 'with *whom*.'

Mary stumbled to the nearest chair and sat down, her knees trembling under her. Julia was still speaking, but Mary heard nothing clearly; it was only a hum of words. She was struggling to comprehend what could have happened — how Fanny could have left Mansfield without assistance, or without anyone else in the house having the slightest notion of her purpose was bewildering to her; and with both Henry and Mr Rushworth absent from Northamptonshire, she could think of no gentleman of Miss Price's acquaintance who could possibly have had either the address, or the means, to effect such an audacious and presumptuous plan. Fanny had been much admired at the Sotherton ball, and danced with many young men who would have been only too aware that she was the heiress of a very extensive property, but from that to an actual elopement was in every way inconceivable! Yet even as such thoughts were filling Mary's mind, a small part of her heart could not help rejoicing, despite the grief and scandal that must ensue for so many people she had come to love; for whatever the consequences such a shocking event must produce, one thing was certain: Edmund and Fanny must be divided for ever.

Julia sat down next to Mary, and the two of them continued in silence for a few moments, before Mary roused herself and took the girl's hand. 'How may I assist you? Ask me any thing — I am at your service.'

Julia gave a wan smile. 'You are very good. It is every thing I can do to support my mother. Maria is no help, and as for my aunt — I truly fear she will go distracted. To have the wedding so close — the gowns almost ready — the date all but fixed — and then *this.* I do not think she will ever get over it.'

At that moment they were interrupted by noises from the drawing-room, and amid the confusion of voices the words, 'Where is Julia? I cannot be comfortable without Julia!' were clearly distinguishable.

Julia got to her feet at once. 'My mother is calling for me. Will you do me the kindness of accompanying me? The only comfort I can offer her is to listen and console, but I fear I am in as much need of succour, and as overwhelmed with the enormity of this shocking event, as my poor mother can be. I am sure your good sense alone would be of the greatest utility.'

'Yes of course,' said Mary, rising from her chair.

The rest of the Bertram family were gathered in the drawing-room, but there was little appearance of unity, either in their behaviour to one another, or their positions about the room. Lady Bertram was on the sopha, Mrs Norris had sunk into a chair on the far side of the fireplace, Maria was standing at the window, and Tom Bertram was pacing to and fro. Mary had never seen him look so agitated, or so clearly a young man of a mere twenty-one years.

'I cannot believe that she was not *seen* — that *they* were not seen. And we do not even know *whom* we are pursuing, which gives us but little chance of deducing where they could be.'

'I should have thought London by far the most likely,' said Maria coolly, turning to face her family. 'After all, in three days' time she will be of age. Whomsoever she has gone with, they will then have no need of a Scottish wedding to make the marriage legal — if marriage is, indeed, their object.'

Mrs Norris groaned, and turned her face away, and it occurred to Mary, for the first time since she had heard the news, that in the distress and anxiety occasioned by Sir Thomas's accident, the approach of Miss Price's birthday had gone unnoticed. She was about to come into her whole fortune, a fortune that would, by the terms of her grandfather's will, pass to her husband on the occasion of her marriage. Mary sighed; she did not know whether to rejoice that her brother was safely in Hertford-shire, and beyond the reach of accusation, or regret that if Fanny's estate was to pass out of the family in such a painful and public manner, it should not be Henry, with all his talents and merits, who was to benefit. She quickly dismissed the thought as unworthy, at such a dreadful time, and directed her attention to the matter in hand. It seemed to her that the situation required both method and dispatch, and the longer decisive action was delayed, the greater the likelihood that Miss Price would not be recovered until it was too late. 'O Edmund!' Mary thought, 'how your family miss you now! Tom Bertram has neither your judgment, nor your determination, but I will do what I can, if they will let me.' She took a step further into the room. 'Have you sent out messengers?' she asked.

Tom Bertram looked up at her in some surprise. 'I beg your pardon?'

'I apologise if you consider this an intrusion, but in such a state of affairs a stander-by may be able to see things more clearly than those who are more directly affected. I have read about such cases, and it seems to me that the best course would be to send out messengers to every inn and turnpike between here and London. Furnish the men with a description of Miss Price, and it cannot be long before you will trace where she has gone. Likewise, Miss Price cannot have been acquainted with more than a dozen young gentlemen hereabouts; it is a matter that will require considerable delicacy, but if any of these young men departed the neighbourhood suddenly in the last few days, it would merit further investigation.'

Mrs Norris raised herself with difficulty in her chair. 'Of all the impertinent, insolent —'

'On the contrary, madam,' said Tom, quickly, 'I believe Miss Crawford has hit upon exactly what was wanting. We have been so overcome with shock, that we have done little but stare at each other, and repine at our fate, all the while doing very little to the purpose. But that will not find her. I will go to the steward at once; with luck and expedition we may have news by nightfall.'

So saying, he walked briskly out of the room. Lady Bertram had begun to weep quietly, and Julia being too distressed herself to offer any support to her mother, Mary suggested gently that they might both be more comfortable upstairs. Mrs Norris turning away in a manner so pointed that anger and resentment could not have been more plainly spoken, Mary decided that her presence was no longer helpful, and politely took her leave. As she moved towards the door, she was not a little surprised to find Maria Bertram offering to walk with her a little way towards the parsonage.

'I suppose this will be the talk of the village before the day is out,' said Maria, as they went out through the hall and onto the drive. Mary stole a glance at her, unable to decipher her tone: was it possible that she took pleasure in the fact that Fanny's disgrace must be spread abroad in such a humiliating and public fashion?

'If that is so, it will not be my doing,' she replied, firmly. 'It would be best for everyone if the truth were concealed for as long as it is possible. Your father must be consulted, and it is still possible Miss Price may repent of her hasty decision, and return home on her own account.'

Judging from the expression on her face, Miss Bertram clearly found this prospect absurd, but confined her incredulity to some lines shewn about the corners of her mouth.

'All the same, Miss Crawford,' she pursued, after a moment, 'I am sure *you* must have some idea — some theory — about what could have happened?'

Mary sighed, and shook her head. 'I find it hard to comprehend how, or why, Miss Price left your father's house.'

Maria gave a short, bitter laugh. 'As to the *why*, Miss Crawford, I am sure you know as well as I do. Fanny was desperate to avoid marrying Edmund. Her manner to him of late has been utterly indifferent. Indeed, I am more and more convinced that she never wanted to marry him at all, but merely acquiesced in a plan of others' making. And to *others'* advantage,' she concluded, with a look of meaning.

'But even were that so,' replied Mary, who did not doubt it, 'she must have been desperate indeed to throw in her lot with someone she hardly knew.'

Maria looked at her archly. 'Why should you say that? I can think of at least *two* gentlemen she knows quite well enough — either one of them might have found her fortune, if not her person, sufficient inducement.'

Mary coloured in shame and vexation. 'Miss Bertram may not have heard that my brother left Mansfield some days ago for

Hertford-shire. I expect to hear from him presently.'

'I am pleased to hear it,' replied Miss Bertram, 'for *your* sake, if not for his. But there is still Mr Rushworth to be considered.'

Mary looked at her in some surprise. 'I was told he had departed for Bath?'

Maria raised an eyebrow. 'So was I. So were we all. But we do not *know* that is where he is. Do we, Miss Crawford?'

And with that she gave a brief bow, turned on her heel, and walked quickly back towards the house.

CHAPTER X

If Mary had been concerned how to keep
the matter secret from her sister, her fears
proved of little consequence; as Miss Bertram had suspected, there was not a house
in Mansfield that had not heard the news of
Fanny's elopement by Monday evening. It
was not to be expected that a lady of such
an open and inquisitive temper as Mrs
Grant would not find much food for conjecture in so extraordinary and uncommon an
event, and Mary had to endure many hours
of such speculation from her sister, as well
as observations of a more severe and moral-
ising character from Dr Grant. The only
event to enliven the quiet and anxious days
that followed was a letter from Henry, much
longer and gayer than his usual communica-
tions, and full of such entertaining accounts
of mud waded through, and deluges averted,
that could not but make Mary laugh despite
herself. Once, and once only, was she able

to see Julia, when she was persuaded to leave her sorrowing mother to her sister's care, and sit for an hour with Mary in the Mansfield flower garden. Mary saw at once that although her young friend had grown even thinner, her looks were greatly improved; the explanation for this gratifying change was soon forthcoming.

'We have heard from Edmund,' she said, slipping her arm through Mary's. 'He writes that my father is in every respect materially better — the fever has all but abated, and although he still has all the weakness and debility of such a serious illness, the physician believes he will make an entire recovery.'

Mary expressed her sincere relief at such welcome news. 'And how is your cousin?' she continued, in a guarded manner.

Julia sighed. 'If what you really mean to ask is whether Edmund has been told the news from Mansfield, then the answer is yes. My father is as yet too weak and nervous to withstand such a shock, but Edmund has sent a letter of advice and assistance to Tom, which has been an inestimable support to him. He has also promised to leave Cumberland as soon as he may, my father being out of danger, and Edmund's presence being so much wanted here. As to his own feelings on the matter, I cannot tell. My cousin has always been reserved, and a frank expression of his sentiments was not to be expected in such a letter, at such a time.'

'No indeed,' thought Mary, who felt a respect for him on the occasion, which only gained him ground in her good opinion. Even were she to suppose him heart-broken by the news of Fanny's duplicity, his digni-fied restraint under such a trial could not but augment her tenderness and esteem.

A few moments later they turned from the garden into the green shade of the lime walk, which stretched beyond the garden to the boundary of the pleasure-grounds. It was a charming walk, leading to a belve-dere, which, by reason of its position on the top of a considerable bank, afforded a delightful view towards the stream and the valley beyond. When they had seated them-selves on the bench, Mary ventured to introduce the subject of Compton, and enquire of Julia what it was that she had wished to discuss with her.

'I know it seems a long time ago, and so much has happened since then, but I can-not forget how distressed you seemed. It appeared to be a matter of some urgency.'

Julia bit her lip and looked down, avoiding Mary's eye. Did she imagine it, or had a shadow passed across the girl's face at her words?

'Miss Bertram? Have I said some thing to offend you?'

'It was nothing — a — a misunderstanding,' said Julia quickly. 'My apologies, my dear Miss Crawford, but I find the walk has tired me more than I expected. Perhaps we could return to the house?'

'By all means,' replied Mary, quite at a loss to know how she had transgressed.

Julia rose to her feet, and stood for a moment looking over the balustrade. The workmen were clearly visible on the far side of the stream, as was the cart in which their tools were stored; they had already completed the first length of the channel, and an ugly black gash was perceptible against the verdant green bank.

Julia's brow darkened. 'How long, do you suppose, Miss Crawford, before they start to fell the avenue?'

Mary went to her friend's side, 'I am afraid I do not know. It will depend what instructions my brother has left in his absence.'

'So there may still be time,' said Julia, her voice dropping to a whisper. 'Time to prevent it.'

They returned to the house in time to see a messenger mounting his horse, and departing down the drive. Seeing their approach, Tom Bertram came down the steps to meet them, but it was clear even before he spoke, that the letter had brought nothing of significance, concerning either Fanny, or Sir Thomas's health. Julia took the opportunity to excuse herself, and hastened away into the house without meeting Mary's eye. Still wondering at the sudden alteration in her manner, Mary was about to take her leave, when Tom asked if he might take a turn with her for a few minutes, and consult her on the subject of the message he had just received.

'I would be most happy,' she said, as they moved towards the garden, 'but I am not sure what assistance I can provide.'

'On the contrary,' he replied earnestly, 'the advice you were previously so good as to offer, was exactly what Edmund suggested in his letter. Your happy interposition saved us at least three days. We are all — the family — most grateful.'

Mary wondered for a moment at that 'all', suspecting that Mrs Norris was in all likelihood experiencing quite another emotion, but she knew better than to voice such a sentiment aloud.

'All the same,' she replied, 'I gather from Miss Julia that following my advice has not advanced you very far.'

Tom shook his head. 'The messengers made every possible enquiry on this side of London, renewing them at all the turnpikes, and at the inns in St Albans and Barnet, but without any success; no-one answering to Fanny's description had been seen to pass through. I believe a carriage *was* seen early that day on the turnpike road, three miles from here, which may, or may not, have contained the fugitives. It was travelling at speed, with the blinds drawn, and bore no livery. But beyond Northampton it cannot be traced.'

'But it was going south? To London, I mean, and not to Scotland?'

'Indeed. And as far as I have been able to ascertain, it was not hired any where hereabouts.'

'I see,' said Mary. 'That suggests to me that it may have been brought especially from London for the purpose, which places the matter in a rather different light.'

Tom stopped, and looked her in the face. 'How so?'

Mary sighed. 'I believe it proves that this was not the impulse of a moment. No sudden decision, but a premeditated plan, carefully conceived. I fear that whomsoever she has gone with, has made the most careful arrangements, and finding the two of them will be all the more difficult as a consequence. And yet she left Mansfield with nothing beyond her purse and the clothes she was wearing. It is all so very strange!'

Tom nodded. 'I can only concur. But thanks to your kind hint, we have also made enquiries throughout the surrounding neighbourhood, and all the young gentlemen of our immediate acquaintance are either in residence, or accounted for, save one. Tom Oliver is thought to be at Weymouth with a party of friends, but there was some uncertainty about his plans, and my letter to an acquaintance in the town has not, as yet, met with a reply. It is, however, unlikely — I would be much surprised if Fanny had spoken to him more than twice in her whole life. Indeed, Miss Crawford, at times I am almost forced to conclude that she did not elope at all, but left here alone, and under her own direction.'

'But even were she the sort of young woman who might contemplate doing such a thing,' said Mary, 'surely she would have taken more of her belongings with her? That circumstance alone seems to argue for the presence of a protector and companion.'

'If that is indeed the case, we can, at least, remove one name from our list of possible seducers,' replied Tom. 'The letter I have only now received was from my father's friend, Mr Harding, in London. He has been making discreet investigations on our behalf, and while he has found no trace of Fanny, he was able to inform me that an engagement has just been announced between Mr Rushworth and a Miss Knightley, who has a fortune of over thirty thousand pounds. The two families' estates lie immediately adjoining one another in Surry, and it seems that Mr Rushworth's father has long hoped to unite them by means of this marriage.'

'Mr Rushworth did not behave as a man who considered himself on the brink of matrimony,' said Mary hesitantly, wondering how much Tom Bertram had noticed of what had passed between Mr Rushworth, his sister, and Fanny. He had never struck her as particularly discerning, but the frown her words occasioned suggested that he had been rather more observant than she had previously guessed.

'No indeed,' he said. 'Some part of his conduct I cannot excuse. Had we known of the existence of this Miss Knightley, both

Maria and Fanny might have been on their guard, and dismissed his behaviour as mere flirtation. But whatever else we might justly accuse him of, he bore no part in Fanny's disappearance. All the rest is irrelevant now.'

Mary could not be so sanguine. She had seen looks exchanged between Fanny and Miss Bertram in public, and could imagine the words that might have accompanied them in private. It was clear to her that they had never been friends, and once rivals, they had quickly become the greatest of enemies. How would Maria take this latest news from London? She might well have hoped that, with Fanny out of the way, Mr Rushworth would be free to return to her. If so, the news of his forthcoming marriage would be a bitter blow.

'You must understand now why I wished to consult you,' continued Tom. 'On the day Fanny went off, the prospect of an alliance with Rushworth, begun under circumstances such as these, filled us with horror; at any time it would have been unwelcome, given her longstanding engagement to Edmund, but to have it so clandestinely formed, and at such a period, would have been the severest of trials. But as the days have crept slowly by, and no news has come, we have all been reduced to the faint hope that it would indeed be Rushworth, and no worse a scoundrel, who would prove to be guilty in this affair. My father might have been brought, in time, to forgive the foolish precipitation of such a match, and receive him into the family. But now, our fears can only increase with each hour that passes.'

'And Miss Price is now twenty-one,' said Mary thoughtfully. 'If she was determined upon marriage, there is no impediment now to prevent her.'

Tom nodded grimly. 'Fanny's coming of age should have been a day of celebration, especially now that my father's health is improving. It was instead marked by the most bitter recriminations. I know I can trust to your discretion, Miss Crawford, when I say that we are all angrily blaming one another for being blind to the truth and strength of Fanny's feelings, which now seem only too obvious. It is a wretched business, and I do not know what else we can do. What do you advise?'

'*I* advise, Mr Bertram! I will be as useful as I can; but I am not qualified for an adviser.'

'You should have a juster estimate of your own judgment, Miss Crawford. I know Mr Norris holds you in very high regard. He himself suggested, in his last letter from

Cumberland, that I might turn to you for counsel, and rely on your good sense.'

'I — I hardly know what to say,' she stammered, her cheeks in a glow, wondering what she should make of such a gratifying compliment. 'I truly believe you have done all that could be expected of you. And your letter to Weymouth may yet lead to some thing. In the mean time we can only wait, and hope for the best.'

Mr Bertram took her hand, and shook it warmly. 'Thank you, Miss Crawford. I do not know what we should do without you. My younger sister, in particular, will, I fear, continue to need your help in the coming days. She is not strong, and the strain of this dreadful situation, coupled with the burden of supporting my mother's enfeebled spirits, is more than her own delicate constitution can withstand. I am sure it would be a great relief to her if she could confide in you, as a friend.'

'Pray tell her I am at her disposal; she has only to ask,' replied Mary but as she watched her companion return at a brisk pace to the house, she wondered, not for the first time that afternoon, if Julia really wished to have her as a *confidante* or whether there was, in fact, some thing preying upon her friend's mind that she had decided to keep to herself, and reveal to no-one.

CHAPTER XI

With the rain returning in full force that evening, the weather added what it could to the mood of gloom and despondency at Mansfield. A storm raged all night, and the rain beat against the parsonage windows, but by eight o'clock the following morning the wind had changed, the clouds were carried off, and the sun appeared. Mary had never been so eager to be out of doors, and walked to the village before breakfast to fetch the letters, a task usually assigned to the groom. She was disappointed in her hopes of a line or two from Henry, but consoled herself with the prospect of a day in the sunshine and fresh air, and offered to assist Mrs Grant in cutting what remained of the roses. The two ladies spent the morning in calm, sisterly companionship, and were just beginning to think with pleasure of luncheon and a glass of limonade, when they were startled by shouts and cries of alarm from the other side of the hedge. They hastened to the gate, to find one of the workmen, with a dozen others at his heels, and in his arms, the apparently lifeless body of Julia Bertram. Her clothes were clinging to her thin frame, her lips were blue, and her eyes closed; she did not even seem to breathe.

'She was like this when we found her,' the man stammered, his face white and terrified. 'We didn't know what else to do, but bring her here.'

'Quickly!' cried Mary. 'Carry her into the house, and have the maids fetch blankets and hot tea. I fear she has been quite soaked through.'

'You mean she b'aint dead after all?' said the man, as he followed them inside. 'It took us so long to free her, and all the while she neither moved nor spoke. I don't mind telling you, we feared the worst.'

'Bring her through here, if you would,' said Mrs Grant briskly. 'Lay her on the sopha — gently now! Mary, rub her temples, and send a maid to find my salts. Heaven only knows how long she has been in this state.'

Mary looked up at the man, who was standing in the doorway, twisting his hat in his hand. She had seen him before — a tall,

197

handsome fellow, who had touched his hat to her once or twice when she had encountered him in the park.

'Did I hear you aright — did you not say some thing about *freeing* her?'

He nodded. 'Yes, miss. We saw her as soon as we got to the avenue — she'd gone and chained herself to one of those old trees. How she managed such a thing on her own, God alone knows, but I swear she weren't there when we left the place last night.'

Mary wondered for a moment why they had not sent immediately to the Park for help, given the much greater distance to the parsonage, but she had seen the trepidation in the man's eyes; in the face of what must have seemed to be a fatal catastrophe, he had no doubt feared that his employer would be only too ready to lay the whole blame of it at his door.

'You have nothing to fear,' she said quickly. 'You have acted quite properly. But I am very much afraid that Miss Julia is extremely ill. We must dispatch a messenger for the apothecary at once, and send word to the Park. Her family will already have missed her.' Even as she uttered the words, her heart ached for the distress the Bertrams must be in — first Fanny, and now Julia, gone from the house with no explanation.

What must they be thinking?

Mrs Grant was clearly of the same mind; she went immediately to her writing-desk, and penned a short note to Lady Bertram. 'If you will be so good as to take that to the Park,' she said, holding it out to the workman. 'And with all speed, if you please.'

'Yes, ma'am,' he said, bowing, and with a parting look at Mary, he was gone.

The apothecary was not long in arriving thereafter; it was lucky for them that he was close by, having been attending a case of pleurisy in Mansfield-common, and he was able to give his opinion on the invalid without delay.

'I am afraid, Mrs Grant, that it is a very serious disorder,' he said, shaking his head. 'Her strength has been much weakened, and in consequence the danger of infection is very great. I will prescribe a cordial for you to administer, and you must convey her upstairs to bed at once. On no account should she be moved unnecessarily. I will call again later today.'

'Thank you, Mr Phillips, you may rely on us,' said Mrs Grant. 'I will see you to the door.'

When Mrs Grant returned to the parlour she found Mary sitting at Julia's side, her eyes filled with tears. 'I should have foreseen this!' she said. 'I knew she had been neglecting her health — I knew she was half frantic about the felling of the avenue — I should have talked to her — comforted her —'

Mrs Grant sat down next to her, and took her hands in both her own. 'I am sure you did every thing you could, Mary. I know your kind heart, and I know your regard for Miss Julia. This latest folly of hers was in all probability the whim of the moment — how could you possibly have anticipated she would do such a thing? And on such a night!'

Mary wiped her eyes. 'It was her last chance,' she said softly. 'They were to start the felling today. She must have been truly desperate.'

'Come, Mary,' said her sister, kindly, 'the best way for us to shew our concern is by ensuring she is well cared for. The maids have prepared the spare room, and lit a good fire. Let us ask Baker to carry her upstairs.'

Mrs Grant went in search of the man-servant, and Mary was left for a few moments to herself — a few moments only, for she was soon roused by a loud knocking at the door, followed, without announcement, by the unexpected appearance of Mrs Norris. This lady looked exceedingly angry, and seemed to have recovered all her former spirit of activity; she immediately set about giving loud instructions to the maids, and directing her own servants to carry Julia to the waiting carriage. Mary intervened most strenuously, citing the apothecary's advice, her own concerns, and the certainty of the best possible care under Mrs Grant's good management, but to no avail. Mrs Norris was not to be denied, and even the re-appearance of Mrs Grant herself could not dissuade her. The two were seldom good friends: Mrs Norris had always considered Mrs Grant's housekeeping to be profligate and extravagant, and their tempers, pur-suits, and habits were totally dissimilar. One of the Mansfield footmen was already lifting Julia in his arms, when Mary made one last attempt to prevent what must, she believed, be a wretched mistake.

'I beg you, Mrs Norris, not to do any thing that might endanger Miss Julia any further. Mr Phillips was most definite — she was not to be moved.'

'Nonsense!' cried Mrs Norris, turning her eyes on Mary with her usual contempt. 'What can *you* know of such things? I have been nursing the Mansfield servants for twenty years — Wilcox has been quite cured of his rheumatism, thanks to me, and there were plenty who said *he* would never walk again. And besides, we have our *own* physician to consult — quite the best man in the neighbourhood, I can assure you. Not that it is any of *your* concern. What are you standing there gaping for, Williams? Hurry up, man — take Miss Julia to the carriage!'

'In that case,' said Mary firmly, 'I hope you will permit me to accompany you back to the Park. It would comfort me to know that Mr Phillips's instructions were conveyed correctly.'

'That is quite ridiculous!' cried Mrs Norris, her face red. 'Absolutely out of the question! Even if there were room in the carriage, how dare *you* suggest that *I* cannot comprehend the instructions of a mere apothecary, or that the Bertrams are incapable of caring properly for their own daughter!' And with that she turned, and without the courtesy of a bow, swept out of the room.

Mary was about to follow her when Mrs Grant put a hand on her arm. 'Let her go, sister. You know it is useless to remonstrate with her when she is in such a humour as this.'

But Mary was not to be restrained, and shaking herself free, she ran out of the house towards the carriage, only to stop a moment later in amazement and confusion. For who should she see helping to settle Julia into the carriage, and arranging the shawls gently about her, but Edmund! She had been thinking him two hundred miles off, and here he was, less than ten yards away. Their eyes instantly met, and she felt her cheeks glow, though whether with pleasure or embarrassment she could not have told. He was the more prepared of the two for the encounter, and came towards her with a resolute step, ignoring his mother's agitations to be gone.

'Miss Julia is most unwell,' faltered Mary. 'The apothecary — he was concerned at the harm that might be caused by such a removal — I do not think Mrs Norris —'

'My mother can be very resolute, once she has determined on a course of action,' he replied, with a grim look, 'but once I understood her design in coming here, I insisted on accompanying her. You may trust me to ensure that the journey causes Julia the least possible discomfort, and that she will have every attention at the Park.'

'And your own journey?' she asked quickly. 'You must have arrived very recently.'

'This very hour,' he said, with a look of consciousness. 'I am sure you will be relieved to hear that Sir Thomas improves daily, but Mansfield is a very different place from the one I left. You, I know, will understand —'

At that moment they were interrupted once again by the sharp voice of Mrs Norris from her seat in the carriage. 'I thought *Miss Crawford* professed herself concerned for Julia's health. In which case I cannot conceive why she is deliberately delaying our departure in this way, and forcing the carriage to wait about in this heat. *That* will do Julia no good at all, you may be sure of *that.*'

Edmund turned to Mary. 'Perhaps you would do us the honour of calling at the Park in the morning?' he said quickly, with a look of earnestness. 'You will be able to enquire after Julia, and perhaps I might also take the opportunity to have some minutes' converse with you, if it is not inconvenient.'

'Yes — that is — no, not at all. I will call after breakfast.'

He bowed briefly, and the carriage was gone.

Mary kept her promise; indeed, she could not suppress a flutter of expectation as she dressed the following morning, and rejoiced that the continued sunshine made it possible for her to wear her prettiest shoes, and her patterned muslin. She knew she *should not* be happy — how could she be so when the family at the Park was labouring under a threefold misery? Even if the news from Cumberland continued to improve, there had been no tidings of Fanny, and at that very moment Julia might be dangerously ill; but whatever Mary's rational mind might tell her, her heart whispered only that she was to see Edmund — and an Edmund who was now, for the first time in their acquaintance, released from an engagement to a woman who had evidently never loved him, and whom, perhaps, he had never loved. Whatever her feelings ought to have been on such an occasion, hope had already stolen in upon her, and Mary had neither the wish nor the strength to spurn it.

But whatever joyful imaginings might captivate her in the privacy of her chamber at the parsonage, every step towards the house reminded her of the wretched state the family must be in, and her duty to offer what comfort she could, without thought for herself. By the time she rang the bell at the Park she had reasoned herself into such a state of penitent selflessness, as to almost put Edmund out of her mind, only to find that all the ladies of the Park were indisposed, and unable to receive visitors. She should, perhaps, have expected such a reception, but she had not, and stood on the step for a moment, feeling all of a sudden exceedingly foolish, her good intentions as vain and irrelevant as her good shoes. She recovered herself sufficiently to leave a message enquiring after Julia, but the very instant she was turning to go, the housekeeper happened to cross the hall with a basin of soup, and glimpsing Mary at the door, hurried over at once to speak to her. She was a motherly, good sort of woman, with a round, rosy face. Even had Mary been in the habit of chatting with servants, Mrs Baddeley was rather too partial to gossip for Mary's fastidious taste, but the circumstances being what they were, she swallowed her scruples and accepted the offer of a dish of tea in the housekeeper's room. Mrs Baddeley was soon bustling about with cups and saucers, while Mary listened to her account of Julia's restless and feverish night with growing concern.

'I don't think the poor little thing slept a wink all night, that I don't, Miss Crawford. Tossing and turning and moaning she was, babbling one minute, and as good as dead the next. And that terrible rash all over her poor arms. Mr Gilbert came again at first light, and has been with her these two hours, but I doubt he has seen ought like it, for all his notions and potions.'

'I am very sorry to hear it, Mrs Baddeley,' Mary replied, her heart sinking.

'Between ourselves,' said the housekeeper, moving a little closer, 'I think you was right to tell Mrs Norris she shouldn't have been moved. That will be at the root of the mischief, you mark my words.'

Mary flushed. 'I am not sure I take your meaning — how did you know that I —'

Mrs Baddeley gave a knowing look. 'Servants may be dumb, Miss Crawford, but we be not deaf into the bargain. Young Williams, the footman who carried Miss Julia to the carriage, he told my Baddeley what you said, and *he* told *me*. There be no secrets in the servants' hall, whatever our betters might choose to believe.'

Mary had never doubted it; she had once been a housekeeper herself in all but name, and had learned more about human nature from those few short years than she had from all her books and schoolmasters, even if it was an experience she now preferred not to dwell on, at least when among genteel company.

'If you ask me, the ladies could do with having someone like you in the house, Miss

Crawford,' continued Mrs Baddeley. 'The whole place is at sixes and sevens. Are you sure I cannot fetch you a piece of cake? Very good cake it is, made to my mother's own receipt.'

'No, thank you, Mrs Baddeley.'

Her companion settled her ample form more comfortably into her chair. 'I'm sure I don't need to tell you that her ladyship is of no use in a sick-room, and Miss Maria isn't much better — from the moment they brought her sister back yesterday she's been all but frantic — crying and falling into fits, and needing almost as much attention as poor Miss Julia.'

'And Mrs Norris? As I understood it, she was to take charge of the nursing.'

'Well, if you call it taking charge. There's been a lot of shouting and bawling, and calls for footmen in the middle of the night, but not much of any use, in my opinion. If you ask me, she's never got over the shock of Miss Fanny taking off like that. That marriage was going to be the making of her. Her and Mr Norris both.'

The mention of Edmund's name recalled Mary to herself, and she hastened to thank Mrs Baddeley for her tea and depart, before she found herself made the *confidante* of observations of an even more awkward nature.

She had almost given up any hope of seeing Edmund, but as she went back up the stairs she saw him at the outer door in the company of Sir Thomas's steward. The two were deep in serious discussion, and it was several moments before they became aware of her.

'My dear Miss Crawford,' said Edmund at once, 'do forgive me. I have been engrossed, as you can see, with Mr McGregor.' He stopped, momentarily discomfited. 'I recall now that you were so good as to agree to call on us today. I have had so much to attend to since my return that my mind has been too much engaged to fix on any thing else. Were you able to see my cousin?'

Mary shook her head. 'Miss Julia is not well enough to be disturbed. I am afraid it is as I feared.'

Edmund nodded, his face grave. 'My reason hopes you are wrong, but my heart tells me otherwise.'

It was the first time she had ever heard him speak so; his manner was as serious as ever, which was only to be expected, but there was a composure in his mien that she had not seen before. She was still pondering what this might signify when he enquired whether she might like to accompany him to inspect the channel for the new cascade.

'I am sorry that my time is so occupied this morning, but Mr McGregor wishes to consult me on a number of practical matters before he allows work to resume. It is a fine morning for such a walk, and it may interest you to see the progress made on your brother's plans? I am sure the paths will be quite dry.'

As Mary well knew, the path a gentleman considers to be dry enough for walking, may still prove ruinous for a lady's shoes, but she elected to keep her concerns to herself, and the three of them made their way into the garden and across the park. She thought regretfully of the *tête-à-tête* she had so fondly imagined; no doubt it had been fanciful to expect Edmund to open his heart to her, when so much remained uncertain, and his family was in such affliction, but the presence of a third person prevented any conversation beyond the most commonplace remarks, and Edmund was soon deep in discussion with Mr McGregor on the subject of the excavations.

'This first channel was cut some days, ago, sir,' the steward was saying, as they approached the place, 'but there has been so much rain since then that we were obliged to desist. I became concerned when one of the side walls began to fall away. In Mr Crawford's absence, I thought it best to wait until I might consult with you on the wisdom of proceeding.'

They had just reached the edge of the chasm, and the base of the channel came into view. Many times thereafter Mary would try to recapture the exact order of events, but however hard she strove, the picture always remained confused in her mind. She remembered seeing what appeared, at first sight, to be a dirty bundle of clothes, lying at the bottom of the trench; she remembered wondering how they came to be there; but she could never remember whether it was the stench, or the sight of that terrible face, that revealed the true nature of what lay before her.

She saw McGregor start back in dismay, and cry 'What the devil —', but then her head began to spin, and there was a buzz in her ears. She turned and stumbled a few yards, before sinking on her knees in the damp grass, without the least thought of the injury to her gown. 'Please God,' she thought, '— not again — do not ask me to endure such a thing again.'

She could hear Edmund's voice behind

her, and even in her confusion, it struck her how oddly his calm and measured tone jarred with the horror that now filled her mind.

'Mr McGregor,' he was saying, 'could I prevail upon you to return to the house at once and summon the constable? You should also send a messenger to Mrs Grant at the parsonage — Miss Crawford has been taken ill.'

'No!' Mary cried wildly. 'Do not distress her! I am quite well — quite well!' Edmund was at her side in an instant; she heard his voice, and felt his hands lifting her up.

'You are *not* well.' he said firmly, 'nor could anyone expect you to be so. Mr McGregor will accompany you back to the house. Pray believe me that I would escort you myself, if it were at all possible, but I have a duty to await the arrival of the constable.'

'There is no need — I can remain here,' she said weakly, but her knees trembled under her, and she could not deny it.

'Indeed you cannot remain — you *must not* remain,' he continued. 'This is no place for a lady. Mr McGregor? Your arm, if you please.'

How long it took them to attain the house, Mary had no idea, and likewise she retained no recollection of what happened subsequently. The next few hours passed in a haze. She had some visionary remembrances of figures passing to and fro before her sight, of screams and cries that seemed to come from a great distance, of lowered voices, and a cup of tea pressed into her hand that tasted dull and cloying in her mouth. When at last she came to her senses, she was lying on a bed she did not recognise, in a room she had never seen. But the young woman sitting quietly sewing by the bedside, she had seen before. It was Rogers, one of the Mansfield Park housemaids.

'Oh, miss! You're awake!' she cried, as Mary struggled to sit up. 'We were that worried about you — Mr Gilbert came and every thing. It's just as well Miss Julia is a little better — he's had his hands full enough with you, and all the other ladies. Your sister's been sitting with you above three hours, but Mr Norris just persuaded her to go home and get some rest. She was looking almost as pale as you do. Give me a minute, and I'll go and call Mrs Baddeley —'

'If you please, Rogers,' said Mary, her voice thick, 'tell me what has happened — I have only the dimmest recollection as to how I came to be here.'

Rogers sat down heavily in the chair, her face grim. 'Are you sure, miss? Mr Norris said you weren't to be upset. Most insistent, he was.'

'I am sincerely grateful to Mr Norris for his consideration,' she said, treasuring the thought, 'but you need not worry. I was, I admit, overcome by a fit of nervous faintness, but I do not usually suffer from such things, and I am quite recovered now. I would much rather know exactly what has occurred.'

'If you say so, miss,' said Rogers, who clearly still had her doubts on the matter. 'It was Mr McGregor who brought you back. You was leaning on his arm and you looked so queer! Of course, none of us knowed why *then,* and Mr McGregor barely had time to tell Mr Baddeley what it were all about before he was off again on horseback to fetch the constable, though what use they think old Mr Holmes is going to be is beyond me. He must be sixty if he's a day. Anyway, that's when we knowed it were serious, but we didn't find out what was really going on until the footmen came back. They'd covered it over as much as they could, but there was this one hand hanging down, all spattered in mud, and jolting with every move of the cart. Gave me quite a turn, I can tell you. Young Sally Puxley fainted clean away.'

Mary turned her face against the pillow, and closed her eyes. So it had not been a dream; it had seemed so shocking, that her heart revolted from it as impossible, but she knew now that the sickening images that had floated before her in her stupor were not, after all, some hideous concoction of memory and imagination, but only too horribly real.

'Are you all right, miss?' said Rogers quickly. 'You've come over dreadful pale again.'

'So it's true,' Mary whispered, half to herself. 'Fanny Price is dead.'

Chapter XII

When Mary opened her eyes again, the morning sun was streaming through the window. For a few precious moments she enjoyed the bliss of ignorance, but such serenity could not last, and the events of the previous day were not long in returning to her remembrance. She felt weak and faint in body, but her mind had regained some part of its usual self-possession, and she dressed herself quickly, and went out into the passage. She was in a part of the house she did not know, and she stood for a moment, wondering how best to proceed. It then occurred to her that she might take the opportunity to locate Julia Bertram's chamber, and try if she might be permitted to see her. To judge from Rogers's words the preceding day, Julia might even have recovered sufficiently to rise from her bed. Mary made her way down the corridor, hearing the sounds of the mansion all

around her; the tapping of servants' footsteps and the murmur of voices were all magnified in a quite different way from what she was accustomed to, in the small rooms and confined spaces of the parsonage. A few minutes later she saw a woman emerging from a door some yards ahead of her, carrying a tray; it was Chapman, Lady Bertram's maid. The woman hastened away without seeing her, and Mary moved forwards hesitatingly, not wishing to appear to intrude. As she drew level with the door she noticed that it was still ajar, and her eyes were drawn, almost against her will, to what was visible in the room.

It was immediately apparent that this was not Lady Bertram's chamber, but her daughter's; Maria Bertram was still in bed, and her mother was sitting beside her in her dressing gown. Mary had not seen either lady for more than a week, and the change in both was awful to witness. Lady Bertram seemed to have aged ten years in as many days; her face was grey, and the hair escaping from under her cap shewed streaks of white. Maria's transformation was not so much in her looks as in her manner; the young woman who had been so arch and knowing when Mary last conversed with her, was lying prostrate on the bed, her handkerchief over her face, and her body racked with muted sobs. Lady Bertram was stroking her daughter's hair, but she seemed not to know what else to do, and the two of them formed a complete picture of silent woe. Mary had no difficulty in comprehending Lady Bertram's anguish — she had supplied a mother's place to Fanny Price for many years, and the grief of her death had now been superadded to the public scandal of her disappearance; Maria's condition was more perplexing. Some remorse and regret she might be supposed to feel at Fanny's sudden and unexpected demise, but this utter prostration seemed excessive, and out of all proportion, considering their recent enmity.

Mary was still pondering such thoughts when she became aware of a third person in the room: Mrs Norris was standing at the foot of the bed, observing the two women almost as intently as Mary herself. A slight movement alerting that lady to Mary's presence, she moved at once towards the door with all her wonted vigour and briskness.

'I do not know why it was necessary for Miss Crawford to remain in the house last night,' she said angrily, to no-one in particular. 'She seemed perfectly recovered to me, and in my opinion it is quite intolerable to

218

have such an unnecessary addition to our domestic circle at such a time. But I did, at the *very least,* presume we would be not be subjected to *vulgar* and intrusive *prying.*'

'Sister, sister,' began Lady Bertram, in a voice weakened by weeping, but Mrs Norris did not heed her, and seized the handle of the door, with an expression of the utmost contempt.

'I beg your pardon,' said Mary. 'I did not mean — I was looking for Miss Julia's chamber —'

'I doubt *she* wishes to see you, any more than *we* do. Be so good as to leave the house at your earliest convenience. Good morning, Miss Crawford.'

And the door slammed shut against her.

Mary took a step backward, hardly knowing what she did, and found herself face to face with one of the footmen; he, like Mrs Chapman, was already dressed in mourning clothes.

'I am sorry,' stammered Mary, her face colouring as she wondered how much of Mrs Norris's invective had been overheard, 'I did not see you.'

'That's quite all right, miss,' he replied, his eyes fixed on the carpet.

'I was hoping to find Miss Julia's room.

Perhaps you would be so good as to direct me?'

' 'Tis at farther end of t'other wing, miss. By the old school-room.'

'Thank you.'

The footman bowed and hurried away in the opposite direction, without meeting her eye, and Mary stood for a moment to collect herself, and still her swelling heart, before continuing on her way with a more purposeful step.

Nearing the great staircase, she became aware of voices in the hall below, and as she came out onto the landing, she was able to identify them, even though the speakers were hidden from her view by a curve in the stairs. It was Edmund, and Tom Bertram.

'It is scarcely comprehensible!' Edmund was saying. 'To think that that all this time we have been thinking her run away — *blaming* her for the ignominy of an infamous elopement — and yet all the while she was lying there in that dreadful state, not half a mile from the house. It is inconceivable — that such an accident could have happened —'

'My dear Edmund,' interjected Tom, 'I fear you are labouring under a misapprehension. You were absent from Mansfield, and cannot be expected to be aware of precise times and circumstances, but I can assure you that the work on the channel commenced some hours, at least, *after* Fanny was missed from the house. It is quite impossible that there could have been such an accident as you have just described.'

There was a pause, and Mary heard him pace up and down for a few moments before speaking again. She had already drawn a similar conclusion; moreover, she had private reasons of her own for believing that the corpse she had seen could not have lain above a day or two in the place where it was found.

'And even were that not the case,' continued Tom, 'you cannot seriously believe that the injuries we were both witness to, were solely the result of a fall? You saw it, as much as I did. Surely you must agree that there was a degree of malice — of *deliberation* — in the reckless damage done to —' he hesitated a moment. 'In short, it can only have been the work of some insane and dangerous criminal. It is of the utmost importance that we arrange at once for a proper investigation.'

'But the constable —'

'— has done every thing in his power, but even were he a young man, which he is not, he has neither the men nor the authority to pursue the rigorous enquiries demanded by such an extraordinary and shocking case. You must see that — just as you must acknowledge that we have only one course available to us.'

'Which is?'

'To send for a thief-taker from London. Mr Holmes himself as good as begged me to do so — he knows as well as I do, that this is our best, if not our only, hope.'

'A thief-taker?' gasped Edmund. 'Good God, Tom, most of those men are little more than criminals themselves! I have read the London newspapers, and I know how they operate. Bribery, violence, and extortion are only the least of it. Do we really want to open our most private and intimate affairs to such a man? To the public scrutiny such a course of action must inevitably occasion? I beg you, think again before you take such a perilous and unnecessary step.'

'Unnecessary?' replied Tom coldly. 'I am afraid I cannot agree. You, of *all* people, must want the villain who perpetrated so foul a deed to be brought to justice? And there is but one way we can hope to achieve that. I have made careful enquiries, and have received a most helpful recommendation from Lord Everingham. His lordship has suffered a number of fires on his property, and this man was instrumental in the discovery and detention of the culprit.'

'For a handsome reward, no doubt,' said Edmund, dryly.

'Of course. That is how such men earn their bread. But they are not *all* base rogues and villains, as you seem to believe. It appears this fellow gave distinguished service as a Bow Street Runner, before setting up on his own account, and Lord Everingham was willing to vouch not only for his proficiency, but for his complete discretion.'

'But surely we should delay until we have the opportunity to consult my uncle? We should not contemplate such a proceeding without his permission. In our last communication from Keswick there was some expectation that he might be sufficiently recovered to commence the journey homewards within a few days. Can we not await his arrival?'

'You know full well, Edmund, that my father is not as yet deemed well enough to receive the news of Fanny's death, coming as it does, so soon upon the shock of her disappearance, which has already provoked a dangerous relapse,' replied Tom. 'And even if he *is* able to set out from Cumberland as promptly as you hope, he will have to travel in slow stages, and will not return to Mansfield for at least a fortnight. We cannot afford to wait so long. I am grateful for your advice, Edmund, but in my father's absence *I* am master at Mansfield Park. I have sent for this Charles Maddox, and I expect him later this afternoon. Good day to you.'

Mary had, by this time, crept to the edge of the gallery and she saw Tom bow coolly to his cousin and turn away, before Edmund caught his arm.

'Can we, at least, have the body properly attended to? They have conveyed her to the old school-room — it faces north, and is cold without a fire, even in summer.' He hesitated, and seemed to be struggling for composure. 'I have had candles lit there, and flowers brought from the garden —'

His voice broke, and Mary leaned against the banister, unsure how to interpret his evident distress of mind; she had been so sure that he no longer cared for Fanny — perhaps had never truly done so — but —

'— but to speak frankly, there is no disguising the smell. In a day or so it will be through the whole house. And we should not forget that Gilbert has urged us to keep this latest misfortune from Julia for as long as possible — he was most concerned that she should not suffer further anxiety at this present, and most delicate, stage of her recovery. For her sake — for decency's sake — let me arrange for the body to be washed and laid out.'

There was a pause, then Tom acquiesced: 'Whom would you suggest we entrust with so repugnant a task?'

Edmund shook his head, 'To tell you the truth, I do not rightly know. Your mother and sister are out of the question, and my own mother is not quite herself. She has been suffering from the head-ache for some days past. I believe we will have to call upon Mrs Baddeley, though that would not be my first preference. Even the footmen who brought back the body recoiled at the sight, and Mrs Baddeley is prone to nervous palpitations. Would that Miss Crawford were well enough — there is no-one so steady, so capable as Miss Crawford.'

'Indeed,' said Tom, 'she is a young woman of rare strength of mind. And we might have relied absolutely on her prudence.'

Mary retreated into the shadows, her mind overcome with a confusion of feelings, in which fear, compassion, and gratification all had their place. She saw in a moment what she must do: Edmund had need of her; there was a service she could perform for him, and if she loved him, then she must face it, and without shrinking.

She did not stay to hear any more, and made her way as quickly and quietly as she could to the room Edmund had referred to, at the farthest end of the east wing. She hesitated a moment on the threshold, but summoned up her courage and threw open the door. The windows were shuttered, and the candle-flames wavered in the sudden draught, throwing monstrous shadows across the walls. Her senses were assailed by a gust of suffocating odours, in which the heavy scent of the cut roses was mingled with another, more sickly sweetness that Mary knew only too well. The body lay a few feet away, the face covered by a white sheet, but there was a dark and spreading stain that spoke of horrors beneath — horrors that would be only too dreadfully out of place in this homely little room, with its writing-desks and ill-used chairs, its map of Europe, and its charts of kings and queens. Mary shivered suddenly; Edmund had not been mistaken when he had said that the room was cold. She went briskly to the door and rang the bell, and sent the footman with a message to Mrs Baddeley. A few minutes later the housekeeper appeared at the head of a procession of maids bearing aprons, hot water, sponges, and, as Mary observed with a suppressed shudder, a linen shroud that looked but newly made.

'Thank you, Mrs Baddeley,' she said briskly, doing her best to shield the maids from the sight of the corpse. 'Are you aware if any arrangements have been made with respect to a coffin?'

Mrs Baddeley's rosy face lost a little of its colour. 'Yes, miss. Mr Norris has commanded one from Dick Jackson. A simple one, as might serve until the family decide what they prefer.'

'I see that Mr Norris has thought of every thing. Pray arrange for it to be brought up, would you? And is there some where the body might lie until the funeral? There is no question, in this case, of visitors being permitted to see the corpse, but there is still a need for an appropriate resting place.'

Mrs Baddeley nodded. 'There's the small sitting-room next to the parlour. That's never used at this time of the year.'

'Thank you, Mrs Baddeley, that sounds most suitable. I will ring again when I have finished.'

The housekeeper looked doubtful. 'Are you sure you don't want me to stay, Miss Crawford? I don't know as I'd be much use, what with my heart being as it is, but I don't like to think of you up here all alone. Quite turns my stomach, that it does. Such a duty is bad enough at the best of times, but having to look at —'

Mary smiled. 'You are very kind, but you need not be concerned,' she said firmly. 'The dead are at peace, Mrs Baddeley, however terrible the manner of their demise.'

When she was once again safely alone, Mary stood for a moment with her back to the door, then took a deep breath, and started to pin back her sleeves. She hoped to harden herself to the undertaking before her by beginning with those parts of it that she might accomplish without trepidation. Leaving the face covered for as long as possible, she first cut the clothes away, and folded them carefully. The skin beneath was cold and waxy, and its paleness had begun to acquire a greenish tinge, while dark purple patches had spread underneath, where the body had been lying against the damp earth. Mary had always been observant, and now, as once before, she wondered if this quick-sightedness were not a positive curse; she feared that every tiny detail of that terrible hour would be etched forever on her mind, but she endeavoured to dismiss the thought, and turned her attention instead to the heavy toil of washing the body, and dressing it in a simple white night-gown. The limbs had become stiff and rigid, and she wondered once or twice whether she should indeed have insisted that Mrs Baddeley remain behind to assist her, but another moment's thought told her that such a request would have been ignoble. She must shift as she could, and do the best she was able.

It was a long task, and an arduous one, but at last the moment came when the sheet must be removed; she could avoid it no longer. She took hold of the cloth, and lifted it slowly away. She had prepared herself, but she could not suppress a gasp. The right side of the face was much as she remembered it, though drawn and distorted, and its features sharpened by death; but the rest was merely a dark mass of crusted flesh, with here and there the pale glimmer of naked bone. The eye that remained was dull and clouded, and seemed to stare up at her with an expression of unspeakable reproach. Mary reached blindly for her handkerchief, and held it to her face, stifling a spasm of nausea. It was so horribly akin to what she had seen once before; but *then* it had been merely the impression of a moment, which she had laboured to forget; now she must confront this horror without flinching, and do what she could to assuage it. Steady nerves achieved a good deal, soap and water even more; and as the dirt and dried blood were eased away, Fanny's face regained a little of its human shape. When it was done, Mary smoothed the hair, secured the jaw with ribbon, and wound the body in its shroud, securing it neatly at head and foot. She had never undertaken any task she had dreaded more, or relished less; but she had probably never done a thing more needful, or one she might be prouder to own.

She washed her hands carefully, then rang the bell for Mrs Baddeley. A few moments later Mary was ushering in the carpenter and a group of footmen, and instructing them how to place the body within its plain oak coffin. As they lifted the lid and made to secure it, Mrs Baddeley took a small package from her pocket, and laid it quickly at the feet of the corpse. Seeing Mary's enquiring look, she hastened to explain herself.

' 'Tis nought but a little Bible, miss. Mr Norris gave it me and asked me to place it there. A last gift, he said.'

Mary could not help remembering another gift he had bestowed on Fanny — a gift she had passed to Mary, with no other thought than to ensnare and humiliate her. The necklace still lay in her trinket-box at the parsonage, but she would never now be able to wear it. At that moment the sound of the great clock striking two carried home to Mary's mind the full duration of her task, and she recollected that she had eaten neither breakfast nor luncheon. Some thing of the kind had clearly occurred to Mrs Baddeley, and she whispered to Mary that tea and bread and butter had been prepared for her in her own room; Mary thanked her; she owned that she should be very glad of a little tea. The housekeeper took her kindly by the arm, as they watched Dick Jackson nail down the lid, and the footmen shoulder their sad burden. They were all so wholly occupied in their progress out of the school-room and into the narrow corridor, that the opening of an adjacent door passed un-noticed — unnoticed, that is, until the silence was rent by a shriek of so terrifying a pitch as to be scarcely human. It was Julia Bertram; her face was white, and she had sunk to her knees, her eyes wide with awe and terror.

'No! No!' she screamed. 'Tell me she is not dead! She cannot, *cannot* be dead!'

'Oh my Lord!' cried Mrs Baddeley, rushing to Julia's aid. 'This is just what I tried to prevent!'

Mary turned at once to the footmen, who were standing motionless, half stupefied. 'Go at once,' she said quickly. 'Make haste with the coffin, if you please. Miss Julia should never have seen this.'

'Did I not tell you, not an hour since,' said the housekeeper, casting a furious look at the maid who had just appeared at Julia's side, 'that on *no account* was Miss Julia to be allowed to leave her bed this afternoon? Heavens above, girl, what were you thinking of?'

The maid was, by this time, almost as horror-struck as her young mistress, and stammered between her tears that 'They would have stopped her had they only known, but Miss Julia had insisted on rising — she said she wished to see her brother, and she seemed so much better, that they all thought some fresh air would do her good.'

'As to that, Polly Evans, it's not for you to think thoughts, it's for you to do as you're told. Heaven only knows what Mr Gilbert will say. It will be a miracle if serious mischief has not been done.'

This did little to calm the terrified maid,

who looked ready to fall into hysterics herself, and Mary motioned to Mrs Baddeley to take the girl to her own quarters, while she helped Julia back to her bed. She was by this time in a state of such extreme distress that Mary sent one of the servants to fetch Mr Bertram, with a request that the physician be summoned at once. But as she waited anxiously for his arrival, it was not Tom Bertram, but Edmund, who appeared at the door. When he saw his young cousin lying insensible on the bed, moaning and crying indistinctly, his face assumed an expression of the most profound concern.

'Is there any thing I can do to assist?'

Mary shook her head. 'I have administered a cordial, but I fear some thing stronger is required.'

Edmund nodded. 'I concur with your judgment. Let us hope Gilbert is not long in arriving.' As he spoke the words his eyes stole to her face, and he saw for the first time that Mary, too, was wan and tremulous. A glance at the apron, with its tell-tale stains, lying disregarded on the chair, told him all that was needful for him to know.

'So it was *you!* You were the one who —' He stopped, in momentary bewilderment. 'When I saw the coffin being carried through the hall I thought — at least, I had no conception that it was *your* kindness —'

Mary had borne a good deal that day, but it was the gentleness of his words, rather than the horror of what she had seen and endured, that proved her undoing. She turned away in confusion, hot tears running down her face. Edmund helped her to a chair, and rang the bell.

'You are overcome, Miss Crawford, and I can quite comprehend why. You have over-taxed yourself for our sakes, and I am deeply, everlastingly, grateful. But *I* am here now, and I can watch with my cousin until Mr Gilbert arrives. You look to stand in great need of rest and wholesome food. I will ring for it directly.'

Being obliged to speak, Mary could not forbear from saying some thing in which the words 'Mrs Baddeley's room' were only just audible.

'I understand,' said Edmund, with a grim look, and not wanting to hear more. 'I understand. I have allowed this unpardonable incivility to continue for far too long. I will arrange for you to take a proper meal in the dining-parlour, as befits a lady, and one to whom we all owe such an inexpressible obligation.'

Such a speech was hardly calculated to compose Mary's spirits, but he would brook no denial, and within a few minutes she was settled in a chair by the fire downstairs, being helped to an elegant collation of minced chicken and apple-tart. Both her head and her heart were soon the better for such well-timed kindness, and when the maid returned with a glass of Madeira with Mr Norris's compliments, Mary enquired at once whether Mr Gilbert had yet been in attendance.

'I believe so, miss. Mrs Baddeley said he'd given Miss Julia some thing to help her sleep.'

Mary nodded; such a measure seemed both prudent and expedient; they must all trust to the certainty and efficacy of some hours' repose. She thanked the maid, and sat for a few minutes deliberating whether it would be best to return to the parsonage; her sister must be wondering where she was. She was still debating the matter when she heard the sound of a carriage on the drive, and went to the window. It was a very handsome equipage, but the horses were post, and neither the carriage, nor the coachman who drove it, were familiar to her. The man who emerged was a little above medium height, with rather strong features and a visible scar above one eye. His clothes, however, were fashionable and of very superior quality, and he stood for a moment looking confidently about him, as if he was weighing what he saw, and putting the intelligence aside for future use. He was not handsome — or not, at least, in any conventional manner — but there was some thing about him, a sense of latent energy, of formidable powers held in check, such as might command attention, and draw every eye, even in the most crowded of rooms. As she observed him ascend the steps to the door, Mary did not need to overhear the servant's announcement to guess that the man before her was none other than Mr Charles Maddox.

A few moments later, this impressive and uncommon personage was being shewn into Sir Thomas's room, where Mr Bertram and Mr Norris were awaiting him. The former had taken up the post of honour behind his father's desk, while his cousin was standing by the window, evidently ill at ease. They had both been to Oxford, and no doubt considered themselves men of the world, but such a creature as Maddox was far beyond their experience.

'Good day to you, sirs!' said their visitor, with the most perfunctory of bows. 'I admire your discernment. This will do admirably.'

'I am not sure I understand you,' said Tom, who had not expected such extraordinary self-assurance from a man who was to be in his employ.

But Maddox had already assumed a proprietorial air, and was wandering about the room, running his hand over the furniture, and inspecting the view from the windows. 'This will make a very suitable "seat of operations", as I like to call it. I will have my assistants set up in here.'

'But this is my father's room —' began Tom, looking at him in consternation.

Maddox waved his hand. 'You have nothing to fear on that score, Mr Bertram. His house shall not be hurt. For every thing of that nature, I will be answerable. And my men are good men. They know how to behave themselves, even in such a grand house as this one.'

Tom and Edmund exchanged a look in which there was as much anxiety on the one side, as there was reproof on the other; the door then opened for a second time, and two men appeared, carrying a large trunk. One was tall and thin, with a pock-marked face; the other short and stout, with a reddened and weather-beaten complexion, and his fore-teeth gone. They set down their burden heavily on the carpet, then departed as they had come, without a word, but leaving behind them a distinct waft of tobacco. Maddox, meanwhile, had installed himself comfortably in an elbow-chair, without staying to be asked.

'And now to business,' he said, genially. 'You agree to my terms, both as to the daily rate, and the reward in the event of an arrest?'

Tom endeavoured to regain the dignified manner suitable to the head of such a house, and to reclaim the mastery of the situation. 'We consider ourselves fortunate to be able to call upon a man of your reputation, Mr Maddox. Indeed, we are relying on you to bring matters to a prompt and satisfactory conclusion.'

'My own aim, entirely,' said Maddox, with a smile. 'And in the pursuit of same, may I begin by examining the corpse?'

The two gentlemen absolutely started, and for a moment both seemed immoveable from surprise; but Edmund shortly recovered himself, and said in a hoarse voice, 'You cannot possibly be in earnest, Mr Maddox. It is quite out of the question.'

Mr Maddox frowned. 'I assure you I am in the most deadly earnest, Mr Norris. The precise state of the body — the nature of the injuries, the advancement of putrefaction, and such like matters — are all of the utmost significance to my enquiries. It is the *evidence,* sir, the *evidence,* and without it, my investigation is thwarted before it even commences.'

'You mistake me, Mr Maddox,' said Edmund coldly, a deep shade of crimson overspreading his features. 'It is out of the question, because the coffin has already been sealed. To open it again — to break open the shroud — would be a sacrilegious outrage that I cannot — *will not* — permit.'

'I see,' said Maddox, eyeing him coolly. 'In that case, may I be permitted to speak to the person who laid out the corpse? It is a poor substitute, but in such a circumstance, secondhand intelligence is better than no intelligence at all.'

Tom hesitated, and looked to his cousin. 'What think you, Edmund? May we impose so much on Miss Crawford's kindness?'

'Could such an importunate interview not wait a few days?' said Edmund, angrily. 'It has been a distressing day for us all, and for none more so than Miss Crawford. She finished laying out the body not two hours ago.'

'So much the better,' replied Maddox. 'The lady's memory will be all the fresher for it. You would be surprised, Mr Norris, how quickly one's powers of recall weaken and become confused, especially in cases such as this, when the mind is exerting itself to throw a mist over unpleasantness. We all believe our faculties of recollection to be so retentive, yet I have questioned witnesses who would swear to have seen things that I know, from my own knowledge, to be absolutely impossible. And yet they sincerely believe what they say. Which is why it is essential that I speak with this Miss Crawford without delay. There is not a moment to lose.'

Edmund turned and went to the window, and remained there some moments. This did not fail to attract a considerable degree of interest from Mr Maddox, though he said nothing, and appeared to be absorbed merely in contemplating the set of family portraits that hung on the wall behind.

A moment later Edmund turned to face them; his features had assumed an air of grim determination, but his voice was steady.

'I will ask Miss Crawford to join us. I am sure you will find her to be both accurate and reliable in her observations.'

He bowed hurriedly, and left the room. There was a short silence, in the course of which, Mr Maddox got up from his chair, and strolled with apparent unconcern towards the paintings.

'Is this the victim?' he asked.

'I beg your pardon?' said Tom, who had not been accustomed to such language as this.

'Fanny Price — is this her?'

'Yes,' said Tom, stiffly, bridling at the familiarity. 'That is indeed a likeness of Miss Price.'

'And is it a good one?'

'I believe it is generally thought to be so. It was drawn some two years ago.'

'I see,' said Maddox, thoughtfully. 'A handsome woman. A very handsome woman, if I may say so. And an heiress, into the bargain. Your Mr Norris was a lucky fellow. And to lose such a prize, in such a way — it would be a wonder if his life were not ruined. Would it not, Mr Bertram?'

Tom was saved from the necessity of a reply by the sound of the door opening, and the reappearance of Edmund, accompanied by Mary.

'I have explained the circumstances to Miss Crawford,' he said, 'and she has kindly agreed to answer any questions you may have. But I would beg you to recollect that we have already made more demands on her than we can claim any right to, and she is, as a consequence, quite exhausted. Pray do not tire her unnecessarily, or distress her without good reason.'

Edmund made to take a seat, but Maddox prevented him. 'I would much prefer to speak with Miss Crawford in private, Mr Norris.'

'Why so? Surely *that* is not necessary?'

'In my experience, Mr Norris, people find it easier to be completely frank and open in their disclosures, when their family or acquaintances are not listening to every word they say. All the more so, when the questions to be asked are of such a delicate and, shall we say, squeamish nature. So if Miss Crawford permits — ?'

Mary held his gaze for a moment, and he perceived the slightest lift of her head as she replied, with some self-possession, 'Thank you for your concern, Mr Norris, but I am quite content. I will speak to Mr Maddox alone.'

Mary had been both surprised and pleased when Edmund had sought her in the dining-parlour, but she had instantly perceived him to be wholly preoccupied by some thing that seemed to have little to do with her; his manner was distant, and had she not become well acquainted with his character and temper, she might have considered him to be almost uncivil. He had explained his errand in some haste, barely meeting her eye, and she could not tell if he was vexed or relieved when he met with a ready acquiescence to his request. He had asked her to accompany him with scarcely another word, and she had barely enough time to collect her wits before she was led into the presence of Charles Maddox.

When the door had closed behind the two gentlemen, Maddox directed her to a chair beside the fire, and took one facing her. It might have been accident, or design, but the seat he had chosen afforded him a clear view of her face in the light from the window, while his own features remained shadowed and obscure.

'Now, Miss Crawford,' he began. 'I am most grateful for your assistance in this sad affair. I am sure you are as anxious as any body to have it elucidated.'

'I will do any thing in my power to help.'

'Quite so, quite so. Perhaps you might begin, then, by giving me your impressions of the corpse. In your own words, of course.'

This was not what she had expected — in so far as she had expected any thing — and she sat for a moment without speaking, wondering how, and where, to commence.

She was aware that Maddox was eyeing her closely all the while, but before she had the chance to begin her relation, he took matters into his own hands.

'Perhaps it might expedite the business if I began by putting one or two questions of my own?'

Mary blushed in spite of herself; she had not thought to find an intellectual superior in such a man as this, but he already had the advantage of her.

'If you would be so good. I have no experience of such things, and do not know what, precisely, you wish to ascertain.'

'Quite so. I would have been astonished if it had been otherwise,' he replied with what he clearly believed to be an affable smile. 'As far as I have been informed, Miss Price met her death as the result of an accident.'

Mary shook her head. 'That is simply not possible. Such injuries could not have been sustained in a simple fall.'

'You say injuries, in the plural. Was that deliberate?'

Mary looked at him archly. 'I am always most precise in my use of words, Mr Maddox. You may take it that what I say, I mean.'

He bowed. 'I am glad to hear it. Indeed, I wish more of my witnesses demonstrated such precision of thought. So, we may

244

conclude her assailant inflicted more than one blow?'

Mary nodded. 'Six, or seven, in my estimation.'

'You saw evidence of that?'

'Not at first, but once I had washed the blood and dirt away, several distinct wounds became clearly visible. They were all close together on the left side.'

Maddox sat back in his chair, and joined his finger-tips under his chin. 'So there was a great deal of blood,' he said thoughtfully, before continuing in a louder tone, 'and what sort of blows, do you imagine, might have produced those wounds?'

Mary frowned. 'I do not take your meaning.'

'Were they, for instance, caused by the blade of a knife?'

'Oh, I see. No, it was most definitely *not* a knife. It must have been much thicker and heavier than that. But with a pointed edge.'

'Like a hammer, would you say?'

Mary considered for a moment. 'Yes. That would be possible. Some thing of that kind. There was also a mark on the right-hand side of the face, but that was little more than a bruise.'

Maddox smiled again. 'Excellent. You are a most observant young woman, Miss

Crawford. Just as Mr Bertram said you were. Now, shall we pursue the same fertile train?'

It was not a very happy turn of speech, but Mary had already perceived that she would do well to keep her private opinions to herself, in the presence of the watchful Mr Maddox.

'Were there any other marks or blemishes on the body, Miss Crawford,' he continued, 'that particularly engaged your notice?'

Mary's feelings had been in such a tumult, that she could not have articulated a sensible answer, had the same question been put to her on the spot; but now, under the influence of his questions, her mind was becoming calm, and her recollections exactly defined.

'I did notice her hands.'

'Her hands?'

Mary nodded slowly. 'Miss Price was always rather vain of her hands. But her finger-nails were broken, and there was mud under them. And there were cuts on both her palms.'

'And you concluded from this?'

Mary could not remember concluding any thing at all at the time, but she found herself replying before she was aware, 'I suppose it

246

is possible that she attempted to defend herself.'

'Quite so, quite so. That is very likely, I should say.'

'There was also the question of the clothes,' continued Mary, hesitatingly.

'Go on.'

'She was wearing a very handsome pelisse, trimmed with fur, which I believe had been given to her by her uncle, just before he left for Cumberland. And underneath that, a white muslin gown. Her boots, also, were of very fine leather —'

Maddox waved his hand. 'I am sure all this is most fascinating for you young ladies, but —'

'If you would allow me to finish Mr Maddox, I was going on to say that her boots were caked in mud. They were not designed for walking any great distance, but I believe that is what she must have done. The weather had lately been very wet.'

'I see —'

'Moreover, the front of the gown was stained with mud. In particular, there were two large dark patches on the skirt.'

It was Maddox's turn to look bewildered.

'Do you not see the significance, Mr Maddox? Miss Price was discovered at the bottom of the trench, lying on her back. I was present at that dreadful moment, and I can attest to that. But the marks on her gown would suggest that she had also, at some point, fallen *forwards,* onto her knees.'

Maddox looked at her with new respect. 'Was there any thing else about her appearance that you noted? Was she, for instance, wearing a wedding ring?'

'No.'

'Was she carrying a purse?'

'No. Nor, I believe, was one discovered in the trench.'

'So she had no money about her at all?'

'No, Mr Maddox, none.'

This exchange was succeeded by a silence of some minutes. Mary was suddenly aware of the sound of the clock on Sir Thomas's desk, and the crepitation of the subsiding fire.

'Now, Miss Crawford,' said Maddox at length, 'we come to what we might call the heart of the matter. It is clear that you are not a young woman given to fits of the hysterics. Nonetheless, these are not pleasant subjects. Not pleasant subjects, at all. Would you like me to fetch you a glass of water, before we proceed?'

'No, thank you, Mr Maddox. I am perfectly composed.'

'Quite so, quite so. My next question,

then, returns to the subject of her clothes. You have given ample proof of a discerning eye, Miss Crawford, so tell me, was her dress in such a state as you might expect to find it?'

'How so, Mr Maddox?'

'Was it, shall we say, torn, or rent in any way?'

'There was, I believe, a small tear to the collar of her pelisse. The trim had come away in one place.'

'It was her dress I enquired after, Miss Crawford, not the pelisse.'

'In that case, the answer is no. Apart from the stains I described, it was unharmed.'

'And when you washed the body, you noticed no other injuries, beyond those you have described? None, shall we say, of a more *intimate* nature?'

Mary shook her head, feeling her face must be like scarlet; so this was why he had wanted to question her alone. Much as she resented being indebted to him on any account, she could not but be grateful that Edmund was not in the room at that very instant. Maddox gave her no time to recover her composure; indeed, he gave no sign of having perceived her confusion.

'And what state was the body in,' he continued, perfectly collected, 'when you laid it out? Let me be absolutely clear, Miss Crawford. How advanced was the progress of decomposition?'

Mary looked at him, but her gaze was steadier than the beatings of her heart. 'You do not mince matters, do you, Mr Maddox?'

Maddox spread his hands. 'I did warn you I would be candid, Miss Crawford. In my experience, there is little to be gained by evading the truth. Not in cases of murder, at any rate.'

Mary took a deep breath. 'Very well. Let us say that the — the — natural process — had commenced, but I do not believe it had advanced more than one or two days.'

'Indeed? And why should you say that? There are those in the household, I am told, who believe that she must have lain there above a fortnight. Nay, sixteen full days, if my own computations are correct.'

Mary shook her head. 'That is quite impossible,' she said quickly. 'As you are already so well informed, Mr Maddox, you must also know that the work on the channel did not commence until *after* Miss Price was missed from the house.'

'Indeed,' he said, with a look that confirmed that it was, indeed, exactly as she had surmised, and she was so much vexed at this manner of proceeding as to be betrayed into uncharacteristic carelessness. 'And even were that not the case —'

She stopped at once, suddenly conscious of where her words were tending.

'Do go on, Miss Crawford,' he said. 'I am all agog.'

Mary wished it unsaid with all her heart; he had provoked her into imprudence, and she had allowed herself to be taken in. She was mortified by her own lack of caution, but there was no help for it now. If Maddox was at all aware of what was passing in her mind, he gave no outward sign, and sat quietly in his chair, exercising his excellent teeth upon his thumb-nails.

'You were saying, Miss Crawford?' he asked quietly.

Mary lifted her chin, and held his gaze. 'If Miss Price had been lying in the open air, during a period of inclement weather, for more than two weeks, the body would have been in a quite different state from the one in which we found it. Is that plain enough?'

Maddox took out a gold snuff-box, tapped it, and let the snuff drop through his fingers, then shut it, and twirled it round with the fore-finger of his right hand. Mary watched with rising irritation, perfectly aware that this was precisely the response he hoped to induce.

'And you base this assertion on personal experience?'

Mary swallowed. 'Yes. I have been unfortunate enough to have seen such a corpse once before. It is not an event I wish to recall.'

Maddox leaned back in his chair. 'No doubt. But it might assist me to know a little more of the circumstances.'

'Really, Mr Maddox,' she said angrily, 'it can have no possible relevance here.'

'Perhaps. Perhaps not. Humour me a little, Miss Crawford.'

She saw at once that opposition to a man of Maddox's stamp would be of little use, and might indeed prove perilous; she did not want this man as her enemy.

'As you wish,' she said, taking a deep breath. 'My brother owns a small house in Enfield. After our parents died we lived for some years with our uncle near Bedford-square, while a housekeeper took care of the Enfield house. However, when our uncle died we were obliged in due course to leave London, and made arrangements to return to Enfield, as a temporary expedient until we might find some where more commodious. The housekeeper wrote to say she

252

would expect us, and my brother came to fetch me and convey me to the house. It was — quite dreadful. Thieves had broken into the property, and taken every thing of any value. The doors were broken open, and some of the windows shattered. We found the young woman lying dead in the parlour, covered in blood. She had been beaten to death, and her skull crushed. Henry believes that she must have surprised the villains in their heinous crime.'

'Henry?'

'My brother. He is at present at Sir Robert Ferrars's estate in Hertford-shire. He left here some days before Miss Price's disappearance.'

'You hear from him regularly?'

Mary frowned. 'Of course.'

'Quite so. Pray continue, Miss Crawford.'

'There is little left to tell. The culprits were never apprehended, and I have never set foot in the house from that day to this. It brings back memories I have striven to forget. Until now.'

Maddox nodded slowly. 'I can quite see that all this must be a painful reminder of what happened to poor Mrs Tranter.'

Mary started. 'But how — I did not tell you her name — how could *you* possibly know such a thing?'

253

Maddox gave her a knowing look, and tapped the side of his nose. 'Someone in my profession comes to know many things, Miss Crawford. Some good, some bad. And some that other people believe to be secrets that they alone possess. You would — *all of you* — do well to remember that.'

Chapter XIII

'The steward was summoned after you left. It appears this Maddox fellow insisted upon seeing that accursed trench with his own eyes.' Dr Grant nodded to the servant to refill his glass, and sat back in his chair.

'Would to God your brother had never conceived of such a foolish plan, Mary. No good can come from such unwarrantable and vainglorious interference in the works of God. We should be content with what He has seen fit to bestow, and not attempt what we call "improvements", which are nought but monuments to our own arrogance and folly. Sir Thomas will rue the day he set out upon such an injudicious enterprise. Indeed, I remarked as much at the time.'

'How did you come to hear of this, my dear?' enquired Mrs Grant, who was accustomed to such pronouncements at the dinner-table, and was rather more preoccupied with how little her sister had eaten of the excellent turkey the cook had dressed specially that day.

'I met with McGregor myself, as I was coming back from Mansfield-common. He informed me that Maddox spent above an hour on his hands and knees, examining the dirt. Let us hope he is equipped with such boots and breeches as may withstand such barbarous treatment. But it was of no avail; he did not find whatever it was he was seeking. I believe the word he employed' — this with some thing of a sneer — 'was *clues*.'

'You do not surprise me, Dr Grant,' said his wife. 'As if there could be any thing still lying there, after all this time. I do not see why such a man as this Mr Maddox is needed, at all. To my mind, the whole dreadful business is easily enough explained — it will be those gipsies I told you of, Mary. They were seen at Stoke-hill two days ago, and accosted a party of ladies in a lane not three miles from here. There were half a dozen children, at least, as well as several stout women, and a gang of great rough boys. The ladies were frightened quite out of their wits.'

Mary had said little during dinner, and her spirits remained agitated and distracted after her encounter with Maddox, but her sister's words drew her attention; she had been imagining all kinds of dreadful possibilities, any one of which would make grievous inroads on the tranquillity of all, but might the answer be far more simple and common-place than that? Might the blame lie with a group of common gipsies? Mary could well see such a throng demanding money, and Fanny refusing in all the disdain of angry superiority, which would only have served to enrage them all the more.

'It is an interesting little theory, my dear, but, I fear, rather wide of the mark,' said Dr Grant, his sonorous tones breaking through Mary's thoughts. 'Not least because Mr Maddox seems to have discovered the ghastly implement.'

Both the ladies looked at him in shock and dismay. 'What can you mean, Dr Grant?' said his wife.

'He may not have found very much in the mud, but I gather that a search of the nearby workmen's cart was rather more productive. One of the mattocks was found to bear distinct traces of —'

Mrs Grant gave a loud cough, and cast a look of meaning at her husband. Dr Grant was a sedentary man, but his intellectual tastes and pursuits were exceedingly various, and he devoted many of his lengthy leisure hours to the study of scientific matters; he had, therefore, felt all the curiosity of a interested party in the steward's description of the fragments of human brain and flesh discovered on the blade of the mattock, and would have proceeded to give them a detailed account thereof, but a glance at Mary shewing her to have turned as pale as she had been on first returning from the Park, he contented himself with remarking, 'Well, well, I shall merely say that it was quite clear that this was the instrument with which the deed was done. Moreover, there had clearly been a rather clumsy attempt to disguise the fact. It had been wiped, but some traces still remained.'

'And what did the family have to say to that?' said Mrs Grant, who had poured a glass of wine for Mary, and was obliging her to drink the greater part.

'I believe he has asked to question the servants, and to carry out a search of the house, but the latter has been absolutely refused. Miss Bertram has declared that her mother is in no fit state to accede to such a request, and Mrs Norris was, as one might have expected, particularly loud in her outrage at such an idea; all the more so since — in *her* opinion — it is now palpably obvious that one of the labourers must be responsible. She is all for having the whole lot of them carted off to Northampton assizes, but I suppose we should not have expected any thing like reason or logic from *that* lady.'

'How so, Dr Grant? I am hardly an admirer of Mrs Norris, *in general,* but surely there is some thing to be said for such a view of the matter?'

Dr Grant shook his head. 'It is no more plausible, my dear,' he said patiently, 'than your picture of a gang of murderous gipsies marauding unchecked and unnoticed across the Mansfield lawns. A mere five minutes' mature deliberation should be sufficient to remind you that the workmen are always under supervision of one kind or another when they are in the park, and share sleeping quarters in the stable block. I doubt any one of them could have slipped away and committed such a crime without one or other of his fellows noticing, especially as there would have been a great effusion of blood, which could not possibly have been concealed. And what could be the motive for such a deed? I believe Maddox has agreed to question the men concerned, if only to appease Mrs Norris, but I suspect that he knows as well as I do, that he will have to look elsewhere for his assassin.'

It had not escaped Mary's notice, that Dr Grant's initial contempt for their London visitor had modulated into some thing very like respect, and she was still wondering over it, when her sister spoke again.

'If only it were possible,' mused Mrs Grant, 'to tell for certain who had handled that mattock. Then all would be made clear in a matter of moments.'

Dr Grant gave a smile that expressed all the indulgence of self-amusement in the face of feminine irrationality. 'Now you really *are* growing fanciful. If you are both ready to withdraw, I will retire to my study.'

Mary and her sister sat over the fire in the parlour, both absorbed in their own thoughts.

'It still does not make sense to me,' said Mrs Grant at length. 'Even if the workmen indeed prove to be innocent, I cannot believe that this Mr Maddox can possibly suspect any of the family of complicity in this dreadful deed. Surely some delinquent vagabond or escaped criminal is far more likely? Whatever Dr Grant says about it being improbable that strangers could go undetected about the park, I find it equally unbelievable that anyone at Mansfield could be guilty of such a brutal outrage against a defenceless young woman.'

'You do hear of such things,' said Mary with a sigh. 'And no doubt a London thief-taker like Mr Maddox has had experience of them, if anyone has.'

Like her brother-in-law, she had to acknowledge a grudging admiration for the man's energy and penetration. She had not given these qualities their proper estimation at first, to her cost, but she now suspected him to be a man with an extraordinary talent for stratagem and manoeuvre, who would likely prove to be a fearsome adversary. God forbid she should find herself in such a position! She shivered a little, and Mrs Grant got up to stir the fire.

'That said, I do not envy Mr Maddox the task of questioning the servants. You know how such people are, Mary — if they are not idle and dissatisfied, they are trifling and silly, and gadding about the village all day long. It will be an insufferably tedious task, and I doubt he will end up with very much to shew for it.'

Mary watched the flames leap up in the grate, and reflected on her sister's words. To judge from her own experience, the Mansfield servants would be only too susceptible to Maddox's method of questioning, and even if the Bertram family might fondly believe that their private affairs would remain private, she feared that Maddox would soon be in possession of a far fuller, and less palatable, version of the truth.

At that very moment, indeed, Mr Maddox was settling Hannah O'Hara into a similar chair, by a similar fire. He had been interested to discover that, alone of all the ladies at Mansfield, Fanny Price had had two maids to her own use; a little, sallow, upright Frenchwoman, who clearly fancied herself as much superior to Maddox, as she must feel herself to be to the rest of the servants; and a young girl who had until very recently made one of the housemaids, and owed her elevation to her skill at her needle. He had quickly established that this girl would be far more convenient for his purpose than the taciturn Madame Dacier, and elected to begin his interrogations with her.

O'Hara had never previously entered Sir Thomas's room, far less been invited to sit down in one of his imposing chairs, and Maddox was relying on the little flutter of self-importance that such an unlooked-for event must provoke, to put her off her guard. The glass of wine he had offered her, 'to steady her nerves', would doubtless have no insignificant contribution to make in that regard. He had already perceived her to be a quick-looking girl, with such an abundance of freckles and red hair as to confirm her Irish parentage before she had uttered a single word. Maddox had no quarrel with the Irish — indeed he had once been much enamoured of a girl from Baly-craig, and young O'Hara's native volubility might be of singular value to him; after all, if anyone was privy to what had been passing in Fanny Price's mind in the days before her disappearance, it was the young woman before him. He had also taken the wise precaution of erecting a small screen at the farther end of the room, and installing his assistant Fraser there, with a memorandum book and pencil. It was his usual practice, and had been of the greatest utility in a number of previous engagements of a like delicate nature: his own memory was first-rate, but Fraser's notebook had often proved to be even more reliable. Maddox had not deemed it necessary to inform the maid that her words were being recorded; he rarely accorded such a courtesy even to those who employed him, and never, yet, to a servant.

'So, Hannah. What can you tell me about your mistress?' he began, in what he designed to be a fatherly manner.

'Miss Fanny, sir?'

'Come now, Hannah, who else would I mean?'

The girl coloured, and gripped her glass a little tighter. 'I'm sorry, sir. I'm a mite nervous, that I am.'

'I quite understand. But there's nothing to fear. All you have to do is tell the truth. I'm sure you can do that, can't you, Hannah — a good God-fearing girl like you?'

'Yes, sir.'

'So. Miss Price. Was she a kind mistress?'

If he had thought the girl was blushing before, it was nothing to the scarlet that flooded her face now.

'We-ell,' she said, 'that's not quite the word as I'd have chosen. She was very partic'lar — *very* partic'lar. Every thing always had to be just so. 'Specially with her clothes. Many's a time I've sat up all night sewing, mending some thing as she'd torn, or finishing some thing as she wanted to wear the next day.'

Maddox smiled, a picture of sympathy. 'Young ladies can be most trying, can they not? Ever prey to the most petty whims and caprices, and it is people like us who stand the brunt of it. But in my experience, even the mistress who is a tyrant to her maids, may appear quite differently among her equals. Would that apply to Miss Fanny, would you say?'

O'Hara gave him a look he could not at first decipher. 'You could say that, I suppose. When she was wit' her family she was like a different person. Then it was all "Yes Sir Thomas", "No, Sir Thomas", "Three bags full, Sir Thomas". Eyes always down, that prim mouth of hers set in plaits.'

'Indeed?' said Maddox, wondering, not for the first time, at the verbal ingenuity of the Irish. 'How very interesting, Hannah. And which, would you say, was the *real* Miss Fanny?'

O'Hara gave a short laugh. 'Mine, to be sure! She might 'a looked as if butter wouldn't melt, but I've seen the looks she gave Miss Maria, when she thought she'd stole that Mr Rushworth from her. We all thought as it were him she ran off with, but it seems it must 'a been someone else entirely.'

'You have no suspicion of who that might have been?'

O'Hara drained her glass, and put it down; her cheeks were somewhat flushed. 'If it 'a been *me,* I'd 'a gone off with that Mr Crawford as soon as look at him. He's a fine gentleman, and no mistake.'

'But since Mr Crawford was not in the neighbourhood at the time —'

O'Hara shrugged her shoulders. 'All I can say is she definitely meant to meet *someone* that morning. That pelisse she was wearing? It was the best she had, and she had some beautiful things. She wouldn't 'a worn *that* for a walk in a muddy garden with no-one round to see.'

Maddox nodded thoughtfully; Mary Crawford had made a similar observation, but it had taken this girl's rude simplicity to make its full meaning manifest. He decided it was time to question her more minutely on the matter in hand.

'Do you know of anyone who might have wished Miss Fanny harm?'

O'Hara's eyes widened in alarm. 'Killed her, you mean? I can't tell you any thing about that — I don't know nothing about it, and that's God's honest truth.'

Maddox cursed himself; terror would only petrify her into silence. 'No, no, do not fret about that. I only wish to know the real state of things between Miss Fanny and her relations.'

O'Hara gave him a narrow look. 'I suppose there's no harm in telling what everyone here knows —'

'No, indeed, Hannah, and especially when it is what everyone *knows,* but no-one will *say.* No-one in the family, that is.'

O'Hara gave him a penetrating glance. 'They didn't know the half of it. Not Sir Thomas and her ladyship, anyways. It always looked peaceful and good humoured enough on the surface, but underneath it was a different story, make no mistake about it. At least as far as the young ladies was concerned. Miss Fanny had a cunning way of her own of causing quarrels without seeming to, if you take my meaning. And as soon as Miss Maria set her cap at Mr Rushworth, well, you can just imagine what Miss Fanny thought 'a that — I think it truly was the first time in the whole course of her life that she'd ever wanted some thing and not got it at the first time of asking. The bickerings that man caused! Miss Maria did what she could to stand her ground, but she never had cat's chance — Miss Fanny would bawl at her like a trollop when they were out of hearing of the rest of the family, however dainty and demure she made sure to look in the drawing-room.'

O'Hara sat back in her chair, and eyed Maddox in a conspiratorial manner. 'If you ask me, some thing happened on that jaunt to Compton. I can't tell you as to what, but every thing changed after that and it weren't just the news about Sir Thomas. You see if I'm not wrong.'

Maddox did not rise to the bait. 'And what about Mr Norris — how did he feel about all this?' he continued.

O'Hara did not appear to be particularly interested in Mr Norris. 'Oh, you never could tell, with him. He's a deep one — keeps his feelings to hisself. But one of the footmen saw what happened when he got back from Cumberland the first time and caught Miss Fanny and Mr Rushworth at that play rehearsal. She was in his arms, so Williams said. Almost *kissing,* he said. Not at all what a man like Mr Norris would have expected, I can tell you. Williams said his face was black as thunder, and he insisted the whole thing was stopped, right there and then. It was the talk of the servants' hall for days after.'

Maddox could well believe it; O'Hara, meanwhile, was still speaking.

'All the same, if you ask me, he was as tired of her, as she was of him. It wasn't just about Mr Rushworth, either. They *both* preferred someone else.'

Maddox sat forward in his chair; he had already discovered, or guessed, much of what O'Hara had told him, but this he had not heard before.

'Oh, he did his best to hide it,' she said, 'being so strict and all, but you only had to look at him when she was in the room. He was in love with her. It was written all over his face.'

'It is most important there is no misunderstanding about this point, Hannah,' said Maddox choosing his words with care. 'To whom are you referring?'

'Why, Miss Crawford, of course. Who else could it be?'

Even though the hour was late, Maddox sent Stornaway to fetch Maria Bertram's maid, and sat over the fire while he awaited her arrival, perusing the notes Fraser had taken. He also read once again the observations he himself had recorded after his conversation with Mary, in the light of O'Hara's last and most suggestive revelation.

It was all very interesting, very interesting indeed.

Chapter XIV

Mary, needless to say, knew nothing of this; and she set out for the Park the following morning with a heart much lighter than it would have been, had she been privy to all that was going through Maddox's mind at that same moment. The house seemed quiet enough, and if the servants were more circumspect than usual, Mary scarcely noticed in her eagerness to enquire after Julia, and her relief at hearing that if she was no better, she was likewise no worse. The girl had been given another sleeping draught, and Mary sat with her for some time, deriving considerable comfort from seeing her in such a quiet, steady and seemingly comfortable repose. From the window she could still see the view that had been so much cherished by her young friend. Mary could not but find it most affecting that, even if it had come about in a way she could never have foreseen, Julia had, indeed, succeeded in her desperate attempt to save her beloved trees: they had been judged sufficiently close to the Park to make the task of felling them too productive of noise and commotion for the abode of a patient in her precarious state of health. A temporary stay of execution had since become indeterminate; the workmen had been confined to their quarters since Mr Maddox's arrival, at his express request, and Mary now doubted whether the improvements at Mansfield Park would ever be resumed.

She was still pondering the effect all this might have on Henry, as she made her way down the main staircase some time later, and saw Maddox in deep conversation with his two assistants in the entrance hall; Maddox was wearing yet another fine and expensive frock-coat, while the men were in riding-dress, and to judge by their appearance, had been on horseback that morning. They were evidently discussing a matter of great import with their employer, and the taller of the two pointed more than once at a piece of paper he held in his hand. As Mary drew closer Maddox made towards her, with a smile that spoke of a development of some significance.

'My dear Miss Crawford!' he said, with a smile. 'You will be pleased to hear that I have already made considerable progress. My men have been enquiring at local inns hereabouts, and have discovered that a young lady answering Miss Price's description was seen at the White Hart in Thornton Lacey some four days past. She was observed alighting from the London coach that evening, and, given the foul weather, decided to take a room for the night. The landlord says she would not give her name, and seemed concerned to muffle herself up in her cloak as much as she was able, and avoid all intercourse with other guests. She then hired a pony and trap early the following morning, but has not been seen since; indeed the landlord begins to be somewhat incommoded by the vast quantity of trunks and band-boxes she left behind.'

It took some moments for Mary to comprehend the full import of his words, and her thoughts returned at once to her conversation with Tom Bertram. She knew that Fanny had been in no want of money when she left Mansfield, but the purchase of such a number of new clothes and effects seemed, once again, to argue for an elopement. And yet she had returned alone just as she had left, and wearing no ring. It was inexplicable. But at that moment, Mary became aware, on a sudden, that Maddox's eyes were fixed upon her.

'I congratulate you, sir,' she said quickly, wondering whether this was the response he had expected, 'you have been most thorough. What did the owner of the pony-trap have to say?'

Maddox inclined his head. 'It is my turn to congratulate *you,* Miss Crawford; that is exactly the question I myself asked. Happily, Stornaway encountered no difficulties in tracking the man down, and has only recently returned from examining him. The man was barely coherent, I am afraid, and a little the worse from spending most of last night in the inn, but it seems the young lady demanded to be set down at the back gate of the estate; the man has not lived long in the neighbourhood, and had no idea that his early morning passenger was the celebrated Miss Price of Mansfield Park. He did remember that it had been raining hard, and the weather still looked ominous, and the young woman did not seem to be shod for walking — as you yourself pointed out to me only yesterday, Miss Crawford. He expressed some concern for her boots as Miss Price was getting down from the trap, but all he received by way of reply was a rather tart little remark about there being "plenty more where those came from".

Curious, would you not say? And now, if you would be so good as to accompany me to the drawing-room?'

'I do not understand —'

'Fear not,' he said cheerfully, already some yards ahead of her. 'It will all become clear, soon enough.'

When the footmen threw open the doors Mary was startled to see that the whole family was assembled, with the sole exception of Julia Bertram. Lady Bertram and her elder daughter were sitting silently on the sopha; Mrs Norris was in her customary chair; Edmund stood by the French windows, his back to the company; and Tom Bertram was standing before the fire, his hands behind his back, in just such a position as his father might have assumed. All were wearing deep mourning, which only served to add to the portentous mood of the room.

Mary turned at once to Maddox. 'There must be some mistake — you cannot require my presence here —'

'On the contrary, Miss Crawford,' he said, taking her firmly by the arm, 'I have a question I must put to everyone at Mansfield, and it will save a good deal of time if I may ask you that question now, rather than being compelled to make a separate journey to the parsonage later in the day.'

'Very well,' said Mary. She knew she must look as confused and perplexed as any of them, and with an attempt at self-possession that was far indeed from her true state of mind, she walked silently towards the sopha, and sat down next to Maria.

Maddox assumed a place in the centre of the room, and began to pace thoughtfully up and down the carpet; his mind seemed elsewhere, but he could hardly be unaware of the eyes fixed upon him, or the painful apprehension his behaviour was occasioning. Mary looked on, conscious of the variety of emotions which, more or less disguised, seemed to animate them all: Maria seemed concerned to affect an appearance of haughty indifference, while a dull grief was discernible in her mother's face; Tom Bertram looked serious, and Mrs Norris furious and resentful; of Edmund's humour she could not judge.

'May I begin by thanking you for your prompt compliance with my request for an audience this morning,' Maddox began, in a manner that was perfectly easy and unembarrassed. 'As I have been explaining to Miss Crawford, I have just now received certain most interesting information. We have, at last, a witness.' He stopped a moment, as if to ensure that his announcement would produce the greatest possible effect.

'Miss Price was seen by a local man, at the back gate to Mansfield, three mornings ago, some time between eight and nine o'clock. Since she never reached the Park, I believe we may safely presume that she met her death at, or around, that time.'

There was a general consternation at this: Edmund turned abruptly round, his face drawn in shock and dismay; Maria gasped; and Lady Bertram drew out her handkerchief and began to cry quietly. Mary was, perhaps, the only one with sufficient presence of mind to observe Maddox at this moment, and she saw at once that he was equally intent on observing *them*. 'So he has contrived this quite deliberately,' she thought; 'he plays upon our feelings in this unpardonable fashion, merely in order to scrutinise our behaviour, and assess our guilt.' But angry as she was, she had to own a reluctant admiration for his method, even if it owed more to guile and cunning, than it did to the accustomary operations of justice. There doubtless were inveterate criminals so hardened to guilt and infamy as to retain control over their countenances at such a moment, but the members of the Bertram family could not be numbered among them. Maddox had succeeded in manoeuvring them all into displaying their most private sentiments in the most public fashion.

'My purpose, then,' he continued, his calm and composed manner providing the most forcible contrast with the state of perturbation all around him, 'is to ask you all, in turn, where you were that morning. It will be of the utmost usefulness to my enquiries. So, shall we begin?'

This was all too much for Mrs Norris, who had sat swelling for some minutes past, and now shewed two spots of livid colour on her cheeks. 'This is the most extraordinary impertinence! Question *us,* indeed! And in such a barbarously uncouth manner! When it is as plain as it could possibly be that it must have been one or other of those blackguardly workmen — why we do not cart the lot of them off to the assizes at once I *still* cannot conceive. A night or two without bread or water and we would soon have our confession — I never did like the look of that tall one with the eye patch —'

But here she was interrupted. 'My dear aunt,' said Tom, 'I am sure we all wish to see this dreadful matter cleared up as soon as possible, do we not? If it will assist Mr Maddox, what objection can we have? It is, after all, quite impossible that any of *us* were responsible.'

Mary wondered whether Tom's readiness to accede to Maddox's request owed more to his knowledge of his own complete innocence in the affair, or to a recognition that he had brought this man into the house, and would be the one answerable if the enterprise should fail.

'I shall set the example, Mr Maddox,' he said. 'You may begin with me. I was in my room until ten o'clock, and after a late breakfast I spent an hour with my father's bailiff, Mr Fletcher. He will be able to confirm that.'

Maddox nodded. 'And her ladyship?'

Lady Bertram looked up; her eyes were heavy, and she seemed not to have heard the question. 'I am sorry, were you speaking to me?' she said, in the languid voice of one half-roused.

Tom turned towards his mother. 'Mr Maddox wishes to know how you occupied your time on Tuesday last, ma'am. Most particularly the time before breakfast.'

Lady Bertram seemed bewildered that anyone should even ask such a thing. 'I was in my room, where else would I be? Chapman came to dress me as usual, and I had a dish of chocolate. I do not understand —

what can this have to do with poor dear Fanny?'

Her tone was becoming agitated, and Tom endeavoured to soothe her, saying at once, 'Oh no, ma'am — I am sure nobody suspected you!'

'Quite so,' said Maddox, with the most deferential of bows. 'I seek merely to obtain the fullest possible picture of where everyone in the house was at that particular time. There is no cause to distress yourself, your ladyship.'

'I am very happy to tell you where I was, Mr Maddox,' said Mary, in an effort to draw attention away from Lady Bertram. 'I spent the morning in the garden with my sister, cutting roses.'

'Indeed,' said Maddox in a steady tone. 'And *before* that, Miss Crawford?'

Mary flushed; she had quite forgotten her fruitless excursion to the post-office, and the conviction was of a sudden forced upon her that Maddox was already fully apprised of every aspect of her movements that day. 'Well, I did walk to the village that morning —'

'So I have been informed. I am delighted that you have elected to be so thorough in your disclosure. Did you see anyone during this no doubt pleasant little walk? Aside from the post-boy, of course?'

Mary shook her head. 'No, I did not.'

The expression on Maddox's face was unfathomable. 'That is a pity. Let us hope it does not prove to be significant.'

Mary opened her mouth to reply, but Maddox had already turned his attention to Maria. 'Perhaps Miss Bertram might now be so good?'

Maria might look a good deal thinner and paler than she had used to do, but she appeared to have assumed once more all the hauteur owing to a *Miss Bertram;* it was with the pride and dignity of a daughter of a baronet that she met the thief-taker's gaze. 'I was somewhat indisposed, as I recall. I remained in my room all morning, with my maid in attendance.'

'You did not speak to anyone during all that time? Aside from your maid, of course.'

Maria shook her head. 'No. I saw no-one.'

Maddox gave a broad smile, and linked his hands behind his back. 'Your clarity is admirable, Miss Bertram. And you, ma'am?' he said, turning to Mrs Norris. 'Perhaps you also took a walk in the park? I gather Miss Crawford was not alone in seeking air and exercise that morning — I am told Miss Julia was also some where in the vicinity.'

'Well, I most certainly was *not.* I have better things to do than wandering about on wet grass catching my death of cold. I was in my store-room, sir, as any respectable matron would be at that time of the morning. And you need not trouble to question my son, neither. *He* did not return from Cumberland until just before luncheon, and he left for the parsonage almost immediately, when we heard what had happened to Julia.'

Maddox was not the only one in the room to turn towards Edmund at this; he was still standing in the window, but Mary saw at once that his demeanour was not as collected as it had been.

'Is this true, Mr Norris?' asked Maddox genially. 'The briefest of discussions with the stable-hands, would, of course, resolve all doubt.'

'For heaven's sake, tell him, Edmund,' said Mrs Norris impatiently. 'Let us have done with this, once and forever.'

Edmund gave a slight cough. 'Mr Maddox will have no need to trouble the grooms. As it happens, I arrived in Mansfield somewhat earlier than my mother might have supposed. The difference is easily accounted for: I was glad to be released, after such a journey, from the confinement of a carriage, and ready to enjoy all the luxury of a walk in the fresh air, to collect my thoughts.'

Maddox gave a disarming smile. 'It seems that the park was more than usually crowded on Tuesday last. You had, I conclude, much on your mind?'

Edmund appeared to hesitate, before regaining his confidence. 'Evidently. But my private cogitations are my own affair, and can have no conceivable bearing on your enquiries, Mr Maddox.'

Maddox was unperturbed. 'I will determine what does, and does not, have a bearing on my enquiries, Mr Norris. So how long did you devote to this perambulation? Let me be absolutely clear: at what time, precisely, did you return to Mansfield that day?'

Edmund flushed. 'I am not entirely sure. Perhaps eleven o'clock.'

Maddox took a memorandum book from his pocket, and opened it with a theatrical flourish. 'According to the information supplied to my assistant yesterday by the stable-boy, you arrived just before *nine* o'clock. He is quite sure of this, because the great clock at Mansfield happened to chime as he was unharnessing the horses. I say again, it was not eleven o'clock, as you claim, but *nine*. Having employed one of Sir Thomas's carriages for the journey, you naturally came

282

directly to the stables here, but then, rather than going into the house, you told your valet that you would, instead, walk across the park to the White House. Rather an irregular way of proceeding, would you not say?'

'What do you mean to imply by that?'

Maddox snapped his pocket-book shut. 'I imply nothing; I enquire merely. However, I am sure I would not be alone in regarding it as rather curious for a gentleman in your position, returning to a house in turmoil, and a family in dire need of him, to dawdle among the delphiniums for upwards of three hours.'

Edmund's colour was, by this time, as heightened as Mary had ever seen it, and it had not escaped her notice that, whether he knew it or not, he had reverted to the stiff and officious mode of discourse that had characterised his manner on their first acquaintance, and which her brother had once found so entertaining. There was no possibility of entertainment now; knowing him as she did, Mary feared, rather, that the alteration in his elocution betrayed a mind profoundly ill at ease.

'I was not aware it was so long,' he stammered.

Maddox linked his hands behind his back.

'You are an educated man, Mr Norris, and as such you will be aware that, given these facts, it would have been quite possible for you to have seen Miss Price — and not only seen her, but met with her, and talked to her. Indeed, it almost defies belief that such an encounter did *not* take place. And it would hardly have been a congenial reunion. You would, indeed, have had good cause for resentment on Miss Price's account. To be subjected to the shame of a public jilting — what man of any character could submit to that with equanimity? And there is, of course, the small matter of her very considerable fortune.'

'You need not concern yourself about *that*,' said Mrs Norris quickly, her face red. 'My son has plenty of money of his own.'

'In my experience, madam,' said Maddox coolly, '*all* men covet money, however lofty their professed indifference; many are willing to die for it, and some are prepared to kill for it. So, Mr Norris, I repeat: what, precisely, happened in the park that morning?'

Mary felt quite sick with fear and apprehension; she could not dispute Maddox's reasoning, but her heart shrank from what that reasoning implied. She did not — could not — believe Edmund guilty of such an act of horror and violence, however cruelly provoked, but she could not deny that his actions had driven him into the *appearance* of such guilt. She could quite believe that Maddox found his story incredible; she alone, of all the family, might have been able to account for such uncharacteristic perturbation of mind, but how could she, with propriety or delicacy, supply Maddox with the explanation he lacked? And even if she overlooked her own scruples, was it not equally possible that Maddox might consider that if Edmund was in love with her, and not Fanny, that would only serve to provide him with an even more cogent motive for committing the very act from which she hoped to exonerate him? She could barely keep still, terrified of what Maddox might say next. Would he have Edmund apprehended there and then? Were his odious assistants even now summoning magistrates and constables from Northampton? It was altogether horrible, and in her anxiety for Edmund, it did not occur to her to fear for herself: not until much later did she perceive that what Maddox had said of Edmund, he could equally well have said of her.

Edmund, meanwhile, appeared to have regained his composure. He looked first at his family, and then at Maddox. 'You have my word, sir, as a gentleman, that no such encounter with Miss Price took place, either then, or at any other time. I can offer no corroborating circumstances or exculpatory evidence; my word alone will have to suffice.'

His voice was both cool and steady, and the two men remained stationed thus for what seemed to Mary to be an age, gazing upon one another in silence. Then Maddox suddenly gave a brief bow. 'Thank you,' he said, 'I have all I need. For the present.'

Having uttered these words, he walked so swiftly to the door as to forestall the footmen, and were the notion not so ludicrous, Mary might have been tempted to think he did so to ensure that no-one inside the room should perceive that there had been some-one listening outside. There was certainly nobody in evidence when Mary followed Maria Bertram through the door and into the hall; Edmund had departed without another word, and as she was endeavouring to determine where he might have gone, her thoughts were distracted by the sight of Mr Gilbert descending the stairs.

Maddox stood in the door of the drawing-room, and observed as the family went their several ways. It had been a most rewarding morning, and it was not done with yet. He had read widely on the subject of physiognomy, and to this theoretical knowledge of facial features, the pursuance of his profession had added a practical proficiency in the interpretation of gesture and demeanour. He regularly derived considerable amusement from scrutinising people at a distance, and deducing the state of relations between them, and many times, as now, this faculty had proved to be of the greatest service in the course of his work. He, too, had noted the appearance of the physician, and he now watched his meeting with Miss Bertram and Miss Crawford with the keenest interest. It was evident that Gilbert had promising tidings to impart, and the satisfaction writ across his face was quickly communicated to one, at least, of his companions: Miss Crawford's relief was immediate and unfeigned; Miss Bertram's response to the news, however, was rather more finely chequered. She seemed to be very much aware that she ought to *look* happy, without really being so; it was the impression of a moment only, but Maddox thought he discerned some thing that looked, to his trained eye, very much like fear. 'Now why,' he thought to himself, 'should that be so?'

As Mr Gilbert turned to spread his happy news to the rest of the family, the two young women went out onto the sweep; Miss Crawford began to walk down the drive towards the parsonage, while Miss Bertram appeared to be making her way to the garden. Maddox followed them out of the house and lingered a moment, watching the retreating figure of Mary Crawford, and suppressing the urge to follow her; something told him that this young woman had a role to play yet, in this affair. What that might be, he could not tell, but he owned himself engrossed to an unprecedented and possibly dangerous degree with the captivating Miss Crawford. For a moment the man strove with the professional, but the professional prevailed. He turned away, and walked briskly in the direction of the garden.

Maria had taken a seat in the alcove at the farther end from the gate, and although she had drawn a piece of needlework from her pocket, she let it fall in her lap when she saw Maddox approaching. Her position afforded each the opportunity of observing the other as he drew near. *He* looked all confidence, but Maria's feelings were not as easily discerned as they had been in the hall; she knew herself to be under scrutiny, and was more guarded as a consequence.

'May I?' said Maddox.

'It appears you have little regard for the niceties of common civility, Mr Maddox,' she replied archly. 'I dare say you will sit down whether I give my permission or no.'

'Ah,' he said with a smile, as he sat down beside her, 'there you are wrong, Miss Bertram, if you will forgive me. There are few men who are more watchful of what you term "niceties" than I am. Many of my former cases have turned on such things. In my profession it is not only the devil you may find in the detail.'

Maria replied only with a toss of her head; she seemed anxious to be gone, but unable to take her leave without appearing ill-mannered. Maddox smiled to himself — these fine ladies and gentlemen! It was not the first time that he had seen one of their class imprisoned by the iron constraints of politeness and decorum.

'To tell you the truth, I followed you here, precisely so that we might have this chance to talk privately,' he continued. 'I wished to elucidate one or two points, but felt that you would prefer to discuss these matters when the rest of your family were not present.'

He received a side-glance at this, but nothing more.

'You stated, just now, that you remained

in your own room for the whole morning on Tuesday last, and that your maid was with you. You still hold to that? There is nothing you wish to add — or, perhaps, modify?'

'No,' she said, her colour rising. 'I have told you every thing you need to know.'

'I fear,' he said, with a shake of the head, 'that that is not the case. But let us leave the matter there for the moment. Why are you so concerned that your sister may soon be in a position to speak to me?'

A slight change in his tone ought to have been warning enough, but she had not heeded it.

'I — I — do not know what you mean,' she stammered, her face like scarlet.

'It is not wise to trifle with me, Miss Bertram, and even more foolish to attempt to deceive me. I saw it with my own eyes only a few minutes ago. Mr Gilbert told you that Miss Julia may soon be recovered enough to speak, did he not? I saw the effect this intelligence had upon you — and how intent you were to disguise it.'

'How could you possibly —'

Maddox smiled. 'Logic and observation, Miss Bertram, logic and observation. They are, you might say, the tools of my trade. Mr Gilbert had good news, that much was obvious; *ergo,* your sister is recovering. And if your sister is recovering, she will soon be able to speak. This intelligence clearly disturbs you; *ergo,* you must fear what it is she is likely to say. Simple, is it not?'

She was, by now, breathless with agitation, and had her handkerchief before her face. 'I am not well,' she said weakly, attempting to rise, 'I must return to the house.'

'All in good time,' said Maddox. 'Let us first conclude our discussion. You may, perhaps, find that it is not quite as alarming as you fear at this moment. But I have taken the precaution of providing myself with salts. I have had need of them on many other like occasions.'

Maria took them into her own hands, and smelling them, raised her head a little.

'You are a villain, sir — not to allow a lady on the point of fainting —'

'Not such a villain as you may at present believe. But no matter; I will leave it to your own conscience to dictate whether you do me an injustice on that score. But to the point at hand. I will ask you the question once again, and this time, I hope you will answer me honestly. I can assure you, for your own sake, that this would be by far the most advisable way of proceeding.'

She hesitated, then acquiesced, her hands twisting the handkerchief in her lap all the while.

'Good. So I will ask you once more, what is it that you fear your sister will divulge?'

A pause, then, 'She heard me tell Fanny that I wished she were dead.'

'I see. And when was this?'

'At Compton. The day we visited the grounds.'

Maddox nodded, more to himself than to his companion, whose eyes were still fixed firmly on the ground; one piece of the puzzle had found its correct place.

'I was — angry — with Fanny,' she continued, 'and I spoke the words in haste.' Her voice dropped to barely a whisper. 'I did not mean it.'

Maddox smiled. 'I am sure we all say such things on occasion, Miss Bertram, and from what I hear, your cousin was not, perhaps, the easiest person to live with, even in a house the size of this. Why should such idle, if unfortunate words have caused you so much anxiety?'

It was his normal practice to ask only those questions to which he had already ascertained the answer, and this was no exception; but even the most proficient physiognomist would have been hard put to it to decide whether the terror perceptible in the young woman's face was proof of an unsophisticated innocence — or the blackest of guilt.

Maria put her handkerchief to her eyes. 'After Fanny and I quarrelled in the wilderness I ran away — but — but — my eyes were full of tears and I could hardly see. I stumbled on the steps leading up to the lawn, and made my nose bleed. I did what I could to staunch it, but the front of my dress was covered with blood. I was mortified to be seen so in public, so I concealed the stain with my shawl, that no-one should perceive it. As a result I alone know how and when the blood came to be there.'

'You did not ask your maid to launder the gown?'

She shook her head. 'Not at first. I had not spirits to bear even her expressive looks. Insolence would have been intolerable, but pity infinitely worse. And when Fanny's body was found, it was too late. I became more and more terrified. It was as if some frightful trap had been laid for me. I thought that if —'

'— if I searched your room I would discover this dress, and draw the obvious — indeed the natural — conclusion. I confess I did wonder why you were so adamant in your refusal to permit such a search.'

'How could I have proved that the blood was my own? Such a thing is impossible.'

'Quite so,' said Maddox, who reflected to himself in passing that, unlike any other injury, a nose-bleed offered the invaluable advantage of leaving no visible scar or sign thereafter, which made Maria Bertram either transparently guiltless, or quite exceptionally devious. He had his own ideas on that subject, but he had not finished with her yet. 'I can quite understand why you should have been concerned, Miss Bertram. And, if I may say so, your explanation seems most convincing.'

Her head lifted, and she looked at him in the face for the first time. 'O, how you do relieve me!' she burst out. 'I have not slept properly for days — not since —'

Maddox held up his hand. 'There is just one more thing, Miss Bertram. One last question, if I may. If you are indeed as innocent as you claim, why did you induce your maid to lie?'

Her eyes widened in terror, and he saw her lips form into a *no,* though the sound was inarticulate.

'There is nothing to be gained by denying it, Miss Bertram — I have spoken to the young woman myself. Do not blame her, I entreat. Your Kitty is one of the most loyal creatures I have ever encountered in her station in life, although I own the ten shillings you gave her would have been a most efficacious reinforcement of her natural tendencies. It was an admirable amount to fix upon, if I may say so — not too large, not too small. Bribery is always such a tricky thing to carry off, especially for a novice: pay too much, and you put yourself in the power of a servant, offer too little, and a greater price — or a greater threat — may be your undoing. And, I am afraid, it proved to be so in this case. Kitty Jeffries was proof against my pecuniary inducements, but even she could not withstand George Fraser. He has never failed me yet.'

He paused; he was not proud of what he had done, but the wench had suffered no real harm, and he had got the truth from her. Maria Bertram was, by now, sobbing as bitterly as her maid had done not twelve hours before.

'I see that you are unwilling — or unable — to speak. I, then, will speak for both of us. I have a little theory of my own, Miss Bertram, and with your permission, I will indulge myself by expatiating on it for a moment. I believe that you did, indeed, leave your room that morning, and your maid saw you go. I believe you were still angry with your cousin, and this anger had festered for many months, nay, possibly even years. Matters drew to a crisis over Mr Rushworth, and contrary to what one might have expected, your cousin's disappearance, and the news of Mr Rushworth's engagement, did nothing to assuage your fury and resentment. Rationally or not, you blamed his defection on Miss Price, and in your eyes, this was only the last of a long series of incidents in which you had been demeaned and humiliated, thanks to her. I believe you were in this same bitter and revengeful state of mind that morning, when, to your enormous astonishment, you saw Miss Price walking towards you near the channel being dug for the new cascade. What you said to one another, I cannot at present divine, but whatever it was, it ended with you striking your cousin a blow across the face. The rest, I admit, is conjecture on my part, but I surmise that whether from pain or shock, Miss Price fell to her knees before you, under the force of this blow, leaving you ashamed, appalled, and perhaps a little exhilarated, at the enormity of what you had done. Doing your best to contain these tumultuous feelings, you returned to the house at once, without daring to look back.

Having regained your room, you remained there in a state of the utmost fear and expectation, dreading every moment to hear a commotion in the hall, as Miss Price arrived to accuse you, but time dragged on, and nothing of the kind occurred. By nightfall you were forced to conclude that she must have returned from wherever it was she had come. But the following day her body was discovered, and you were compelled to face the unspeakable possibility that the blow you had struck was far worse than you had perceived, or meant. You had, in fact, committed murder.'

He had never yet used that word, and it had the predictable effect on the already high-wrought nerves of his companion. He sat back in his seat and took out his snuffbox. 'Now, Miss Bertram. Perhaps you can tell me whether my theory requires some emendation?'

She took a deep breath. 'Very little, Mr Maddox,' she whispered. 'You are correct in almost every particular. Except one.'

'And that is?'

'I did look back. I could hardly bring myself to do it, but some thing — some impulse — made me turn around. She was still there — lying on the ground where I had left her, screaming at me. I cannot get the sound out of my head. It haunts me, both sleeping and waking.'

Maddox could well believe it; her spirits were clearly quite exhausted. 'So when they found the body, you presumed that she must have fallen into the trench, and been unable to save herself, dying a lingering and terrible death, from the effects of hunger, no more than a few short hours thereafter.'

Maria put her head in her hands, and her slender frame was racked with sobs.

Maddox took a pinch of snuff. 'This is not the first time I have had cause to remark on the deficiencies of young ladies' education, particularly in relation to what we might term the human sciences. A well-nourished young woman like Miss Price could not possibly have succumbed to starvation in so short a period, and certainly not if she retained the use of her lungs, and the ability to call for help. Now tell me, Miss Bertram, did you see the body when they brought it home?'

She shook her head, and murmured some thing in which the words 'my cousin Edmund' were distinguishable.

Maddox nodded; it was of a piece with every thing he knew of the public character of Edmund Norris to have stipulated that the young ladies should be protected from such a shocking and distressing spectacle, but on this occasion his interference had had terrible and unintended consequences.

'Your cousin's consideration for you has, for once, done you a grave disservice. Had you been permitted to see it with your own eyes, rather than relying for your information on rumour and servants' gossip, you would have saved yourself many hours of needless grief and self-reproach. The wounds inflicted on Miss Price were far more grievous than any thing you describe. The blows that killed her were made by an iron mattock, not a human hand.'

Maria raised her head and stared at him, daring, for the first time in days, to allow herself the possibility of hope. 'But how do you know that I am telling the truth — that I did not pick that mattock up and wield it, just as you say?'

Maddox shook his head, and smiled. 'You have the proof, there, in your own hand.'

Her expression of uncomprehending amazement was, he had to admit, exceedingly gratifying, and one of the subtler pleasures of his chosen profession.

'I do not take your meaning. I have nothing in my hands — nothing of relevance.'

'On the contrary. Before I intruded upon you, you were engaged in needlework, were you not?'

'Yes, but —'

'— and, if I am not mistaken, you hold your needle in your left hand? And your pen, when you write?'

She nodded. 'It is not the common way, I know — indeed, when I was a girl, my aunt Norris insisted that our governess school me to use my right hand instead, "as all but idiots do". Every thing was attempted, including tying my left hand behind my back in the school-room, but it was to no effect. Not for nothing does my aunt call me *gauche*.'

'I fear the effort was always doomed to failure, Miss Bertram. Such preferences are in-born, and cannot easily be changed — if at all. But you are correct in noting that it is not a common trait. It is so *un*common, in fact, that according to my observations, you are the only person I have encountered at Mansfield to exhibit it. A fact which is most significant, in the circumstances.'

He could have carried on in the same vein a good deal longer, but elected to be merciful; this girl had suffered enough, and all to no purpose.

'I have considerable experience in the art and act of killing, Miss Bertram. It is not a suitable subject for young ladies' ears, and I myself am frequently shocked and sickened at the extremities of cruelty and pain that human beings are capable of inflicting on one another. But such a long and intimate acquaintance with the many methods by which my fellow men have met an untimely death, allows me to be quite categorical as to certain critical aspects of the horrible crime I have been asked to investigate here, including the full significance of the exact position of the wounds that killed Miss Price. In consequence, I know for a fact you did not take your cousin's life. The person who wielded that mattock did so with their *right hand*.'

It took several more minutes to convince her, and even longer to quiet her into any thing resembling a composed state of mind, but Maddox was patient. He had one more question to ask, and a demand to make, and he required her to be both rational and sensible when he did so.

'Before I allow you to depart,' he said presently, 'I must enjoin you to absolute secrecy as to the nature of our discussion this morning; I have already commanded as much from your maid. I am sure Miss Bertram will find herself more than willing to accede to this request, in exchange for a reciprocal silence on my part. After all, I cannot believe she would wish to submit her mother, in particular, to further unseemly revelations about the goings-on in her own family.'

There was a blush at this, and she bent her head with downcast eyes.

'Good. I was sure we would understand one another. My final request will not, I am sure, surprise you. Would you be so good as to inform me what *exactly* Miss Price said to you that morning?'

Maria stared into the distance, as if to force her attention to the reviving of such a distasteful memory.

'It was very much as you surmised. I was astonished to see her — and see her in such high spirits, into the bargain. I asked where she had been, but she told me that was her affair, and none of mine. She said this in that arrogant, imperious way she had when we were alone, and out of the hearing of either of my parents — as if I was little better than a servant, or one of her pitiable underlings. I had been angry before, but her words and her tone aroused a fury such as I had never felt before. I thought of all the distress she had caused — the scandal in the neighbourhood — my mother's grief — and yet there she was, parading about in her finest clothes, with no thought for the fact that she had put the whole family through days of doubt and misery on her account. Some part of this I think I said — my recollection is somewhat confused — but I do recall her laughing. Laughing out loud, and saying that she did indeed doubt that the like alarm would have been raised if *I* had been the one to go off with a man, instead of her. They would not have missed *me* half so much, she said, or wasted half the effort to discover *me,* always assuming I could have persuaded any man of fortune or distinction to take me in the first place.'

A single tear rolled down her cheek at this, and Maddox was moved to pity her; he could only imagine what submitting to the incessant spite and ascendancy of her cousin had been to a temper like Maria Bertram's, an evil which even the comfort and elegance of such an eligible home could not have entirely atoned for. He had never met Miss Price, but every thing he had heard of her declared her to have been a monster of complacency and pride, who, under a cloak of cringing self-abasement, had succeeded in dominating Mansfield Park, and everyone in it. And without presuming to judge whether she had merited such a fate, he suspected, nonetheless, that Maria Bertram was not the only member of the family who might have yearned for a world without Miss Price, however much they might have shrunk from such a savage and brutal way of achieving it.

'Go on, Miss Bertram,' he said softly. 'We shall soon have done.'

'I know she meant those words as provocation; I know she meant to insult and offend; but that was no excuse. I will think of what followed with shame and regret for the rest of my life. I struck her, Mr Maddox. I struck her full across the face, and she staggered. She had not expected it — how could she? She could not conceive of anyone having the audaciousness to raise a hand to *her* — to Miss Price, the heiress of Lessingby. I could scarcely believe it myself, and as I watched her sink on her knees before me in the mud every thing seemed to be happening with strange and unnatural slowness. And then the full horror of what I had done rushed in upon me, and I ran away.'

The two sat in silence for a moment, each lost in their own thoughts. At last Maria rose to her feet, and made as if to return to the house. She was a few feet away when Maddox called her back.

'You are quite sure she said she had left here with a man — that she had eloped?'

Maria nodded.

'But she did not say with whom? You do not know who it was?'

'No, Mr Maddox. I am sorry, but I cannot assist you. She never told me his name.'

Some time before this, Mary had returned to the relative peace of the parsonage, and, finding both Dr Grant and her sister departed on business to the village, she sat down in the parlour to write to Henry. She had not heard from him for some days, and had not written herself since Miss Price's disappearance: as catastrophe had succeeded catastrophe she had not known how to begin, or how best to convey such terrible and unexpected news; preparing him for the disappointment to be occasioned by the cessation of all work on the improvements was only the least of her concerns.

She had arranged her paper, pen, and inkstand, and even gone so far as to write 'My very dear Henry', when she was suddenly aware of an unusual noise in the hall. A moment later the door of the room was thrown open, and Henry himself rushed into the room, his clothes bespattered with the dirt of the road, and his hat still in his hands.

'Is she here?' he cried, in a state of agitation. 'Have you seen her?'

'What can you mean?' said Mary, rising to her feet in dismay. '*Whom* do you mean?'

'My wife, of course — who else? I've come back to find her — I've come back to find Fanny.'

Chapter XV

Mary would remember the hour that followed to the end of her days. She could only be grateful that they were accorded the luxury of spending that hour alone, without even her sister or Dr Grant to overhear or intercede. It was hardly possible to take in all her brother had to say, and it was many, many minutes before she could form a distinct idea of what had occurred. It seemed that while Henry had, indeed, travelled to Sir Robert Ferrars's estate, he had staid there no more than two days; hearing of Mr Rushworth's engagement, he had decided, in a moment of rash impetuosity, to return to Mansfield in secret, and contrive to see Fanny. She, as Mary well knew, had taken to walking in the garden alone in the morning, and it was there that he had met her — met her, made love to her, and persuaded her, at last, to run away with him. It was clear that, on her side at

307

least, it was a decision owing nothing to passion, and every thing to hatred of home, restraint, and tranquillity, to the misery of disappointed affection, and contempt of the man she was to have married. Having a man like Henry Crawford wholly in her power had likewise offered its own allurements, as had the idea of a romantic elopement, and all the bustle and excitement of the intrigue — not merely travelling by night, and bribing innkeepers, but imagining the uproar that must have ensued at Mansfield, as soon as she was missed. More than once did Mary shake her head as she listened to this narration; more than once did she picture, with horror, the awful consequences of this rash marriage, had Fanny lived. But she had *not* lived, and Mary had not yet had the courage to say so. She watched as her brother paced up and down the room, his face haggard and anxious, despite the unaccustomed richness of his attire.

'We were married in London four days later,' he said, at length. 'The day after she came of age. She was happy — ordering new clothes and viewing houses in Wimpole-street. She has a quite extraordinary talent for spending money — nothing is too good, nothing too expensive — but little more than a week later I awoke in our lodgings to find she was gone. I have spent every waking hour since looking for her.'

He threw himself into a chair, and cast his hat onto the table.

'I come here at last in desperation, Mary. Knowing her as I now do, I cannot believe she would have returned here willingly. Not alone, at any rate. In triumph perhaps, to make a point. But the carriage is not yet ordered, the house not yet taken, the announcement in *The Times* not yet made. No, no, I do not believe it, it is not possible.'

He fell silent, and they heard the distant sound of the great clock at Mansfield, striking the half hour. Mary stirred in her chair. She hardly dared trust herself to speak, yet it was now absolutely necessary to do so. But even as she was collecting her thoughts and wondering how to begin, the door opened for a second time.

'You see, my dear,' Dr Grant was saying to his wife as they came into the room, 'I was quite right. I knew the presence of such a horse in the yard could betoken only one thing. I will see to it that more claret is brought up from the cellar. I am glad to see you again, Crawford, even if you do return to a neighbourhood in mourning. We will all be very thankful when Sir Thomas resumes his customary place at Mansfield, and the funeral can at last take place; so protracted a delay is disrespectful, and serves only to amplify what is already the most lamentable circumstance. Indeed, I cannot conceive a situation more deplorable.'

'In *mourning?*' said Henry, rising again from his chair. 'I do not understand — that is, Mary did not say —'

Mrs Grant looked first to Henry, and then to her sister. 'Mary? Surely you have been most remiss — there has not been such an event as this in these parts for twenty years past. You will scarce believe it, Henry, but we have had a murder amongst us. Miss Price is dead.'

Dr Grant was the only one among them capable of any rational thought or deliberation in the course of the extraordinary disclosures that must naturally follow, though Mary could have wished his remonstrances less rigorous, or at the very least, rather fewer in number. Dr Grant had, indeed, a great deal to say on the subject, and harangued Henry loudly and at length for having so requited Sir Thomas's hospitality, so injured family peace, and so forfeited all entitlement to be considered a gentleman. Mrs Grant needed her salts more than once, during this interminable philippic; while Henry, by contrast, seemed hardly to hear a word of it. He was not accustomed to allow such slights on his honour to pass with impunity, even from his brother-in-law, but his manner was distracted, and his whole mind seemed to be taken up with the attempt to comprehend such an unspeakable turn of events; he had started that day a husband, even a bridegroom, but he would end it a widower.

Dr Grant had not yet concluded his diatribe. 'And now we have this wretched man Maddox in our midst, poking and prying and intermeddling with affairs that in no way concern him, in what has so far proved to be a fruitless quest for the truth. He will want to see you, sir, without delay; that much is abundantly clear. There will be questions — and you will be required to answer. And what will you have to say for yourself, I wonder?'

There was a silence. Henry did not appear to be aware that he was being addressed. He was staring into the bottom of the glass of wine Mary had poured for him, his thoughts elsewhere.

Dr Grant cleared his throat loudly. 'Well, sir? I am waiting.'

Henry looked up, and Mary saw with apprehension that his eyes had taken on a wild look that she had seen in them once before, many years ago. It did not bode a happy issue.

'What did you say?' he cried, springing up and striding across the room towards Dr Grant. 'Who is this — *Maddox* — you speak of? By what right does he presume to summon *me* — question *me*?'

The two men were, by now, scarcely a yard apart, and Henry's face was flushed with anger, his fists clenched. Mary stepped forward quickly, and put a hand on his arm. 'He is the person the family have charged with finding the man responsible for Fanny's murder,' she said. 'It is only natural that he should wish to talk to you — once he knows what has occurred.'

Henry shook her hand free; he was still staring at Dr Grant, who had started back with a look of alarm.

'Henry, Henry,' said Mary, in a pleading tone, 'you must see that it is only reasonable that Mr Maddox should wish to talk to you. You may be in possession of information that could be vital to his enquiries. You must remember that you saw her — spoke to her — more recently than any of us. It may be that there is some thing of which you alone are aware, which may be of vital significance — more than you can, at present, possibly perceive.'

She stopped, breathless with agitation, and watched as Henry stared first at her, and then at her sister and Dr Grant.

'So that is what you are all thinking,' he said, nodding slowly, his face grim. 'You think *I* had some thing to do with this. You think *I* was responsible in some way for her death. *I* — her husband — the man she risked every thing to run away with — you actually believe that I could have —'

He turned away. His voice was unsteady, and he looked very ill; he was evidently suffering under a confusion of violent and perplexing emotions, and Mary could only pity him.

'Come, Henry,' she said softly. 'Your spirits are exhausted, and I doubt you have either eaten or slept properly for days. Let me call for a basin of soup, and we will talk about this again tomorrow.'

'No,' said Henry, with unexpected decision. 'If this Maddox wishes to see me, I will not stay to be sent for. I have nothing to hide.'

Dr Grant eyed him, shaking his head in steady scepticism. 'I hope so, for your sake, Crawford.'

The two ladies turned to look at him, as he continued. 'We here at Mansfield have

313

spent the last week conjecturing and speculating about the death of Miss Price, but it seems that we were all mistaken. It was not Miss Price at all, but *Mrs Crawford*. That puts quite a different complexion on the affair, does it not?'

Mary's eyes widened in sudden fear. 'You mean —'

'Indeed I do. Whoever might have perpetrated this foul crime, it has made your brother an extremely rich man. As Mr Maddox will no doubt be fully aware.'

At that very moment, Charles Maddox was sitting by the fire in Sir Thomas's room. It was a noble fire over which to sit and think, and he had decided to afford himself the indulgence of an hour's mature deliberation, before going in to dinner. He had not yet been invited to dine with the family, but such little indignities were not uncommon in his profession, and he had, besides, gathered more from a few days in the servants' hall than he could have done in the dining-parlour in the course of an entire month. They ate well, the Mansfield servants, he could not deny that; and Maddox was a man who appreciated good food as much as he appreciated Sir Thomas's fine port and excellent claret, a glass of which sat even now at his elbow. He got up to poke the fire, then settled himself back in his chair.

Fraser had completed his questioning of the estate workmen, and although he had assured his master that there was nothing of significance to report, Maddox was a thorough man, and wished to read the notes for himself. There were also some pages of annotations from Fraser's interviews with the Mansfield servants. Maddox did not anticipate much of use there, either; he had always regarded both maids and men principally as so many sources of useful intelligence, rather than probable suspects in good earnest. Moreover, only the female servants had suffered that degree of intimacy with Miss Price that might have led to a credible motive for her murder, and he could not see this deed as the work of a woman's hand. Stornaway, by contrast, had spent the day away from the Park, interrogating innkeepers and landlords, in an effort to determine if any strangers of note had been seen in the neighbourhood at the time of Miss Price's return. Now that Maddox knew she had indeed eloped, it was of the utmost necessity to discover the identity of her abductor. If Stornaway met with no success, Maddox was ready to send him to

London; it would be no easy task to trace the fugitives, and Maddox was mindful that the family had already tried all in its power to do so, but unlike the Bertrams, he had connections that extended from the highest to the lowest of London society; he knew where such marriages usually took place, and the clergymen who could be persuaded to perform them, and if a special licence had been required, there was more than one proctor at Doctors-Commons who stood in Maddox's debt, and might be induced to supply the information he required.

It was little more than ten minutes later when the silence of the great house was broken by the sound of a commotion in the entrance hall. It was not difficult to distinguish Mrs Norris's vociferous tones in the general *fracas,* and knowing that lady was not in the habit of receiving visitors any where other than in the full pomp and magnificence of the Mansfield Park drawing-room, he suspected some thing untoward, and ventured out to investigate the matter for himself. The gentleman at the door was a stranger to him, but first impressions were Maddox's stock-in-trade. He prided himself on his ability to have a man's measure in a minute, and he was rarely wrong. This man was, he saw, both weary and travel-soiled, but richly and elegantly attired. Maddox was some thing of a connoisseur in dress; it was a partiality of his, but it had also proved, on occasion, to be of signal use in the more obscure by-roads of his profession. He could, for example, hazard a reasonable estimation as to where these clothes had been made, by which London tailor, and at what cost. This was, indeed, a man of considerable air and address; moreover, the set of his chin, and the boldness of his eye, argued for no small measure of pride and defiance. Yet, in spite of all this, it piqued Maddox's curiosity not a little to see that Mrs Norris accorded the newcomer neither courtesy nor common civility, and her chief object in leaving the sanctuary of the drawing-room for the draughtiness of the hall seemed to be to compel the footmen to expel the intruder without delay.

'May I be of some assistance, Mrs Norris?' said Maddox, with a bow. 'And perhaps you might do me the honour of introducing me to this gentleman.'

'There will be no call for that,' said Mrs Norris quickly. 'And I can assure you, he is *not* a *gentleman.* Indeed I cannot think what Mr Crawford is doing here, unless it be to enquire what we intend to do about the improvements. The time is not convenient, sir. We cannot stay dinner to satisfy the importunate demands of a *hired hand.* I suggest you call on the steward in the morning.'

'So this,' mused Maddox, 'is the Henry Crawford of whom I have heard so much.' His person and countenance were equal to what his imagination might have drawn, but Maddox had been in Mary Crawford's company sufficiently often to make a tolerable guess as to the number of her gowns, and the constraints on her purse. He had not expected a brother of hers to have the means to equip himself so handsomely; an idea was forming in his mind, and he began to have a faint glimmering of suspicion as to what was to ensue.

'Forgive the intrusion at this late hour,' said Henry, 'but am I correct in supposing that I am addressing Mr Charles Maddox? I am but recently arrived at the parsonage, and have only now been informed about —'

'We have no need of *your* sympathy, Mr Crawford,' said Mrs Norris, drawing herself up more stiffly than ever. 'Who knows, or cares, for what *you* have to say? The death of Miss Price is a private family affair, and can have nothing whatsoever to do with such as *you.*'

'I beg to differ, madam,' said Henry,

318

coldly. 'I rode up here directly, as soon as I heard the news. It became absolutely necessary that you should all know the full truth, and from my own lips.'

'What truth, sir?' demanded Mrs Norris, peremptorily.

'The truth that Fanny —'

'Fanny? *Fanny?*' she gasped. 'By what right, sir, do you *dare* to call Miss Price by her Christian name?'

Henry stood his ground, and did not flinch. 'The best right in the world, madam. A *husband*'s right.'

There was a instant of terrible silence, then she threw up her hands before her face, uttered a piercing shriek, and sank down prostrate on the floor. Maddox had anticipated the revelation by some moments, and knowing some thing of Mrs Norris, and conjecturing pretty well what a blow this must be to the family's pride and repute, he feared that she might succumb to a fit. But Mrs Norris had a strong constitution, and quickly found a vent for her fury and indignation in a vehement bout of crying, scolding, cursing, and abuse.

'You are a *scoundrel,*' she screamed, pointing her finger in Henry's face, 'a felon — a lying, despicable *blackguard* — the most infamous and depraved *villain* that ever debauched innocence and virtue —'

This invective being interspersed by screams so loud as must soon alarm the whole house, Maddox made haste to lift Mrs Norris to her feet, and turning to the butler, interposed with all necessary authority, 'I think, Baddeley, that Mrs Norris would benefit from a glass of water and some moments lying down; perhaps the footmen might attend her to the parlour? See that her ladyship's maid is called, and inform Mr Bertram and Mr Norris, if you would be so good, that I will beg some minutes' conversation with them after dinner. I will be with Mr Crawford in Sir Thomas's room.'

The door closed and peace restored, Maddox poured two glasses of wine, and handed one to his companion, noting, without surprise, that he held it in his right hand. He then took up a position with his back to the fire. Crawford was standing at the French windows, looking out across the park; the sky was beginning to darken, but it would still be possible for him to make out the alterations that had already been imposed on the landscape at his behest; the transformation about to be wrought inside the house might prove to be even more momentous. Maddox wondered how long it would be before the news of Miss Price's scandalous marriage had spread throughout the whole household, and made a wager with himself that the last and least of the housemaids would know the whole sorry story long before most of the family had the first notion of the truth about to burst upon them. He wondered, likewise, whether he might now be on the point of elucidating this unfortunate affair, but abstained from assailing his companion with questions, however much he wished to do so. He had long since learned the power of silence, and knew that most men would hurry to fill such a void, rather than allow it to prolong to the point of discomfiture. He was not mistaken; Henry Crawford stood the trial longer than most men Maddox had known in his position, but it was he who broke the silence at last.

'You will expect me to be particular.'

Maddox took out his snuff-box and tapped it against the mantel. 'Naturally. If you would be so good.'

'Very well,' Crawford said steadily, taking a seat before the fire. 'I will be as meticulous as possible.'

He was as good as his word. It was more than half an hour before he concluded his narration; from the first meeting in the garden, to the hiring of the carriage, the nights on the road as man and wife, the taking of the lodgings in Portman-square, and the wedding at St Mary Le Bone, on a bright sunny morning barely two weeks before.

'So what occurred thereafter?' said Maddox, after a pause. 'Listening to what you say, one would be led to expect this story to have a happy ending, however inauspicious its commencement. How came it that Mrs Crawford returned here alone?'

Henry got to his feet, and began to pace about the room.

'I have already endeavoured to explain this once today, but to no avail. The simple answer is that I do not know. I woke one morning to find her gone. There was no note, no explanation, no indication as to her intentions.'

'And when, precisely, was this?'

'A week ago. To the day.'

'I see,' said Maddox thoughtfully. 'But what I do *not* at present see, is why — given that Mrs Crawford arrived here so soon thereafter — you yourself have not seen fit to make an appearance before now.'

'I had no conception that she would choose to return here, of all places. She abominated this house, and despised most of the people in it. To be frank with you, sir, I find it utterly incomprehensible.'

Maddox took a pinch of snuff, and held his companion's gaze for a moment. 'May I ask what you have been doing, in the intervening period?'

Henry threw himself once again into his chair, and Maddox took note that, consciously or not, Crawford had elected a posture that obviated any need for him to meet his questioner's eye, unless he actively wished to do so.

'I have been searching for her,' he said, with a frown. 'I spent two fruitless days scouring London, before resorting to the dispatch of messengers to Bath and Brighton, and any other place of pleasure that might have offered her similar novelty or enlargement of society. She did not lack money, and could have taken the best house in town, wherever she lighted upon. Nor would she have seen any necessity for the slightest discretion or subterfuge. I calculated that this fact alone would assist me in finding her. But it was hopeless. I could discover nothing.'

'And you conducted these enquiries where, exactly?'

'From our lodgings in Portman-square.'

'So I take it you come directly from

London?'

Henry hesitated, and flushed slightly. 'No. Not directly. I come from my house at Enfield.'

Maddox looked at him more closely; this was an interesting development indeed. 'Now that, sir, if you will forgive me, strikes me as rather odd. Capricious even.'

'I do not see why,' retorted Henry, sharply. 'I had decided to return to Mansfield, and Enfield is in the way from London.'

'Quite so,' said Maddox, with a smile. 'I do not dispute your geography, Mr Crawford. But I *do* ask myself why a gentleman in your position — a man of means, with horses and grooms at his disposal, and the power to command the finest accommodations in the country — should voluntarily, nay almost wilfully, elect to lodge in a house that, as far as I am aware, is barely larger than the room in which we sit, and has not been inhabited for years. Not, indeed, since the regrettable death of poor Mrs Tranter.'

Henry started up, and stared at his companion. 'How do *you* come to know of that?'

Maddox's countenance retained its expression of impenetrable calmness. 'You will not be surprised to hear that your delightful sister asked me exactly the same question,

Mr Crawford. But it was a brutal and notorious crime, was it not? And not so very far from London. You would surely expect a man in my line of work to have heard tell of such an incident. The gang was never apprehended, I collect.'

Henry shook his head. 'No, they were not.'

Maddox turned to stir the fire. 'I gather your sister finds the house so retentive of abhorrent memories that she will not set foot in it. You, by contrast, elect to stay under that very roof, when you might have had your pick of lodgings without stirring a finger.'

He turned to face Crawford once more, but received no reply.

'But perhaps I am unjust,' he continued. 'Perhaps you found yourself in the immediate neighbourhood just as twilight descended. Perhaps it was easier to put up for the night there, than search for more suitable quarters after dark. And, after all, I have no doubt that you stayed not a minute longer than was absolutely necessary. You must have been in such haste to be gone that you left with the light the following morning. Am I right?'

Henry shook his head, his eyes cast down.

'At noon, then? Surely no later than three?'

Henry drained his glass. 'I left the next day.'

Both men were silent.

'There was no particular reason for this otherwise unaccountable delay?' said Maddox at last.

'No reason I am prepared to divulge to you, Mr Maddox. I do not choose to enlarge upon my private concerns. All I am willing to confirm is that I stayed two nights on the road at Enfield. That is all.'

'No matter, Mr Crawford. I am happy to take the word of your grooms and coachman. Unless, of course, you came on horseback?'

He had not needed to ask the question to obtain the answer; and it had not exercised any great intellectual faculty to do so: his companion was in riding-dress, and the hem of his great-coat was six inches deep in mud. The facts were not in dispute; he only wished to see how Crawford addressed them, and on this occasion it was with some self-possession.

'To use your own phrase, Mr Maddox,' he replied, with a scornful lift of the brow, 'I would expect a man in your line of work to have taken notice of my boots.'

Maddox inclined his head. 'Quite so, Mr Crawford, quite so.' Had he known it, he had just had a glimpse of another Henry Crawford, the witty and charming Henry Crawford who had succeeded in persuading one of the country's foremost heiresses to elope with him. Maddox smiled, but never had his smile been more artificial, nor his eyes more cold than when he next spoke.

'You were, I believe, examined by the constables after the death of your housekeeper.'

It took a moment for the full implications of the question to be felt.

'You are well informed, sir,' Henry said at last, in a purposely even tone. 'And that being the case, you will also know that they were more than satisfied with the information I was able to impart. After all, what possible reason could I have had for committing such a repugnant crime?'

'None at all, I grant. Though the present case is somewhat different, is it not? You would, I contend, have *every* possible reason to murder Mrs Crawford. You will now take full possession of a very considerable fortune, without the concomitant inconvenience of a demanding, and from what I hear, rather unpleasant wife.'

Henry flushed a deep red. 'I will not allow you, or any man, to insult her. Not before my face. I loved her, sir.'

'Perhaps you did; perhaps you did not. That does not materially alter the facts. Nor does it explain why you tarried two days in an empty house when you claim you were desperate to find her.'

'I have already addressed this. I told you — it is none of your concern. And besides, I hardly knew what reception I might expect when I did arrive. I was not certain how the family would receive the news.'

Maddox adopted an indulgent tone. 'Come, come, Mr Crawford, you are disingenuous. I am sure you knew perfectly well how the Bertrams would view such a marriage. To see Miss Price's fortune pass out of the family, and in such a fashion! So shortly before the union that had been planned for so long, and was so near consummation! Mrs Norris may not, I own, be a fair sample of the whole family,' he continued, as Henry shifted uncomfortably in his chair, 'but did you really imagine Sir Thomas would embrace you with rapture, and congratulate himself on the acquisition of such a nephew? But we digress. Let us return for a moment to the unfortunate Mrs Tranter.'

Henry leapt to his feet and paced to the farther end of the room, before turning to face Maddox. '*Must* you continually harp on that string? It has nothing whatever to do with what happened to Fanny. It is nothing but an unlucky coincidence.'

'That may, indeed, be one explanation. But there are some noteworthy similarities between the two cases, I think you will find. Not least the extreme and unnecessary violence with which each attack was perpetrated.'

'True or not, that has nothing whatever to do with me. What possible reason could I have had for murdering the unlucky creature? She was a mere servant, nothing more.'

'There, I am afraid, we disagree. Hetty Tranter was far more than a *mere servant,* at least as far as you were concerned. Indeed, it is quite alarming how often the women you seduce meet their deaths in such a cruel and brutal fashion.'

Crawford turned away. 'I do not know to what you refer.'

'Come, Mr Crawford, we are both men of the world. This Hetty Tranter was your mistress. Oh, there is little point in denying it — your countenance has already betrayed you. Indeed, you may have papered over your debaucheries by calling her your 'housekeeper', but the real truth is that you had installed this girl in the Enfield house for your own sordid convenience. At a discreet distance from town, far from the prying eyes of your loftier acquaintances, and the rather juster remonstrances of your sister. *She* is still in ignorance of this particular aspect of the affair, is she not?'

'And I had rather she remained so,' said Crawford quickly — too quickly, as the expression on his companion's face immediately testified.

Maddox nodded. 'I can see that it would, indeed, be most trying to have to explain your squalid depravities to someone as principled as Miss Crawford. So trying, in fact, that you might well have been tempted to silence the Tranter girl once and for all — especially if she were becoming importunate in her demands. Or if, shall we say, she had told you she was with child, or threatened to expose you to your sister. Or even, poor wretch, if you had merely tired of her, and wished to rid yourself of an incumbrance which had, by then, become nothing more than a source of irritation.'

Crawford's face had turned very red. 'How *dare* you presume to address me in this manner — there is absolutely nothing to substantiate a single one of these vile and disgusting accusations, and I defy you to do so.'

Maddox remained perfectly calm. 'You are

quite right. If there *were* such proof, no doubt even the rather slow-witted constables of the parish of Enfield might have been expected to uncover it.'

Crawford took a step nearer. 'And if I find you repeating any of these base and unfounded allegations to my sister —'

He had, by now, approached so close as to be less than a foot from the thief-taker, but Maddox stood his ground, even in the face of such encroachment. 'I have no wish to distress her, sir. Unless, of course, it is absolutely necessary. I am sure that she — like you — would prefer to forget the whole horrible affair; but *unlike* you, she may one day be successful in that endeavour.'

'And what do you mean to insinuate by that?'

'Merely that unresolved murders of this kind have a habit of coming to light, even after the lapse of several years. The law may seem to nod, Mr Crawford, but she is not wholly blind, especially where unanswered questions persist, and when the persons involved subsequently find themselves entangled in circumstances of a similar gruesome nature. It is interesting, is it not, that then, as now, you cannot confirm your whereabouts at the time of the killing?'

Crawford turned away, and Maddox

watched with interest as his companion perceived, for the first time since he had entered that room, that he was face to face with his dead wife. Maddox had wondered, when he elected to use Sir Thomas's room for this interview, whether Crawford had ever entered it, or seen this portrait, and now he had his answer. It was, he believed, a striking likeness of the late Mrs Crawford. The painter had no doubt yielded to the young lady's demands as to the pink satin gown, the bowl of summer roses, and the small white dog leaping in her lap, but he was evidently a good hand at drawing a likeness, and there was a certain quality in the set of her head, and the curl of her lip, that belied the outward charm and sweetness of the *tout ensemble.*

Crawford was still standing before the portrait, lost in thought. He seemed to have forgotten the presence of his interlocutor; it was the very state of mind that Maddox had hoped to induce, and too fair an opportunity for a man of his stamp to let pass.

'I wonder, did the constables ever resolve the mystery of the shirt?'

Henry turned slowly, his countenance distracted.

'If you recall, Mr Crawford,' continued Maddox, 'the hammer with which Mrs

Tranter was so cruelly done to death was subsequently discovered in the garden of the house, wrapped about in a blood-stained shirt.' He paused. 'Her blood, but *your* shirt.'

Henry shook his head, as if to banish the thoughts that had begun to beset him. 'It was an old shirt,' he said. 'One I had deposited in a trunk in the house. I cannot explain how the ruffians came to discover it.'

'Any more than you can explain why a witness claimed to have seen you in the neighbourhood that day? A washer-woman, was it not?'

'She was mistaken, God damn you! She was old, half-blind and very likely in liquor. She was *mistaken.* Indeed, as I recall, she withdrew her story only a few days later.'

'So there is no danger of a similar sighting in the vicinity of Mansfield on the day your wife was battered to death?'

Henry Crawford's face, which had been flushed, was now as pale as ashes. 'Absolutely none. I was, as I said, still in London. You may make whatever enquiries you choose.'

Maddox drained his own glass, and placed it carefully on the table. 'Thank you, Mr Crawford. I would have done as much whether you consented or not, but this is a rather more civilised way of proceeding, is it not?'

Mary was alone in the parlour when Henry returned. The impetuous and defiant demeanour had gone, and been replaced by an expression she might almost have called fear. As she handed him a glass of Madeira she noticed that his hands were cold, even though the evening was warm.

'Come, Henry, sit with me by the fire.'

He sat for some moments in silence, until prompted by her once more.

'Did you see the family — Mr Bertram, her ladyship?'

'I saw Maddox, mostly. He it was who has detained me so long. The man is a veritable terrier, Mary. Heaven help the guilty man who finds himself in his power, for he can expect no quarter there. Would to God that you had told me he knew so much of Enfield — he had all the facts at his fingers' ends as if it had happened only yesterday. It was like living the whole atrocious business through a second time. I had thought we had left it behind us in London, and now it returns to haunt us once more — will we never be free of it?'

Mary put a hand on his arm. 'I am sorry.

I should have said some thing. But our sister and Dr Grant were in the room at the time, and we agreed never to speak of it to anyone. No good can come of doing so now. It would only —'

'— give my brother-in-law yet further reason to suspect me, and fix me even more firmly at the head of whatever list it is that Maddox is busily compiling. Good God, Mary, it appeared as if every word I uttered only made me seem the more guilty.'

'Do not lose courage. If Mr Maddox is ruthless, that should only reassure us that he will, at the last, discover who really committed this crime.'

Henry shook his head sadly. 'I am afraid you do not appreciate how such a man Maddox is accustomed to operate. He will receive a fine fat reward for bringing the culprit to justice, but what will happen if he cannot find the real villain? Do you imagine he will merely doff his hat to Tom Bertram, and admit he has failed? Depend upon it, he will deliver *someone* to the gallows, and whether it is the right man or no will not trouble him unduly.'

They sat in silence for a long while after this, until Mary ventured to ask him, once more, if he had seen the family.

'I saw Mrs Norris, who was intent on seeing me off the premises with all dispatch. I am heartily glad you were not there to see it — or *hear* it, given the choice turn of phrase she chose to avail herself of. The only thing that distinguishes that old harridan from a Billings-gate fishwife is a thick layer of bombazine, and a thin veneer of respectability. No, no, my conscience is easy on the score of Mrs Norris; she has never shewn me either consideration or respect, and I will requite her insolence and contempt in equal measure. But I do have cause for self-reproach on Lady Bertram's account. You know I have always thought her a silly woman — a mere cipher — interested only in that vile pug and all that endless yardage of fringe, but she has a kind heart, for all that, and has borne a great deal of late, without the strength and guidance of Sir Thomas to assist her. I am afraid to say that this latest news has quite overcome her, and she has taken to her bed. I am heartily sorry for it, and all the more so since I discovered how ill Miss Julia had been these last few days.'

'And the gentlemen — Mr Bertram?' and, this with a blush, 'Mr Norris?'

'I saw Bertram very briefly. He left me kicking my heels for upwards of half an hour, but I had expected no extraordinary politeness, and suffered my punishment with as good a grace as I could, feeling all the while like a naughty if rather overgrown schoolboy. He was angry — very angry — but he neither called me out, nor threatened me with all the redress the law affords, which I confess, I had at times been apprehensive of, even though Fanny was of age and the marriage required the consent of neither parent nor guardian. I verily believe he did not know whether to address me as his cousin's ravisher, her widowed husband, or her probable assassin. We none of us have the proper etiquette for such a situation as this. Norris did not appear at all, and I confess I was not sorry. I have had my fill of doleful and portentous prolixity for one day — indeed I often wonder if Norris has not missed his vocation. If Dr Grant should succeed to that stall in Westminster he endlessly prates of, our Mr Norris would make a capital replacement, and could hold forth in that pompous, conceited way of his every Sunday, to his heart's content.'

It was, for a moment, the Henry of old, and Mary was glad of it, even if it came at such a price; but her joy was short-lived.

'And besides,' he said in a more serious tone, 'I do not know what I should have said to him. My marriage has become a source of regret to me, Mary, and not least for the pain it has caused to others — a pain that I cannot, now, hope to redress.'

He sighed, and she pressed his fingers once again in her own, 'You must tell me if there is any thing I can do.'

'There is certainly some thing you can do — for the family, if not for me. Good Mrs Baddeley took me to one side as I departed, and begged me to ask you to go to the Park in the morning. It seems Miss Bertram is taken up with nursing her mother, and Miss Julia is still in need of constant attendance. Mrs Baddeley was high in her praise of you, my dear Mary, and I trust the rest of the family is equally recognisant. Indeed, I hope their righteous fury at the brother's duplicity does not blind them to the true heart, and far more shining qualities, of the sister.'

Mary's eyes filled with tears; it was long since she had heard such tender words, or felt so comfortable in another's company. Having been alone in the world from such an early age, the two had always relied on each other; her good sense balancing his exuberance, his spirits supporting hers; his pleasantness and gaiety seeing difficulties nowhere, her prudence and discretion ensuring that they had always lived within their means. She perceived on a sudden how much she had missed him, and how different the last weeks would have been had he been there. But it was a foolish thought: had Henry been at Mansfield, none of the events that had so oppressed her would ever have occurred.

'I will go, of course, but I meant to ask if there was any thing I could do for *you.*'

'Nothing, my dear Mary,' he said, with a sad smile, 'but to take yourself off to bed and get what sleep you can. You will need your strength on the morrow. Do not worry, I will be up myself soon.'

He watched her go, and settled down into his chair, his eyes thoughtful; and when the maid came to make up the fire in the morning, that was where she found him; in the same chair, and the same position, hunched over a hearth that was long since cold.

Chapter XVI

Nothing but the assurance that her presence was both necessary and wished for would have reconciled Mary to calling on the Bertrams, after such revelations as her brother's return had precipitated, but she gathered her courage, and presented herself at the Park at an earlier hour than common visiting would warrant. Mrs Baddeley received her in a rapture of gratitude, and she was glad, for once, to encounter no-one but the housemaids on her way upstairs. She had soon installed herself by Julia's bedside, happy to feel herself useful, and knowing that she brought comfort to at least some of the inmates of Mansfield Park. The household was slow to stir that morning, and Mary was probably the only person, besides the servants, to observe the departure of George Fraser. Hearing sounds on the drive she had stepped to the window, to see him emerge from the house, carrying a

knapsack of such a size and bulk as anticipated at least one night's absence. She was
watching him mount, when the door
opened, and Julia's maid entered with a pile
of clean sheets for the bed. She saw Mary
at the window, and stopped for a moment
at her elbow.

'The footmen say he be heading towards
London, and then to another place in the
same direction. Some wheres beginning
with N?'

'Enfield,' said Mary, her heart sinking. 'I
imagine he is going to Enfield. My brother
has a house there.'

Evans's eyes widened. 'So it's true, miss!
Miss Fanny — she upped and went off with
your Mr Crawford! I always did say he was
a lovely-looking gen'leman. Always a smile
for the likes of us — and a thank you, as
well — you can't say that for everyone who
comes a-calling here.'

The girl's cheeks had, by now, grown very
pink, and her eyes had strayed from Mary's
face. Mary sighed; she knew her brother occasionally indulged himself in harmless gal-
lantries with maid-servants, but she had
never approved of such careless conduct,
and liked it even less when it concerned
girls of Polly Evans's youth and *naiveté*. She
was wondering whether it was necessary to

caution her, however gently, to be rather more guarded in future, when hooves sounded on the gravel, and Polly turned to the window once again, her pretty features darkening into a frown. 'Let's hope that's the last we see of that evil villain — and fair riddance. Poor Kitty Jeffries hasn't risen from her bed since he was set loose on her. She won't eat, and sobs as if her heart would break.'

Mary turned to her aghast. 'What can you mean, Polly?'

Polly clapped her hand to her mouth. 'Oh miss, I shouldn't have said nothing! She made me promise on the Bible not to tell. That Maddox, he put the fear of God on her if she so much as breathed a word.'

'But is she harmed — is she in need of a physician?'

Polly shook her head. 'Not now. Mrs Baddeley took a look at her, and said there was nothing broke, and the marks would heal. Don't fret, miss,' she said, seeing Mary's horrified look, 'it's no worse than what her pa used to do to her when he was angry and in drink. Kit's a tough one — she's used to it.'

Mary felt for a chair, and sat down heavily, her mind in a tumult; what justification could there be for the use of such extremes of violence on a blameless servant? What could Maria Bertram's maid possibly know that would force Maddox to resort to such desperate measures to extort it from her? She looked up at Evans, who was wringing her hands in a state of extreme agitation.

'Please don't say nothing, miss. That man Maddox is still in the house, and if he were to hear of it —'

'You have no need to fear, Polly,' she said firmly. 'I will see to that. But have you no idea *at all* what it was that Kitty told this man Fraser?'

Polly looked exceedingly awkward. 'Not really, miss. Though I did hear her murmur some thing about — well, about Miss Julia.'

Mary turned involuntarily to the figure lying unconscious on the bed; the girl had not, to Mary's knowledge, spoken a word since the day she saw Fanny's coffin carried past her room. But *Julia?* How could such an innocent young girl possibly be involved in this dreadful affair?

Mary sent Evans away with renewed promises of silence and complicity, and closing the door quietly behind her, sat down by the bed to ponder and deliberate. As the morning wore away, however, she was obliged to put her own concerns aside; she began to perceive that though Julia's

343

pulse had initially been much stronger, and her condition more favourable than on her preceding visit, she was slowly growing more heavy, restless, and uncomfortable. Mary asked for Mr Gilbert to be sent for, and waited anxiously until Mrs Baddeley ushered him into the room.

'I cannot comprehend it,' he said, a few moments later, his face anxious, 'every sign was growing more propitious, and I saw no cause to apprehend a relapse. Not, at least, a relapse such as this. You are sure —' this to Mrs Baddeley '— that only the cordials I prescribed have been administered, and in the correct doses?'

'I would stake my life on it, sir,' said Mrs Baddeley, her pink face somewhat pinker than usual. 'I have given the maids the most strict instructions.'

Gilbert shook his head. 'Only yesterday I was offering the family my felicitations on a recovery surpassing even my expectation, but now a recovery of any kind is most doubtful, most doubtful indeed. We will have to redouble our vigilance — and our prayers. Miss Crawford, can we prevail upon you to assist us yet further?'

Mary assured him of her complete willingness to watch the rest of the day, and the night if needed. It was a period of almost equal suffering to both. Hour after hour passed away in increasing pain and discomposure on Julia's side, and in the most cruel anxiety on Mary's, which could only be augmented by the new sense of unease that had arisen since her conversation with Evans.

She made a hasty dinner in the housekeeper's room, and returned to relieve Mrs Baddeley. Julia was tossing to and fro, and uttering frequent but inarticulate sounds of complaint. Her face was flushed, and she seemed to be breathing with difficulty.

'I do so hate to see her in such a pitiable state, Miss Crawford,' said Mrs Baddeley, with tears in her eyes. 'I do believe she is worse even than when you went downstairs.'

Mary put her hand on her arm, and offered words of reassurance that were very far from the forebodings in her own heart.

'Mr Gilbert has promised to call again in the course of the next three or four hours, Mrs Baddeley. Let us endeavour to support our hopes and spirits until then. We will be of more assistance to Miss Julia if we can remain calm.'

At that moment Julia started up in the bed, and in a near frenzy, cried out, 'No! No! It cannot be! It cannot be!'

Mary was at her side in an instant, and

advising Mrs Baddeley to send for Mr Gilbert without delay, passed her hand over the girl's brow.

'I am here, Julia. There is no cause for alarm. You are quite safe.'

'No! No!' she moaned, 'You must tell them — I can trust you — I did not mean — did not mean — an accident — an *accident* —'

'Hush, Julia, do not distress yourself so,' Mary said imploringly, as she attempted to persuade her to lie down again, but when she clasped the girl's shoulders, she felt her thin frame grow rigid against her.

'So much blood! — never knew — so *much* — her dress — her hands — never, never wished for that — let me be rid of it — let me forget it — never, oh never — no hope — no hope —'

She threw herself back on her pillows, as if exhausted, and lay for some moments neither moving nor stirring. Mary, too, was unmoving, half stupefied between horror and incredulity. Was this the explanation of the reprehensible conduct of Maddox and his associate? Was it indeed possible that Julia had been responsible, even if accidentally, for the death of her cousin? She knew the strength of her youthful passions, and the weak hold of more temperate counsels over the immoderation of youth and zeal;

she knew, likewise, that Julia had been frantic to prevent the felling of the avenue, and in her high-wrought state, weakened by recent illness, the event had no doubt taken on a disproportionate enormity in her child-like mind.

As Mary sat retrospecting the whole of the affair, and the conversations she herself had witnessed, she began to perceive — all too late — that Julia might, indeed, have come to regard Fanny as wholly to blame for the disaster about to befall her beloved trees, believing her cousin could have prevented it, had she been prepared to intercede, and use her considerable influence to compel her uncle to alter his plans. Much as her heart revolted from the possibility, Mary's imagination could easily conceive of a meeting between the two cousins in the park that ill-fated morning — the very morning that the work was due to commence. She could picture Fanny listening to her cousin's pleas with contempt and ridicule, and Julia, provoked beyond endurance, striking out in desperation and fury, if only to put an end for ever to the scorn in that voice. She did not want to believe it, but her heart told her that it was possible, just as her mind acknowledged that it would explain many things that had puzzled her hitherto; it would render Julia's despairing decision to chain herself to the trees more readily comprehensible; and it would account for her terror at the sight of her cousin's coffin. Mary thought back to that dreadful scene, and recalled, with a cold shudder that carried irrefutable conviction, the actual words Julia had used. She saw her in imagination, standing in the door of her chamber, her hand to her mouth, crying out, '*She* is not dead, *she* cannot be dead.' But how could she possibly have known whose coffin it was? The family had been careful to conceal the news of her cousin's death from her. There was only one answer, only one explanation.

How Kitty Jeffries had come to discover the secret, Mary could not guess; all she did know, was that discover it she had, and Maddox had wrung it from her. Even now, she thought, he must be waiting only for Julia's recovery to question and apprehend her, and she recalled with a tremor of sick dread her own brother's words as to the fate that must inevitably attend the perpetrator of such a crime. She started up and began to pace the room, unable to keep her seat with any composure. She could see no way to obviate such terrible consequences, no other way to explicate what she had heard than by casting Julia — all unlikely as it seemed — in the repellent light of her cousin's murderess.

She stopped by the window, and pulled aside the heavy curtain. It was moonlight, and all before her was solemn and lovely, clothed in the brilliancy of an unclouded summer night. She rested her face against the pane, and the sensation of the cool glass on her flushed cheeks made her suddenly aware how stifling the room had become. She went across to the door, flung it open, and stood for a moment on the threshold. The great house was still and noiseless — or was it? She knew her nerves were more than usually agitated, but she thought, for one fleeting instant, that she had detected a movement in the dark shadows, beyond the wan circle of light cast by the lamp. It was not the first time she had felt such a sensation in recent days, and she suspected Maddox was deploying his men as spies. Had Stornaway been deputed to listen at Julia's door, and if he had, what had he heard?

She wavered for a moment, wondering whether to seek the man out, and challenge him, but a few minutes' reflection told her that nothing she could do would make any difference, and whatever the man might have gathered by stealth, would no doubt only serve to confirm what his master had already obtained by violence. She returned into the room with an even heavier heart, and took her place once again at the bedside. Julia had recommenced her feverish and confused murmurings, and Mary was so preoccupied, and so fatigued by her many hours of watching, that it was some moments before she discerned that the tenor of the girl's ramblings had undergone a subtle but momentous change.

'I can never be free of it — never erase it — never blot it out — that face, those eyes — cannot bear it — pretend I never saw, pretend I never heard — no, no, do not look upon me — I will not tell! I will not tell!'

The precise import of these words forced itself slowly but inexorably upon Mary's consciousness. It was not *Julia* who had killed Fanny, but *someone else*. Julia's previous burst of feeling did not signify her own guilt, but her horror at having seen her own cousin being brutally done to death, and by someone she herself knew. It was no wonder the girl was distraught — no wonder she was in terror —

Mary's heart leapt in hope — and as soon froze, as the girl sprang up suddenly in the bed, her lips white, and her eyes staring sightlessly across the room. 'Do not look

upon me! — I will not tell — a secret —
always, always a secret! — Edmund —
Edmund!

Chapter XVII

Charles Maddox was, at that moment, standing in silence on the garden terrace. He was not a man who required many hours of repose, and it had become his habit to spend much of the night watching, taking the advantage of peace and serenity to marshal his thoughts. Living as he did in the smoke and dirt of town, he could but rarely, as now, enjoy a moonlit landscape, and the contrast of a clear dark sky with the deep shade of woods. He gazed for a while at the constellations, picking out Arcturus and the Bear, as he had been taught as a boy, while reflecting that moonlight had practical as well as picturesque qualities: a messenger could ride all night in such conditions as this, and that being so, Maddox might, with luck, receive the information he required in the course of the following day. He had sent Fraser to London, to enquire at Portman-square as to the exact state of affairs between Mr and Mrs Crawford during their brief honeymoon; the husband had claimed they were happy, but every circumstance argued against it. Maddox had seen the clenched fist, the contracted brow, and the barely suppressed anger writ across his face. He would not be the first man Maddox had known, to conceal violent inclinations beneath a debonair and amiable demeanour, and this one had a motive as good as any of them: not love, or revenge, but money, and a great deal of it.

Maddox could not have told, precisely, how long he had been standing there, meditating the histories of his past cases, when he heard the sound of an approaching horse, the echo magnified unduly in the stillness of the air. He abandoned his reverie at once, and proceeded to the front of the house, to find a man dismounting in some haste. He was a medical gentleman, to judge by his bag, but he was not the physician Maddox had seen at Mansfield before.

'Do I take it Mr Gilbert is unavailable?' he asked.

The man looked at him with suspicion, as if wondering at his impertinence. 'I am sorry, sir. I do not recollect that we have been introduced.'

'My apologies. My name is Charles Maddox. The family have requested my assistance in resolving the unfortunate business of Mrs — that is — Miss Price's death.'

The man nodded. 'I had heard as much in the village; indeed, they are talking of little else. I am Phillips, the apothecary. Mr Gilbert has been detained at a lying-in at Locking Hall. He sent word to me to attend here in his stead.'

'The patient is worse, I apprehend?' said Maddox.

'Indeed so, sir,' said Phillips. 'I must hasten to examine her. A great deal of time has already been lost.'

He handed his mount to the stable-boy, and began to hurry towards the house, but Maddox kept pace with him.

'Have you been informed as to the symptoms?'

'Of course. The message was most precise, though I do not see that it is any concern of yours.'

'Nonetheless, if you would.'

'Very well,' said Phillips, stopping for a moment before the door, his gloves in one hand. 'The pupils are contracted, the patient flushed about the face, the respiration raucous, and the pulse slow. Now if you will excuse me, I am expected.'

Maddox caught his arm; his face had assumed a sudden and uncharacteristic gravity. 'Will you permit me to accompany you, Mr Phillips?' he said, quickly. 'It may prove to be of the utmost importance.'

The apothecary hesitated a moment, and Maddox made a shrewd guess that he was only too conscious of his subordinate and substitutionary status at the Park, and would, in consequence, lack the confidence to refuse such a request, or to question the authority of a man who appeared to enjoy the full confidence of Sir Thomas, and to be residing in his house.

'Very well,' he said at last. 'Follow me.'

Had Maddox known no better, he might have presumed that it was Mrs Baddeley Mr Phillips had been summoned to attend. She it was, at first sight, who appeared to be most in need of medicinal assistance; her face was pale, and she had sunk breathless into a chair, one hand at her side, and her aromatic vinegar in the other. Miss Crawford, he could see, was divided between her desire to alleviate the housekeeper's immediate distress, and a more painful concern for Julia Bertram, who seemed to be in a state of profound stupor. More alarming still, the young girl's countenance was dark with suffused blood, and her features utterly still and seemingly lifeless.

'How long has this present condition persisted?' asked Phillips, forestalling Maddox's own enquiry.

'An hour — perhaps two,' replied Miss Crawford. 'Immediately prior to that she became suddenly agitated and distressed — she began to talk for the first time in days. But,' she faltered, her cheeks flushed, 'there was no sense in the words. Since that time I have watched her sink into the pitiful state in which you now see her. I have given her two further doses of the cordial Mr Gilbert prescribed, but it seems only to make her worse.'

Maddox noted her countenance as she spoke these words, just as he had noted her start back with a frown at his approach; he wondered at it, but he had not then the time to ponder its meaning. To his eyes, it was evident, only too evident, what afflicted the patient, and he watched Phillips commence a prolonged physical examination with increasing impatience, succeeding in checking his anger only by reminding himself that the symptoms were, indeed, easily mistaken for those of common fever, and the alternative was hardly likely to have formed part of the experience of a country apothecary.

'She has been poisoned, man,' he cried at last. 'Can you not see that? She shews all the signs of having ingested an excessive — indeed fatal — dose of laudanum. The initial excitement under the effects of the stimulant, and then the slow lethargy — the strident breathing — the dreadful colour of the face.'

'I beg your pardon, Mr Maddox,' said Phillips. 'I did not know you included a medical proficiency among your many other accomplishments.'

'I do not, sir. But I have had considerable experience of unnatural death, and the means by which it may be brought about. I have, alas, seen cases like this before. If I am right, we will soon see her succumb to an even deeper lassitude, and her breath and pulse will slow to the point of absolute torpor. If we do not act at once, this deadly listlessness will become irreversible; she will sink lower and lower, and we will not be able to bring her back.'

All the time he was speaking he had kept his eyes fixed on Mary Crawford's face, and had seen the grief and horror his words occasioned; he saw, too, that if she did not like him, she did, at least, believe him, and her first action, when he had concluded, was to turn at once to Phillips, and beg him with passionate ardour to comply with whatever he suggested. Mr Phillips, however, was extremely reluctant to cede the right to determine the correct mode of treatment to someone completely unqualified to pronounce in such cases. Nor, it seemed, did he agree with the diagnosis.

'I cannot concur with you, sir,' he said, coldly. 'I attended the young lady some days ago, at the onset of her present indisposition. I am of the decided opinion that this is merely a particularly virulent case of putrid fever. I propose to bleed her, in order to suppress the fever in its forming state, and relieve the vascular congestion. I have complete confidence in the efficacy of this method of proceeding, as I do of Mr Gilbert's agreement with what I propose.'

'It seems to me, sir,' retorted Maddox, 'that you are more afraid of deviating from Mr Gilbert's opinion, than you are of losing your patient. Bleeding will not help her now — indeed, it is very like to kill her, in the weakened state to which she is now reduced. We must apply a purge, and hope to expel the poison from the gut before it can be absorbed into the body. There is no time to lose — we do not even know when the fatal dose was administered. It may already be too late.'

He had hoped to shock the man out of his timid complacency, and his words had their effect — though not, at first, on the apothecary.

'What do you mean, sir?' cried Mrs Baddeley in terror, rising unsteadily from her chair. 'Do you talk of *poison?* And in this house? The poor girl has had nothing but Mr Gilbert's cordial, administered with my own hands.'

'That may very well be the case,' said Maddox, striding to the table of medicines, and beginning to examine them. 'But are you in a position to swear that there was never a moment — never a single moment — in the last two days, when Miss Julia has been left alone?'

Mrs Baddeley flushed, and the two women exchanged a glance.

'I see you cannot,' continued Maddox. 'And here, I believe, is the result. This bottle breathes faintly of laudanum. Mr Phillips — your opinion, if you please.'

The apothecary came forward, and lifted the bottle to his nose, before looking up with an expression of horror. 'This is most alarming — someone has clearly tampered with the cordial. Heaven knows what Mr Gilbert will have to say to this —'

'Your efforts would be better directed to assisting your patient, Mr Phillips. Mrs Baddeley, do you happen to have a supply of ipecacuanha in the house? It may serve, as an emetic.'

'I believe so, sir. It is long since I have had need of that evil physic, but there may still be a small quantity in the chest in my room. I will need to fetch the key.'

'Then if you feel strong enough, I would ask you to make haste there with Mr Phillips, so that he may make up a tincture.'

'Mrs Baddeley is not well, sir,' intervened Miss Crawford, as the door closed behind them. 'I know the chest to which she refers, and could just as easily have gone in her place.'

'I wished to speak to you alone, Miss Crawford,' said Maddox, 'and prepare you for what is to come. Once the emetic has taken effect, we must try to get Miss Julia from her bed, and revive her a little by moving her about the room. With luck, we may prevent the onset of the final stupor. But it will not be an easy task, and may tax even your strength and fortitude. If you do not feel yourself equal to it, I will send for one of the servants, but, for reasons that will no doubt become clear to you when you have had time to reflect, I would prefer to keep the matter between our four selves, at least for the moment.'

She did not answer at once, and when he

turned his eyes towards her white and horrified face, he perceived that she was already blaming herself. She had administered the last doses of the cordial; she — all unwitting — had therefore been the purveyor of the poison; how she might feel if the girl were to die, he had not, then, the energy to contemplate.

He did not think it likely that either of them would forget the night they endured together, at Julia Bertram's bed-side. The darkness without was nothing to the grim work they undertook within. The ipecacuanha brought upon such violent reachings as seemed to tear the girl's frail constitution in pieces, and more than once he wondered whether the cure might not be more deadly than the malady, and he would prove, at the last, to be a murderer, not a saviour. He saw, too, that Mary Crawford was beset by doubts of a similar melancholy order, but she never uttered a word of doubt or misgiving, and directed her efforts to assisting Mr Phillips, and accomplishing the charge before them. And it was a soul-harrowing task; the reachings were soon followed by a foul-smelling vomit, and a sudden gush of liquid smelling strongly of laudanum, and even when the basins had been removed, and the patient cleansed, there was no possibility of rest. Knowing the state of prostration which would necessarily follow, and the stimulant measures necessary to counter it, if death were to be averted, Maddox had them take her bodily from the bed, and toil hour after hour by turns, half-carrying, half-dragging her cold and insensible body about the room.

As the dawn rose behind Sir Thomas's woods, the two women began to fancy there was some slight improvement in the girl's pulse: they waited, watched, and examined it again and again, and when the first rays of sunlight revealed a lightening of the venous darkness that had flooded her face, they dared at last to hope that she might be out of danger. Even Mr Phillips acknowledged a temporary revival, and ventured to give encouraging assurances, but Maddox was not so sanguine; he had seen this flattering symptom before, and knew that all too often it proved to be but the harbinger of a final and more fatal crisis; he did his best to keep the women from indulging the expectation of an amendment that might never come, but he could not dissuade them. Within the hour the girl's breathing began to slow, until there was a considerable interval between the successive inspirations, and a cold sweat had broken out over her body; and then the pulse that had shewn such a decided improvement began to diminish gradually in fullness and strength. Mrs Baddeley could not be shaken from the hopes that had been so cruelly raised, but Maddox knew that they had laboured in vain, and he saw that Mary Crawford knew it too.

Julia Bertram died at exactly fifteen minutes after five o'clock, as by her watch on the table.

Mrs Baddeley burst at once into a torrent of grief, kissing the girl's hands, and raising them to her own face, and sighing as if her heart would burst. 'I never thought to see her depart this world before me — I used to dance her on my knee when she was a tiny child, and I thought one day I would do the same with her own babes, when she became a wife. But that will never be. Oh my sweet, sweet lady!' she sobbed, murmuring some other words, which her tears made inarticulate. And then, as if recollecting herself, 'Forgive me, sir. I am quite overcome, as you would be yourself if you had known the poor dear young lady as I did, and as Miss Crawford did. And after all the other terrible things to have befallen this family — what will her ladyship and Mr Bertram have to say? And poor Sir Thomas, when he returns?'

'As to that, I will answer,' said Maddox gently, raising her to her feet. 'You would do best to take some rest and endeavour to restore your enfeebled spirits. I will have them send up chocolate and some thing nourishing to eat, but I charge you to speak to no-one — not even your husband — of what has occurred here this night, and remain in your room until I send for you.'

Mr Phillips was not long in following the housekeeper from the room, and as he prepared to depart, Maddox laid upon him the same injunction with which he had dismissed Mrs Baddeley.

'You will appreciate that I must demand absolute secrecy as to the true cause of this piteous event. As far as the family are concerned, for the moment, this was merely the sad culmination of many weeks of previous indisposition. When the time is right, and only then, I will divulge the truth. You know, as well as I do, Mr Phillips, that the contamination of that cordial was calculated and deliberate, and that being so, I now have another murder to resolve at Mansfield Park, and by the same hand as the first. I must condition for the broadest possible freedom of movement and decision if I am to find the man responsible, and bring him to justice. I trust we understand one another?'

Mr Phillips nodded, and with a curt bow, took his leave. Maddox turned to Mary Crawford, who was sitting silently in the window-seat.

'And you, Miss Crawford? Do you agree to the same terms?'

She said nothing, and fixed her eyes instead on the sunlight now streaming across the lawns, and touching the woods with gold. It occurred to him that the repugnance he had seen in her countenance the evening before, when he had first entered the room, and which had vanished in the face of the far more pressing need to sink their differences for the sake of her friend, had now returned with renewed vigour. There was some thing else, too, beyond her immediate and understandable anguish, to which he could not yet put a name; but whatever had occasioned it, there were questions he would have to ask, and they could not wait.

'I need to speak to you, Miss Crawford, and in private, but perhaps it would be best if we were both to take some repose and refreshment. With your permission, I will call at the parsonage this afternoon.'

And with that, he was gone.

Chapter XVIII

It was as much as Mary could do to summon the strength to walk back across the park to the parsonage. The ordeals of a day and night passed in such exertion were nothing to her grief and exhaustion of mind; her limbs were trembling, and she was faint and giddy from a want of proper rest and food. It was too early to expect her sister or Dr Grant to be up, and she was glad to be spared the necessity of lengthy explanations, in which she would be obliged to conceal as much as she revealed, trusting that the Mansfield gossips would supply her sister with the sober facts of the case as well as she could do. But if she wished to avoid society in general, she most earnestly sought the company of her brother. He alone would understand some thing of what she was suffering, and he alone would have the words with which to console her; but a search of the house revealed only that his bed was empty, and his horse gone.

She asked the cook for a dish of tea, and made her way slowly to the privacy of her own room, where she finally gave way to a violent outburst of tears. It was some time before this excess of suffering had spent itself, and even longer before she could trust herself to appear before the Grants in a tolerable ease of mind, so she sent word that she was indisposed and lying down. And lie down she did, though with such a head-ache as precluded all hope of sleep. Never had she wanted the bliss of oblivion more, and never had she more need of it; she knew her impending interview with Charles Maddox would tax all her reserves of watchfulness and caution, and yet she could not quiet her thoughts. Between the horror of Julia Bertram's senseless and untimely death, and her own unconscious part in it, and the words she had heard from the girl's own lips, only hours before she died, she could not tell if her heart were more oppressed by sorrow, guilt, fear, or foreboding.

When Maddox arrived shortly after three o'clock, she was sitting in the shrubbery. He saw at once the paleness of her face, and the slight tremor in her hands, and guessed some thing of what she had been suffering in the hours since dawn. He pitied her, but he could not afford to shew it; she, by contrast, could think of him only in the guise of a man prepared to resort to torture, to intimidate an innocent servant. He would have taken her hand, had she offered it, but she remained seated, and would not catch his eye. He said nothing immediately, but took a seat on the bench beside her.

'I see we do not meet as friends, Miss Crawford. I am at a loss to know how I have so far forfeited your good opinion.'

'You have only to search your own conscience, Mr Maddox.'

'Even so, I would prefer to hear it from you.'

'Really, sir,' she said angrily, turning to face him, 'do you have no recollection at all of the atrocious way you behaved towards Kitty Jeffries? Setting your brute of an assistant upon her like a dog?'

He sat silent for a moment, and it occurred to her that he had supposed her ignorant of the incident, and was even now debating how best to excuse it. She had never seen him frown before, and she was struck by how much it served to alter his face, as the scar above his eye deepened, and cast shadows along the strong lines of his chin and jaw, sharpening them to an edge. She had known him to be a formidable adversary; now, for the first time, she saw him without the mask of geniality or politeness. It may, perhaps, have been due to her extreme weariness, but she felt the power of his presence as she had never done before; she had been used to condemning him as arrogant and domineering, but now, sitting by him in such close proximity, and after such an experience endured together, she found herself affected in a way that was wholly new to her.

'It was — necessary,' he said at length. 'Regrettable, but necessary. The girl will take no lasting harm, and I fancy her mistress is already remembering me in her nightly prayers.'

Mary gathered her wits, and called to mind why she had been so displeased with him. 'Lest you have already forgotten, Mr Maddox, Miss Bertram has this very morning lost her beloved sister.'

'My apologies, Miss Crawford, I am properly reprimanded. We are both of us, I suspect, somewhat fatigued. I meant merely to say that Miss Bertram is far from sharing your resentment. She does not approve of the method, any more than you do, but it has been the means of exonerating her from all suspicion, and relieving her mind from an intolerable burden. I see from your expression that you do not know the story. I will be brief. At a certain point during your pleasant little party to Compton, Maria Bertram told her cousin that she wished her dead. She did not know, then, that her sister had overheard these words, and when Mrs Crawford's body was found, Maria was seized with panic, fearing she would be suspected if the story became known. Her fears were all the greater because she had suffered a nose-bleed while at Compton, and had blood on her dress.'

'I remember,' said Mary, slowly. 'On the journey home she held her shawl close round her shoulders, even though the night was warm.'

Maddox nodded. 'Thank you for your corroboration, Miss Crawford. This same incident also accounts for Miss Bertram's inordinate reluctance to consent to a search of her chamber — she knew my men would find that gown, and —'

'— she would not be able to prove the blood was her own.'

'Quite so. She bribed her maid to keep her silence. Had she trusted me from the start, I would not have been forced to such disagreeable measures.'

'Can you blame her, Mr Maddox? Your

methods and demeanour hardly inspire confidence.'

He inclined his head. 'You may be right; I do not court popularity. But whatever the rights and wrongs of my means, the end is always the same: the truth. I know now that Maria Bertram did not kill her cousin, just as I know she did not kill her sister. Julia Bertram did not die because she heard or saw some thing at Compton, but because she heard or saw some thing at *Mansfield Park,* on the day of Mrs Crawford's death. Some thing or *someone.*'

Maddox saw his companion grow yet paler at these words, but he said nothing. Many things might have provoked such a reaction, particularly in her current nervous state; nonetheless, he still felt sure that this young woman had a part to play in elucidating this crime, even if she would neither help nor trust him in his own efforts to do so.

They sat for a while in silence, a silence that was merely accidental on her part, but had been calculated with some exactness on his. It interested him to try whether she, a mere woman, could bear the oppression of silence longer than her brother, and his respect for her only increased when it became clear that, although there must be questions she wished to ask him, she could hold her tongue longer than many a vice-bitten London felon he had known. He stored away the insight for future perusal, shrewd enough to know that such a degree of self-composure was not only rare, but, at least in one respect, a rather ambivalent quality in any person caught up in the investigation of such a crime. At length, he spoke again. 'I do not need to ask you if you saw someone tamper with the cordial. If you had, I am sure you would have informed me already. And if you had tampered with it yourself, you are hardly likely to confess it to me now.'

She looked at him briefly, then resumed her contemplation of Dr Grant's garden. 'I will not dignify that remark by addressing it. Anyone in the house might have entered that room without arousing suspicion. Nor was it a crime that required undue premeditation. There was a vial of laudanum among the other medicines. It would have been the work of a moment to pour the contents into the cordial.'

'I see that you have given the matter some thought, Miss Crawford. Your ratiocination is admirable.'

'I deserve no compliments, Mr Maddox,' she said, tears filling her eyes. 'I will never forgive myself for not perceiving it sooner. The odour was palpable. *You* recognised it at once.'

'*I* was looking for it; you, on the other hand, had no reason to suspect it. You were fatigued with watching, and anxious for your friend. Do not blame yourself.'

'That is easily said, sir.'

'Quite so.' There was a pause, then he continued, 'Given how closely you have examined the question, Miss Crawford, I am sure it has occurred to you to wonder when, exactly, the lethal dose could have been added to the cordial. Judging by the quantity remaining, it must have been but lately opened?'

'I gave the first dose from it myself, yesterday afternoon.'

He saw the look on her face as she spoke, and when he resumed it was in a gentler tone. 'I had presumed as much. In my experience, it would have been a matter of some hours only before the symptoms became unmistakable. And the bottle itself was not sealed?'

'No. None of them are. I dare say Mr Gilbert does not consider it necessary. It was only a cordial, after all.'

'*Was,* yes. Quite so.'

She looked at him for a moment, but said

nothing. Maddox sat back in his seat. 'We have made some progress, but not, as yet, advanced very far. As you yourself said, Miss Crawford, anyone in the house might have committed this crime; moreover, the same reasoning appertains to anyone who has entered the house since the bottle was left there.'

She turned to him quickly, then looked away. Maddox continued, 'I have had word from Gilbert. He says he left that bottle by Miss Julia's bed two afternoons ago. He left it there, indeed, only a few short hours before Mr Crawford returned from his long absence, and hastened to pay his visit to the Park.'

'Oh, you need not concern yourself about my brother, Mr Maddox. He did not remain in the house long enough, and was certainly *not* alone.' She smiled, but it seemed to Maddox that she was struggling to maintain a corresponding lightness of tone, an effort somewhat belied by the slight flush to her cheek.

'On the contrary,' he said, 'I recall that Mr Bertram kept him waiting upwards of half an hour. A petty gesture, I grant, but perhaps we might forgive him, when we consider the injuries the family has suffered at your brother's hands. And as you said, only a few minutes ago, it would have been the work of a moment to slip up to Miss Julia's chamber.'

'Perhaps,' she said, with enforced patience, 'if he had known where he was going. Do you ask me to believe my brother to be acquainted with the whereabouts of the sleeping-rooms of the young ladies of the house? I doubt he has even been upstairs. It is a ridiculous theory.'

Maddox was undeterred. 'He might have made a shrewd guess, based on all those other great houses in which he has been employed, or he might simply have followed Mrs Baddeley, without her being at all aware of it. It is not quite so ridiculous a theory as you maintain, Miss Crawford. Indeed, I wondered at the time why Mr Crawford was so determined to pay his call that evening, late and dark as it was. It might have waited until the morning, might it not? But for reasons of his own, your brother insisted on presenting himself at the Park without delay. Having gone thus far, let me postulate a little further. Let us say that your brother returned to the Park some days earlier than he would have us believe, and that he encountered his wife, fresh off the coach from London. Let us say that they argued — argued so bitterly that he was moved to strike her. Faced with the full enormity of his crime, he flees the estate, but not without first perceiving Miss Julia in the park. He does not know what she has seen — or if she has indeed seen any thing — but when he returns some days later, feigning to have arrived directly from Enfield, he discovers that this possible witness has been all this time unconscious. He has an unlooked-for opportunity to silence her for ever, and he seizes it. Without remorse.'

There was no doubt of the colour in her cheeks now, but the reason for it was not entirely clear to him. It might be anger at his impertinence, but it might equally be fear of discovery. Ever since he had learned that Crawford was Miss Price's abductor, he had been convinced that he was by far her most likely killer. Logic, observation, and experience all argued for it, and if it was indeed so, he had no doubt that this young woman was in her brother's confidence; Crawford would have confessed every thing to her on his return, even if she had not known of his plans for the elopement until after it had taken place. Indeed, Maddox could easily see Mary Crawford as far more than a mere *confidante;* he knew she had loved the girl, but she loved her brother more, and if Julia Bertram's silence was the only means to save him from the gallows, then it was a price she would be prepared to pay. If there was a woman in existence, who would have the courage, the resolution, and the *sang-froid* to carry through such a crime, he could believe Miss Crawford to be that woman.

'I do not believe him capable of such a thing,' she said at last, in a tone of utter dejection, as if all her strength were gone.

'You did not believe him capable of lying, and yet he did.'

She turned to look at him, as he continued, 'He lied to you about being at Sir Robert Ferrars's estate — indeed, I believe he even wrote you a letter that he claimed to have sent from there, which can only have been designed to deceive you. And if that were not enough, he lied to you about his marriage. I am sorry to be the bearer of such news — believe me, or not, as you will, but it gives me no pleasure to tell you this. I have just this hour received word from Fraser in London. He has spoken to Mrs Jellett, the gentlewoman who keeps the lodgings in Portman-square, and it is not a pretty story she had to tell. There were vehement arguments almost from the day they moved in — arguments loud enough to wake the rest of the house, and to make Mrs

Jellett apprehensive for the reputation of her establishment. And that, I am sorry to say, was not all. The day before Mr Crawford departed — without settling their bills — there was a quarrel of such ferocity that Mrs Jellett was constrained to call the constable. She saw the marks of violence with her own eyes. And yet he told me — as he no doubt told *you* — that they were happy.'

He watched her for a moment, awaiting a response, but she kept her eyes fixed firmly ahead.

'All things considered, Miss Crawford,' he said at last, 'I believe my enquiries are nearing their conclusion. Having spoken to you, I am more and more confident of that. An event is imminent. Yes indeed, an event is imminent.'

Henry did not return from his ride for some hours, and the shadows were lengthening across the parsonage lawn, when Mary at last heard the sound of a horse in the stable-yard. Her sister had tried in vain to induce her to come indoors and take some rest, and had only with the greatest reluctance been persuaded to return to the house. Mary walked to the archway that led from the drive to the yard, and stood watching

Henry, as he dismounted. He had provided himself with a black coat and arm-band, and she saw at once, and with inexpressible pain, that the assumption of formal mourning appeared to have deprived him of his quick, light step, and the poised and confident air that had so distinguished him in the past; he seemed weary to his very soul, and when he looked up and saw her, she knew from his face that the same desperate weariness was also visible in her own.

'Will you walk with me, Henry? Mr Maddox has been here.'

He looked at her, and then nodded gravely. 'Of course. But take care *how* you talk to me. Do not tell me any thing now, which Mr Maddox would not want you to disclose. I would not wish you entangled in my own difficulties any more than is absolutely necessary. I would protect you from that, even if I can do nothing else.'

She sighed. 'I do believe he spoke to me with the express intent that I should convey every word of it to you. The more I see of him, the more I think this to be the most insidious of all his schemes. He issues information, little by little, here and there, and then sits back to watch how it takes its effect — how we behave, what we do, what we say. It is as if we are all his puppets —

mere clockwork toys, or pawns on a chess-board he can manoeuvre at his pleasure.'

'In that case,' said Henry, with a gloomy smile, 'I cannot be afraid of hearing any thing you wish to say. Do not check yourself. Tell me whatever you like.'

It was not long in the telling. The death of Julia Bertram, the suspicions of Maddox, and the news from London, were all told in a very few words. Such was the sympathy between brother and sister, so deep their mutual love and understanding, that she needed only to relate the facts, for him to comprehend all that she had suffered, and all that she now feared.

When she had finished, he drew her arm through his, as they walked, and she could see that he was troubled.

'I do not know what pains me more, Mary: the grief you are feeling on account of Julia Bertram, or my own shame at having lied to you.' He flushed. 'In that respect, if no other, Maddox told you the truth — which is more than I can say on my own account. I did lie about being at Ferrars's place, but I did so because I did not want to put you in an invidious position, by asking you, in your turn, to conceal where I really was from our sister and the Bertrams. And I lied about the true state of relations between myself and Fanny because — well, because I was ashamed. Embarrassed and ashamed — that is the truth of it. I did not want to admit that a course of action I undertook from motives of sheer mercenary selfishness, and which has injured so many, did nothing but bring misery on her, and humiliation on myself. When all the excitement of the intrigue was over, a few — a very few — days were sufficient to teach me a bitter lesson. I learned to value sweetness of temper, purity of mind, and excellence of principles in a wife, because I knew by then I would never find them in the woman I had married. I had thought such qualities insignificant compared to the far greater misery of pecuniary distress; I had thought the comforts of rank, position, and money would far outweigh the little inconveniences of a bitter and spiteful wife, who would forever be reminding me that I had dragged her down from the exalted sphere of life to which she might have aspired. Barely two days in London proved to her that she might have bought herself a title with a fortune as large as hers, and she never thereafter allowed me to forget it.'

They walked a little further in silence, before he turned to her. 'Are you cold, Mary? Your hands are shaking.'

'Our sister will scold,' she said, attempting a smile. 'I have, as usual, forgotten to bring my shawl. Please, go on.'

'There is not much else to tell. You know my character, Mary — you know my faults, as well as I know them myself. In short, I could not trust myself. Indeed, I should defy any man of warm spirits and natural ardour of mind to govern his temper in the face of such incessant and violent recriminations. She had raised her hand to me once; I did not stay to be tempted to pay her back in kind.'

Mary looked at him in horror, only now comprehending the full import of what he was saying, and how it related to what Maddox had told her. '*She* raised her hand to *you?*'

He nodded. 'I do not cut a very manly figure, do I?' he said, with grim irony. 'A man beaten about the face by his own wife — how could I hold my head up in public ever again? I would be laughed out of every club in London, and pilloried for a hen-pecked husband and emasculated milksop.' He laughed, but the sound was hollow, and his smile was forced.

'And so, you left her?' she said, gently.

'To my everlasting shame. She did not leave me, *I* left *her* — left her alone in town, where she had no friend but me. *My own wife.* I only found out that she had gone when I had a letter from Mrs Jellett, asking me for the money owed on our lodgings. She had presumed — why should she not? — that Fanny had followed me to the address in Drury-lane I had confided to her. I knew better. I returned to Portman-square, and began to search for her. That part, at least, is true.'

'And Enfield? I still cannot comprehend why you should have chosen to go there.'

'It was the only place I could think of where I might hope for a moment's peace and solitude — some where I might gain a little breathing time, while I prepared myself to face the Bertrams.'

He stopped and turned to face her, his face grey with unease. 'All I can say is, that it did not seem such an injudicious choice *then.* But as a consequence I cannot prove I was not here in Mansfield when she arrived. I cannot prove I did not kill her. I cannot even say — with truth — that I did not want to be free of her; that I did not, in some small and shameful part of my heart, *want* her dead. Maddox has his motive, Mary, and he is gaining on me — he is closing in. If he does not soon find the true perpetrator of this crime, I am a dead man.'

CHAPTER XIX

Mary went to her bed that night in such an agony of mind as she had never yet suffered. The tumults of the last dreadful weeks were nothing to what she endured now; she had not known the human mind capable of bearing such vicissitudes. She saw, only too clearly, what she should do; it was not merely her knowledge of her brother that told her he was guiltless, but the words that she had heard from Julia Bertram's own lips, and which no-one else would ever hear now, if she herself were not to communicate them. But was she prepared to take such a terrible step? Was she willing to send the man she loved to certain death on the gallows? Because that, she believed, would be the inevitable consequence of her disclosure. Henry might have more obvious motives for killing his wife, but she knew that some might consider Edmund Norris to have reasons that were scarcely less cogent, and he, like Henry, had no alibi for the morning of Fanny's death. Were Julia Bertram's last words to become generally known, the evidence against him would appear all but conclusive. It was an appalling prospect: say nothing, and watch her innocent brother condemned; speak, and see Edmund hang in his place.

She could not imagine any possibility of sleep, and lay awake for many hours, passing from feelings of sickness to shudderings of horror, and from hot fits of fever to cold. But shortly before two o'clock her bodily weakness finally overcame her, and she slipped into a shallow and disturbed slumber, only to wake at dawn in a terror that made such an impression upon her, as almost to overpower her reason. She had fallen into a dark and wandering dream, in which she was barefoot, walking across the park, as the mist rose from the hollows, and the owls shrieked in the dark trees. All at once she found herself at the edge of the channel — the dank and fetid pit yawned beneath her very feet. She was overcome with fear, and dared not go any farther, but some thing drew her on, and she saw with revulsion that the body was still there at the bottom of the chasm, still wrapped in its crimson cloak and bloody dress, the face already rotting, and maggots eating at the suppurating flesh. She turned away, sickened, but Maddox stood behind her, and took hold of her arm, forcing her to look, forcing her to the very brink. And now she saw that Henry and Edmund were standing at either end of the trench — she saw them face each other, their countenances blank of all expression, then draw their swords with a rasp of polished metal. Minute after minute they fought over the body, notwithstanding all her prayers and tears, trampling the dissolving carcase beneath their feet, and staining their shirts with runnels of blood that smoked in the cold air. Then in the space of a moment, Henry was suddenly in the ascendant, pinning his opponent against the earth, and holding his sword across Edmund's throat; Mary cried out, 'No! No!' and as her brother looked up to where she stood, Edmund drew back his sword, and ran his rival through the thigh. Henry slipped to his knees, his eyes all the while on Mary's face, fixing her with a look of unutterable agony and reproach. She turned to Edmund for mercy, but he rejected her pleas with arrogant disdain, and pushed the point of his sword slowly, slowly through his adversary's heart. She crawled towards him, as Maddox threw earth and dirt down upon her dying brother, and the rotting corpse of his dead wife; then she awoke in a cold sweat, real tears on her cheeks, and the frightful images still before her eyes.

She did not know how long it was she lay there, trembling and weeping, before she felt able to sit up. It was still dark outside. She had never given any credence to dreams, deeming them to be but the incoherent vagaries of the sleeping mind, and no prognostic or prophecy of what was to come; but while her intellect might attribute her vision to the uneasiness of a weakened and disturbed constitution, her conscience told her otherwise. Her imagination had forced her to contemplate the true nature of the choice she must now make; her heart shrank from the dread prospect, but her mind was clear; she was quite determined, and her resolution varied not.

As soon as the servants were awake she sent a message to the Park, requesting an interview at the belvedere that morning, then made a hasty breakfast, and went out into the garden.

By the time she heard the great clock at Mansfield chime nine, she had been waiting at the appointed place for more than an hour, and the bench offering an uninterrupted view to the house, she was able to watch him approaching for some moments, before he was aware of her presence. His step, she saw, was measured, and his comportment upright. When she rose to her feet and walked to meet him, she perceived, with a pang, that his step quickened.

'Good morning, Miss Crawford.'

'Mr Norris.'

'I must thank you, once more,' he continued, 'for the kind service you have afforded my family at this sad time. I have heard from Mrs Baddeley of your exertions in the last stages of Julia's illness, and I know that you did all in your power to nurse her back to health. We are all, as you might imagine, quite overcome. To lose a daughter and a sister in such terrible circumstances, and so soon after the death of her cousin, it is — well, it is intolerable. My poor uncle will come home only to preside at a double funeral, though his presence will, at least, be an indescribable comfort to my aunt. We expect him in a few days.'

There was a silence, and he perceived, for the first time, that she had not met his gaze.

'Miss Crawford? Are you quite well?'

'I am very tired, Mr Norris. I will, if you permit, sit down for a few minutes.'

They walked back, without speaking, to the bench, too preoccupied by their different thoughts to notice a figure in the shadows, just beyond the wall of the belvedere, listening intently to every word they spoke.

Mary took her seat, and was silent a moment, endeavouring to quiet the beating of her heart.

'I have dreaded this moment, Mr Norris, and more than once I felt my courage would fail me before I came face to face with you. Now that I am here, I beg you will hear me out. I asked to see you because there is something I must tell you. It relates to your cousin.'

He frowned a little at this, but said nothing.

'Some hours before Julia lapsed into her final lethargy, she became very distraught, and began to talk wildly. I did not perceive, at first, what had distressed her to such a dreadful extent, but I am afraid it soon became only too clear. As you know, she was walking in the park the day Miss Price returned; I now know that she saw something that morning, and she was frightened half out of her wits by the memory of it. I believe, in fact, that she saw quite clearly who it was who struck her cousin the fatal blow. She was talking incoherently about the blood — on her face, on her hands. It must have been a barbarous thing for such a young and delicate girl to witness.'

She rose from her seat and walked forward a few paces, unable to look at him; she had hardly the strength to speak, and knew that if she did not say what she must at that very moment, she might never be able to do so.

'She — she — mentioned a name. I am sure you do not need me to repeat it. It is — too painful; for you to hear, or for me to utter. I only tell you this now because I am convinced that Mr Maddox is about to arrest my brother for this crime. I, alone of everyone at Mansfield, know that he absolutely did not do this thing of which he will be accused. I therefore have no choice but to go to Mr Maddox and tell him what I have just told you. Once I have done so, you and I will probably have no opportunity to speak; indeed,' she said, in a broken accent, 'we may never see each other again.'

Had Mary been able to turn towards him and encounter his eye, she would have seen in his face such agony of soul, such a confusion of contradictory emotions, as would have filled her with compassion, however oppressed she was by quite other feelings at that moment. He rose and moved towards her, and made as if to put a hand on her shoulder, but checked himself, and turned away.

'I am grateful,' he said in a voice devoid of expression, 'for the information you have been so good as to impart. I wish you good morning.'

He gave an awkward bow, and walked stiffly away.

She had enough self-control to restrain her tears until he was out of hearing, but when they came they were the bitterest tears she had ever had cause to shed. Notwithstanding Julia's dying words, notwithstanding the seemingly incontestable nature of what Mary had heard, she had never entirely lost the hope that he might have an innocent explanation. That he would seize her hands, and tell her she was mistaken, that he was as blameless as her brother. But he had not. She had not seen him for some days, and in that time her knowledge of his character had undergone so material a change, as to make her doubt her own judgment. How could she have been in love with such a man — how could she justify an affection that was not only passionate, but also, as she had thought, rational, kindled as it had been by his modesty, gentleness, benevolence, and steadiness of mind? She must henceforth regard him as a man capable of murder, a man who could kill the woman to whom he was betrothed in the most brutal manner, without any apparent sign of remorse. And even if it were possible for her heart to acquit him, in some measure, of the death of Fanny, on the grounds of a sudden wild anger, or insupportable provocation, how could she ever forgive him for the part he had played in Julia's demise — a gentle, sweet-tempered girl for whom he had appeared to feel deep and genuine affection? And when she had confronted him with the evidence of his guilt he had merely reverted to the cold and impenetrable reserve that had characterised their first acquaintance.

She wondered now whether Henry's estimation of him had not been correct all along, and she had seen in Edmund some thing she had wished to see, but which bore little relation to his true character. And much as she had tried to dismiss it, she had never fully rid herself of a slight but insistent unease she had felt ever since the dreadful day when they had discovered Fanny's body. Even in the midst of her terror she had thought his behaviour singular: she had told herself since, that his composure was that of a rational man, undaunted by the horrors of death, and concerned only to alleviate her own distress; but now she knew, beyond question, that it was not so: he had known all along what he would find in that trench, and prepared himself, however unconsciously, to behold it without recoiling. And yet she could not entirely quell the bewitching conviction that he had loved her, nor forget how she had felt with his eyes upon her. Whatever his fate, whatever his crime, she could not imagine thinking of another man as a husband. Was it an attachment to govern her whole life?

It was enough to shake the experience of twenty. And though she knew it to be her duty to go at once to Maddox and put an end to this suspense, she did not yet feel capable of such an irrevocable deed, and sought the most retired and unfrequented areas of the park, hoping by prayer and reflection to calm her mind, and steel herself against the final act of absolute condemnation. It was near the hour of luncheon when she returned to the parsonage, and she was in hopes that her walk in the fresh air had sufficed to wipe away every outward memento of what she had undergone since she was last within its doors. But she need not have been uneasy. Her sister came running towards her, as she entered the garden gate, her handkerchief in her hand, and her face in a high colour.

'Oh Mary, Mary! Such news, such shocking news! Mr Norris has confessed! He has told Mr Maddox that he killed Fanny! Who would have believed such a frightful and incredible thing?'

Mary was not quite so unprepared for this intelligence as her sister might have supposed, but it was not without its effect; she staggered, and felt she might faint, and a moment later felt Henry's arm about her waist, supporting her.

'Come Mary,' he said softly. 'This is a most dreadful shock, and you have already had too much to bear. Come inside, and I will send for some tea.'

She did not have the energy to refuse, and a few minutes later found herself sitting by the parlour fire, with her sister fussing about her, chattering all the while about the astonishing developments at the Park.

'Mrs Baddeley told me about it herself, when I encountered her in the lane. It appears Mr Norris went to Mr Maddox this very morning, and told him the whole appalling tale — how he met Miss Price that morning by accident, and they had the most terrible quarrel. He claims he never intended to harm her, but when she told him she was married, he was seized of a sudden by a desperate anger. It seems he does not remember much of what ensued, and it was not until the body was found, that it was brought home to him exactly what he had done.'

'That being the case,' said Dr Grant heavily, 'it is a pity he did not make his confession then and there, and save us all a world of trouble and scandal.'

'He has saved my neck, at least,' said Henry. 'I owe him a debt of gratitude for that.'

'*You*, sir,' replied Dr Grant, 'have almost as much cause for remorse and repentance as Mr Norris can have. *You*, sir, deserve, if not the gallows, then the public punishment of utter disgrace, for your own part in this infamous affair. *You*, sir, have indulged in thoughtless selfishness, and cold-hearted vanity for far too long. *You*, sir, would do better to take this unhappy event as a dire warning of what God apportions to the wicked, and hope by sincere amendment and reform, to avoid a juster appointment hereafter.'

'A pretty good lecture, upon my word!' said Henry, sarcastically. 'Was it part of your last sermon?'

'Come, come,' said Mrs Grant, quickly, 'I am sure Henry is well aware that he has a good deal to answer for. I must say,' she

395

continued with a sigh, 'I never thought to hear myself say such a thing, but it's Mrs Norris I pity. I cannot imagine what she must be suffering.'

'She will have to bear much worse if he is convicted,' said Dr Grant. 'As a gentleman, Norris might hope to avoid being dragged through the public streets to the taunts of the mob, but birth and fortune will not preserve him from the gallows. He deserves no better, and should expect no less; it will be a meritorious retribution for a crime so obnoxious to the laws of God and man.'

Mary could endure no more, and leaping from her chair, ran out of the room. It was one thing to act as she had done, from the heroism of principle, and a determination to do her duty; it was quite another to hear Edmund's fate so freely, so coolly canvassed. She took refuge in a far corner of the garden, which offered no view of the Park, feeling the tears running down her cheeks, without being at any trouble to check them. It was some minutes before she heard the sound of footsteps, and looked up to see her brother walking towards her.

As soon as he reached her, he took her hand, and pressed it kindly. 'I am no great admirer of our brother-in-law, but you must forgive him, if you can, on this occasion. I do not think he has the least idea of your feelings for Mr Norris. Whatever our sister says, I believe you are more to be pitied than his unspeakable mother.'

Mary nodded, a spasm in her throat. 'It must have been the work of a moment — a temporary insanity — under sudden and terrible distress of mind —'

Henry looked away, uncomfortable.

'What is it, Henry?' she cried, catching his arm. 'Tell me, please.'

She would not be denied, and he did, at length, capitulate. 'Very well. It was not, perhaps, so unpremeditated an act as you have just described. I have not told you this before, as there seemed no necessity to do so, but when we were in Portman-square, Fanny wrote to Mr Norris, to tell him of her marriage. I heard her give the messenger the directions to the White House.'

'And what did she say in this letter?'

'I did not see it all, only some scraps. What I *did* see was couched in the scornful and imperious language that I was, by then, coming to expect from her. I do, however, recall one phrase. It was some thing to the effect that "I wonder now if my fortune was always the principal attraction on your part, given that I have now discovered that you are very much in need of it".'

'I do not understand — Edmund has an extensive property.'

'Not, perhaps, as extensive as we have all been induced to believe. And it seems that this is not the only matter about which Mr Norris has dissembled. Having received that letter, he would have known that Fanny was married, but he said nothing of this to anyone at the Park.'

Mary's heart sank still further. 'I suppose no killer would willingly draw such attention upon himself.'

Henry pressed her hand once more. 'But he has, at least, confessed. That can only assist him at the assizes. We must hope for clemency.' He stopped, seeing the expression on her face. 'Mary?'

She took a deep breath, and looked him in the eyes. 'He did confess, but not voluntarily. I myself forced his hand.'

She had, until that moment, adhered to Maddox's request to keep the manner of Julia Bertram's death a secret, but she saw no reason to respect his wishes any further, now that he had apprehended his killer. She saw at once that her brother was shocked and disgusted at what she had to tell him, far more shocked and disgusted, indeed, than he had been at the death of his own wife.

'But she was a mere child — an innocent *child* —'

'I know, I know — but if she did indeed see what happened that day — if he feared she was recovering and would soon tell what she knew —'

Henry dropped her hand and walked away, pacing across the grass, his face intent and thoughtful.

'Did you hear what our sister said, Mary? There was no mention, as far as I can recall, that Mr Norris has confessed to killing Julia. Fanny, yes, but not Julia. That is curious, is it not?'

It had not occurred to her before, and she hardly knew how to explain it. 'I cannot tell, Henry, nothing seems to make sense.'

'But this, indeed, does *not* make sense. From what you say, aside from good Mrs Baddeley, no-one at the Park is aware how Julia died — with one exception: our friend Maddox. So why has he not confronted Mr Norris with that fact? Why has he not extorted a second confession?'

Mary looked helpless. 'I do not know. It is unaccountable.'

Henry was still pacing, still pensive. It was some minutes before he spoke again, but when he did, his words made every nerve in her body thrill with transport. 'Do you really believe him to be guilty of these terrible crimes?'

'I do not want to believe it, but what choice do I have? I heard what Julia Bertram said.'

'But from what you say, she only cried out his name — that does not prove any thing in itself. Is it at all possible, do you think, that she was calling to him for help? We know he was in the park at that time. Might she have seen him at a distance, and called to him, even if he never heard her — even if he never even knew she was there?'

'Then why has he confessed? Why admit to a crime he did not commit?'

Henry took her hands in both his own. 'Has it crossed your mind, even for the briefest of moments, that he may have been protecting *you?*'

'But why? Why should I need his protection?'

'Come and sit down, and tell me, as exactly as you can, what you said to Mr Norris this morning.'

She sat down heavily on the bench, her mind all disorder, trying to recapture her precise words. 'I — I told him that Julia had spoken a name, but that I did not need to repeat it. I said I could not allow you to be falsely accused, and that I had no choice but to go to Maddox. And I said,' her voice sinking, 'that he and I might never see each other again.'

She was by now crying bitterly, but her brother, by contrast, was in a state of excited agitation.

'So you never, at any point, accused him directly?'

She shook her head.

'In fact, my dear Mary,' he said, coming to her side and taking her hand, 'every thing you said might have led him to believe that *you* were confessing to *him*.'

It was gently spoken, but every word had the force of a heavy blow. She gazed at him in amazement, her mind torn between bewilderment and mortification. The shock of conviction was almost as agonising as it was longed for; he was not guilty, but he was willing to appear so for her sake, and she alone had placed him in this peril.

'But Henry, this is dreadful!' she cried. 'I must explain — how could he have believed me capable of —'

'You believed *him* capable, did you not?'

'I must go to him — to Maddox — I must tell him —'

'Calm yourself, my dear sister. You are not thinking clearly. We do not even know where Mr Norris is at this moment. He may, even now, be on his way to Northampton. And as for Mr Maddox, I fear you will need more proof than this to convince a man of his make. He has his reward money already in his sights, and he will not relinquish a suspect who has so conveniently confessed, unless we can present him with another equally promising quarry. Our best course will be to convince Mr Norris that his heroic concern for you is not necessary; if he can be persuaded to withdraw his confession, we may be better placed to counter Maddox.'

'But how are we to do such a thing? If we do not even know where he is?'

'Leave that to me, my dear Mary. I will go at once to the Park, and see what I may discover. I do not expect the family to see me — that would be too much of an intrusion — but the steward, McGregor, will be as well-informed as any body, and he still has regard for me, even if some others at the Park do not. You, in the mean time, should take some rest. I will return as soon as I am able.'

She had no better plan to propose, and returned to the house after watching him mount his horse, and head down the drive. She heartily wished to avoid going into company, but she knew that any further absence would only attract more notice and enquiry, so instead of retiring to her room she joined her sister and Dr Grant in the parlour. She could not hope for restraint from her sister, in the face of such extraordinary news, but she did hope that, by suggesting a game of cribbage before dinner, she might limit the scope of her speculations. The cards were brought, and for the next hour the reckonings of the game were interspersed with Mrs Grant's wondering conjectures.

'And that makes thirty-one, Mary. And to think, all this time the killer was right under our very noses — and for it to be Mr Norris too! — it just shews that you can never judge by appearances — I always thought him such a placid and agreeable gentleman! Four in hand and eight in crib. And to think, anyone of us might have fallen prey to his murderous urges, and been slaughtered in our beds at any moment!'

'I think that most improbable, my dear,' said Dr Grant, looking up from his copy of *Fordyce's Sermons*. 'According to the eminent authorities on the subject whose works I have perused, Norris does not exhibit any of the recognised characteristics of lunacy, and is therefore most unlikely to be an indiscriminate killer of the type to which you refer.'

'That may very well be the case, Dr Grant,' replied his wife, 'but Mrs Baddeley told me his own servants are now afraid to go near him, fearing that he is more than half-crazed. You are to deal, Mary; shall I deal for you?'

The time passed heavily, and Mary was impatient for sounds of her brother's return; indeed, she could not comprehend why such a simple errand should have taken him so long, but when Henry did, at last, present himself in the parlour, the explanation was not tardy in coming forth.

'I hope I have not been the means of delaying your dinner,' he said, as he handed his gloves to the servant, 'but I have been unavoidably and unexpectedly detained. Sir Thomas has returned to Mansfield.'

'Sir Thomas returned!' exclaimed Mrs Grant. 'But I thought he was not expected for another two days at least?'

'It seems that he made rather quicker progress on the road than he had originally hoped — or than his physician had advised. But I am afraid he had distressing news to hear on his return. Having so far outstripped his expected course, the intelligence had not yet reached him of his daughter's death. It must have been a cruel blow.'

'And a heavy aggravation to what he will already have suffered upon hearing of Miss Price's murder,' said Dr Grant. 'Not to mention her unseemly marriage. I imagine he had words to say on that subject to *you*, sir.'

Henry flushed. 'Once I learned of his return, I went directly to offer Sir Thomas my respects. He was, indeed, so good as to receive me.'

Mary could only imagine the particulars of that interview, and her brother's conscious and awkward manner served to confirm her suspicions; Dr Grant might be overly condemnatory in his reproofs, but impartiality would not have denied that Sir Thomas had good cause to be aggrieved, and Henry as good cause for self-reproach.

'He was not pleased — how could he be? — but I can assure you, Dr Grant, that he remained both just and reasonable throughout, even in the face of such provocations as he has suffered. Indeed, I do not think I have appreciated, till now, the true benevolence of his character. He has such a fine and dignified manner, that one scarcely distinguishes the man, from the head of the house. He did not scruple to give me his opinion of my conduct, but he was prepared to listen to what I was able to say in my defence, and concluded by observing that the one consolation he has derived since his return,' this with a side glance at Mary, 'is the discovery that I am no longer suspected of any involvement in the death of my wife.'

'I imagine that will be but poor solace for the loss of her fortune,' retorted Dr Grant, with a sniff.

'And what about Mr Norris?' interjected his wife. 'Did you discover any more on that subject?'

This time Henry did not meet Mary's eye. 'He is to be taken to Northampton in three days' time. There are, it seems, some matters of procedure to be resolved with the magistrate, and Mr Maddox is reluctant to hand over his charge until they are settled. I fancy Sir Thomas was not much pleased to find his room — and his claret — had been appropriated in his absence, and by such a man as that. I do not think he had been at home more than an hour when he saw me, but it had sufficed to return his room to all its previous peace and stateliness.'

'So where is Mr Maddox now?' asked Mrs Grant.

'He has moved, as a temporary expedient, into lodgings with the steward, my old friend McGregor. Mr Norris remains, for the moment, at the White House, under guard.'

'Let us hope *he* is dispatched bag and baggage long before the funerals,' said Mrs Grant. 'Imagine the scandal if it were otherwise! Even Northampton would be too close.'

'That, I am afraid, is not very likely, my dear sister,' said Henry. 'Indeed, sir,' turning to Dr Grant, 'Sir Thomas bade me inform you that, if it is convenient, he wishes the burial services to take place the day after tomorrow.'

CHAPTER XX

Much as Mary might have hoped for an opportunity to see Edmund the following day, Henry was skilful enough to dissuade her from it, arguing that, even if she had no care for propriety, she could not hope to see him alone in a house full of servants, and when he was under close surveillance by one of Maddox's underlings. In her brother's view, there was nothing for it but to await the day of the funerals, when the White House domestics would be absent at church, and Henry might be of service in distracting Stornaway for a few moments while she slipped into the house. They had talked, and they had been silent; he had reasoned, she had resisted; but she had ended by acquiescing.

She spent, as a result, a miserable and restless day, unable to work, unable to read, and reluctant even to leave the house. Henry was absent in Northampton on business with Sir Thomas's attorney, and Mrs Grant, perfectly unaware of what was passing in her sister's mind, encouraged her to take advantage of the dry weather and walk up to the Park.

'Even if her ladyship is not well enough to see you, you might sit for an hour with Miss Bertram, or see the corpse of poor Miss Julia, and tell me how it appears.'

Mary could barely repress a shudder; she had never told her sister that it was she who had prepared Fanny Price's disfigured body for the grave, and she could not face such another experience, not even to pay a final farewell to her sweet dead friend.

By late afternoon the weather had changed; the clouds rolled in, and the sky grew dark. Mary sat at the window watching the first dismal drops of rain, wondering if Edmund might also be looking out, as she was, and whether his thoughts were drawn to her, as hers were, so irresistibly, to him. She could not bear even to contemplate how she must now appear in his eyes: the cold-blooded murderess of the woman he was to have married, driven to an unforgiveable transgression by the basest motives of jealousy and resentment, and too craven to admit to what she had done. Any esteem, any respect, he might once have accorded her must now be utterly done away, and yet he loved her still. He must do so, or why would he be prepared to forfeit his own life in place of hers? To face the gallows without flinching, for love of her. She could not bear to contemplate the pain he must be suffering, and was racked the more from the knowledge that it was in her power to relieve it, could she but find five minutes to speak with him, and tell him the truth.

But that all-satisfying moment would have to wait. She had first to endure an evening with the Grants, without even her brother's company to support her. Her mind was abstracted and dissatisfied; she could hardly eat any thing at dinner, and could only with difficulty govern her vexation at the tediousness of her brother-in-law, who elected to prepare them for the morrow's solemnities by filling the interval before bed-time with a peroration from Bishop Taylor's *Holy Living and Dying,* concerning 'the Contingencies and Treatings of our departed friends after death, in order to their Burial', which he delivered in a tone of the most monotonous pomposity. The good Bishop had provided numerous remedies against impatience, but none that were of any efficacy in stilling Mary's eagerness, or calming her longing to be some where else altogether.

It continued to rain all night, and Charles Maddox was woken the following morning by the sound of the wind in the trees outside his window. He no longer had such a view as he had enjoyed at the Park, but the steward's wife was hospitable, and the food only a little inferior to that served in the servants' hall. By the time he had breakfasted, and spoken at some length to Fraser, who had returned to Mansfield the night before, the funeral bell was already tolling from the tower of Mansfield church. He had dressed in his black coat, and now added the arm-band of crape, which was always carried with him in his luggage, and had seen much service over the years, before making his way to the Park to join the rest of the household now assembling in the hall. He did not put himself forward to pay his respects; indeed, it suited his purpose to remain silent and unattended to, and observe how the family conducted itself at such a pass. Sir Thomas, he saw, looked thin and haggard, the marks of his recent illness given stronger emphasis by his mourning clothes, and his son stood at his side, ready to offer his arm should that become necessary. Maddox had not thought to see the

411

ladies of the house; in his experience, fashionable London ladies were never expected to attend family obsequies, but he suspected that the absence of Lady Bertram and her daughter might be attributed more to genuine feeling, than the mere observance of the proper etiquette. A few moments later a deeper and almost unnatural silence began to take possession of the room, and as the whispers died away, Maddox heard the sounds of the approaching horses.

The carriages came to a halt before the open door, the two hearses drawn by plumed horses, the first curtained in black, the second in maiden white. Maddox saw, with no little consternation, that the cortège was accompanied by Henry Crawford on horseback. The master of the house then took his place in the family carriage, and a few moments later the solemn procession began to make its slow way down the sweep. By the time they reached the church, the long line of servants following on foot had been considerably augmented by tenants from the Mansfield estate, and the carriages of the best local families, their blinds pulled down.

As the Mansfield footmen carried the two coffins into the nave, and Maddox took his own seat near the back of the church, he saw that Mrs Grant and her sister were already seated in the parsonage pew. He found it hard to believe that it was only a few days since he had last seen Mary Crawford, so changed was her appearance. Her face was drawn, and there was a hollowness about her eyes that did not augur well. He wondered, for a moment only, whether he might not be following the wrong course, but told himself that he was allowing his partiality for this woman to impede his professional judgment. Knowing what he did of Dr Grant, he could not hope for brief eulogia on the deceased, but all the same, he found himself unexpectedly affected by the signs of genuine grief that attended the clergyman's account of Julia Bertram's short life; her father and brother were visibly distressed, and her young maid, Polly Evans, wept inconsolably in Mrs Baddeley's motherly arms.

When Dr Grant turned his attention to the late Mrs Crawford, Maddox was aware of an immediate and decided change in the mood in the church; there was little evidence of sorrow now, whether real or feigned, and the few murmurings that came to Maddox's ears were expressions of sympathy for the plight of Mr Norris, a fact which he found both surprising and instructive. Nor did Maddox envy the clergyman his task: it was clear that, were it any other young woman but Sir Thomas's niece, Dr Grant would have deemed it his Christian duty to present her fate as an awful warning to the congregation, and a caution against the evils of lust and avarice, but he was painfully constrained by the presence of his patron, and the demands of common politeness. It demanded all the ingenuity of a casuist to steer a safe course through such dangerous waters; to bury Mrs Crawford without praising her, and give an account of her life without referring to the husband who had seduced her, or the cousin who would be charged on the morrow with having done her to death. The husband, at least, had the good grace to appear abashed, and while Henry Crawford held his head high in the family pew, there was a spot of colour on each cheek that spoke either of a considerable suppressed anger, or an inner regret rising to wretchedness; even Maddox, with all his aptitude for physiognomy, could not determine which. It was of a piece with what he had come to know of the man, and he laid up this latest observation alongside the new intelligence Fraser had brought with him from Enfield. Henry Crawford was a conundrum that appeared to grow more complex the more closely he examined it; he had yet to decide if the solution to that conundrum was a matter of intellectual curiosity, or some thing more significant, but he hoped he might not have to wait very much longer to obtain his answer.

When the service was concluded, the gentlemen rose to accompany the coffins down into the family vault, and the assembled mourners waited in respectful silence; a silence broken only by the quiet weeping of Evans, and the whispered words of comfort offered by the housekeeper. Several minutes elapsed before Sir Thomas reappeared, his own face as white as if iced over by death. His halting progress down the aisle, supported by his son, was pitiful to see, and Maddox wondered whether the old gentleman's health might never recover from the series of shocks he had sustained. Maddox was one of the last of the mourners to attain the door, and what he saw outside did not surprise him: there was a crowd of people thronging the churchyard, but both Henry Crawford and his sister were gone.

The knell was still tolling behind her as Mary made her way quickly to the rear gate of the White House. She had only visited the house once, quite early in her stay at the parsonage, but she remembered it very clearly, having spent an extremely tedious hour being taken through every room by Mrs Norris, who did not scruple to point out every chair, table, silver fork, and finger-glass, and who could enumerate the price of every item with as much facility as an agent shewing the house to a prospective tenant. Henry had warned her to remain out of sight until she saw him on the terrace with Stornaway; the man was said to be partial to snuff, when he could get it, and Henry had still a plentiful supply of fine Macouba that he had purchased in St James's. It was hardly subtle, by way of a bribe, and should the man prove suspicious, Henry was not at all sure how he was to explain his sudden presence in the house; if pressed, he intended to claim he bore a message from Sir Thomas, enquiring as to the arrangements for Mr Norris's removal, but it was, at best, a poor excuse, as any astute sentinel would know; they must hope that Maddox chose his subalterns for their physical not their mental prowess.

The minutes passed slowly by, and Mary began to fear that the White House servants would return long before she would have the opportunity to see Edmund; but just at the moment when she was about to give up hope, the door opened and she saw her brother and Stornaway emerge onto the terrace. Her heart was by this time beating so hard and so quick, that she could scarcely draw breath, far less move, but move she must; there was no time to be lost. She waited until the two men had disappeared round the side of the house, then slipped up the garden path, and through the open door into the drawing-room. She could hardly believe that she had actually attained the house without being detected, and stood motionless on the threshold, hardly knowing what to do next. She and Henry had spent so long discussing how she might gain access to the house, that they had barely touched upon what she should do once she had achieved it. But her customary self-possession did not fail her; she went quickly to the door, and stood in the hall, listening intently. At first the whole house seemed utterly quiet, but as her senses adjusted to the silence, she perceived that there was a strange, low, rasping sound emanating from a room quite close by; were it not for the time of day, she might have supposed there was someone sleeping there. She crept softly along the hall and stopped at the foot of the staircase; to her left the breakfast-parlour, to her right the dining-room, its door standing ajar. The sound, whatever it was, originated from there. Some thing impelled her forward, she knew not what, and almost without daring to breathe, she placed her hand to the door and pushed it open.

He was there. At the table, as if to eat — and there was, indeed, a plate at his side — but he was no longer sitting, no longer upright; he was slumped over the table, his head between his arms, his face half-concealed. She made a move towards him, then stopped, noticing for the first time the bottle and empty glass at his hand. She had never known him intoxicated — had thought, indeed, that he had an aversion to strong liquor in all its forms — and yet here he was, in the middle of the day, in a state of apparent drunkenness. Her first feeling was one of guilty remorse — had she really brought him to this? — but a moment's further observation led her to question her first response. There was still more than half a bottle of wine remaining, and he could not possibly have been reduced to such a state after imbibing so small a quantity. He bore all the signs of intoxication — the stertorous respiration, the flushed face — but as she moved closer, she could not discern the breath of wine.

'Mr Norris?' she said, hesitatingly. 'May I speak to you for a moment?'

There was no reply.

Summoning all her courage, she put out a hand and took him by the shoulder, and spoke again, as loudly as she dared, 'Mr Norris? Are you awake?'

Once more, she received no reply, but the propinquity in which she now stood allowed to observe him more closely, and she perceived that his stupefaction did not so much resemble the effects of drink, as the terrifying torpor into which Julia Bertram had descended, and from which they had not been able to reclaim her. She reached for the glass at once, and seized it with fumbling fingers; her suspicions were correct — there was a strong odour of laudanum.

'My God!' she cried. 'What have you done — what have you *done?*'

She dragged him to an erect position, his head lolling over one shoulder, and saw, with terror, that his face was beginning to take on the same deep suffusion of blood that she had seen only a few days before. This time, at least, she knew what to do. She moved first towards the bell to ring for assistance, before she recollected that the servants were all absent; she turned towards the door, thinking to call for aid from her brother and Stornaway, but she never reached it. There was already someone standing there, with her hand to the door-handle, and a basket of cutlery over one arm.

'Oh Mrs Norris!' cried Mary, running towards her. 'Thank God that you are here! You must help me — I think Edmund has taken poison — he must have despaired in the face of — but no matter — I fear I am not making myself very clear, but this is exactly what happened with poor Julia — we must act *quickly* — it may already be too late!'

Mrs Norris looked at her for a long moment, then shut the door quietly behind her.

'You would do better to sit down and calm yourself, Miss Crawford. These theatrical performances of yours serve no useful purpose.'

'But — did you not hear me?' she stammered. 'Your son has taken *poison* — we must procure him an emetic — I know what to do — and with your knowledge of remedies you must have such a thing in the house — there is a chance — if we intervene at once that we may —'

'We may *what,* Miss Crawford? Preserve his life so that you may tighten your grip yet further on his heart?'

'I do not know what you mean —'

'*You* were more than half to blame,' she said, advancing towards Mary. 'If it had not been for you, and that blackguard brother of yours, they would be married by now. Once Rushworth was out of the way I thought everything would return to how it should be, but oh no. Your contemptible brother resorted to the most vile arts, to the most depraved, wicked contrivances to lure her away —'

'But even if that were true,' interrupted Mary, 'it is not important *now*, not at this moment. We must act quickly to help Edmund or we will *both* lose him. Please, Mrs Norris — he has taken laudanum — a very great deal of laudanum —'

'I know exactly what he has taken, and I know better than *you* can do what the consequences will be.'

Mary took a step back, hardly knowing what she did. It occurred to her, for the first time, that Mrs Norris did not look quite her usual self; there was an involuntary twitch under one eye, and she seemed to be labouring to catch her breath.

'It was *you*,' said Mary slowly, as the horrifying truth flooded her mind. 'All of this — from the beginning — was *your* doing.'

'You need not look so shocked, Miss Crawford. You are a woman of spirit yourself; indeed, it is the single admirable quality you possess. Do not try to pretend to *me* that you are not capable of resolution and premeditation in the pursuit of what you desire. I have seen you at it every day for months.'

'So it was you who tampered with Mr Gilbert's cordial.'

'I could not risk the girl waking up and accusing me. I could not be sure what she had seen. As soon as Gilbert told me that she might make a full recovery, I knew what I must do.'

'And you are now prepared to do the same to your own *son?*'

Mrs Norris's face became hard and closed. '*He* is no child of *mine*. And in any case, it will be better thus. I do not know what you said to him at the belvedere, but when he returned he was like a man possessed. I tried to explain, but he would not *listen*. He was out of the house before I could stop him, and straight to that odious ruffian, Maddox. But I need not tell *you*, that any sort of trial is completely out of the question. Even to contemplate that a son of my dear late husband's — a *Norris* — might be paraded through the streets of Northampton to the jeers of the common rabble — it is in every way unthinkable. This way it will all be hushed up, and soon everyone will have forgotten that any thing ever happened.'

'*Forgotten?* How can the Bertrams ever forget their daughter? How will any of us forget what happened to Fanny? And to resort to such *violence* — I saw what you did to her, and the memory of it sickens me.'

'As to that, I will admit to falling prey to a momentary impulse — a mere freak of temper. She wrote to me, you know, flaunting her patched-up marriage — rejoicing in the fact that I would probably succumb to an apoplexy when I discovered the name of her husband. Congratulating herself for having escaped Edmund — and the next moment stating that she was even more thankful to have escaped *me. Me!* Do you know what I have done for that girl all these years? Petted and cosseted and brought her forward, day after day, even at the expense of my sister Bertram's children. And all for nothing — *nothing!* And when I met her that morning she threw it all in my face — with such *pleasure* — such malicious enjoyment of my ignominy and humiliation.'

'And did she take an equal delight in your

imminent ruin?' said Mary quietly.

'What's that?' snapped Mrs Norris.

'My brother saw parts of that letter, Mrs Norris. I know that Mrs Crawford referred to your very great need of money — *her* money. That was the real reason why you were so keen on the marriage, was it not? It had nothing to do with your son's happiness, and every thing to do with her vast fortune. It was not the family honour that my brother destroyed, but your own hopes of ever rectifying your perilous financial position. All your scrimping and penny-pinching, *they* were real enough, but this house, your style of life, it was all a sham — a blind. There is no money, is there, Mrs Norris? It has all gone.'

Every thing was clear to Mary now: even the smallest elements of the riddle had found their true place. 'Indeed, it was not merely insults she threw in your face, was it? I have wondered from the start why she had no purse when she was found, but now I think I understand. She actually dared to offer you money. Was that not the final insult? To receive a few miserable shillings from someone who had robbed you of so much, and sealed your ruin? And yet you were so desperate for money, that you kept it, little as it was.'

'How dare *you* stand there and talk to me in such a fashion! What can *you* possibly know of such things?'

Mary began to edge slowly round the edge of the table towards the window. She had already perceived that her sole hope lay in someone hearing their voices, and coming to investigate. If not her brother, then the White House servants; she must do all in her power to keep Mrs Norris talking — even to reason with her, if she could; though one glance at the woman's haggard, ill face was enough to make Mary fear whether she were not already far beyond the reach of either reason or persuasion.

'I know a good deal of such things, Mrs Norris,' she said, in a placatory tone. 'I, too, have struggled to maintain the proper appearances on a straitened income. I, too, have been forced to measures I deplored, merely to make ends meet. We are not so very unlike, you and I.'

'Do not presume to compare *your* situation with *mine*,' she cried, pointing a trembling finger at Mary. 'You are *nothing,* a *nonentity* — scarcely better than a servant, and with the manners and wardrobe to suit — an impudent upstart without birth, connections, or fortune.'

'Oh, but there you are wrong,' said Mary.

'Even if I allow that I may lack some of those things — though I resent your insolence just as much as you resent my supposed impudence — I am not, now, without *fortune.* Indeed, thanks to his marriage my brother will henceforth be one of the richest men in England, as well as the legal inheritor of Lessingby Hall.'

She had hoped to plead a rational case — to present the prospect of a marriage between herself and Edmund as the only way to recover the family's lost prosperity, and therefore grounds enough for Mrs Norris to spare Mary's own life, and help her save her son. But she had miscalculated. She could not have known that the mere mention of Lessingby would smite such a raw nerve. It was the summation of every thing that Mrs Norris had hoped for, and to which she had deemed herself entitled; to her mind, it remained the pattern of perfection for all that was gracious, elegant, and desirable, that she had been denied for so long; had it taken place, her son's marriage would have brought this dream of felicity within her reach at last, and made her, *de facto,* the mistress of the Hall. It had been the darling wish of her heart for many, many years, and she had not relinquished it without much pain, and even greater bitterness; it had been torn from her like the child she had never borne, and here, before her very eyes, was the woman to whom so much of the blame could be attributed.

She threw down the basket upon the table, and seized one of the silver knives within it.

'No!' cried Mary, backing away. 'You are not thinking clearly — someone will be here at any moment — they will discover you — you cannot hope to escape —'

'Your brother, perhaps? Or that piece of vermin Stornaway? When I last saw them they were chatting away quite comfortably in the alcove. Which does not surprise *me*; it is clear your brother is quite at home with men of *that* class.'

'Then your own servants — they will be returning from the Park.'

'I have already had the foresight to allow them a half-holiday, out of respect to the dear departed. I did not want my step-son disturbed — not before matters were brought to their inevitable conclusion. You see, you underestimate me, Miss Crawford, as you always have. You and that reptile Maddox alike. *He* thinks only a man could be capable of what I have done, just as *you* think I am so weak-minded as not to have anticipated this very possibility, and planned accordingly. I knew you might eventually piece together who was really responsible for Fanny's death, and I have been prepared to act for some days past.'

She stopped, and smiled, a smile that froze Mary's very soul. 'In fact, I am indebted to you, Miss Crawford. You have made it easier for me than I could have ever hoped. I will only have to say that I found you dead when I opened the door. My step-son is already accused of a crime no less violent, and it will not be difficult to induce people to believe him capable of another act of equal savagery. Indeed, it will merely make it easier to explain his regrettable decision to take his own life.'

All this time Mary had been edging along the side of the table, hoping to attain the French door, and praying that it would not be locked; but she was too slow, and Mrs Norris too quick. Time and time again Mary had heard tell of this woman's energy and vigour, but she had never seen it put to such dreadful use. She seized Mary by the arm, and twisted it so brutally that she fell back against the table, gasping in pain, and then in fear, as she felt the cold blade of the silver knife pressed against her throat. Overcome with panic, she wrenched herself away and reached in desperation for the empty glass on the table — any thing that might serve to defend herself — but it span away from her on the polished wood, and she felt fingers in her hair, and an arm dragging her back and down. She put up her hands to shield her face, but she was too late. The blade flashed before her sight, and as the hot blood ran on her skin, and the icy metal cut into her flesh, her eyes filled with darkness, and she knew no more.

Maddox had heard enough. He pushed his fist through the window-pane and threw open the door. He had relied on surprising her, and it did indeed buy him a few precious seconds. The old woman looked up at him, and at the burly figure of Fraser at his heels. Her eyes narrowed, and she raised her hand to strike, just as Maddox seized her wiry wrist, and forced the blade from her grasp. As the knife clattered onto the floor he dragged her away from the insentient body of Mary Crawford, and pushed her, none too gently, into Fraser's muscular clutches. She began to shriek and kick, the spittle dripping from her mouth as she hurled a stream of such rank and obscene insults, as would not have disgraced one of the more brazen Covent-garden whores of Maddox's acquaintance.

'Secure this harpy's hands, and take her

down to the cellar,' he said, with an expression of disgust. 'She is not fit for decent company. And make sure to lock the door behind you.'

'Aye, sir. It'll be my personal pleasure.'

'And call Stornaway in from the garden. I need to send him at once in search of the physician.'

Fraser nodded, and hoisted the screaming woman over his shoulder, and made towards the door, while she all the while hurled invective at anyone prepared to listen.

'And you can tell that slattern *Mary Crawford* that I insist she cleans that blood off the carpet before she goes, even if it means getting down on her hands and knees and scrubbing it herself. That carpet is genuine Turkey, I'll have you know, and cost me fifteen shillings a yard from Laidler's, and *that* does not even include the cost of carriage —'

As soon as the door had closed behind them, Maddox went to Mary Crawford and knelt down beside her. The wound on her brow was bleeding profusely, and she was still unconscious; Norris remained sprawled over the chair, his head thrown back, and his mouth hanging open. Maddox took out his handkerchief, and folded it into a wad. The blood seeped into the fine linen, as he

430

pushed her smooth dark hair away from the gash; he had never touched her before, beyond the briefest of hand-shakes, and his fingers trembled at the contact with her skin. If he had tried to deny his emotions before that moment, he could do so no longer.

He was still bent over her when he heard the sound of footsteps, and saw Stornaway's tall thin frame at the door, followed hard by Henry Crawford. The latter could not possibly have had any apprehension of what he was about to see, and he stood for a moment, gazing in horror at the scene before him — the man with his sister's head in his lap, the blood on her face, and on his hands. A moment later Maddox found himself hauled up by the collar, and pushed violently against the wall.

'What the devil has happened here?' cried Crawford. 'What have you done to my sister? If she is harmed, I swear to God I will kill you with my own bare hands —'

Stornaway had by this time seized Crawford by the shoulders, in an endeavour to pull him away, but Crawford was the stronger, and his hands began to tighten round Maddox's neck.

'I am waiting, Maddox,' he hissed, his eyes fixed on the thief-taker's.

431

'You would do better to release my throat, sir, and allow me to send my man for the physician. Mr Norris's life, if not your sister's, may depend upon it.'

The grip slackened, and Crawford took a step back. Maddox nodded to Stornaway, who turned at once, and left the way he had come.

'What in heaven's name is going on?' said Crawford, as he sank to his knees, and took Mary in his arms.

'The person who killed your wife has just attempted to murder your sister. Thankfully, I was close by, and able to intervene in time.'

'But who? *Why?*'

Maddox looked down at his distraught face, 'All in good time, Mr Crawford. The more urgent necessity at this moment is to convey Mr Norris upstairs to his bed. And then we will do whatever is necessary to assist your sister. She is a remarkable young woman, sir. A remarkable young woman indeed.'

CHAPTER XXI

When Mary opened her eyes it was to see Charles Maddox sitting at her side. She was lying down, with a blanket about her, and there were lamps burning in the room. Some thing was obscuring her left eye, and she put up her hand to find a thick cloth bandage had been wound about her head. She stared at Maddox for a moment, her vision still blurred, then endeavoured to sit up.

'Have a care, my dear Miss Crawford. You have had a terrible shock, and are not yet fully recovered.'

She looked around at the room; her head was painfully heavy, but her mind clearing; she was starting to remember what had happened — and why she now found herself lying on a sopha in the drawing-room at the White House. Mrs Norris had attacked her, and Edmund —

'Where is he?' she said quickly. 'He needs

help — he was given —'

'— a fatal dose of laudanum, I know. Fear not, Miss Crawford; he is in the best hands. Mr Gilbert and Mr Phillips are upstairs with him now. We were able to get help to him quickly, and purge the system before the poison took full effect. He is still very ill, but they are in hopes that no mortal damage has been done. If he lives, he will have much to thank you for.'

Mary turned away, her eyes filling with tears; it was too much. Charles Maddox watched her for a moment.

'I am afraid I cannot offer you the use of my handkerchief; I had to use it to staunch the bleeding. The cut you have sustained is deep, and you lost a quantity of blood. Mr Gilbert has done his best to dress it, but you have, I fear, quite ruined your gown.' He smiled. 'This time, at least, there is no need to prove that the blood is indeed your own.'

'You have cuts on your own hand,' she said weakly.

Maddox shook his head dismissively. 'I have borne far worse in the past. These are mere scratches, incurred in the process of unlawful entry into Mrs Norris's house.'

Mary nodded slowly; she had no memory of such a thing, but it must indeed have been so, though in all her girlish dreams of a princely rescuer riding to her deliverance on a milk-white palfrey, he had never taken on such a shape as Maddox.

'How can I thank you,' she began. 'Had you not happened to be there —'

He got up and went to the side-table and poured a little wine, all the while avoiding her eye. 'I think you should drink what you can of this,' he said. 'As to my presence, you will find out soon enough that it was not quite so fortuitous as it might seem. This case has been one of the most demanding of my career. The evidence pointed first one way, and then another. I will confess, Miss Crawford, that until very recently I was fully convinced that it was your brother who was responsible. No-one had a better motive than he.'

'But —'

Maddox held up his hand. 'As I said, that was what I *had* thought. You may possibly be aware that I have deployed my men to gather information.'

'To listen at doors, you mean.'

'On occasion, yes. You look reproving, and no doubt it is not a very commendable activity, but murder is not a very commendable activity either, and as we have discussed together once before, I am sometimes forced to employ methods that fine ladies and gentlemen find distasteful, in order to discover the truth. This was one such circumstance.'

He took the empty glass from her hand, and sat down beside her once more.

'When you met Mr Norris at the belvedere, your *tête-à-tête* was not, as you believed, *à deux,* but *à trois.* My man Stornaway was listening.'

Mary flushed, and she felt the wound above her eye begin to throb. 'That was an outrageous intrusion, Mr Maddox —'

'Perhaps. Perhaps not. It has, however, been of the most vital importance in elucidating this case. Stornaway could not hear every word, but he did discern enough. Thus when Mr Norris came to me and confessed, I knew at once that it was a complete invention from beginning to end. A few pertinent — or impertinent — questions on my part were enough to put the matter beyond question. Unlike almost everyone else in the house, Mr Norris had actually seen Mrs Crawford's body, so he was able to describe the injuries he had supposedly inflicted with tolerable accuracy. However, he had absolutely no idea that Miss Julia Bertram had died any thing other than a perfectly natural, if lamentable, death. I knew, then, that he was lying.'

'So why did you arrest him? Why confine him here like a criminal, and let us all believe him guilty? How could you do such a thing?'

'Because I had no alternative. And if you recall, I did go to great lengths to ensure that he would not be removed to Northampton, nor suffer the indignities of the common jail.'

Mary turned her face away, and he saw, once more, the thinness of her face, and the hollowness under her eyes; she had clearly suffered much in those two days.

'Besides,' he continued, 'I wished to keep him here in Mansfield for my own reasons. Given that Mr Norris had clearly *not* committed the crime, there was only one possible reason why he should have chosen to confess to it. He was protecting someone; someone for whom he felt either duty and responsibility, or great affection. Someone he perceived to be weaker than himself, and less capable of enduring the punishment that must attend such a heinous crime. In short, a woman.'

He got to his feet and began to walk about the room, his hands clasped behind his back. 'I was convinced, for some time, that this woman was *you*, Miss Crawford. I had you watched at all times, I intercepted your letters, and subjected your behaviour to the most intense scrutiny. I know your habits, I know all your ways; what time you prefer to breakfast, and where you prefer to walk. I know every thing about you — I have made it my business to know. Despite all my efforts, I saw nothing to indicate that you yourself were guilty. You were distressed, but I was forced to acknowledge that this was the natural distress of a woman who knows the man she loves is about to sacrifice himself needlessly for her sake.'

Her face was, by now, flushed a deep red, but she did not turn to look at him.

'And so I turned my attention elsewhere. I had initially dismissed Mrs Norris as a possible murderess, on account of her age, but it seems I did not fully appreciate her physical strength, nor her formidable capacity for jealousy and resentment. It was the poisoning of Julia Bertram that forced me to think again. The killing of Mrs Crawford had always seemed to me to be the work of a man — the brutality, the bodily vigour it required — but poisoning is, in my experience, very much a woman's crime. And who was better placed than Mrs Norris to perpetrate the act? The whole household went to her with their coughs and sore throats and arthritic joints, and no-one — not even you, Miss Crawford — would have questioned her presence in the sick-room.'

Mary looked at him in consternation, unable to take in all this new information. 'Then why in heaven's name did you not arrest her at once?'

'I needed *proof,* Miss Crawford, *proof.* I needed to *hear her say it* — admit what she had done in the presence of a witness. You were my only hope. I guessed that you would try to see Mr Norris, and having let it be known that he would be moved on Thursday, I made sure that today was your last opportunity. I knew, likewise, that if Mrs Norris was indeed guilty, she would have to intervene to prevent you speaking to him. And knowing how much she hated you, I relied on that hatred to make her voluble.'

'And while you waited for this confession of yours, you stood idly by and watched her try to kill her own *son?*'

For the first time in their acquaintance, she saw Maddox flush. 'That, I confess, was an error on my part. I had not expected her to act so soon. I attended the funeral, as you did, having left Stornaway overseeing matters here.'

'And he did *nothing* whatsoever to prevent her?'

'I have not yet had the opportunity to question him fully, but I suspect he did exactly what I instructed him to do. Watch and wait. But I had not, I regret, anticipated either the speed, or the method she would employ. If she resorted to laudanum a second time, I relied on Mr Norris being able to discern the taste; I did not bargain for the dulling effect of curried mutton. No doubt she chose it for precisely that purpose.'

'That does not excuse you, Mr Maddox. You put Mr Norris in deplorable danger, and I can never forgive you. He may, even now, be dying at her hands.'

Maddox looked grave. 'I will regret that, Miss Crawford, for as long as I live. But there is some thing I regret even more. That I should have so endangered *you.* You are brave, and you are capable, and I thought that would be sufficient to protect you. To my infinite regret, I found that it was not, and I am more sorry for that than I can say.'

They looked at one another for a moment, then she looked away. 'You saved my life,' she said, her voice breaking.

He smiled gently. 'You are most welcome, Miss Crawford. And now I will leave you. I hear a little commotion in the hall, and I fancy your brother has returned with Mrs Grant.'

He gave a deep bow, and went out into the garden, leaving her wondering at what had happened, and wondering still more at what was yet to come.

Chapter XXII

A week later, Mary was sitting in the garden at the parsonage, a parasol at her side, and a book, unopened, in her lap. It was such a lovely day that her sister had finally relented and permitted her to take the air outside. It was the first time she had been out of doors since the events at the White House, and she breathed the fresh air with the purest delight, noticing how the last flowers of the summer had already started to fade, and the first edges of gold were appearing on the leaves. But her pleasure was not wholly unalloyed. She had not yet been able to visit the Park, whither Edmund had now been removed, and she knew that his recovery was neither as complete, nor as swift, as Mr Gilbert had hoped. They had kept it from her at first, fearing a relapse in her own condition, but Mrs Grant had, at last, admitted that while Mr Norris was now out of danger, the family were apprehensive for his future health. Mary had not yet heard from Mr Gilbert that morning, and when she saw her sister approaching from the house, she presumed at first that she was coming with a message from the physician.

'There is someone to see you, Mary,' said Mrs Grant. 'I have explained that you have already seen Sir Thomas today, and are still too delicate to receive so many visitors, but he will not be gainsaid.'

Mary smiled. 'Let me hazard a guess — it is, perhaps, Mr Maddox to whom you refer?'

'The man has scarcely been out of the house since the day you — well, since the day of your accident. I am more than half tempted to start charging him board and lodging.'

'I do not recommend it!' laughed Mary. 'I am sure our table is better stocked than Mr McGregor's, so he will very likely take you at your word, and then where will you be?'

Mrs Grant smiled, despite herself. 'With an unwanted lodger taking up the only spare room, that's where I would be. How do you go on with your book?'

Mary smiled. 'Not well. It is very entertaining — the author blends a great deal of sense with the lighter matter of the piece, and holds up an excellent lesson as to the dangers of too great a sensibility, but I fear my spirits are not yet equal to the playfulness of the style.'

'Well, if you do not wish to read, perhaps you have energy enough for conversation? Shall I fetch Mr Maddox? He says there is some thing he wishes to discuss with you. I'll wager it's about what is to be done with Mrs Norris — there have been messages going to and fro between him and the magistrate for the best part of a week. Mrs Baddeley told me she is to be shut up in a private establishment in another part of the country — some where remote and private, by all accounts, and with her own mad-doctor in constant attendance. If you ask me, she should have paid the price for what she did, but it appears she has quite lost her reason, and become quite raving, and Dr Grant says that even if there were a possibility of her ever standing trial, the jury would be forced to acquit her by reason of insanity. As you might imagine, Sir Thomas will not hear of a public asylum.'

'I am not surprised at that. I have acquaintances in London who have visited Bedlam, and I would not wish even Mrs Norris incarcerated in such a terrible place. People make visits there as if it were some sort of human menagerie — they even take long sticks with them, so that they can provoke the poor mad inmates, purely for the sake of entertainment. It is unforgiveable. Sir Thomas would never permit such inhumane treatment, even for the murderess of his own daughter.'

Mrs Grant stood up and touched her sister on the shoulder. '*You* have become quite the daughter to him, these last few days.'

Mary blushed. 'I think he wished, in the beginning, to thank me for what I have tried to do for the family, and especially for Julia. But since then we have spent more time in conversation, and have found we enjoy one another's company.'

'I am sure that you are more than half the reason why he seems to be becoming reconciled to Henry as a nephew.'

Mary shook her head. 'I have scrupled to plead Henry's cause directly — that is not my place. Sir Thomas knows I do not approve of what my brother has done, but I do believe Henry to be sincerely desirous of being really received into the Bertram family, and very much disposed to look up to Sir Thomas, and be guided by him. For his part, Sir Thomas has acknowledged to me that he feels he should bear some part of the blame for what happened — for the elopement, at least. He feels that he ought never to have agreed to the engagement with Edmund in the first place, and that in so doing he allowed himself to be governed by mercenary and worldly motives. He is too judicious to say so, and too mindful of the respect owing to the dead, but I think he had very little knowledge of the weak side of Fanny's character, or the consequences that might ensue from the excessive indulgence and constant flattery she received from Mrs Norris. As for Henry, if he knew Sir Thomas as I now do, he would value him as a friend, as well as someone who might supply the place of the father we lost so long ago. Sir Thomas and I have talked together on many subjects, and he has always paid me the compliment of considering my opinions seriously, while correcting me most graciously where I have been mistaken. I admire him immensely.'

'As he does you, no doubt. And as *Mr Maddox* does also,' said Mrs Grant with a knowing look. 'Good heavens! That gentleman will be wondering where I have got to! I will shew him into the garden, and fetch you some thing to drink from the kitchen. And then I must return to unpacking the new Wedgwood-ware. The pattern is pretty enough, in its way, but I think they might have allowed us rather larger leaves — one is almost forced to conclude that the woods about Birmingham must be blighted.'

Despite all her other cares, Mary could not but laugh at this, and she was still smiling a few minutes later when Maddox appeared, carrying a tray and a pitcher of spruce-beer.

'I come bearing gifts,' he said, 'but I am not Greek, and you need not fear me.'

'*Timeo Danaos et dona ferentes.* I did not know you read Virgil, Mr Maddox.'

'And I did not know you read Latin, Miss Crawford. There is a good deal, I suspect, that we do not yet know of one another.'

Mary noticed that 'yet', but she did not remark upon it.

'My sister says there is some thing you wish to discuss with me?'

'Quite so. May I?' he said, indicating the chair.

'Of course. Pray be seated.'

He sat for a moment, looking at her face, and she became self-conscious. The wound had started to heal above her eye, but there would always be a scar. It was little enough in itself, considering what might have been, and she had never prided herself on her beauty alone, seeing it as both ephemeral and insignificant; but she had not yet become accustomed to her new face, and his intent gaze unsettled her.

'My apologies,' he said quickly. 'I did not mean to stare in such an unmannerly way, only —'

'Only?'

'It occurred to me, just then, that we have a good deal in common, besides a liking for Virgil. And a scar above the left eye.'

Mary laughed. 'That is no way to ingratiate yourself with a lady, Mr Maddox! You should be thankful that your profession does not require you to obtain information under cover of flirtatious gallantry. You would never resolve a crime again.'

She had meant it as a joke, but his face fell, and she felt, for a moment, as remorseful if she had chosen her words on purpose to wound him.

'I am sorry, Mr Maddox, I did not mean —'

He waved his hand. 'No, no. Think nothing of it. I was merely momentarily discomfited. The conversation is not going in the direction I had intended.'

'And what did you intend, Mr Maddox?'

'To ask you to marry me.'

She could not pretend it came as a surprise; she had been aware, for some time, of a particularity in his manners towards her, and since her convalescence, his attentions had become so conspicuous that even Dr Grant could not avoid perceiving in a grand and careless way that Mr Maddox was somewhat distinguishing his wife's sister. But all the same, as every young lady knows, the supposition of admiration is quite a different thing from a decided offer, and she was, for a moment, unable to think or speak very clearly.

'I see I have taken you by surprise,' he said. 'You will naturally wish for time to collect your thoughts. Allow me, in the mean time, to plead my case. It is, perhaps, not the most romantic language to use, but you are an intelligent woman, and I wish to appeal, principally, to that intelligence. I know you have an attachment to Mr Norris —' she coloured and started at this, but he continued, 'I have no illusions, Miss Crawford. *My* affections are, I assure you, quite fervent enough to satisfy the vanity of a young woman of a far more trivial cast of mind than your own, but I have known for some time that I would have a pre-engaged heart to assail. I know, likewise, that you will now be a woman of no inconsiderable fortune. But what can Mr Norris do for you — what can even your brother do — compared to what *I* shall do? I am not the master of Lessingby, but I am, nonetheless, a man of no inconsiderable property. If such things are important to you, you may have what house you choose, and have it completely new furnished from cellar to attic, and dictate your own terms as to pinmoney, jewels, carriages, and the rest. But I suspect such things are *not* important to you. My offer to you is independence. Heroism, danger, activity, adventure. The chance to travel — to see the world. All the things that men take for granted, and most women do not even have the imagination to dream of, far less embrace. But you, I fancy, are an exception. What would be tranquillity and comfort to little Maria Bertram, would be tediousness and vexation to *you*. *You* are not born to sit still and do nothing. Even if he makes a complete recovery, which is by no means certain, you are no more fitted to be Edmund Norris's sweet little wife than I would be. And if he does *not* recover, you will waste your youth and beauty pushing an invalid in a bath chair, buried in a suffocating domesticity. Do not make the mistake of marrying a man whose understanding is inferior to your own — do not hide your light under a bushel, purely to do him credit. You are worth more than that — you can *achieve* more than that. I know enough of you already to be quite sure that you would be an inestimable support to me in my profession — and not merely a support, but a partner, in the truest, fullest sense of the word. Your eye for detail, your capacity for logical thinking and lucid deduction, surpass any thing I have seen, even among men whom I admire. You have a genius for the business, Mary, and if you do not choose it, it seems that *it* chooses *you*.'

She drew back in confusion, aware that she ought to be displeased at the freedom of his address, but he had already taken her hand — not with lover-like impetuosity, but with cool deliberation; he lifted her fingers slowly to his lips, his eyes on hers in a gaze of passionate intensity. Some thing passed between them, that Mary felt all over her, in all her pulses, and all her nerves. Denial was impossible; there was a connection between this man and herself; an attraction that she had long been blind to, and even longer denied.

Such reflections were sufficient to bring a colour to her pale cheeks; a colour that Maddox saw, and seized upon. But he knew better than to press her.

'I am very sensible of the honour you are paying me, Mr Maddox,' she began, dropping her eyes.

'But?'

'But I will need some time to consider it.'

'Of course,' he said, getting to his feet, and preparing to go. 'Pray take all the time you need. My own affections are fixed, and will not change. I love you, Mary Crawford, and I give you my word, that in marrying me, you will lose nothing you value that is associated with that name, and you will gain a freedom that only Mary Maddox could dream of attaining.'

The effect of such a conversation was not to be underrated, especially for a mind that had suffered as hers had done, and it required several hours to give the appearance of sedateness to her spirits, even if they could not bring serenity to her heart. She did not know what to think; she was flattered, tempted, disarmed. She could not deny that the prospect he described held an irresistible attraction for her; having done so little, and travelled so little, to have a life so full of novelty and endeavour! To be at once active, fearless, and self-sufficient — to move, at last, from a state of obligation to one of such brilliant independency! And yet, did she love him enough to marry him? Did she, indeed, love him at all? She had a regard for him, she admired his intellect and esteemed many of his fine qualities, but she also knew him capable of acts that were abhorrent to her principles, and she had challenged and condemned his gross want of feeling and humanity where his own purposes were concerned. Pity the wife who might fall victim to such barbarous treatment, and all the more so as she suspected that, however high she appeared to stand in his regard, he had no very high opinion of her sex in general. If he became her husband, would she not be more than half afraid of him?

With a mind so oppressed, she longed for the calm reflection of solitude, and after a quiet dinner with the Grants, she professed herself equal to a short walk in the park, and having allayed their very natural concerns, she set out at a gentle pace. The harvest moon had already risen, and was nearly at the full, hanging like a pale lantern over the sheep grazing peacefully on the farther side of the ha-ha. On the other side of the valley the labourers were once again at work, and she had no doubt that her brother was present to direct and dictate; Sir Thomas having determined that the improvements should, after all, be completed, Henry had insisted, to Mary's very great pleasure, on offering his services.

Though the triumph and glory of his scheme would never now be realised: Sir Thomas had decreed that the avenue was to remain, in lasting tribute to the daughter he had lost.

How it happened, she could not tell, but Mary found her footsteps were drawn towards the White House. It was not in hopes of seeing Edmund, for she knew that could not be; nor was it to recall what had happened there only a few short days ago. Had she been asked her purpose, she could not have told, she had only a sense of some thing unfinished, and incomplete. She unlatched the garden gate, and walked slowly across the lawn. The late summer shadows were lengthening under the trees, and she did not perceive at once that she was not alone. He had his back to her, his head resting against the chair, and a rug draped across his knees. It was so like the posture in which she had last seen him, so awful a reminder of what had been, and what might have been, that she stood for a moment, unable to move, her hand at her breast, and her heart full. Perhaps she made a sound, but at length he moved, and half-turned towards her.

'Mrs Baddeley? Is that you?'

She hesitated; then took a step closer.

'No, Mr Norris. It is not Mrs Baddeley.'

There was a pause.

'Mary?' he whispered.

She had heard her name from another's lips not three hours before, and she could not, at that moment, have told if she had longed or feared to hear it now. She went quickly forward, and stood before him. The change in his appearance clutched at her heart. His face was white and pinched, and his eyes had a hectic feverishness that did not seem to be solely the consequence of his recent misfortune; some thing more profound was amiss. Neither spoke for some moments, then he roused himself, and gestured towards the chair beside him.

'I am so much reduced, Miss Crawford,' he said, in a bitter tone, 'that I cannot even do the necessary courtesy to a lady by standing in her presence.'

'In that case, Mr Norris, I will sit.' They remained in silence a moment, but it was not a companionable silence; the minds of both were over-taxed.

'I had not thought to see you here,' she said at last.

'Mrs Baddeley was so good as to wheel me to the garden. I wanted to take a last look at the place.'

'Last? Are you going away?'

He shook his head. 'Only as far as the Park. This house is to be sold, and every thing in it. And it will still not be enough — nowhere near enough — to clear away all the claims of my creditors. My father's wealth derived almost entirely from his estate at Antigua, and it is only now that I have discovered that it has been making heavy losses for a number of years. In consequence I find I have debts far greater than I could ever have conceived of, and no way to pay them with any degree of expedition, except by the sale of all I have.'

She noted the formal character of his discourse, and felt it at her heart.

'It is a wonder,' she said, at length, and with a break in her voice, 'that your mother was able to keep up the appearance of affluence for so long.'

He smiled sourly. 'She has — *had* — a will of iron. But even she could not endure such a terrible burden for ever; the pressure was too great. That day in the park — the unexpected encounter with Fanny — it was not so very much, in itself. But it brought her to the brink of the abyss. She had already seen the wreck of all her hopes of my marrying Fanny; our debts had mounted to the point of imminent ruin; and now she had to endure contempt and disdain from

456

the very person from whom she expected the utmost deference, gratitude, and respect.'

He paused, and gazed across the lawn to where the moon was rising in the late afternoon sky.

'When you spoke to me at the belvedere, I knew at once. When you talked about the blood — the "blood on her hands" — I knew. That day, when I returned from Cumberland, she had not expected me; when I surprised her at the house, she was in a strange mood — excitable, nervous — she could barely keep in one place for a minute together. You know her character, and you know such behaviour to be quite unlike her usual self; I, certainly, had never seen it before. And when I went into the parlour, I found rags in the fire. Blood-stained rags in a fire that did not need to be lit so early on such a warm day. She told me she had dropped a jar in the store-room, and cut her hand, and there were indeed some marks that might have testified to such an incident. But how could I have suspected their real cause? Even later, when it became horribly, indisputably clear, I still could not believe —'

He swallowed, and went on, 'When I confronted her, she said she had done it for *me* — for *us*. I saw at once that, even if *she* were the actual perpetrator of the crime, *I* bore my own terrible responsibility for what she had done. I should have made it my business to enquire into our pecuniary circumstances years ago; had I done so, I would have known the strain under which she had been labouring for so long, and been in a position to take action to alleviate it. Any man of the least decision of character would have done so, and more. How could I, knowing that, allow *her* to pay the price for *my own* blindness and incompetency? I did the only thing left to me. I went to Maddox, and confessed to every thing.'

'Not quite every thing. That was how he knew you were not telling him the truth.'

He turned to look at her. 'So you knew? About Julia? And yet you said nothing.'

'I was there when she died. It was impossible *not* to know. But I was bound by a solemn promise of secrecy. And besides, that day at the belvedere, I believed *you* to be the murderer. It was your name I had heard on Julia's lips — it was *you* I thought had killed her. To keep her from betraying you.'

His astonishment appeared to be beyond what he could readily express; he stared at her, then looked away. 'There is a fine irony

458

here, could I but appreciate it. Here I have been, thinking you despised me for a fool, a coward, and a dupe, and all the time you believed me capable of killing two defenceless young women in the most brutal, cold-blooded manner.' He laughed, but it was a chill and hollow sound. 'I should, I suppose, be flattered you deemed me capable of acting with such resolution! And yet, believing that, you trusted yourself, alone, in my company, that day at the belvedere. You took such a terrible risk — merely to warn me?'

Mary shook her head. 'I do not think I really believed you guilty. I longed to hear you give a plausible explanation — to tell me some new fact that would prove you innocent.'

'And yet no such fact was forthcoming. Indeed, your worst fears must only have been confirmed, when you heard of my subsequent confession.'

'I do not wish to speak of that,' she said with a sigh. 'It is past, and should be forgotten.'

'And you wish to think only of the future.' It was a statement, rather than a question.

'I do not take your meaning.'

'Come, Miss Crawford. The housemaids at the Park can talk of little else, and in my pitiful invalid state I cannot easily escape from their chatter. Mr Maddox is, I gather, growing extremely particular in his attentions.'

She flushed, but would not meet his gaze. 'I have received a proposal of marriage, yes.'

'And when am I to wish you joy?'

'I have not yet made my decision. There are many things to consider.'

Had Mary been able to encounter his eye, she might have seen a faint colour rush into his cheeks; the herald of an infinitesimal hope, when all before had been utterly hopeless.

'If things were different, Miss Crawford,' he said slowly, 'if I were a proper man — a man able to stand on his own feet, and not the useless, vacillating weakling my step-mother always said I was — then I would ask you myself — I would say —' He threw up his hands in anguish. 'But how can I do so? Look at me — confined to this damned chair — with no money and no prospect of gaining any. How can I ask any woman — far less a woman like you — to make such a sacrifice? I can live on comfortably enough at the Park — Sir Thomas has been very kind — but a man should give a woman a better home than the one he takes her from, not condemn her to a miserable dependence on the benevolence of others. And it is not only my fortune I have lost. My reputation is gone — quite gone. As far as the world is concerned, I will for ever be a man who confessed to murder, and there will no doubt be some who will always question whether I did not, in fact, commit those dreadful crimes. And if that were not enough, how can I ask another woman to become Mrs Norris, in the shadow of what has happened to the last woman to bear that name?'

They were silent.

'It is true,' she said gently, after a pause, 'that you are not the happy and prosperous Mr Norris whom first I met.'

'In truth, Miss Crawford, I was neither, even then. I did not know, at that time, that my prosperity was as much a chimaera as my happiness. You, by contrast, might now have both. You might marry whom you choose.'

'And I *do* choose, Mr Norris. Do you think my feelings are so evanescent, or my affections so easily bestowed? Do you think I care for what people think? And though I have lived all my life under the narrow constraints of comparative poverty, I am now in the happy position of discarding such wearisome economies for ever. You talked just now of fine ironies; here is another: the fortune that will now provide for me, is the fortune *you* should have had. Had *you* married Fanny, as everyone wished, *you* would be the master of Lessingby now, and not my brother.'

He shook his head. 'Your words only serve to remind me of my own shame. I should never have allowed the engagement to persist so long. It was cowardice — rank cowardice. I should have spoken to Sir Thomas long ago; had I done so, he would never have allowed the connection to endure as long as it did. I would have been released, and she — she might still be living today.'

'But everyone — every *thing* — was against you. Duty, habit, expectation. Such an arrangement — established when you were so young, and supported as it was by your whole family — it would have taken great courage to give it up.'

'A man should always do his duty, Miss Crawford, however difficult the circumstances. Indeed, there is little merit in doing so, unless it demands some exertion, some struggle on our part. Long standing and public as was the engagement, I had a duty to her, as well as myself, not to enter knowingly into a marriage without affection — without the true affection that alone can justify any hope of lasting happiness.'

His words struck her with all the force of a thunderbolt. She knew — had always known — how wretched she would be if she were to marry a man she did not love, and yet only a few hours before she had been giving serious consideration to just such an alliance. She had even reasoned herself into believing that Maddox might be the only man in the world who could place a just value on her talents, and that they might — as he had insisted — have much in common; not merely a shared literary taste, but a general similarity of temper and disposition. But now the truth of her own heart was all before her. Whatever the inconveniences that might lie before them — whatever the attractions of another course — she loved Edmund Norris still; loved him, and wished to be his wife.

She rose to her feet. 'I will detain you no longer, Mr Norris. I must find Mr Maddox, and beg a few minutes' conversation with him in private.'

Had she doubted his affection before, she could do so no longer; the expression of his face sank gradually to a settled and blank despair. It was as if a lamp had flickered and gone out.

'I hope you will be happy, Miss Crawford,' he said, in a low voice, turning his face away.

'I hope so too, Mr Norris; but it will not be with Mr Maddox, if I am.'

It was said with some thing of her former playfulness, and when he looked up at her, he saw that she was smiling.

'I have decided to refuse him. After all, how can I marry Mr Maddox when I have already given my heart to another?'

CHAPTER XXIII

It was a very quiet wedding. Neither Mary nor Edmund had any inclination for needless ostentation, but it would not have escaped the notice of those schooled in matters of fashion, that the refined elegance of the bride's gown owed as much to the generosity of her brother, in sending for silks from London, as it did to her own skills as a needlewoman. They had been obliged to wait until the three months of deep mourning were over, but that period had been, all things considered, a happy time; Mary had worked on her wedding-clothes, and wandered about the park with Edmund all the autumn evenings, under the last lingering leaves, raising his mind to animation, and his spirits to cheerfulness. His health improved so well under this agreeable regimen that by the time the couple met at the altar he was able to walk from the church unaided, with his bride on his arm. Sir Thomas was not the only onlooker to observe the effect of real affection on his nephew's disposition, nor the only one to attribute it to Mary's lively talents and quick understanding. Mr Maddox had been cruelly disappointed by her rejection, even if he had not ranked his chances of success very high, but his self-control in her presence had been punctilious, and when he departed the neighbourhood some few days thereafter, he had called at the parsonage to bid her the farewell of one who wished to remain always her friend.

They had stood on the sweep before his carriage, his trunks and notebooks neatly stowed, and his assistants waiting at a discreet distance.

'I hope you are leaving us with the reward that is owing to you, Mr Maddox,' she said.

He smiled. 'I would rather be leaving with some thing quite different. But, yes, my pockets are well enough lined; Sir Thomas has been very generous. Though he had no compunction in pointing out that there was another, to whom he was almost equally indebted, for bringing the full truth finally to light.'

'I did very little.'

'You are, once again, under-valuing your talents. It is a habit I would have cured you of, had I been given the chance.' He paused. 'I hear you are to remove to Lessingby with your brother, after you are married.'

'Indeed so. There is a small house on the estate that we may have — Henry tells me it sits by the side of a lake, and has its own garden leading down to the water. It is peaceful, and the views are said to be beautiful. I think it will be exactly calculated to please us.'

'And Mr Crawford will take possession of the Hall?'

'He has already done so — he arrived three days ago, and will return in time for the wedding. He writes that the house is large and draughty, and the grounds are happily in great need of improvement. I imagine he has work enough for two summers at least.'

'I am glad to hear he will be so usefully employed, with so much money at his disposal, and so little to provoke him.'

It was a strange turn of phrase, and she had seen his dark brows contract. 'What do you mean, Mr Maddox?'

Maddox looked at her joyful, unsuspecting face, and made a decision. Ever since Fraser's return from Enfield, he had been debating with himself whether to tell her what his assistant had discovered. Henry

Crawford may, or may not, have killed his mistress, but he had lied from the first about his whereabouts on the day of her death. It had not been difficult for a man like Fraser to find the old washer-woman who had claimed to have seen him, nor had it taken long to persuade her to divulge why she had decided to retract her story: Crawford had bribed her, and bribed her very generously, considering his own straitened circumstances at the time. It was enough to make Maddox uneasy, but it was not enough to hang the man, or destroy his sister's happiness for ever.

'It is nothing,' he said at length. 'A momentary distraction, that is all. You have my most sincere good wishes, Miss Crawford,' he continued. 'I hope Norris values you as he should. And you are no empty-headed girl — you understand the nature of the choice you have made, and I am sure you will make the best of it, and not repine for what you might have had.'

'You do not need to pity me, Mr Maddox,' she said with a smile. 'I am sure I shall be quite as happy as I deserve.'

'But what will you *do,* when you are not submerged in conjugal duties and household chores? How will you occupy yourself?'

'Oh, as to that, I think I will try my hand

at writing. If the book I am reading is aught to go by, there might be an opportunity there for an intelligent woman, with a modicum of wit, to apply her mind, and even, perhaps, earn her own bread.'

'I wish you luck,' he said, as they shook hands. 'I will scour the London booksellers in search of your name.'

'I fancy I would prefer to remain merely "a lady",' she laughed, as he opened the carriage door, 'but I will most assuredly send you a copy, and with the greatest of pleasure. If I am successful, of course.'

Three months later the happy event took place that was to take her from Mansfield, and in the course of the year that followed she pursued her plan, and sketched out a design for a novel that might appeal to a reader such as herself. Two or three families in a country village seemed the very thing to work on, and once commenced she made rapid progress, and found to her surprise and delight that the work was accepted by the first publisher she approached. Edmund, meanwhile, had found the beauty of the Lakes, and the glory of the scenery, most conducive to productive reflection, and having retrospected the course of his life, the errors he had made, and the lessons he had learned, he began to consider whether he might not make himself useful to others, and secure an income large enough to support his family, without relying on his brother-in-law's generosity, by taking orders. It was a decision that Mary heartily approved; she had, in fact, long wondered whether becoming a clergyman might not suit him in every respect, and do full justice to his kind heart, gentle temper, strong good sense and uprightness of mind. The resolution taken, all that remained was to find him a suitable living, and here they were indebted to a stroke of good fortune. After talking of the possibility for many years, and almost ceasing to form hopes of it ever coming about, Dr Grant finally succeeded to the stall in Westminster that had long been the object of his ambition, and he and his wife removed to London. The living at Mansfield now falling vacant, Sir Thomas was most heartily gratified to be able to offer it to his nephew, and no less heartily did he welcome the young couple home, having formed such an attachment to Mary, in the weeks after his return from Keswick, as had made him miss her as much as if she had been his own daughter. After settling her in her new home with every kind attention to her comfort, the object of almost every day was to see her there, or to get her away from it.

One might suppose that the prospect of living at the parsonage would revive some painful memories, but these were quickly done away. Mary had always thought it a pretty little house, and now every window in it afforded fine views of a landscape that, thanks to her brother's improvements, was fast becoming established as one of the beauties of the county. With her husband's love, and her own rising fame to sustain her, the parsonage soon grew as dear to her heart, and as thoroughly perfect in her eyes, as every thing else, within the view and patronage of Mansfield Park, had long been.

ACKNOWLEDGEMENTS

My first and greatest debt is, of course, to Jane Austen herself — not just her wonderful novels, but her letters as well, which I have both mimicked and mined in an effort to recreate her characteristic combination of elegant turns of phrase and delightfully ruthless observations. As a lifelong fan of her work I've tried to remain faithful both to the spirit of her writing, and the actual language she used — I'd like to think that if she'd turned her hand to murder it might just have turned out something like this.

Some readers will also have recognised the deliberate reference to Kingsley Amis's famous condemnation of the original Fanny Price as "a monster of complacency and pride, who under a cloak of cringing self-abasement, dominates and gives meaning to the novel". This comes from an article originally published in *The Spectator* in October 1957, entitled 'What became of

Jane Austen?'

Finally, I'd like to thank my husband Simon for all his support, and my agent, Ben Mason, for everything he did to make this happen — without him, it would never have been published at all.

474

Jane Austen...

READING GROUP QUESTIONS

1. There have been many sequels and pre-quels written to Jane Austen's novels over the years. Do you think it's legitimate to re-work Austen in this way? Does *Murder at Mansfield Park* shed any new light on the original book?

2. Fanny Price in *Mansfield Park* is very un-like a typical Austen heroine — in fact it's Mary Crawford who is much closer to Elizabeth Bennett or Emma Woodhouse. What do you think about the role and idea of the heroine, both in Austen's novel(s) and in this one?

3. Two of the central episodes of *Mansfield Park* are the theatricals and the visit to Sotherton, both of which are echoed and re-worked in this novel. How do these scenes advance the plot, and develop our understanding of the characters in

both books?

4. One of the consequences of the murder in this novel is that the servants at Mansfield Park suddenly take on a new role and importance. What effect does this have?

5. The laying out of the corpse in Chapter XII could be seen as a nineteenth century version of the post mortem scenes that are now common in modern detective fiction. Are there other episodes or aspects to the plot of this book that also recall contemporary thrillers?

6. Kingsley Amis famously described the Fanny Price of *Mansfield Park* as "a monster of complacency and pride who, under a cloak of cringing self-abasement, dominates and gives meaning to the novel." These words have been deliberately echoed in this book, as a reflection on the Fanny Price of *Murder at Mansfield Park*. What do you think about the character of Fanny in both books?

7. Do you think the Henry Crawford of *Murder at Mansfield Park* committed the earlier killing at Enfield? Why? Or why not?

8. Many critics have suggested that Jane Austen interferes with the plot of *Mansfield Park* towards the end, to achieve the ending she wants, when the natural trajectory of the story would have had Mary marrying Edmund, and Henry marrying Fanny. What do you think?

9. Do you think the Mary Crawford of *Murder at Mansfield Park* makes the right choice of husband at the end? Who would you have chosen?

10. Jane Austen had a very close relationship with her brothers and sister, and in *Mansfield Park* she makes a point of stressing the importance of the ties of blood between "children of the same family . . . with the same first associations and habits." What do you think about the relationship between Mary and Henry as sister and brother in the two novels?

NOTES